DRY STERILE THUNDER

Also by Jim Accardi

Saigon Landing
The Rosette Habit
The Movie Moon (and other stories)

DRY STERILE THUNDER

Jim Accardi
Author of Saigon Landing

7/1/06
BILL & DEBBIE
Hope ya'll enjoy!

Jim

iUniverse, Inc.
New York Lincoln Shanghai

Dry Sterile Thunder

iUniverse, Inc.

For information address:
iUniverse, Inc.
2021 Pine Lake Road, Suite 100
Lincoln, NE 68512
www.iuniverse.com

ISBN: 0-595-31908-4

Printed in the United States of America

In loving memory of Pam and Faye.

To all the warriors in the never-ending struggle for justice.

Acknowledgments

My sincerest thanks to all the folks who helped this project happen, especially:

Marian, as always, for her love, patience, and editorial assistance
Tim Morgan: a gentleman, friend, great D.A, and font of information.
Burns, for the inspiration, advice, and cover concept/design
Rodger Morrison
Rob Broussard
Angie Lane
Allison Palmer
Jeff Bennett
Shirley Lee
Gary Rigney
Bryan and Heather Douglas
David Stephens
Rebekah Callahan
Jeannie Cole
John Shaver
And Reta McKannan for her PR help with *Saigon Landing* and *The Rosette Habit*

And to everyone else who inspired, enlightened, or informed me—thank you all
so much.

CHAPTER 1

▼

In less than ten minutes, Kerry Grinder would become the driver's second victim. She would never know that her death had been coded to a few lines of eighty-odd-year-old verse. Or that the killer had already designated victims for the remaining sections of the cryptic, fragmented poem. The only muted perception she had as the jostling van nudged her closer to consciousness was that something was terribly wrong.

She'd been nearly comatose for several hours. As she had begun to emerge from the heavy, drug-induced sleep, a vivid and disturbing image assembled itself in her mind. She envisioned herself trapped and on fire—a helplessly bound figure enveloped in a chrysalis of orange flame. She had no idea how or why she'd become thus imperiled. She only knew she had to free herself.

But it soon became apparent that escape wouldn't be possible. She sensed that she was paralyzed, her limbs incapable of even the slightest movement. Not that it would have mattered: her body seemed encased in a dense matrix that burned intensely from every side.

The van swerved and shuddered, bringing her even closer to consciousness. Her perception of pain, distant and theoretical until that moment, was beginning to seem more immediate, more real. She tried, even immersed in that frightening half-sleep, to logically evaluate her own predicament: Were these intensifying sensations the result of an actual and recent physical injury or did they exist only in some stimulated site on her neural map? Was it even possible for her brain to independently generate such agonizing sensations? And what about the other all-too-real symptoms? The tremendous difficulty she was having breathing, just for one. Although she was managing to access air in clipped, ineffectual breaths, there clearly wasn't enough to sustain her for long. She commanded herself to awaken completely, to shed herself entirely of the bad dream. But her drugged brain wouldn't cooperate; she remained partially submerged in the murky pool of unconscious experience. Even worse, the pain continued to increase in intensity. She reached the inescapable conclusion that she had somehow been condemned to a slow and torturous death.

As the general numbness receded, Kerry began to feel each aching area of her body: her head throbbed, a searing pain radiated outward from her spine to the tips of her fingers and toes, and her left cheek and shoulder felt like they were on fire. She realized that she was lying on her left side on a surface that was hard and warm and irregular in texture. She processed the layer of sensations—the warmth beneath her, the low familiar rumble, the rocking and jostling, the feeling that she was hurtling through space-time.

She was in some type of moving vehicle.

She struggled to remember why this would have been so. Had she been out partying with friends? Had she gone overboard with the chemicals again, drinking and smoking until she'd finally passed out? That particular scenario wasn't totally unfamiliar to her. But she wasn't able to recall anything about the preceding hours. It occurred to her that, whatever she had consumed, it must have been some very powerful stuff. She found this notion almost amusing. She'd never been so wasted that she was incapable of remembering *anything*.

Next came the terrifying realization that she couldn't see. Her eyes were open—she consciously forced herself to blink, just to make sure—but there was nothing but blackness. Then she tried to move her arms and legs only to discover that her ankles were bound and her wrists had been secured behind her back. When she attempted to call out, she found that something—tape or some other sticky substance—had been stretched across her mouth. Panic engulfed her. She bucked and kicked, but only succeeded in changing her position. She was now lying face down, her chin resting in a warm, metallic groove. The pain in her shoulder eased but her neck and chin began to ache. Her voice, swelling into a confused cry for help, only echoed in the cavities of her head.

She could still hear, but the only thing to be heard was the low rumble of the vehicle's engine and drive train, the steady hum of tires on asphalt. This combination of hypnotic sounds continued for what seemed like an hour, possibly longer. She wondered how far she might be from her apartment. From her friends. She imagined that her mobile prison, efficient machine that it seemed to be, had already devoured hundreds of miles.

She began to frantically explore her environment, first by trying to inch her way along the floor, then by rocking from side to side, finally lurching violently to her left. She landed on her back, wincing as a new wave of pain washed over her. When this discomfort subsided, she continued to explore. She discovered that the floor was fairly sizable and had more than the one groove. At that moment, she determined that she was in a large, enclosed vehicle, probably a van.

Kerry arched her back, lifted her hips and tried to extend her arms toward her ankles. She had hoped to pass her bound wrists under her feet—she was sure that she'd seen escape artists use this technique—but quickly realized that it would be a physical impossibility for her. She lay there for a moment and tried to recover from that exhausting task. When her hands, now compressed beneath her, began to ache, she turned herself again. She landed on her side, but continued to push back onto her chest when the shoulder pain returned. She laid her face flat, trying to rub the blindfold off on one of the floor grooves. If she just were able to see, she thought, she'd be able to figure out how to extract herself from her predicament. She swiped her face repeatedly against the burning metal, desperately sucking in air. The blindfold moved a fraction, but she still wasn't able to see. Her panic turned, at least for the moment, to anger. She exploded in a rage-filled animal growl that resonated in the empty van.

There was an unexpected jolt, as if the vehicle had hit a pothole or some solid object. The side of her face smashed against the floor, gashing her chin. Before she could react, the vehicle swerved again, throwing her to the side. Her head struck something hard and rounded—she assumed it was a wheel well. She cursed and thrashed angrily. The pain was intense now, almost unbearable. It seemed like every part of her body was bruised or lacerated.

The engine rumble fell in volume. Kerry sensed that they were slowing down, then turning slightly. She thought she could hear gravel snap under the tires.

And then the vehicle stopped. Abruptly and, as far as Kerry was concerned, utterly unexpectedly. Inertia propelled her violently forward. With her hands tied behind her, she was unable to protect her head. Once again, her face smashed against something hard. She rolled over on her back and, using her right shoulder, continued to try to peel the tape from her face.

A door slammed. Kerry stopped what she was doing and focused on the sounds. One door, most likely on the driver's side. She waited for another slam, but it didn't come. She heard the crunching of gravel at the side of the vehicle. There was a pause, then the sound continued toward the back of the van. *One person.* Her heart was pounding wildly now. She sucked air into her nostrils in wild, panic-driven bursts.

Kerry knew that she only had moments to free herself. She tried again to pull her hands under her legs, but again found that she lacked the flexibility to accomplish that task. Enraged by her helplessness, she pulled savagely against her wrist restraints. At last, nearly spent, she collapsed against the floor. Tears began flowing, pooling in her eyes and soaking the fabric of her blindfold.

Another door—she assumed that it was the van's rear door—began to open. Oppressively humid air and exhaust fumes washed over her. She remembered now that it had been a brutally hot Alabama afternoon. Her heart was crashing savagely now; she feared it might just explode.

"Okay, Kerry," a gruff voice said. "We're here."

She tried desperately to place the voice. Was it someone she knew? Somebody she'd met that day? Some guy she'd partied with? Could this all be some sort of cruel prank? She tried to force her mind to assemble the details of her recent social history. Where had she been? Who had she been with? Someone with access to a van, someone with little regard for the feelings and physical well-being of others. She gritted her teeth and shook her head. That could be any one of a dozen guys she hung out with.

Powerful hands gripped both her ankles. With a single, savage tug, she was dragged several feet along the van's floor. She flexed her knees and with all the strength she could muster, tried to kick out at her assailant. Most of the force of the kick was absorbed by the powerful arms.

"Please don't," the driver said. The voice was low and even. There was no malice apparent, not even a hint of menace. "This is just part of the game. You *do* like to play games, do you not?"

She gathered to attempt another kick, but the driver's grip tightened on her ankles. There was another powerful tug and she felt her legs clear the van floor.

"Don't do that again," the voice commanded.

Suddenly there was something around her neck, a loop of some kind, leathery and pliant. She thought she could feel the strap cut into her skin. She attempted to scream in the remote hope that somebody, anybody, might hear.

The loop tightened, stretching her neck upward. Her muted scream became a high-pitched whine.

"If it rains," the voice rasped, "we'll play a game of chess. That's what we agreed on, wasn't it?" The loop tightened even more, and Kerry was yanked upright. "Trouble is, it doesn't really look like rain."

She tried to speak, but only a muted hissing sound managed to escape her lips.

"But we'll play anyhow," the driver growled, as Kerry was pulled from the van. "I'll be the king and you'll...be...my...pawn."

Kerry crashed to the ground, her upper back and arms absorbing most of the shock. She screamed out in agony. Feeling consciousness slipping perilously away, she made another attempt to strike out at her attacker. She thrust her bent legs upward, but couldn't generate any force, and the blow landed on the driver's shins without doing significant damage. She fought desperately for air.

The driver yanked violently on the leather strap. Kerry gagged, feeling as though her head was about to be pulled from her shoulders. It was now impossible to get any air at all. She was aware that her body was being dragged although she no longer felt pain in her lower extremities. Her awareness had contracted into a montage of fleeting, discrete snapshots: her brother and two sisters, friends from high school, her first boyfriend, an old stuffed giraffe. These images quickly faded and were soon absorbed by a blinding mental luminary.

She realized then that she was about to die.

"Hurry up, please," the voice intoned. "This evil bitch-pawn has been captured. Captured and disposed of. Hurry up, please, it's time."

The belt twisted and tightened even more, and was held in that position until Kerry quit twitching.

"Goo-night, Bill," the driver said. "Goo-night, Lou."

Kerry's limp body was dragged slowly away from the roadside, through lifeless grass and wilted ox-daisies into a parched strawberry field at the base of a kudzu-enshrouded hillock.

The driver yanked the duct tape from the young woman's face, then, in a voice that seemed pleasant, almost cheerful, said: "Goo-night Kerry."

CHAPTER 2

▼

The witness reclined in his chair, seeming to savor the nervous laughter rippling through the courtroom gallery. He rested his chin on his right hand, his index and forefinger arranged in a "V" on his cheek. He seemed entirely pleased with the progress of this question-and-answer drill. He'd been able to easily handle everything the district attorney had thrown his way, especially the last series of questions concerning compensation for his testimony. Of course he'd been paid for his professional services, he had testified: "Fifty dollars an hour—about half what I pay my plumber." Each time the prosecutor had regrouped to attack his testimony on the grounds of bias, the witness had discharged defensive salvos of oral chaff, deflecting any potentially lethal strikes. Each measured response provoked a sprinkling of laughter from the spectator section.

The witness, psychologist Britton McHugh, Ph.D., was a venerable presence, with his varnished tussock of silver hair, a pleasant and expressive face marked with razor-creased lines of experience, and his generally noble bearing. His eyes were pale blue and darted from juror to juror over the half-lenses of his tortoise-shell reading glasses. He wore an impeccably tailored charcoal heather suit with a red silk tie. His white cotton shirt was crisply pressed. He spoke in his resonant and reassuring "therapy voice," and anchored his words with strong and strategically deployed hand gestures.

Rabon Creasey, the defense attorney, seemed particularly gratified by the vocal reaction from the gallery. As an experienced trial advocate, he surely understood that such sudden changes in momentum, especially those which occurred late in the presentation of evidence, often influenced the jury deliberations in a most material way. Even more significantly, the jurors themselves seemed to be particularly entertained by this smooth defense witness. They were seen smiling and nodding; a number of them had even joined the gallery in its mirthful appreciation of his clever replies. Creasey certainly had reason to have his spirits buoyed by the progress of his defense.

It was a particularly grim case. Joe Terry Hollins, a twenty-year-old independent landscape worker, stood accused of murdering Marie Anderson, the seventy-three-year-old widow who had employed him. Her body, slashed and punctured by a ten-inch carving knife, had been discovered by a concerned neighbor. Initial suspicion, based solely on Hollins's opportunity to commit the crime, was soon followed by a convincing trail of evidence. A pawn ticket signed by Hollins connected the yard man to the sale of the victim's ruby ring. A bloody latent palm print lifted from the crime scene matched the known file print of Hollins's left palm. When the police arrested him in Birmingham later that same day, he was still wearing sneakers spattered with Marie Anderson's blood. Even though Hollins didn't admit to the crime—he told Richfield investigators that he had no memory of the previous two days—evidence of his guilt was almost overwhelming.

But the focus of the defense had been on Hollins's mental state, specifically his inability to appreciate the criminality of his conduct. This came as no surprise to the D.A.: it was almost a standard defense tactic in brutally violent cases. But Rabon Creasey had never been known for simple solutions. In his illustrious career, now entering its fifth decade, he had won many difficult cases with a combination of persuasive advocacy skills and innovative defense strategies. Indeed, he had unleashed a novel but potent attack on the prosecution's theory of the case in the face of the compelling evidence of guilt.

According to the psychologist, the defendant had endured an extraordinarily abusive childhood and was of "moderately subnormal" intelligence. As the victim's yard man, he had frequently been criticized by his perfectionist employer—several defense witnesses had testified to her harsh and demanding management style—for deficiencies in the quality of his services. In the end, completely in accord with the announced defense theory, he testified that Joe Terry Hollins had simply "snapped." Operating in a dreamlike "fugue" state triggered by the emotional trauma, Hollins had burst into the victim's kitchen and stabbed her fifteen times with a knife he had found on a table there. He was not guilty of murder, McHugh claimed, because he didn't have any idea what he was doing, much less that what he was doing was wrong. And, he reasoned, if he was not guilty of murder, he obviously couldn't be guilty of capital murder. This conclusion, burnished by the witness's experience and, up to that moment, untested by cross-examination, seemed to waft through the courtroom like the scent of some pleasant forensic potpourri.

Not all the courtroom spectators were as pleased with the trial's developments.

The members of Marie Anderson's family seemed particularly disturbed by this alarming shift in momentum. They sat rigidly in their chairs along the wall behind the prosecution table, eyes opened wide with disbelief. What had been, only minutes before this witness's testimony began, a carefully constructed template of guilt, now seemed a hopelessly confusing tangle of arcane psychological issues. This Dr. McHugh, this obvious shaman of psycho-nonsense, had all but instructed the jury that it could not convict the defendant of murder. Mrs. Anderson's son and daughter sat numb and speechless. Their eyes darted back and forth from the witness to his current examiner, the tall, handsome woman sitting calmly at the prosecution table. Panic was beginning to set in with the grim re-emergence of every suppressed doubt concerning a suspect "justice" system. And now, just when long-awaited justice appeared to be mere hours away, the prosecutor, their champion and trusted voice, seemed oblivious to this looming peril.

They could never have truly understood why Bienville County District Attorney Katie Cowan O'Brien didn't seem to share their sense of impending doom. And they certainly couldn't have known that a dramatic reversal in momentum was again about to occur.

Katie had never met this psychologist and she had never had the opportunity to cross-examine him, yet she certainly knew *of* him. "Doctor Brit" was an established Birmingham psychologist, well known because of his "Mental Health Forum" segment on a popular local television morning show. He had an excellent reputation among his peers, had taught at the University of Alabama, and had authored a number of well-received articles on family therapy. Among area prosecutors, however, he had earned a different reputation: a bright and knowledgeable practitioner who could be something of a "whore"—a professional who occasionally testified as a hired defense witness in criminal cases.

But, as is usually the case, the truth here wasn't that simple. McHugh often provided his services for little or no compensation, and this professional largesse seemed to swathe him in bias-proof armor. He made it clear that he believed in his causes—all of them. An intelligent and qualified expert who stated his opinions with great forcefulness and heartfelt sincerity was guaranteed to be a most influential witness. More than anything, he now seemed supremely self-confident, virtually assured that Katie O'Brien possessed neither the particular knowledge of psychology nor the baseline advocacy skills necessary to seriously challenge his testimony. Indeed, she was a virtual unknown quantity to the defense alliance. The psychologist had never heard of her; Rabon Creasey had only tried one case against Katie—when she was a young and quite inexperienced deputy prosecutor.

These miscalculations would work to Katie's distinct advantage.

Of course, the D.A. understood all along that the strength of the evidence couldn't assure her a conviction. If the jury accepted Dr. McHugh's expert opinion, it wouldn't be able to convict Hollins of intentional murder. Felony murder, perhaps, or manslaughter. In the worst-possible-case scenario for the prosecution, he could even be found not guilty by reason of mental disease or defect.

Katie O'Brien had no intention of permitting that to happen.

She rose now from her chair at the prosecution table, an impressive presence—five-feet-nine, lustrous chestnut hair, strikingly attractive. She moved slowly to the edge of the jury box, her eyes meeting those of nearly every juror. It was time, she decided, to start stripping away Dr. McHugh's cloak of invincibility. She began her counterattack by getting the witness to describe Hollins's diagnosed disorder, dissociative fugue, as a "disturbance in the normal functioning of identity and consciousness." Then she procured McHugh's assurance that the diagnosis was based exclusively on the official *Diagnostic and Statistical Manual* criteria and, of course, his own experience as a practitioner.

Katie thanked the man and stared up at the ceiling as if searching for inspiration in the fireproof acoustical tiles. When she glanced at the witness again, she noted that he was resting his chin on the tips of steepled fingers. *Good,* she thought. His body language, particularly this hand gesture, suggested that he was feeling confident, secure. She wanted him to march triumphantly into the trap she was setting for him. If she could extract his unqualified endorsement of the lure along the way, so much the better. Trapping an expert witness in a cage built by his own spurious testimony was all well and good; watching him set himself afire with the torch of his own ego was infinitely more satisfying.

Katie wanted to be careful about this particular attack. She knew dozens of people whose quality of life had been enhanced through the assistance of psychiatrists, psychologists, and other trained therapists. She also was acutely aware that several of these jurors had family members who'd been successfully treated for depression, sleeping disorders, and attention-deficit disorders. A broad and ill-conceived attack on all mental health professionals would not only be unproductive, it could absolutely alienate members of the jury.

At the same time, she was also well aware of the weaknesses in this science's foundation. For example, she knew that the *Diagnostic and Statistical Manual,* the official sources of most diagnostic criteria, had been generated by work groups and committees, had been subjected to blatant political and economic influences, and was a scientific resource only in the broadest construction of that term. Moreover, the manual had been designed and was intended for use in therapeutic situations—its descriptions, definitions, and constructs had little to do with the lexicon of legal insanity. As a result, psychologists who testified in legal proceedings often found themselves trying to wedge square pegs into round holes.

And, while Katie didn't believe psychology was a "voodoo science," she certainly recognized "voodoo testimony" when she heard it. She knew a great deal about personality disorders, in general, and dissociative disorders, in particular. She understood human nature well enough to know that Joe Terry Hollins had not been disabled by such a disorder when he stabbed and robbed Marie Anderson in her kitchen. He might well have had some type of malignant or destructive personality disorder, but this explanation wouldn't legally dissolve his intent to murder. In any event, what attorney Rabon Creasey had wanted was an excuse, not an explanation. For a price, McHugh had supplied a diagnosis that precisely satisfied Creasey's need: he had replaced Hollins's extreme self-centeredness and antisocial rage with some vague psychological fog. And McHugh's testimony essentially amounted to an ambush attack on the state—it was the product of a "secret," *ex parte* defense motion for expert assistance. As a result, Katie was a gladiator in phosphorescent armor sent to fight an unknown and invisible foe in a pitch-black coliseum.

She was, however, far from helpless.

After getting McHugh to concede that he had no firsthand knowledge of the murder itself, she moved in for the kill. The Anderson family had waited long enough.

"This diagnostic manual you've described, is it considered scientifically valid?"

"Oh, yes. Absolutely." McHugh folded his reading glasses and tucked them into a jacket pocket. "Each diagnosis is the end-product of years of research and study, and the criteria are intensively reviewed by expert panels and committees."

Katie moved slightly closer to her table. "And do you rely on these standards when you make diagnoses?"

"Of course. It's the official source—"

"You relied on that book when you diagnosed *this* defendant?"

McHugh paused slightly, as though a hint of suspicion now flickered in his consciousness. His eyes narrowed briefly as he regarded Katie. Then the doubt seemed to evaporate and he answered in a confident voice, "Yes, I did, Missus O'Brien. Of course I did."

"And you applied all the appropriate criteria?"

"Of course."

She moved decisively to her table now and pulled a thick book from her leather attaché. It already was marked with a red exhibit sticker. As she approached the witness stand, McHugh stiffened visibly.

"You do recognize this item, marked 'State's Exhibit Seventy-seven'?" she asked, handing the book to the psychologist.

He opened the volume, examined it briefly, handed it back to her.

"Yes," he said. "This would be the *Diagnostic and Statistical Manual TR Four* that I referenced earlier in my testimony." He made a valiant attempt to maintain the tone of authority in his voice, but it was apparent that he was surprised by the sudden production of the manual. Katie determined that he had considered— and ruled out—the possibility of actually being confronted with the authoritative text.

"This exhibit is an authentic copy of that manual, as published by the American Psychiatric Association?"

"Yes. Or at least it appears to be."

"As such, it will contain the approved categories of mental disorders along with text and diagnostic criteria?"

The color suddenly drained from the witness's face. Katie knew that he now realized what was coming. But it was too late for him to seek an alternate route to safety. He had not only allowed the prosecutor to bait her snare, he had blessed the bait and then marched confidently into the trap. Worse, by previously claiming complete reliance on the manual's diagnostic criteria, he had denied himself a significant "safety net"—the option of claiming that he also relied on groundbreaking, independent research into fugue states in making his diagnosis. The fact that such research may not have existed wouldn't have mattered: nobody in the courtroom, Katie included, would have been qualified to refute his claim. The D.A. noted the abrupt change in Dr. McHugh's body language. The victory "V" was gone from his cheek, the steepled hands were now clenched into tight balls. His arms were wrapped tightly around his accordion file, now his obvious defense structure. He no longer had the bearing of the wise and omniscient teacher. Now he looked like a man whose parachute had just failed to open.

"Yes," he said. "However, I think I should say—"

Katie handed the book back to him and walked a few paces away from the witness stand. "I'm sorry, Doctor," she interrupted. "You've spent the last hour and

a half saying what you think. Right now I'd like you to read to the jury the diagnostic criteria for *Dissociative Fugue State*." She turned obliquely toward the jury.
"Section three hundred point thirteen, if I'm not mistaken."

Rabon Creasey sputtered an objection.

"Overruled."

"You may answer the question," Katie said, politely but insistently.

McHugh retrieved the reading glasses. He positioned them on the bridge of
his nose, stared silently at a page for a moment, then read the criteria aloud.
Phrases such as "sudden and unexpected travel away from home" and "inability
to recall one's past" tumbled awkwardly from his now arid mouth.

"Tell the jury about Mister Hollins's 'sudden, unexpected travel away from
home'." Katie carefully avoided any hint of unctuousness in her voice. She didn't
want to alienate a jury which had clearly taken a liking to this witness.

Blood rushed to McHugh's face. "Well. Away from his home…ah…" He shot
an anxious glance at Creasey. The attorney stared down at his legal pad. "My
understanding is that he left Richfield and went to Birmingham."

"That's correct. He went to Birmingham to pawn a ring he stole—"

"I can't say for certain why he went there."

"—from Missus Anderson, whom he had just stabbed to death?"

"As I said, I can't—"

"He was actually living in Birmingham at the time of the offense, is that correct?"

"Well. You say 'living.' I think he was actually just staying with his mother."

"In Birmingham."

"Correct."

"Do you know the length of time he had been 'staying' with his mother
there?"

The psychologist shrugged. "I really don't know for sure."

"Would you care to consult your notes?"

McHugh fumbled with his file folder briefly, then said, "I believe he had been
there with his mother for some length of time."

"*Some length of time?*"

"I believe it would be at least a year, Missus…Madam District Attorney."

"Could it have been as long as *two years*, Doctor?" She opened a file on her
table and gave the appearance of searching for a particular document.

The witness swallowed reflexively. "A couple of years. Possibly."

Katie turned toward the jury and nodded. "So you would now agree that he
was 'living' there, as that word is commonly understood."

McHugh shrugged. "I suppose so. Dicing and mincing the meanings of words is your province, not mine."

Katie smiled. "You have found, in *your* province, that fleeing the scene of his crime and going directly to the place where he was living constituted *unexpected travel away from home*?"

The witness's embarrassed silence only served to call attention to the new wave of laughter in the room.

Katie continued: "If the evidence was that the defendant immediately left the scene of this murder and went straight to a Birmingham fence to sell the stolen property for drug money, would you say that his behavior was consistent or inconsistent with Dissociative Fugue State?"

McHugh shifted in his chair. "You have to understand…evaluating Mr. Hollins involved a complex series of interviews…He had no recollection of the events of the day in question, of amnesia for that particular event. And he exhibited a great deal of identity confusion as well—"

"Identity confusion? Let's talk about that." Katie now moved closer to the witness stand, compressing the psychologist with her now ponderous proximity. She watched with some amusement as he clasped the accordion file folder to his chest. She handed him a slip of paper. "I hand you an object which has been marked as 'State's Exhibit fifty-six' and which is already in evidence. It has previously been identified as the pawn ticket filled out by this defendant."

McHugh stared sullenly at the exhibit. "Yes," he said, at last.

"Please read the name signed at the bottom of that slip."

"Looks like 'Joe Tee Hollins'." He handed the exhibit back to Katie and glanced at Rabon Creasey. The attorney slumped forward in his chair, his head bowed.

"Is this consistent with someone confused about his identity?"

"I would have to say it was inconsistent, but—"

"Is there any warning or caution listed under three-hundred point thirteen?" Katie asked, again abruptly shifting gears and leaving another defect exposed. "Specifically with respect to malingering?"

"A warning? I believe so," he meekly replied.

"You 'believe so'? Would you like to look at the book and refresh your recollection, Doctor?" She took the *DSM* off the edge of the witness stand and re-offered it to him.

He sighed. "That's not necessary," he said. "There is such a warning."

"What is malingering, Doctor?"

"That would be appropriately diagnosed when the patient feigns his symptoms for some personal benefit," he said.

"And avoiding a death sentence would be 'some personal benefit,' in your opinion?"

"Yes."

"And avoiding punishment totally would be an even greater personal benefit?"

"I—"

"You have no firsthand knowledge of his mental state, isn't that correct, Doctor?"

"I'm not sure what you—"

"You weren't standing in Marie Anderson's kitchen when the defendant unlawfully entered her home? You weren't standing there, observing him or administering diagnostic tests, when he plunged the knife repeatedly into her body?" A pause. "When the defendant butchered Marie Anderson."

McHugh's face flushed momentarily. "I wasn't present, nor did I examine him at that time. But I saw him, at the request of his attorney, a few weeks later and was able to reconstruct his mental state from observation, testing, and examination of the available evidence."

"Relying on the diagnostic criteria we've just reviewed?"

"Yes, Missus O'Brien."

"Diagnostic criteria which, to use your own words, are absolutely reliable, the 'profession's diagnostic authority'?"

Another audible sigh. "That is true."

She paused, debating whether she should take one more step with this witness. She was confident that she had already accomplished her essential cross-examination goals: he had admitted the deficiencies of the diagnosis stated on direct examination, and he had made important concessions to her case. True, Rabon Creasey could, and probably would, make some effort to rehabilitate McHugh on re-direct exam. And Creasey certainly had the oratorical skills to entrance the jury during his closing argument and, at least for the moment, direct its collective eye back to the defense theory. But the damage had been done, and the jury had been witness to it—not even Rabon Creasey could un-ring that bell. To ask even one more question now would violate every rule of effective trial advocacy. Katie understood this, and the risks associated with asking the "one, fatal question too many."

At the same time, she also understood that risks, calculated and foreseen, were occasionally worth taking. She determined that the burnish had been scalded off the good doctor. No longer just an authoritative media personality, perhaps he would respond like that which he really was: simply an intelligent man, well-schooled in a science of constructs and consensus. Perhaps, now given the opportunity to shine as a true expert, he could redeem himself before leaving the stand.

She made her decision.

"One more thing, Doctor McHugh," she said. "Did you ever formulate an opinion about his sanity or not at the time the offense was committed?"

McHugh, seemingly alarmed by the question, shot a look at Rabon Creasey.

"What do you mean…his sanity…?"

Katie, too, glanced at her adversary to gauge his reaction to this question. He twitched slightly, almost imperceptibly, but said nothing. Katie had felt confident that he wouldn't object or otherwise interfere with this line of questioning. For one thing, the judge would probably overrule the objection and would be correct in doing so. For another, it was a question to which the jury would very much want an answer. As an experienced trial lawyer, Creasey would understand that an objection at this point would only call more attention to the answer. All he could do was hope that McHugh would handle it. The discomfort in his eyes told Katie that he had no real expectation that this result would obtain.

"Yes," Katie said. "Apart from the dissociative fugue state that we've already discussed, do you have an opinion, to a reasonable degree of medical certainty, whether this defendant was suffering from a severe mental disease or defect at the time of the offense?"

The witness took a deep breath. "In my opinion, he was not."

Rabon Creasey sagged visibly, and a wave of murmuring rolled through the courtroom.

"He was not?"

"No, ma'am."

Katie paused a moment for effect, then thanked Dr. McHugh and returned to her counsel table. Kevin Rose flashed a smile and slid a note over to her. It read, "I am Woman—watch me kick some Man-ass!" She folded the note and stuck it in her jacket pocket.

"I don't believe I have anything else for this witness," she announced. She allowed her eyes to meet those of several jurors, then rise fractionally to the representatives of the Anderson family.

She was sure she saw relief in every face.

The spectators spilled from the courtroom after Hollins was sentenced, briefly turning the narrow second-floor hallway into a swarming hive of activity. Some of the individuals gathered into small murmuring clusters along the walls; others headed silently toward the broad stairway which led to the courthouse lobby. Most of the media representatives fell into synchronized step behind the district attorney, who, along with her staff and members of the Anderson family, was moving briskly away from the courtroom doors.

The hulking, bearded man in a threadbare plaid shirt had worked his way into the hallway with the other trial spectators. He slouched, slightly compressing himself, and attempted to merge into the rapidly moving human current. He doubted that Katie would even know him now—he had added a shaggy beard and forty-odd pounds of mass in prison—still, he didn't want to risk recognition.

The D.A. turned suddenly and looked right at him—or, more accurately, *through* him. Exactly as he had expected her to do. There was no reaction, no sign of recognition from her. *Nothing.* She turned away, spoke to an associate, flashed a confident grin. She kept on walking and never looked back at him.

The man gave a snort of amused confirmation. She hadn't the first clue who he was. And why should she? After all, he was just another generic dirt clump on the slope of her personal ambition. She had crushed him underfoot, then haughtily marched on. His personal hell, the eight long years of unjustified abuse, meant absolutely nothing to her.

Maybe the state of her general awareness would be changing soon.

He had watched much of the trial from a seat on the back row. He had wanted to observe her in action, evaluate her current performance level. Was she a more skilled advocate now than when she had convicted him? The jury had convicted Hollins, but then what prosecutor wouldn't have seemed competent with such a cut-and-dried case? She *had* shown flashes of brilliance—her cross-examination of the psychologist, for example—but it was evident that there was still a great deal that she didn't understand.

Like her own true self-worth and cosmic importance. Like all those self-involved, spoiled little Carry College women, she imagined herself to be some manner of perfect life form—floating above the lesser world, repelled by all things common. Judging and demanding, acquiring or rejecting with simple waves of the hand. In reality, though, she was nothing more than he was. *Than all humans were.* In the end, she was simply a mortal fabrication of elemental parts: atoms, waves, energy. Drained of that energy, she'd have no more significance than a simple rock. She would never spend time reflecting upon this truth, of course. Few humans would. Unless, of course, they had endless hours, days, and months to sit in a cold cell with nothing but pain and their thoughts to keep them company.

And there were probably other things about which she was clueless.

She probably didn't even know yet about the murders. She'd been too busy shooting fish in a barrel. At that precise moment, Katie was still euphoric from her "conquest." There was no one in her world now but herself, and no news in the world but that of her guilty verdict.

Even when she learned of the killings, she would never truly understand them. She hadn't seen the woman's eyes. *Like he had.* Dull and glazed, to be sure, but still able to recognize the cruel end that was coming.

He paused as he watched the D.A. disappear around a corner. He rubbed his scraggly beard and grinned

The horror, he thought, would catch up to her soon enough. Nothing got the community's attention like an ever-increasing body count. Especially when the killer managed to elude the authorities. It would get Katie O'Brien's attention, too, but would she be able to do anything about it?

Soon, the man thought, all of Richfield would get a chance to see how smart Katie O'Brien *really* was.

CHAPTER 3

▼

Most of Katie's entourage had made it into the second-floor stairwell by the time she was cornered by the clutch of persistent news reporters. Eerie shadows danced on the chipped plaster wall behind her as she squinted into the intense floodlight glare.

The question she had very much wanted to avoid came flying at her like a live grenade.

"Why didn't ya'll ask for the death penalty?" a voice had demanded from beyond the wash of light.

Katie had sagged momentarily. The tension in her jaw confessed her frustration with the case resolution and with this inquiry. She understood that, for the reporters, a manageable morsel of mini-information, compressed for deadline and editing purposes, was far preferable to a lengthy but heartfelt discourse on the complexities of the process. At the same time, there was no sound-bite-sized expression that could fully describe the emotional torture Marie Anderson's family had undergone. In the end, the decision to spare Hollins's life had been based on the family's belief that Marie Anderson would not have wanted her killer executed.

But Katie had also detected latent political and personal implications—real or imagined—in the death penalty question. If the provocations were imagined, nobody could really blame her for her touchiness. After she'd been appointed D.A., remarks allegedly made in barber shops and country club locker rooms had made their way back to her. Among the comments that she had found most irritating was "she doesn't have the stones to put a man in the electric chair." And it was no secret that the Richfield "good ol' boy" establishment had already recruited several young lawyers to run against her. But she had promised on the day of her investiture to follow the law and aggressively pursue drug sellers and violent criminals. She'd publicly declared on many occasions that she wouldn't hesitate to seek the death penalty in an appropriate case.

And then, there she was, at the conclusion of her very first capital case, asking the jury to spare a cold-blooded killer's life.

The truth of the matter was, while she would have no problem asking for death in a fitting circumstance, she really wasn't enthusiastic about the idea of capital punishment as it operated in actual practice. For one thing, it took so long to actually execute someone—twelve-to-fifteen-year delays for appeals weren't uncommon—that it clearly failed in one of its primary stated purposes: deterring others from committing similar crimes. How could a man's execution deter a potential criminal who was only a toddler when the capital crime took place? And the years of imprisonment while the appeals worked their way slowly through the courts made a delayed execution seem almost pointless. If society had managed to endure for fifteen years while the execution order was stayed, how would the killer's death now make the world a better place? Beyond that, there seemed to be a sort of intellectual dishonesty at every level of judicial action regarding capital punishment. The courts all paid lip service to the death penalty's constitutional-ity, yet they bounced death cases around like ping-pong balls, constantly invent-ing new technical reasons to subvert executions. And trial judges, who had been given the power to override jury verdicts sparing a defendant's life, seemed, as elected officials, necessarily wired to a make a substantially political decision.

Because of the complexities of the diverse capital punishment issues, Katie tried to avoid the many related questions inevitably fired at her in situations such as this. Did she approve of the ridiculous and tortured road to executions? *No, absolutely not.* Could she ask a jury to impose a death sentence? *Of course she could.* Those who accused her of being "too soft" had obviously forgotten that she had once killed a man in self-defense. And she had never felt guilty about it either, never had been crippled by post-traumatic stress. The kidnapping of her son by cold-blooded killers had been a frightening ordeal, and she hated the idea of having to end another human life. But her action had saved her life; more importantly, it had saved her son. And she would do it again in a minute if it ever became necessary.

So Katie had reluctantly turned to face the lights, cameras, and tape recorders and had answered the question. She told the shadow reporters lurking in the nimbus of light that it had been a joint decision arrived at by the D.A.'s office, the investigating officers, and the family of Marie Anderson. It had been a hard decision, she had added, but it had been the right decision.

And then, flanked by her top deputies, Kevin Rose and Berry Macklin, she had disappeared into the stairwell.

They climbed, and when they were about to reach the third-floor door, Katie heard a voice echoing in the concrete and steel chamber. She turned and saw a woman clambering up the stairs right behind them. Katie recognized her as *Richfield Ledger* courthouse beat reporter Andrea "Andy" Renauld. Tall and athletic-looking with a thick mane of blonde hair, Renauld climbed two steps at a time even though she had two equipment bags strapped across her shoulders.

"If I could have one more minute, I have a few more questions," the reporter said, barely breathing hard.

"I don't have anything else to say about the case, Andy."

"This isn't about Hollins." She sneaked a glance behind her, as if to ensure that she hadn't been followed.

Katie gave Renauld a puzzled look. What issue could be so pressing that a news reporter would sprint up a staircase after her? No matter. It wasn't about the Hollins case, and that was an immense relief to the D.A.

Katie glanced at her watch. *Twelve-forty.* She had planned to grab a bite to eat, clear off her desk, and spend the rest of the afternoon with her son. She wanted to make up for weeks of neglect brought about by the Hollins case. But another few minutes at the office wasn't going to cause him irreparable emotional harm.

"All right," she said. "Let's get out of the stairwell."

Andy followed the D.A. into the office's cramped reception area. Katie allowed her overstuffed brown accordion case file to tumble into a chair. She sank into another chair and gestured for Renauld to sit across from her. Berry Macklin, the head of the violent-crime unit and the office's first African-American prosecutor, leaned against the wall behind the desk of Laurie Ross, Katie's secretary. Andy sank into a chair and let the two bags slide to the floor.

"Okay, shoot," Katie said.

Renauld tapped the side of her pen on her open reporter's notebook. "I need to get a quick comment on the body they just found out in the county."

Katie shot an alarmed glance at Berry Macklin.

"I'm sorry, Andy," she said. "I don't have the first idea what you're talking about."

"Oh, I'm sorry. I assumed that you would have heard. A call came out about twenty minutes ago on one of the sheriff's frequencies. Someone found the body

of a young woman out in the Hazard Creek area. I picked it up on my scanner."
She held up one of her bags to show Katie the cell-phone-sized police-band scanner protruding from a side pocket. "I'm running out there in a second to see what's going on. I thought, since I was already in the courthouse, I might get a comment from you before I head that way."

"I've been in court all morning," Katie replied, with a look of bemused amazement on her face. "Twenty minutes ago, when you heard the dispatch, I was listening to Rabon Creasey's five hundred post-trial motions. When I finally got out of court, I was answering questions about what took place in court. Then I was in the stairwell with you. When could I possibly have heard about it?"

"Sorry. I just thought someone might have said something to you."

Katie shook her head. "Nope. It takes us a while to transition from one media event to another. So was she buried, lying out in a field…"

"Don't know yet. Like I said, I'm gonna run out there and see if I can talk to someone at the scene."

"Okay, they found a body of a young woman in the county. What's your question?"

"Do you believe that the killer is gonna be the man who kidnapped the women from the Carry College campus?"

Katie's jaw dropped. "Can we talk off the record for a minute here?"

Renauld tapped her pen on the open page and didn't reply.

"Is that a problem?" Katie asked.

"No," Andy replied. "Just as long as I can get something official for my story." She sneaked a quick glance at her wristwatch.

"Andy, I've been in a capital murder trial for a week. The week before that I was getting ready for trial. Right now, I couldn't even tell you what day of the month it is. I don't even know for a fact that these missing women were, ah, kidnapped. And I sure don't know that this woman they just found was murdered. Or that they actually even found a dead woman. Much less that these two things are connected." She shrugged. "I'd like to help you out, but I'm afraid I'm just a little out of the loop on the facts."

"I'm sorry, Missus O'Brien—"

"Call me Katie. Please."

"Sorry. Katie. I don't mean to put you on the spot. Really and truly. I've just gotta write something on the Hollins case and then put a story together on this other thing." She sighed heavily. "Our deadline was actually noon. I'm gonna have to throw something together on the road and call it in." She gave the D.A. a weary smile. "I think I'm in a little over my head at the moment."

Katie smiled back at the reporter. She could certainly relate to Andy's dilemma. When she had been about her age—she guessed Andy was somewhere in the early to mid-twenties—she had worked as a prosecutor in the office's property-crime unit. She could recall times when she carried as many as two hundred active felony cases at a time. On many occasions, she had found herself scrambling madly just to keep her head above water. Just like Andy, she had balanced and juggled and eaten a lot of bad food on the run. Katie knew that Andy had inherited the courthouse and metro beats after the previous reporter left the *Ledger* for a job with the Birmingham paper. In the beginning, she had seemed utterly lost, a virtual deer in the headlights, but she had proved to be a very fast learner.

Katie didn't know her all that well, but she was pretty sure that she liked the young reporter. Andy seemed to be very bright and, from all her courthouse evaluations, she got her job done. She wasn't what one would call obtrusive, but she was extraordinarily persistent. She certainly was an imposing physical presence—tall, attractive, and very much in shape, a former college track, basketball, and softball athlete. But impressive and persistent as she might have been, she had always recognized and respected boundaries. Her pieces, written in stripped-down A.P.-style prose, were standard newspaper fare, but they seemed balanced and, most importantly, factually accurate. In the end, though, Andy Renauld was essentially just another newsdog: a bottom-line fact gatherer with a deadline, someone always composing and pasting on the run. Katie just hoped that she wasn't going to rush into a speculative story that would provoke an already jittery community.

"Are you aware that Kerry Grinder's sister has hired an attorney who's criticizing ya'll's performance in these cases?" Andy asked.

"Her sister?"

"Yeah. Ima Something-or-other." She flipped back through her notebook. "Ima Lee."

"In what way are we being criticized?"

"Well, he said stuff like, this is 'obviously the work of a serial kidnapper' and that your office and the police have 'fumbled the ball' on this investigation."

Katie and Macklin exchanged glances again.

"No, Andy, I wasn't aware of that. Who exactly is this person and when did he make this ludicrous pronouncement?"

Renauld flipped pages in her notebook. "The man's name is Jay Grady Spangler. He's a lawyer in Memphis, or some other kind of official family representative. The press conference was yesterday afternoon." She flashed an uncomfortable smile. "My editor plans to run something in the late edition. You know, a sidebar piece to run with the story about the coed's body being found—"

Katie blinked. "Wait a second. The body's been identified? Already?"

Blood rushed to Andy's face. "Well, no. Not officially. But I think everybody's just kind of assumed that—"

"Who's *everybody*?"

Andy shrugged. "The managing and city editors, just for two. And I think the police have sort of made that connection. At least, that seems to be what I'm hearing." She patted the scanner. "One of the responding officers said that the dead woman seems to match the physical attributes of one of the victims."

"*Seems* to match?"

"Apparently the body's decomposed somewhat over time. And that's another thing. How long has it been since the women disappeared?"

Katie sighed. "I'm not sure, Andy. A couple of weeks. Like I said—"

"I understand your situation completely. It's just that all this is sort of exploding right now. You know, with the angry relatives, the freaked-out Carry folks." Her pen continued to tap out a furious cadence on the metal notebook binding. "And, of course, now the dead body. I think everyone's been dreading this, but sort of expecting it at the same time. That's why I'm kind of desperate for something."

"All right, Andy. This is what I feel like I can say on the record." Katie leaned back in her chair and massaged her temples. "This office has been working, and is prepared to continue to work, with local law enforcement in bringing this offender or offenders to justice." She paused, staring at the acoustical ceiling tiles overhead. "Any information that is brought before the District Attorney—" She suddenly rocked forward in her chair and frowned at Andy Renauld. "Did I just refer to myself in the third person?"

"I think you did," Renauld replied, grimacing. Then the grimace was slowly replaced with a sly grin. "But I'm willing to work with you."

"Thank you. I promised myself I'd quit if I ever did that. And the other quote sounded absolutely retarded."

"Let's try a little question and answer. That might make it easier." When Katie didn't respond, Andy asked, "Do ya'll have any kind of suspect right now?"

"Not that I'm aware of. That doesn't mean the police aren't working on something, even as we speak."

"Do you think there's any connection between the body found at Hazard Creek and the kidnappings?"

Katie made a face. "Off the record again real quick?"

The reporter nodded.

"Andy, the only thing I know about this alleged body is what you've told me. How in the hell am I supposed to comment officially on that?"

"Okay, unofficially…"

"Unofficially, I can't speculate on connections between things I don't even know exist."

"Could you maybe call somebody? The case investigator…"

"No, Andy. They'll call me when they've got something."

"Do you think this might be…" The reporter paused, almost as though dreading the rest of the question.

"Might be…"

"I don't know. The work of some kind of a…serial killer?"

Katie sighed. "Andy. If what you've heard is true, we've got one body. *One.* Even assuming that there's a woman's body and that she was murdered, there's only one victim. It's really hard to characterize anything as serial if there's only one of it."

"But you do have another young woman missing…"

"Missing, but not necessarily kidnapped."

Andy smiled awkwardly, closed her notebook, and got to her feet.

"Okay," she said. "I guess that's all I can think of. I better head out to the scene. I can call in the Hollins story en route." She threw a bag over a shoulder and shrugged. "Maybe I'll get lucky and find out something when I get there."

Katie rose and extended her hand. "Sorry I wasn't much help."

The reporter smiled and shook the D.A.'s hand. "Don't worry, I'm sure there'll be a lot more to talk about in the weeks and months to come." She gave Katie's hand a slight additional squeeze and cut her eyes quickly in Berry Macklin's direction.

"Berry," the District Attorney said. "Could you do something for me?"

"You name it, boss."

"Can you see if you can go round up Kevin?"

"You got it. What's up?"

"The three of us need to get together and talk about something." She winked at her assistant and flashed a quick smile at the reporter.

When Macklin had gone, Andy Renauld said, "Thank you so much, Katie. I'm sorry if I'm interfering with anything important. I just…needed to tell you one more thing."

"You bet. Shoot."

"I didn't really want to say this in front of Berry. It's just that—" Renauld took a deep breath and exhaled slowly. "Okay, it's true that we're running a story on this thing, the dead woman. And it's true that I've got to write something for the final. But, more than anything else, I asked most of these questions for my own personal reasons."

Katie's brow furrowed. "I don't understand—"

"I live in that same general neighborhood, near the college. Plus, I attended Carry on volleyball and basketball scholarships before I transferred to Alabama. Quite frankly, I'm scared to death about all this. Who's doing this? *Why* is he doing it? Who's gonna be next? Why not *me*? Have you noticed that both of the kidnapped women were tall and blonde?" She stared at the floor and slowly shook her head. "I tell you, I come in from work late at night and I'm shaking. I just know someone's gonna jump out of the shadows and grab me before I can get to my door."

"Andy, I really don't think that—"

"I know, I know," the reporter interrupted. "These are probably just two random, unrelated cases. The dead woman probably didn't have anything to do with Carry College." She traced a square floor tile with the toe of her right foot. "It's just that I have this weird…I don't know, *intuition* about all this. Somehow, I just *know* that there's some twisted serial kidnapper and killer on the loose in my neighborhood."

Katie grimaced. "God, Andy, I hope you're wrong about that."

"Me, too. Anyway, I just wanted to explain…I guess I just need to know something for my own peace of mind."

"No explanation necessary. I completely understand your concern. But the city and the campus police have both beefed up their patrols in the area. They've got plain-clothes cops in unmarked cars positioned throughout Southpark. I feel sure that there won't be any more abductions. And I can assure you that we're working on finding the guy and getting him off the street. I wasn't just blowing smoke a while ago when I made that statement."

"I believe you," Andy said.

After an awkward moment of silence, the reporter shook Katie's hand again and then headed out into the main hallway. After a few steps, she stopped and turned back toward the D.A.

"I guess I'll see you and your two deputies out at Hazard Creek Road here in a minute," she said, flashing a confident and knowing grin.

Katie felt the prickle of blood rushing once again to her cheeks, then began smiling herself.

"I guess you will," she said.

Then, as she watched the reporter hustle toward the public elevators, she murmured to herself: *I know one thing, sister—no attacker is ever going to outsmart you.*

CHAPTER 4

▼

Bobby Joe Franks stepped from his black Crown Victoria, and his scuffed black boots sent a puff of dust into the stifling air. He straightened his sturdy frame, grimacing as pain radiated through his lower back. The asphalt road, no more than fourteen feet wide at that point, glittered under the midday sun. The air was alive with the electric drone of dying cicadas.

Franks adjusted his sunglasses and surveyed the area. Crops grew on most of the land in this corner of Bienville County, but here, at this exact point, the cultivated fields ended and rolling wooded hills began. Just to the south, corn seared by a rainless August sagged on a thousand crispy brown stalks. Beyond the corn field lay acres of parched cotton and soybeans—a sea of green, tan, and brown. Imperiled crops simmering in the unrelenting heat. A small crowd of gawking spectators had gathered near the line of trees north of Hazard Creek Road. A deputy, attired in the navy and gray uniform of the Bienville County Sheriff's Department, stood between the crowd and the woods. Three buzzards floated in a menacing circle above the trees.

Franks frowned as he thought of the farmer's wasted hours, the hopes for a bountiful harvest withering with his crop. He knew firsthand the clawing fear of impending ruin, the sense of utter helplessness. You prayed for rain at just the right time, you prayed it would stop raining. Sometimes the weather cooperated; often it did not. It had not been that long ago that this very specter had haunted him, as well. Now he had different problems, a new set of professional difficulties, a new reason to fear failure.

"What're *you* doin' here?" barked a red-faced man standing in the tall grass at the top of the clay bank. He was short but very wide, a virtual vending machine with limbs.

Franks took a long, final drag on his unfiltered cigarette and slammed the Crown Victoria's door. He crushed the cigarette butt under his boot and discharged a defiant stream of smoke in the man's direction.

"Wha'dya mean, what am I doing here?" he snapped. "I'm a taxpaying citizen of this state and county." His voice was deep and coarse, almost a growl. "Give me one reason I can't be here." He took a few steps toward the man then paused, a boot resting on a rock protruding from a thicket of dying sage.

Bienville County Sheriff's Lieutenant Gordon Childs' face seemed to redden even more.

"I ain't saying you *can't* be here, Bobby Joe," he said. "You just off your turf. That's all I'm saying. City jurisdiction ended back yonder, the other side of the highway." He folded his arms, mirroring Franks's defiant attitude. "But, of course, you already knew that."

"I wasn't aware that there were jurisdictional rules for ordinary citizens," Franks said. He trudged up the dirt bank at the edge of the road, crushing dusty Queen Anne's Lace, sage, and goldenrod underfoot as he climbed.

"Is that what you're being, Bobby Joe? An ordinary citizen?"

"You damn straight. Just a citizen who happened to be passing by on a public road." He lifted both hands in the air. "Look, do you see my shield? No, you don't. I'm not even armed."

Childs's eyes narrowed. "What's that in your back pocket?"

Franks glanced at the pocket and shrugged. "Nothing but a harmless old digital camera."

"Fine," Gordon Childs said, at last. "Since you're merely observing, you can stand over there, with all them other nonparticipating citizen-observers." He nodded in the direction of the crowd of onlookers. "I hope you got a real powerful telephoto lens."

Bobby Joe Franks cut his eyes in the direction of the onlookers. A dozen people, mostly farmers who lived along Hazard Creek. The deputy, his thumbs hooked in his leather utility belt, was staring up at the circling buzzards. Franks returned his penetrating gaze to the lieutenant. He watched a sly grin slowly cross Childs's face.

Franks tried to maintain his defiant countenance, but his expression softened, eventually rounding into a grin of his own. He had known Childs for more than twenty years. The two men had been in the same police academy class, had served together as uniformed officers on the Richfield city police force. They had taken their investigator exams together, been handed their gold shields on the same day. For a year and a half, they had sat at adjoining desks in the Homicide-Robbery Unit of the police Criminal Investigative Division. They had waded through gruesome crime scenes together, struggled through the bureaucratic tangle of reports, forms, and investigative supplements. Each had known long nights with suspects and witnesses, followed by bleary-eyed days in Bienville County courtrooms.

But the rising arc of their careers had been collapsed by the harsh gravity of public controversy. On a warm July night five years earlier, Bobby Joe Franks had lost control. An intoxicated and aggressive young strong-arm robbery suspect—a scholarship athlete at Carry College—picked the wrong night to resist arrest. After being physically attacked by the indignant subject, Franks struck the young man several times in the head and face before finally getting him handcuffed. Officially, the arrest report claimed the need to employ certain "striking techniques" in order to bring the man "under control." Privately, however, he confessed to a number of understanding fellow officers that he "had lost it" after having been punched, spat at, and kicked in the groin. The arrestee's outraged family publicly demanded "justice" for their son's "brutalization." The appeals ignited a spark of public indignation; fanned by the steady breeze of media condemnation, a rogue fire of outrage soon raced through the community. *The Richfield Ledger* demanded an investigation while a few individuals and groups angrily called for the filing of criminal charges. Gordon Childs resigned in the wake of the incident, eventually accepting a better-paying job in the plumbing supply business. Franks soon resigned, as well. Although he had eventually been completely exonerated by an inter-agency review board, Richfield Police Internal Affairs, the Justice Department, and a Bienville County Grand Jury, the experience—the requisite, but nevertheless humiliating suspension, the nonstop questioning, the persistently accusatory op/ed polemics—had so embittered him that he felt no desire to remain in policing. It infuriated him that common street thugs were fashioned into martyrs while cops, who placed their lives on the line daily for coolie wages, were hamstrung, muzzled, and universally vilified. He didn't mind aspiring to the impossible performance standards that society had imposed upon his profession; he just wanted to be forgiven for being, in addition to his roles of protector, physician, psychologist, attorney, and clergyman, an ordinary human.

He had turned hopefully to cattle farming, working sixty head of mixed Angus-Hereford cows on two hundred leased acres in the northern part of the

Bienville County. His uncle had been a cattleman and Bobby Joe had learned a little about that business while spending summers on his farm. Franks worked hard at his new career, doing everything from cutting and baling hay to administering shots to ailing cows. He wanted desperately to succeed, to make a living far from perpetual scrutiny and harsh public judgments.

But it had been a brutal time for all farmers. A long-term drought, worsened by crippling heat, officially began the summer before his second crop of calves were due. The clover and fescue pastures were eaten down to bare earth and his three ponds nearly dried up. With only hay from a single cutting on hand, Franks was required to purchase hundreds of bales to feed his animals. By the end of his third full year, he discovered that he was buried in debt with no relief in sight. Exhausting days and anxiety-filled nights had been rewarded by the distinct possibility of long-term financial ruin. Even worse, his fifteen-year marriage soon collapsed under the cumulative weight of his difficulties—the controversy surrounding the brutality accusation, the murderous work hours and economic hardships, his ever-deepening depression, and, finally, accusations of "transient violent behavior." Beaten down now by two separate vocations, Franks knew that he had to find a steady paycheck. He was tens of thousands in debt, and additionally had heavy family support obligations. When a new chief of police offered him his old job—conditioned on successful completion of anger management counseling—he reluctantly accepted.

Now, all these years later, Franks and Childs were both back in policing, Childs as a supervisor with the sheriff's department's investigative division. The two men worked different shifts for different agencies and, therefore, crossed paths only infrequently. Despite this fact, they remained friends and, more importantly, allies—decorated veterans of an undeclared and never-ending war.

Franks had been eating lunch at a nearby barbecue restaurant when he had overheard the first dispatch on the sheriff's frequency. The voice of the dispatcher, flat but urgent in tone, had crackled from the portable scanner sitting on the table. A farmer on a tractor had discovered the remains of a human body. Units from the Sheriff's Department and Alabama Bureau of Investigation, the county coroner, and field agents of the Department of Forensic Sciences had been summoned. Franks had left for the scene without finishing his chicken plate or iced tea. One could never tell when a discovered piece of evidence could end up being the critical piece to the puzzle of an unsolved case. And Franks had a very troubling unsolved case hanging like a guillotine blade over his neck.

A string of vehicles rumbled up the narrow road. Franks turned and watched the procession—an ambulance, followed immediately by a state trooper's patrol unit, followed by the coroner's van, a hearse driven by the deputy coroner, a local television station's remote unit, and three passenger cars—fall into line behind his unmarked Ford.

He tapped a fresh cigarette from the pack in his shirt pocket.

"Ah, hell," he muttered, nodding in the direction of the road. Yet another car, the sheriff's official vehicle, a shiny black Chevrolet, had rumbled into view. "If it ain't the high sheriff himself."

"Oh, yeah. You think he's about to pass up a photo opportunity like this?"

"I gotta go take a look at the scene, Gordy. Seriously. I need to have a look for myself before the buffalo herd tromps it down." The ironic edge in the investigator's voice had suddenly been replaced by an urgent, almost plaintive tone.

"Why? Why do you *need* to go down there?"

"Because I've got some loose ends floating. I've got a potential kidnapping I'm working on. A girl from the college." Franks took off his sunglasses and slid them into his shirt pocket. "Twenty-year-old junior. I know you've seen it on the news—"

"Only like every fifteen minutes."

Franks lit the cigarette and took a deep and pensive drag. He paused, wondering just how much information he needed to give the sheriff's investigator. At last, he said: "There actually may have been two kidnappings. Possible kidnappings, I meant to say."

"*Possible* kidnappings?"

"Chief don't want to call them abductions yet, but that's the way I'm leaning. If this turns out to be either of those girls—" He paused and took another deep drag. "I just need to eyeball the scene before it gets trampled. You know, just in case." His steely blue-grey eyes met Childs's. "I don't need to remind you about what happened on that Fitcheard case."

Childs shifted uneasily. It wouldn't be easy to forget that case. Leon Fitcheard, an ex-convict wanted for a Richfield robbery-murder, had been arrested in a hunting cabin deep in the Bienville County hills. The sheriff's crime scene team claimed primary jurisdiction, and worked the arrest scene before Richfield P.D. was ever notified. When Franks was finally called, he learned that a rookie investigator had destroyed blood-soaked towels and garments—a veritable treasure trove of potential forensic evidence—claiming that they were "biohazards." Investigative supervisor Gordon Childs, infuriated by this appalling lack of professionalism, had quietly accepted complete responsibility for the screw-up.

"I hear what you're saying, Bobby," Childs said, at last. "But things have changed around here. We got a couple of cracker-jack crime scene guys now. I don't think anything like that Fitcheard mess will ever happen again. At least, not on my watch. And you know how the sheriff is about these jurisdictional things. He thinks the county folks ought to work county cases."

Franks nodded. There wasn't a law enforcement officer in Bienville County who wasn't painfully aware of the ongoing feud between the sheriff and the chief of police. It had begun three years earlier when the sheriff had refused to serve a search warrant obtained by Richfield investigators. The city cops had reciprocated by seizing and confiscating an airplane and truck that the county had hoped to seize and condemn. This pathetic failure of cooperation had ultimately led to the withdrawal of city officers from a joint drug task force and a ridiculous sense of territoriality by both departments. The Fitcheard fiasco had only served to harden feelings. Jurisdictional lines now were strictly observed, crime scenes jealously guarded.

"You don't know that this person was killed out in this field," Bobby Franks said, at last. "Have ya'll found any evidence that the murder took place right here?"

"No," Childs drawled, "but it could've been."

"But she could've been killed somewhere else and just dumped here."

"She wasn't just *dumped*, Bobby."

"Why do you say that?"

"Because whoever done it spent some time with her. Yessir. Spent some dadgum time down there with her."

Franks set his jaw. "My girls are still missing and unaccounted for."

Both men watched Sheriff Eddie Walton get out of his car and greet the stream of reporters and cameramen.

"I mean, what difference does it make?" Franks asked. "The district attorney's gonna handle the case no matter which department works it."

The sheriff's lieutenant sighed and said, "If you're going, you better get on it before Eddie gets here."

"Thanks, man. Just give me some kind of idea what I'm gonna find down there."

Childs shrugged. "Basically a nude body. Dead, of course. Female. Not a pretty sight."

Franks stared blankly. He didn't say it, but he had never seen a murder crime scene that was a pretty sight.

"Anyway, a body left like that, you know, out in the elements—" Childs shook his head. "Out there with all the bugs and animals and what have you." He shuddered. "It don't take long in this heat for 'em to get ripe on you."

Franks took another drag off the cigarette.

"Plus, they's some other stuff, too, Bobby. Deeply disturbing stuff."

Franks's brow furrowed. "Like what?"

"You'll see. A bunch of weirdness, if you ask me." Childs's eyes narrowed and lifted fractionally. "You better boot it, hoss. Here they all come."

Franks made a face. "What kind of weird stuff?"

"Hell, I don't know, Bobby. Creepy stuff. I mean, whoever done this didn't just kill the girl. They done stuff to her. Looks like one of them cult killings you see on them police shows. I guarantee you ain't never seen a murder scene like this one." Childs swiped at his face again with the handkerchief. "Go see for yourself."

Franks patted his old friend on the shoulder and began marching toward the trees. A murder scene unlike any he'd ever worked? He had a hard time imagining that. He'd worked so many death cases over the years that he felt like he'd seen one of everything. He'd seen humans who'd been bludgeoned with aluminum ball bats, hacked with axes, blown apart with high explosives. He'd seen teenagers who'd shot their best friends and young adults who had accidently strangled themselves while masturbating with nooses around their necks. He had helped lower hanging victims and fish floaters out of muddy waters. He'd even removed charred bones from a heap of burnt tires.

The one thing he'd never seen was a young woman—a person not dissimilar in age and appearance from his own daughter—murdered as part of some bizarre cult ritual. If that, indeed, was what this was all about. But even that grim prospect didn't cause him excessive concern. A lifeless body was, after all, a lifeless body. He was a professional, and investigating death scenes happened to be his profession. What *did* bother him was the haunting possibility that this particular lifeless body might be one of his kidnapping victims. He had already become so much more than a disinterested fact-gathering bureaucrat in that investigation. He had spent hours with distraught relatives, friends, and anxious school administrators. He had looked at dozens of photographs of the two students, listened to countless stories about their lives. He saw their smiling, very much alive faces at night when he closed his eyes. He felt almost like a member of their extended families, someone with an emotional stake in their safe return. He rarely got an opportunity to close out his cases with happy news for families and friends. Just this one time, he wanted things to be different.

Anjanette Donna Crawley. Her name burned like a firebrand into his consciousness. An interesting name, maybe even a movie star's name. She had been the first to disappear, having last been seen in the campus library on a sultry night on the 4th of August. An outstanding student, a junior in pre-med, Crawley had been active in many campus organizations. A local media "missing person" blitz was about to expand into a national campaign. According to his captain, the woman's mother and father had already been to see the chief of police and were planning to appear soon on a cable news network.

The second coed to disappear, on the other hand, was a different story. From what Franks had been able to patch together from incongruent reports, Kerry Grinder was either a misunderstood genius who had overcome a troubled childhood or a pathological trouble-maker, a manipulative child of privilege who had defrauded her way into Carry College. A sophomore art history major, she had a well-documented track record of disappearances and reappearances. She had last been seen the previous weekend at a nightclub frequented by Carry students. Witnesses reported that she left to "go to the restroom" and never returned. This matter hadn't yet been turned into an official "missing-persons investigation," but it weighed on Franks's mind anyway.

He waded through tall, dry grass and paused at the edge of the trees. He glanced up, then back toward Hazard Creek Road. He clenched his jaw. *Vultures everywhere.*

He took the camera and a cloth handkerchief out of his back pocket, took a deep breath, and headed in.

What he saw, only a few strides into the trees, stopped him in his tracks.

CHAPTER 5

▼

Katie stood at the window of her office and sipped lukewarm coffee from an insulated stainless steel mug. From this vantage on the third-floor of the Bienville County courthouse, she could see most of the Richfield business district and the sprawling residential area beyond it to the north. She was even able to identify, through the ever-thickening curtain of sepia haze, the tower of the deserted cotton mill at the city's edge.

Born, raised, and educated in Birmingham, Katie had found her adopted hometown a most curious place, uncomfortably schizophrenic and tangled in self-contradictions. It was, at once, urban and provincial, elitist and bourgeois, historically languid but increasingly on edge. A community of nearly a hundred thousand, it had made the journey from sleepy cotton town and mercantile center to post-industrial southern city awkwardly, caught in the tension between progress and reaction to it. Richfield, Katie O'Brien had often said, was an example of one of the immutable laws of social physics: A small community will remain at rest until an overwhelming will to change propels it forward.

From all outward appearances, Richfield had finally made its break with the past. Its forward progress, to be sure, could only have been measured in awkward fits and starts. But it was clearly not the same town Katie had found when fate had deposited her there sixteen years earlier. A number of light industrial concerns, including new automobile engine and electronics component assembly plants, a fragrance and cosmetics production facility, and a major computer software producer, had recently chosen to locate there. The suburban collar had expanded to accommodate the ever-increasing population. Malls, free-standing stores and shops, and clusters of restaurants and multiplex theaters now occupied land once dedicated to agricultural use. And Carry College had begun to make a name for itself among southern colleges and universities.

But the crime rate was displaying impressive growth of its own, with the volume of drug offenses, gang-related violence, robberies, and homicides increasing at a disturbing rate. Katie, who had once written about the role of environment, genetics, and superego pathology in formation of the criminal mind, found that she was unable to expound publicly upon the precise psychosocial explanation for the crime surge. For one thing, she no longer had the time to play the role of Beneficent Sociologist. It took all of her office's attention—and most of her energy—just to deal with crime's ugly aftermath. More importantly, the citizens of Bienville County expected her to prosecute criminals and to keep their streets safe, and nothing else. Accordingly, she had resolved to leave public debates concerning social dynamics to the sociologists while maintaining her very private fascination with the sinister processes of the criminal mind.

She watched the silent and orderly passage of pedestrians and vehicles along State and Curran streets, two of the busiest thoroughfares in downtown Richfield. From this sheltered observatory, the city looked peaceful, almost Edenic. But for her years of experience and current office statistics, Katie might have had a difficult time believing that these streets could generate more than a thousand felony cases a year.

And yet, there was the raw evidence of the crime wave—the computer printouts on her desk and the scores of files stacked in the offices of her seven attorneys. She rarely saw the criminals in their milieu, but there could be no doubt that they were out there. There were the angry and insecure adolescents, defiantly opposing the existing order with an almost inexplicable sense of alienation and bitterness. There were the pathetic addicts, no longer in control of any meaningful aspect of their lives. There were the Joe Terry Hollinses of the world—heartless predators who, for whatever twisted motivation, felt compelled to hurt, humiliate, control. There were also, of course, the foolish, the irresponsible, and those simply caught up in the heat of human passion. And, as she knew all too well from her nightmare in a place called Saigon Landing, there were many who would gladly surrender their last vestiges of humanity for a shot—*any* kind of shot—at large amounts of easy money. Katie knew all these people were out there, that they had always been there, and that, no matter how diligently or faithfully she executed her duties, they would persist in abundance.

And now there was a new kind of menace on these seemingly placid streets. But what, precisely, was its nature? The discovery of the mutilated Carry coed's body the previous afternoon had accelerated the wave of public anxiety. The intense media coverage had all but guaranteed that result. As could have been expected, the locally broadcast news stories focused more on framing dramatic but horrible possibilities than on conveying verified facts. Of course, the media couldn't really be blamed for exploiting the tragedy. The sheriff, with his chatty press conference from the Hazard Road crime scene, had set the tone for the information surge that would follow. And the public, more attracted to than repulsed by such events, had devoured the many news reports devoted to the story. Furthermore, the grim televised accounts, all delivered in somber tones by field reporters with appropriately knitted brows, all posed legitimate questions. Was this crime the work of a dangerous local cult? Could the killing have been the isolated act of an acquaintance of the victim, a boyfriend or fellow student? Were the disappearances of the two women related in any way, or merely a chilling coincidence? And the most troubling question of all: could these simply be the first links in what might ultimately be revealed as a chain of brutal crimes?

Katie allowed her attention to be diverted to the graceful curve of the hills. She noticed that many leaves on the oak and hickory trees were already turning brown, prematurely dying from thirst and the relentless heat. It had been nearly three weeks since there had been any significant rainfall. The leaves had actually begun changing colors several weeks earlier. Katie had been so preoccupied with the Hollins trial that she hadn't even noticed.

She turned and walked toward her desk. She paused at her walnut cabinet bookcase and gazed lovingly at each of the framed photographs arranged along the top. There was a picture of Garrett, now nine and nearly five-feet tall, posing in his baseball uniform. Then there was a photo of her husband, Con, in a starched white shirt and silk tie, sitting behind his desk and grinning. The picture had been snapped only weeks before his near-fatal heart attack. This photo would always be one of her personal treasures. Con was more than just her husband and the father of her child. He was her best friend in the world. He had been her friend long before they had ever been lovers. Their frenzied but satisfying family life had almost been instantly converted to a spool of burnished memories when he collapsed in the middle of a trial. She remembered the grim time that had followed: the harrowing days in intensive care, the triple-bypass surgery, the weeks of recovery. But he *had* recovered and had walked away from public office, accepting a new, less stressful, position on the Carry faculty. He was still very much alive and very much a part of their lives; this photo was a constant reminder of how fortunate she and Garrett had been. Her gaze shifted to the next frame, a photograph of her longtime friend and former college roommate, Avery May, taken by Con at their Orange Beach cottage. In the picture, Avery, a photo editor for an area business magazine, was reclining in a beach chair with a *Cosmopolitan* in one hand and an amber beer bottle in the other. The expression on her face—something between a menacing scowl and mischievous grin—had obviously been intended only for Con but, in an appropriately symbolic way, perfectly represented their long, fractured history. Fortunately for all concerned, the two former antagonists were now allied, personal adversity having been the strong binding force. Katie's eyes drifted to the last frame, a glossy print depicting Con and Garrett together, hiking on a mountain trail. This photo, taken the previous spring, was her favorite among favorites in that it provided additional proof that both her "boys"—her two buddies and precious survivors—were still there for her.

Her tired eyes settled on the pile of pink message slips stacked neatly on the desk blotter. Each slip represented somebody's crisis, real or imagined. Crisis management had become her primary function as district attorney. When she accepted the appointment to the position briefly held by her husband, she had held a very different vision of her role as D.A. She assumed that she would be able to handle the office's major administrative tasks, try a few cases, and leave the management of public grievances to her cadre of experienced assistants. It had all seemed so simple back then. But she had soon discovered that, like it or not, she was now officially a public figure. People looked to *her*, not her office, to repress crime and mediate their disputes. So she tried to personally respond to as many of these calls as she could. She knew well that public officials did not stay public for long in Bienville County if the citizens—the *voters*—felt abandoned. And, at that moment, people were demanding to know all the details of this gruesome and bizarre crime.

The message slips returned her thoughts to the kidnappings and to the murder of the young Carry coed. The last, sobering question presented in the news reports and by Andy Renauld haunted her. *Could there be a serial killer loose in Bienville County?* Most of the recent calls to her office were from Carry school officials, the terrified parents of Carry students, and concerned citizens. They all posed the same basic questions: what was the motive for the kidnappings, were they at all connected, what was being done to apprehend the killer, and how safe were the students on the Carry campus? What had begun as a couple of ordinary missing-persons reports had turned overnight into a crisis of local leadership.

The sudden disappearances of college students usually didn't set off official alarms in Richfield. Carry students "disappeared" all the time—to the beach, to the mountains and whitewater rivers, to New Orleans and the Mississippi casinos. Usually, within a day or two, the "missing" students wandered back to campus, unharmed and frankly puzzled over the fuss.

But these two new cases were different. Now everyone knew there had been at least one real abduction with a tragic and very real resolution. The speculation over coed comings and goings, personal motivations, and media sensationalization had all been laid to rest with one shocking discovery. Suddenly, everything had changed. Now everything was real, and as bad as advertised.

And the questions persisted.

At this point, Katie had only one answer. She knew that the local police were highly motivated by the discovery of the young woman's body and were frantically scrambling to put the pieces together.

The door of her office opened and Laurie Ross's head appeared. "Investigator Franks is here for your meeting," she said. "And Kevin and Berry just walked in the door."

Katie nodded and motioned for them to enter.

Chief Deputy D.A. Kevin Rose entered first, took a quick step to his right and sank into his usual spot at the end of Katie's leather sofa. Bobby Joe Franks and Berry Macklin followed in quick succession. Macklin took up a position on the other end of the sofa and Franks carefully settled into one of the leather wing-back side chairs facing the D.A.'s desk. He was holding several notebooks, a vinyl-covered RPD portfolio, two file folders, and a number of loose pieces of paper.

"Congratulations on your verdict," he said to Katie. "There's nothing sweeter than kicking Rabon Creasey's kick-proof ass."

Katie blushed. "I didn't kick anyone's ass, Bobby. First of all, *you* put the case together. All I did was let it unfold."

Franks cut a glance at the two deputies. "Oh, here we go. Welcome, contestants, to today's edition of *The Modesty Game!*"

"I'm serious, Bobby. I mean, I think Kevin and I did a decent enough job of presenting the case. But at the end, while the jury was out, we were all sweating bullets. At least I was. Rabon gave his usual world-class closing. It's like that with all his cases—you think you're winning, then he argues and, *bam*, the bad guys are suddenly ahead on points." She paused, shuffling the message slips. "Besides, Rabon really wasn't on top of his game for this one."

"This was his first case back since his surgery," Rose explained. "The anesthesia must've really laid him out good."

Franks snorted. "I saw him in action, Kevin. He cross-examined me, for crying out loud. He wasn't *that* damned laid-out!"

"Katie did absolutely destroy their star witness. Rabon gave a great closing, but it was already over with by that time, and he knew it."

"See?" Franks said, winking at Katie. "That's what I'm talking about."

"When she finished with Dr. Brit, he shot outa the courtroom like a Tomahawk missile."

"I don't think he even stopped to grab his briefcase," Berry Macklin said. "Straight to his Mercedes and back to Birmingham. I'm afraid he may never visit our quaint little village again."

"Well, I'm sorry I missed the show," Franks said, struggling to suppress a yawn. "I had planned to return to the courthouse after lunch, but I went out to see about the body and never made it back. In fact, I never even made it home last night."

Katie studied the investigator. He looked rough, with dark circles under bloodshot eyes and a salt-and-pepper stubble apparent on his jaw and chin. He was wearing the same permanent-press shirt he had worn the previous day. There was what appeared to be a ketchup stain on a shirt pocket bulging with a pack of cigarettes and a pair of reading glasses.

"You okay, Bobby?" Katie asked.

He shrugged. "I guess so. I'm *real* tired." He glanced at his watch. "Haven't slept in about thirty hours and I have to work tonight. Oh, and I'm in horrible pain. Other than that, I'm great." He shifted in the chair and grimaced.

"Your back still bothering you?" Katie asked.

Franks nodded. "I've sorta learned to live with it. Good thing, too, because none of the doctors I've been to know how to fix it."

"How'd you hurt it?" Kevin Rose asked.

"The first time, I was messing with a bull on my farm a few years back. Then I stepped in a dadgum hole out in the woods yesterday while I was taking pictures of that girl. That sorta got it flared up all over again."

"I've got a little discomfort of my own," Katie said. She held up a handful of the message slips. "Ten calls since yesterday afternoon about the murdered girl. Four are from concerned citizens. Three of the calls are from television reporters. One is from Andy Renauld with the paper. Another is from Joe Wilker, the dean of student affairs at the college." She paused a beat. "The last one is from Robert Crawley, the murder victim's father." She tossed the messages onto her ink blotter. "I guess they all want to know how close we are to making an arrest. I really don't know what to tell them."

"Tell them we ain't close at all. Tell them we—*I*—been busting my butt ever since Miz Crawley disappeared and I ain't got nothing." His tired eyes suddenly burned with indignation. "Concerned citizens, my ass," he growled. "I'll tell you what it is. People watch *way* too much dadgum television. They think you just walk through a murder scene, close your eyes, then have some kind of vision where the computer-assisted brain of a dead cop solves the crime for you." He gave a derisive snort. "You get them same folks on a jury and they suddenly fold up like canvas chairs. And screw a bunch of Andy Renauld. Her and her damn fish wrapper of a paper. They have absolutely no interest in helping us find the killer. All they want to do is profit from everybody's misery."

"You're preaching to the choir, brother," Berry Macklin said.

"I'm not really worried about answering general questions from the community-at-large right now," Katie said. "I know this all is kind of alarming, but I think most reasonable folks understand we're doing all we can. We can issue some kind of general statement if and when there's something meaningful to report." She paused. "So far as Dean Wilker and the other folks over at Carry are concerned, I do understand their anxiety. The fall quarter's about to start and their students are being kidnapped and murdered. Wilker's had calls from about twenty pissed-off parents who're threatening to pull their kids out of school until this is resolved. I'm going to have to do one press conference this afternoon just to reassure everybody that we're working on the problem. But I really don't think Dean Wilker—or, for that matter, Barney Q. Citizen—is entitled to daily updates on the progress of the investigation. We'll give them information when we're able." She paused, staring down at the message slips. "Robert Crawley's a different story. There's not much anyone can do for him at this point. But at least we can keep him up to speed on the investigation's progress." Her eyes met Franks's. "I think we owe him that much."

Her mind drifted back to her last conversation with Crawley, the night after the jury had been empaneled in the Hollins case. His daughter—he called her "Annie," although she was known to her friends on campus as "Donna"—was still officially a "missing person" at that point. At that precise moment, Crawley was still able to suppress the horrible possibilities, although, after weeks of dead ends and unanswered questions, his hope was clearly receding.

"She's all I have," he had said, at last, his voice cracking. He had explained that his wife had died unexpectedly from surgical complications several years earlier. It had become apparent to Katie from their several conversations that this loss had taken a heavy emotional toll on him. The thought of losing his daughter was unbearable.

Katie had attempted to reassure him that all that could be done was being done.

"It's a horrible feeling, thinking that someone's taken her," he had said. "An accident, something like that...that's bad enough. But you could almost accept it. It's like it was somehow God's will. But *this*. God would never will this on anybody. It's just too horrible. And I could never accept it."

"I understand," Katie had said.

"No, ma'am," he had murmured, gently reproving her. "You could never know unless you'd been through it yourself."

She had then debated sharing with Crawley the story of Garrett's abduction. The fact that she had, in fact, experienced these same paralyzing fears and sense of helplessness might help cement a trust-engendering bond with the man. On the other hand, the details of that harsh crime's resolution—Garrett clearly would not have survived but for brute luck, the timely and courageous involvement of strangers, and, she now believed, divine intervention—might have been less than reassuring. In the end, she chose to quietly agree with his assessment and offer her prayers and encouragement.

That had been a week ago. In the meantime, Annie's body had been found. The final act of the drama had been played out, revealing the story as a tragedy. Now there was nothing to offer Robert Crawley but sympathy and the questionable assurance of law enforcement's continued best efforts.

"Whatever you need, Katie," Bobby Franks said. "Although I'm still not sure which direction to turn."

"Tell me what we have and we'll decide together which way to go."

Franks opened his file folder on his lap.

"What we have," he repeated. "Well, there's a lot of stuff—very strange stuff, mostly—but I'm not sure what it all means yet."

Katie nodded and settled back into her chair. She could see a dozen yellow adhesive notes stuck to the inside cover. She found herself smiling at the homicide investigator as he sorted through his materials. Franks had always been one of her favorite investigators. He was bright, inquisitive, and very well read. Their careers seemed to be locked in a strange synchronicity—they started to work for their respective departments during the same year, left to pursue private interests at roughly the same time, and returned to public service within three months of each other. They had spent a lot of time together over the years. At Con's insistence, he'd taught her how to shoot. They spent twenty hours at the police range, training until she could routinely land nine in the target's chest at twenty meters. And he didn't just teach shooting—he required her to be able to assemble and disassemble a Beretta 9mm and its magazine, and taught her ways to remedy jams or misfeeds. She'd never been fond of guns—she'd seen daily reminders of the cruel aftermath of criminal handgun use—but she couldn't deny that she'd enjoyed this time spent with Franks. There was something powerfully attractive about a professional who was strong and confident and good at his job. And Bobby Franks was all of those things. Katie had always found him ruggedly handsome, but as he edged into his forties and his shaggy dark hair became a well-groomed silver thatch, she found him distinguished looking as well. But the thing that attracted her most to him was his character. He had always been rock solid: a hard worker, a team player, and a man who was uncompromisingly, occasionally *painfully*, direct. His major professional flaws seemed to be his aversion to diplomacy and substantial lack of organizational skills. Even now, notes and scraps of paper fell from his portfolio and notebooks as he flipped through the loose pages. Still, as Katie had learned from being on his side and from being his adversary, he somehow always managed to get the job done.

"All right," Franks said, finally, carefully working the pair of drugstore reading glasses onto his face. "The victim's gonna be Anjanette Donna Crawley, white female, age twenty-two. Of course, you already knew all that. She's from a suburb of Atlanta. She was about to be a senior at the college, majoring in lit and history. From all I've been able to find out this morning, she was an absolute gem of a person. Honors student, student government officer, homecoming queen finalist, you name it. Attended the Southpark Baptist Church on a regular basis. Nobody had anything bad to say about her." He paused, flipping through the file until he came up with a wallet-sized color photo. "She was a pretty girl, too." He tossed the photo on Katie's desk. "When I first observed the body, it was partially covered with rocks." He shuffled through a small group of photos, found one and flipped it onto Katie's ink blotter. "I guess ya'll heard all this on the news last night."

"Yeah," Katie said, picking up the picture. "What's up with that?"

"I have no idea. But wait—it gets *much* weirder."

The D.A. sighed and handed the picture to Kevin Rose who, with Berry Macklin, had crowded around the desk in order to get a better view.

"Go ahead," Katie said.

"As you could tell from the photo, the head, parts of the upper torso, and the lower extremities were exposed. Everything else had rocks on them."

"Any idea where the rocks came from?"

"The forensic folks are looking into it. They were packaged up and sent to some specialist somewhere. But it seems obvious to me that the rocks came from a dried-up creek bed nearby. They were all of the same general type—that is, some kind of sedimentary rock, like sandstone—as those in the bed."

Kevin Rose, still peering at the photo, said, "Do you think somebody might have just started to do an above-ground burial, got freaked, and booted it?"

Franks considered this for a moment, then shook his head. "Nah. That doesn't make any sense. Not if you're actually trying to hide the body. Somebody's eventually gonna see the rock pile and get suspicious. Besides, it's probably easier just to dig a hole."

"Well *why*, then?" Katie asked.

The investigator took a deep breath and exhaled slowly, as if he were debating the appropriateness of his next comments. "One thing I'm still considering is that this might have been some kind of cult thing." When he noticed the alarm on the faces of the three lawyers, he quickly added, "I'm not convinced that it is, mind you. I'm just saying that there were some very unusual things about this killing."

"I can see the headlines now," Rose said. "'Murderous Sedimentary Rock Cult Terrorizes Rich White Liberal Arts Students'."

"You're saying we have some kind of killer cult?" Katie asked the investigator. "Right here in Richfield?"

Franks shrugged. "I guess not officially. As you know, my department still hasn't even officially acknowledged that *gangs* exist in this area. But, as far as I'm concerned, any time you have crazy assholes in a community, you got the ingredients for a cult." He turned to Kevin Rose. "Do we have any crazy assholes here in Richfield?"

Rose grinned. "Uh, that would be affirmative. One or two."

"Then you got enough for a cult."

"She was posted yesterday evening, wasn't she?" Katie asked.

"Yep. Doctor Hunter and his crew at Cooper Green."

"Have you gotten a preliminary report from him yet?"

"Yeah, he faxed it to me this morning."

"What does he say about the cause and manner of death?"

Franks peered at Katie from over the frames of his glasses. "Cause of death is gonna be tricky. She clearly had major blunt force trauma to the back and side of the head. I think this is pretty evident from the photo. And in his preliminary report, he says blunt force trauma is the cause of death. But he also notes that the victim had aspirated water at some point prior to dying."

"What does that mean?"

"I'm not sure. To tell you the truth, I'm not sure he's one hundred percent sure himself. I called him right before I came over here. He stops short of saying drowning is the cause of death, but says that he found 'watery fluid' in the lungs and stomach, and some swelling of the lungs. He says this is something they might see in a person who died from other causes just after being immersed in water."

"So he's saying that she took a couple of shots to the head and then toppled over into water and died?"

Franks stifled another yawn. "I guess so. Or something like that. Or maybe she was almost drowned, then was beaten to death." He rubbed his eyes. "I'm too tired for it to make sense right now."

"There's no water at the scene, right?" Berry Macklin asked.

"Nope. Nothing but a dried-up creek bed."

"So then it's not likely that the actual assault took place there?"

"Highly unlikely. There's no water there, plus there would've been a lot of blood and a lot of high-velocity blood spatters in the vicinity. Also, it's pretty obvious that she was dragged to this spot from a logging road about fifteen feet away. My guess is that she was driven there in a vehicle—probably a van or truck—and then unloaded."

"What significance do you think the rocks have?"

Franks shrugged again. "Maybe these folks are a bunch of rock freaks. Maybe it doesn't mean anything. Who knows? I've been on the case for less than twenty-four hours. It might take me until this afternoon to completely solve it." He flashed a quick smile at Katie. "But we haven't even gotten to the weirdest stuff yet."

Katie settled back into her chair. "Okay, shoot…I think."

"For starters, Miss Crawley had words carved into her chest and belly." Franks selected another photo, a shot of the woman's abdomen taken by the pathologist at the autopsy, from his folder and handed it to Berry Macklin. "Doctor Hunter feels like this was probably postmortem because of the lack of bleeding."

Macklin looked at the color image with a look of horror on his face and then handed the photo to his boss.

"Yikes," he said.

Katie stared at the photo with a furrowed brow.

"I can't make out what it says," she complained.

Franks snorted. "It's those cheap-ass cameras the department buys for us. The writing says, 'Here's Your Bella Donna'." He paused, then added, "And, no, I haven't got a clue. Not yet anyway."

"Didn't you say Donna was her middle name?" Rose asked.

"I did."

"And 'bella' means 'beautiful' in Italian, doesn't it?"

"Hell if I know." He slumped in his chair, tossed this information around in his head. "Okay, so let's say that's what the killer had in mind. What would that tell us?"

"Well, it might at least help establish that whoever did this knew her."

"Or knew her name," Franks argued.

Katie looked up from the picture. "You said this was for starters. I'm kind of afraid to ask, but what else is there?"

"The victim had a limp flower stem wadded up in her mouth." He pulled a third photo from his folder and sailed it across the desk to Katie. "A cut-off stem, about six inches or so, with some dried-up ol' flowers. If you've got a theory about that one, I'd sure like to hear it."

She studied the photo carefully. It had been taken by Franks at the scene and showed a wilted spike with a small cluster of dried purple flowers protruding from Donna Crawley's colorless, desiccated lips. One detached wilted petal rested at the base of her throat.

"This is starting to get a little too creepy for me," Berry Macklin said.

"Wait a minute," Katie said, lowering the photo briefly. "Belladonna is also a flower, a member of the lily family, I think. Does anyone know what belladonna looks like?"

"I only know two flowers," Macklin said, "and I can say with some degree of certainty that the flower in that picture is neither a rose nor a dandelion."

"It wasn't in very good shape—pretty old and wilted. We left the whole stalk, whatever, in her mouth until the autopsy. Hunter removed it and sent it back here with one of the forensic sciences guys. I think someone over at forensics is analyzing the stem right now. It's my understanding that the whole flower assembly fell apart when Hunter pulled it out of her mouth." He was unable to stifle a yawn this time. He covered his mouth and apologized. "I'm sorry, ya'll. I'm gonna need a few hours sleep before I'll be any good to anyone."

"It's a hyacinth," Katie announced suddenly. She rocked back in her chair with a look of satisfaction on her face. "A blue grape hyacinth. Also in the lily family. Mom once had them in her garden."

"Okay," Franks said, at last. "I guess that's something. I still don't know what it means—"

"It means we go look for someone with a hyacinth bush in his yard," Kevin Rose said.

"Hyacinths only bloom around here in the spring," Katie replied, "and then only for a few weeks. And they don't grow in freakin' bushes. They're sort of like tulips. They grow from bulbs, they're pretty, and don't blink or they're gone."

Franks and the two attorneys stared at her.

"So I guess that means that this flower was probably cut sometime in March or April. That's why it's all dried up."

Franks said, "Note to self—try to figure this shit out after sleeping for a few hours."

"One more thing," Katie said, sliding the investigator's photos back across the desk to him. "Have you been able to find anything linking these two abduction cases?"

Franks collected the pictures and flashed a quick grin. "Well, actually, I have," he said. "One thing. Maybe it's a small thing. Maybe it's nothing at all. I think you'll probably find it interesting."

"O-*kay*—"

"Miss Crawley and the other lady, Kerry Jean Grinder, hardly even knew each other. They didn't have any of the same classes, didn't belong to the same organizations. Miss Grinder, as I understand it, ran with a totally different crowd." He placed the photos in his folder and got to his feet. "But there's one thing they shared. They both went out with the same dude. Not at the same time—a year or so apart. Dude's name is Jamie Amerson."

Katie stared at Franks. "Jamie Amerson. Why does that name sound familiar?"

"Well, let's see. He's a former Carry student. Works as the shop supervisor now for his daddy's heating and cooling company. Half the folks I talked to think he's the second coming of James Dean, the other half think he's a huge tool. I get the impression that he would include himself in the former category."

Katie rose from her chair and walked around to the front of the desk. "Wait a minute. Amerson Heating and Cooling? I remember that guy now. *James Darren Amerson*. I prosecuted him for—" She paused, her eyes wide and jaw slack. "Oh my God, Bobby. It was an attempted abduction from a shopping center parking lot. He had followed this girl…a Carry student…out to her car and tried to force his way in—"

"Then she screamed and he ran away," Franks interrupted. "I know. It was Gordy Childs's case. I pulled the file off microfiche last night. The stupid machine wouldn't print right. That's one reason I was up all night."

Katie sat on the edge of her desk. "He was, like, a freshman at Carry then. Real smug, spoiled little jerk, I remember that. Childs wanted to make it a kidnapping case, but the magistrate would only give him an unlawful imprisonment warrant. He was convicted in District Court and then Daddy hired Rabon Creasey for the appeal."

"…and the jury cut him loose."

"Yeah," Katie said. Her eyes glazed over as her unconscious mind fed the unpleasant memory of that defeat into her present awareness. "It was a tough case and I was still pretty green. And Rabon, as usual, worked the jury like an evangelist. That's back when he was absolutely on top of his game. We never had a chance. I remember when they left the courtroom, Amerson gave me this look, this evil little smirk."

"Let's go pick his bony, white ass up," Berry Macklin said.

"On what?" Franks asked. "All we've got so far is the fact that he dated both women. That's it. That hardly amounts to probable cause."

"He also tried to abduct a woman—"

"—and was acquitted by a jury."

Katie said, "Well, at least we have *something* now. We have a direction and a possible destination. Ten minutes ago I was convinced there was absolutely nothing."

Bobby Joe Franks shuffled toward the door.

"I'm planning on watching the boy," he said. "I'm gonna be on him like drool on a baby." He paused in the doorway, turned and said, "Maybe I'll poke around in his garden and see what's growing there. But first, I'm gonna catch me a little shuteye."

After Franks had left, Katie asked Macklin and Rose to find out everything they could about Jamie Amerson. No office resource was to be spared. This was about catching a murderer, but there was a lot more at stake. If Amerson was, in fact, the kidnapper, his capture might lead them to Kerry Grinder. And, perhaps of equal importance, he would be stopped from doing it again.

And, despite all precautions, there was no reason to believe that it wouldn't happen again.

Katie slid into her chair and stared at the message slips. She picked up the note with Robert Crawley's phone number and sighed. She dreaded making the call because she knew nothing she could say would make his pain go away.

The harsh sound of the telephone ringer sundered the stillness and jolted Bobby Franks from his sleep. Lids fluttered, sunlight seared his squinting eyes. He waited, hoping he hadn't really heard that sound, but there it was again. He rolled on his side, his huge hand groping in vain for the receiver. He heard his answering machine click on.

"Hey Bobby, it's Blaine Martin. Pick up." The voice of his lieutenant, urgent and insistent.

Franks lunged at the phone and this time managed to pick it up.

"What's up, Lieutenant?"

"You asleep?"

Franks grunted.

"I just got a call from a deputy down in Maynor County. They found a body in a strawberry field there. It's a young woman, maybe nineteen or twenty. Pretty badly decomposed. It looks like she was strangled, at least according to the coroner. They think she might have been there a few days."

Franks struggled to shake the cobwebs from his brain. A body in Maynor County? And how did this concern him? He was already up to his neck in unsolved crimes in Bienville County.

"I don't understand—"

"She had words scratched into her skin, Bobby. Just like that girl yesterday."

Franks bolted upright. "Do you know what the words were?"

"Wait one." There was a pause on the other end. "Yeah, it was, like, 'We'll Play,' or 'We'll Play a Game,' or something along those lines. Whatever it was, it's too damn strange for me."

"Where's the body right now?"

"I think they've got her in the morgue down there. Forensic Sciences is waiting on somebody to authorize an autopsy. They're trying to round up a prosecutor down there. I guess everyone goes home at four down in Rock Spring."

Franks glanced at his clock. It was almost five.

"All right, Blaine. I'm on my way."

"Ten-four. Keep me up to speed."

"Hey, Blaine?"

"Yeah?"

"They didn't say nothing about the girl having a flower in her mouth, or anything, did they?" Franks was on his feet now, trying to slip into his shoes.

"Nah, but it's weird you should say that. They told me they found a chess piece in her mouth."

"A chess piece? What kind of chess piece?"

"Hell, I don't know. I don't play chess. I think maybe it was a pawn. Does that sound right?"

"It sounds possible," Franks said. "It sure as hell don't sound *right*."

CHAPTER 6

▼

Carlyn Bedsole steered her battered Nissan Sentra into a parking space in front of Breaux's Diner. She switched off the ignition and gave a sigh of relief. She was ten minutes late for her five o'clock meeting with her friend, JoEllen. But JoEllen always met her outside the front door, and she wasn't there, so she was obviously running late herself. Staring intently into the repositioned rear-view mirror, Carlyn made two quick swipes with a tube of dark red lipstick. She smacked her lips together and then, after making an expert contouring adjustment with the nail on her right pinkie, she swivelled the mirror back into its original position.

JoEllen hadn't given her a specific reason for wanting the meeting at Breaux's. Her friend had been vague with her on the phone, as she usually was when she called from her workplace. Carlyn had a pretty good idea why, anyway, based on experience and JoEllen's recent personal history. It probably had something to do with Roger, JoEllen's husband, she thought. They had just gone through a very tough year and things hadn't quite gotten back to "normal." Of course, JoEllen was painfully aware that things might never be normal again. Her affair hadn't been much—two or three meetings, at the most—and it was definitely over and done with, but Roger had been absolutely devastated when his wife confessed her infidelity. Of course, JoEllen had to go and tell Roger all about it. Carlyn had advised her against this indiscretion, right there in their booth at Breaux's. Absolutely nothing good will come from it, she had warned. But JoEllen had insisted, saying that "being totally honest is the only chance I'll have to regain Roger's trust." So she had sat Roger down and just confessed. She had told Roger the whole sorry story, beginning to end. Just as Carlyn had predicted, it hadn't turned out well. Roger had listened without interruption, silently absorbing each breath-stealing blow of betrayal. When JoEllen had finished, he had just gotten up and walked away. He never said a word, never even inquired as to the identity of her inamorato. He just walked to their room, packed a single suitcase, and disappeared for about two weeks. Temporary disappearances apparently were a standard strategy in his particular style of crisis management. He returned, as he always had, but he and JoEllen didn't speak for another week or so. They had just glided mutely past each other like two cloistered monks freighted with obligations, if not vows, of silence. When they eventually resumed speaking, communications were strictly limited to matters of great immediacy and took the form of clipped questions and succinct answers. In time, they had gotten back on regular speaking terms, but there was still an incredible amount of tension in the air. JoEllen wondered often if anything would ever be as it once had been. As bored as she had been by her life before the affair, she wanted desperately now to have at least that much again.

Breaux's was where JoEllen had broken the news of the affair to her friend. That precise scenario—the two of them at a table in the shadows at the back of the room, JoEllen dressed in her floral print technician's smock, twisting her napkin as the awkward admission spilled from her mouth—now became a clear visual image in Carlyn's mind. She had been stunned to hear this particular report from her friend, she remembered that. JoEllen had always been the sensible one. Back at Talmadge High, she had been class president and "Most Likely to Succeed." She had never joined Carlyn in any of her "craziness"—skinny-dipping in the reservoir, sneaking into the drive-in, getting drunk, smoking weed, and popping pills. JoEllen had been a good Baptist girl—Girls In Action, the whole deal. While Carlyn spent her evenings chasing boys and getting stoned, JoEllen was doggedly pursuing her G.A. "Queen" Step by learning sixty countries in which Baptist missions had been established. Carlyn even knew for a fact that JoEllen had only dated two boys before meeting Roger her freshman year at Auburn. She assumed that her status was probably the same when they got married, too, about a year later. And *that*, in Carlyn's estimation, was a huge part of the problem. They got married too young, she thought, before either one of them had learned anything about life or the world. And now finally, after thirteen years of marriage, two kids, and the tedium of perpetual obligation, craziness had finally seduced her.

It wasn't that Roger was a bad man, or anything like that. He was ordinary in just about every sense of the word. It had occurred to Carlyn that, if they offered a Nobel Prize for ordinariness, Roger would have certainly been a category nominee. Although, as Carlyn now realized, in a marital relationship, ordinariness wasn't necessarily the worst possible thing. Her own ex-husband, for example, was an extraordinary asshole. He was immoderate in his use of chemicals, gambled to excess, and partied like there'd never be a next day. In the beginning, the marriage had been exciting. Their life together had been one giant celebration; their house was Party Central. There were poker parties, billiards parties, parties to celebrate every televised sporting event. There were tailgate parties for football games and infield encampments at Talladega where he usually got drunk, more than once ending up in a fight with some other extraordinary individual. Then the partying began to get a little old. After a few years, the smell of stale beer and cigarette butts and the sight of his friends passed out on her furniture began to stir feelings of dissatisfaction. When he laughed off her suggestion that they "settle down" and have children, she began to feel angry and resentful. But she stayed with him anyway because she didn't really want to be single again and because life with him *was* exciting. When he began slapping her around, however, she decided that maybe a little less excitement was what she really wanted. She left one night with him passed out on his pool table, and she never went back.

With JoEllen and Roger, she decided, it was different. It was, she once told JoEllen, "like that *Bridges of Madison County* movie with Clint Eastwood and Meryl Streep." The husband, "Richard Johnson or whatever," wasn't a bad person, she had noted, he just didn't "light any fires." Roger was the same way. He went to work every morning and came home every night and helped pay the bills. He took care of the kids when she was detained by work and he didn't fool around on her. They made love on occasion, even though they always followed the "exact identical routine." (She knew that only because JoEllen had told her so, one evening right there at Breaux's). Roger was just an ordinary guy, reliable but extremely, well, *boring*. And that, in her opinion, was the rest of their problem. Because, just when JoEllen became resigned to a life of ordinariness, along came this handsome stranger who paid her attention and treated her like she was somehow unique in all the world. It was, she thought, probably how husbands and wives *ought*, but sometimes forget, to act anyway. And that was basically the story of their affair. A spark had been lit and, left untended for a sufficient length of time, was permitted to swell into an inferno of passion. JoEllen let the blaze go for about a month, then extinguished it. She decided that it was unfair to both Roger and her children. The sensible girl returned and the craziness went away.

Carlyn glanced at her watch again. *Fifteen after five.* It wasn't like her friend to be that late for anything. She was supposed to be coming straight from work. Something had to have come up.

She got out of her car and locked the door. The heat radiated up from the sidewalk and stole her breath. She glanced up and down State Street and checked all the street-side parking places to see if she had somehow missed JoEllen's white Ford van. When she was unable to locate the van, she glanced down Alabama Street to see if it was coming. JoEllen was a technician for a radiologist whose office was on Alabama, about three blocks from there. Carlyn knew that a great deal of her work consisted of making images of the brain. She was even called to the hospital to help with some emergency brain procedures.

It all seemed clear now to Carlyn. She would never have just blown her off or forgotten about their meeting. An emergency had come up, and she had gotten called to the hospital. Either that or some problem at home had suddenly developed. She checked her watch again and sighed in resignation. *JoEllen had never been twenty minutes late for anything in her life.*

Carlyn went into Breaux's and stood at the vacant hostess's podium. She gave a quick glance around the restaurant. It was a pleasant though unassuming place—polished tile floor, a couple of potted plants, a painting on each of the four walls. There were a dozen tables spaced a comfortable distance apart in the center of the room, eight booths along one wall, and a bar running half the length of the wall opposite the booths. A delicious aroma of roasting meat, hickory, and herbs filled the room. Carlyn only saw four customers—one couple at a table in the back of the room and two men sitting together at the bar. She assumed that this was not an unusual circumstance for that time of the day. Things would get much busier later on a Friday night. She and JoEllen usually left before it got too crowded.

The hostess, who was chatting with the bartender, spotted Carlyn and crossed the room to her. She was compact and perky, swathed in layers of starched white, two menus held out in front of her.

"Are you expecting someone?" she asked

"No," Carlyn replied, then quickly added, "I was, but I'm not now." She asked the hostess if anyone had left a message for her.

The hostess repeated the question to the bartender who shook his head.

"Would you like to go ahead and be seated?" the hostess asked.

Carlyn glanced again at her watch, then told the woman no. Feeling vaguely uneasy, she turned and headed back to the door.

She walked to her car and unlocked her door. Something wasn't right, she decided, and she was going to get to the bottom of it.

She headed out, traveling east on State Street, slowly and somewhat reluctantly, as though she hadn't yet made up her mind about which way to go. JoEllen's house was out that way, but she really didn't want to go there. She felt uncomfortable around Roger now. He acted like he held her partly responsible for JoEllen's crime of betrayal. And, of course, if JoEllen *had* forgotten their meeting, it would only be a very awkward and embarrassing scene for her to just turn up at the house. The Sentra crept along, past shoe shops, dry goods stores, and the trendy renovated buildings that now served as offices for architects, accountants, and attorneys. Carlyn found herself examining doorways, alleys, and parking places for any sign of JoEllen while she decided on her ultimate destination. She continued down State, past a long block of old commercial buildings that represented the eastern periphery of the central Richfield business district. Many of these buildings—mostly two and three-story brick masonry Victorian-style commercial buildings with similar cornices, brackets, and decorative medallions—were of interest to historians of late nineteenth century southern architecture. They were absolutely of no interest to Carlyn at that moment. Her only interest was finding out what had happened to her friend.

Abandoning any intention of tracking JoEllen to her house now, Carlyn turned north on Feltner Avenue, then back west on Lee Street. She passed Amerson Heating and Cooling, noting that the lights were out and the business seemed to be closed for the day. She proceeded up the street, past the Central Presbyterian Church, checking the parking lot for any sign of JoEllen.

She was stopped at the corner of Alabama Street and Lee, and was trying to decide where to go from there, when she spotted a white Ford van parked in the alley behind Breaux's. She pulled into the alley to check on the van. It was, indeed, JoEllen's: the Snoopy license tag bracket and the Habitat for Humanity bumper sticker identified it beyond any doubt.

She pulled alongside the van and got out to check it. JoEllen might have gotten there late and gone in the rear entrance.

Then she peered in the driver's side window and felt a sudden jolt. JoEllen's purse was sitting on the front passenger seat.

When she tried the door, it was unlocked. Her heart began pounding. Something was definitely not right.

She got back in her car and sat behind the steering wheel, hands clasped over her mouth. She didn't know what to do. She just knew that something bad had happened. She wanted to lock the van or, at the very least, secure her friend's purse, but she was afraid to touch anything. If JoEllen had been a crime victim, she knew that the police would probably need to dust the vehicle and her belongings for fingerprints.

She decided that the prudent thing would be to call the police from Breaux's and then remain there, keeping an eye on the van.

She jumped from the Sentra and flew up the steps to Breaux's back door, her heart sinking with every step.

CHAPTER 7

▼

"I'm just asking you to consider all the available options, Missus O'Brien. That's all I'm doing here. I'm not trying to step on any toes."

Dr. Joseph Sherman Wilker, Carry College's dean of student affairs, sat in one of Katie's side chairs, slumped obliquely in her direction, hands clasped plaintively in his lap. He had a wide, expressive face and a small mouth that pursed when he was thinking and twisted into odd, quicksilver grins as he established each strategically sequenced point in his argument. The lower half of his face, therefore, seemed to remain in perpetual motion, for he droned on without respite, shifting constantly between apparent rumination and discourse. His heavy brow seemed permanently furrowed above the sturdy black plastic frames of his glasses. He dressed as if he had been outfitted at the Academy Stereotype Store—thirty-year-old blue seersucker suit, ancient square-ended knit tie, rumpled ecru poly-cotton blend shirt. His hands remained clasped as he spoke, although he would from time to time gesture dramatically or brush imaginary lint from his trouser leg.

He reminded her somewhat of one of her political science professors at Birmingham-Southern. She could recall this man, a Doctor Quintus Reynolds, attired in his usual rumpled suit, pacing back and forth in front of the class, extracting his thoughts with the deliberation of a tournament chess player. That image and the hypnotic convergence of Wilker's droning voice, the hum of the computer, and the overhead flourescent light buzz gently eased her into the past, back to the campus on the hill and less complicated times.

Suddenly she was with her history class on a crisp fall afternoon outside Munger Memorial Hall (Avery May and many others called it Ma-vunger Hall, because of the Latinate lettering which substituted a "v" for the "u" on the building's frieze). The class was meeting under the ginko tree with a gentle breeze bearing the sweet potpourri of autumn across the quad. There was a great deal of comfort in this memory of carefree, irresponsible days. Wilker's rambling jeremiad, persisting long after his major points had been made, drove her deeper into the comforting zones of her unconscious.

Sudden awareness of a lingering silence dragged Katie rudely back to the harsh reality of the present.

"Yes, I understand your concerns," she said. "And I think we're keeping all our options open."

The D.A. had gone out of her way to establish a connection with Dean Wilker. She had removed the substantial barrier of her desk, choosing instead to sit with him in the other side chair. She was attempting to mirror his body language, now clasping her own hands and leaning slightly toward him. And she continued to express support for the Carry administration's concerns, even though Wilker clearly hadn't the first clue about investigative protocols or criminal procedure.

Her rapport-building efforts didn't seem to be working, at least not yet. The singular purpose of Wilker's visit was to solve Carry's growing public relations dilemma; his basic persuasion strategy seemed to revolve around badgering Katie and the police into magically producing a defendant, a demon in the dock. To this end, he dieseled on, utterly unresponsive to Katie's openness and apparently unconcerned with his own bridge building. Even his requests for assistance contained blunt insinuations of governmental incompetence.

Of course, Katie couldn't really blame the Carry administration for its anxiety. The two kidnappings and the murder of Donna Crawley had sent the entire campus into a state of shock. Students, faculty members, and school officials staggered numbly through their daily routines, their collective security-delusion ripped apart with a single rude blow. Things this hideous just weren't supposed to happen in such a snug and leafy environment. At the beginning of the case investigation, the administration had earnestly expressed its concern and pledged full cooperation and support. But the continuing threat to the campus served only to raise the anxiety level. As Wilker now made abundantly clear, the fall semester was about to become an enrollment nightmare: At least three young women had already withdrawn from school, dozens more were threatening to follow suit.

"The problem," Wilker said, "is that we're still standing at the starting line. You folks are no closer today to solving these crimes than you were back on day one." He sat back and observed Katie's reaction to his comment. "Is this accurate, or am I mistaken?"

Katie shifted uncomfortably in her chair. It was absolutely true that the police had not "solved" the crimes. Serial crimes committed by clever sociopaths were rarely solved by police investigation alone. Usually it took blind luck, information from the public, a major blunder by the offender, or some combination of these things to bring such a spree to an end. And it was becoming apparent that the Carry kidnapper-killer was no intoxicated buffoon randomly bumbling from crime scene to crime scene. So far, no eyewitnesses had been located, no physical evidence found. He might have left clues—words and rocks and a flower—but their significance, if any, hadn't been established. And, if he had blundered, it wasn't yet apparent.

Of course, there had been one interesting development in the investigation— the established connection between Jamie Amerson and the two victims. But, even though Katie remained hopeful that this lead would prove fruitful, it was still only a lead, and a fragile one, at that. In any event, it certainly wasn't something she could share with either the Carry administration or the general public.

"I'm very confident that we're going to get a break in the case very soon," she said. "The case investigator is a very competent—"

Wilker snorted in derision. "Investigator? You mean *Jimmy Bob* Franks, or whatever his name is? *Competent*? I don't think he's capable of finding his own two feet, much less a serial killer."

Blood rushed to Katie's face. Frustration was one thing, but this uncharitable characterization of the investigator was both unexpected and inappropriate.

"His name is Bobby Franks," she sputtered, finally. "And I can assure you he's very experienced, very bright. Quite frankly, he's RPD's best investigator."

Wilker crossed his legs and gave Katie a patronizing smile.

"I don't mean for anyone to take this personally," he said, again flicking away imaginary lint from the crease in his trousers, "but I believe he's in over his head on this thing." When Katie didn't reply he said, "Who do you think solved the Son of Sam and the Zodiac killer cases? One guy named Billy Bob with cowboy boots?" He retracted his chin into his wrinkled neck and frowned. "And look how many people it took to catch the Beltway snipers. There must have been at least a hundred state and federal officers working around the clock."

"We've had one woman kidnapped and murdered," Katie said. "We've got another woman missing and we really don't know what—"

"And so what's happened on our campus doesn't matter? Because we've only had one of our students zipped up in a body bag so far? Is that what you're saying?"

Katie's fingers dug into the arms of her chair. "Of course that's not what I'm saying. We regard the death of Miss Crawley as a terrible thing, a barbaric act, and we're determined to bring her killer to justice. I'm just saying that we're doing everything that can be done right now to—"

"Have you contacted the federal authorities and asked for their help?"

"At this point, I seriously doubt that the feds would consider this something within their jurisdiction."

"So you're saying you haven't asked for their help."

Katie stared at the man, momentarily rendered speechless by his arrogance and accusatory tone. She had barely had the time and opportunity to review the basic facts of the two cases, much less to formulate a complex, long-term investigative strategy. But she knew Franks and trusted his judgment. He was overworked and exhausted—who wasn't? But if he even *suspected* that he was in over his head, he'd be the first one to admit it.

"I'm saying the investigation is moving forward," Katie said, at last. "Theories have been developed and leads are being followed. We haven't ruled any strategy out—"

"*Theories?* Is that what you said? *Plural?* All that tells me is that Mister Franks doesn't have a single clue about what actually happened."

"I have the utmost confidence in Bobby Franks," the district attorney replied. "I've met with him, I've reviewed the investigation with him, and I think he's on top of it."

Wilker's eyes bore into Katie. "Just like he was on top of that Carry student he battered a few years back? Is this the man in whom we're all supposed to place our confidence?"

Katie's jaw clenched. "I think that's highly inappropriate for you to say, and, if you'll pardon me, extraordinarily ignorant and closed-minded." She met Wilker's steely gaze with a determined, almost defiant, stare of her own. "I'm satisfied now that you really don't know anything about how things work out here in the real world."

Dean Wilker slowly uncrossed his legs and got to his feet.

"Very well," he said. "I'm going to report to the president that I've met with you and your statement to me is that you find me ignorant and closed-minded and you refuse to ask for any help."

Katie stood and took a deep breath. It occurred to her that it was good for this man that Con was not still the D.A.

"I think that report would be partly accurate," she said, finally.

Wilker rocked from heel to toe for a moment, considering her.

"I think you should know that the college has already engaged the services of Charles Nix, Junior." He paused, carefully watching Katie, looking for some reaction. "We're currently studying any available legal recourse."

Katie made every effort not to react visibly. Charles Bruton "Bru" Nix, Jr. was a young attorney with a small but influential firm that had been founded by his grandfather. He was charming and handsome and had been educated at prestigious Virginia schools. It wasn't a huge secret that certain members of Richfield's power elite were grooming him to run against her in the next election.

"I think it's wise to consider every available option," Katie said. "And then, when Franks catches this man and my lawyers take him to trial, perhaps we'll invite Bru to come sit behind them in the courtroom." She flashed a smile and shrugged. "If he wants to do what we do, he should probably learn from the best."

It was Dean Wilkins's turn to burn crimson and sputter. He finally jammed a pale hand in Katie's direction. Katie smiled and gave him a firm handshake.

He muttered something and then disappeared.

Katie was standing at her desk, trying to make some sense out of the dean's visit, when her secretary, Laurie Ross, poked her head in the open door.

"Boy, who jammed a fireplace poker up that dude's butt?" Laurie asked.

Katie laughed. "I don't know, Laurie. I think he was just born that way."

"Oh, well. You did remember to pick up your husband's cake, didn't you?"

Katie shot a startled look at her watch. Panic erupted in her eyes. "Oh hell, Laurie! I completely forgot!"

She was throwing a birthday dinner for Con that night and still had a half dozen errands to run. She grabbed her purse and briefcase and jogged through the reception area toward the elevator. "I hope the bakery's still open," she said.

"Anything I can do?" Laurie called after her.

"Yeah," Katie replied, as she punched the elevator button, "if that pompous son-of-a-bitch comes back for any reason, zap him with your stun gun."

CHAPTER 8

▼

JoEllen Russell's head rolled sharply to the right, cracking loudly against the van's passenger side window. She felt a flash of pain, but it was vague and distant, as though she was merely sampling the discomfort of another person. With great effort, she managed to turn her head away from the window. She closed her eyes and began to giggle. It all seemed so funny to her—the disturbing sound of her head hitting glass, the accompanying flash of light, the strange, dissociated pain. And she was amused by her complete lack of control. She usually had control of everything. Of her life, her workplace, her family. Well, perhaps she had surrendered control of her family. One weak moment and a series of connected moral failures had seen to that. Nearly a year had passed and she had forgiven herself, but she knew she'd never be able to completely distance herself from that infidelity's shameful legacy. The fact that she was there at that moment instead of being at home with her family was proof enough of that. And now she had somehow given up control again. Or had her control been taken from her? After just one drink—she wasn't even sure she had finished the whole drink—she was completely inebriated. Her muscles had turned to gelatin; she seemed to be melting into the car seat. It was not an entirely unpleasant sensation, but, under the circumstances, an entirely inappropriate one. Her day was far from over. Her family was out there somewhere, waiting for her to show up, to shuttle children around, to cook supper. She couldn't recall exactly what was on her after-work schedule for that particular day, but she knew there would be a long list of tasks awaiting her. There always were. Instead, she was doing this—riding somewhere, presumably to revisit her past indiscretions. The thing was, she didn't really care now.

And in the sedated fog that had thickened in her head, this new insouciance was probably the funniest thing of all.

"What's so damn funny?" the driver growled.

"Everything," JoEllen replied, her words slurring badly. Her mouth was dry and her tongue felt huge and numb. "Everything's so damn funny."

She turned her head again and gazed at the countryside blurring by in the failing light. She saw vaguely familiar sights pass: the dairy at the edge of town, the graded bare earth where the new interstate would one day run, a pasture where shadow-cows grazed in a violet haze.

When they came upon the rolling, kudzu-covered hills and dense oak forests of northern Lake County, JoEllen turned toward the driver.

"Where are we going?" she asked.

"To the hotel, like I told you."

"I need to go get my children," she protested. She licked her lips with her numb tongue. "No, really, where are we going?

"To the hotel. Just to talk. Like I promised you."

"What're we gonna talk about?"

"About your impurity, JoEllen. We can talk about that if you like. Although I think you're already aware of your problem. I would especially like to talk about the fire and how it can restore your purity."

JoEllen stared at the driver through heavy lids. "What on earth are you talking about?"

"You'll see. Just be patient. We're almost there."

The van swerved suddenly, violently, onto an abandoned road. Weeds, sage and other grasses that had gone to seed grew as high as the vehicle's fenders. The van plunged on, deeper and deeper into the darkness until the woods closed in on them from either side. The higher tree limbs formed an eerie vault as they seemed to reach for each other across the narrow passage. The moon, a pale crescent sliver set against the growing darkness, flashed in the random overhead interstices. The right front tire found a hole in the road's neglected surface and jostled both driver and passenger.

"I don't feel so good," JoEllen moaned.

"We're almost there."

JoEllen closed her eyes and melted into the headrest. She felt clammy now, her stomach turning over with each bump and jostle. She tried to remember why she was even there. Her best assessment was that it was an expedition with no apparent justification or purpose. Her history with this person, the driver, was another mystery, far too complicated to be reconstructed in her current state of mind. There wasn't a single aspect of her personal world that wasn't blurred beyond recognition. She commanded herself to focus, to identify the critical components of her life. *Her children, Sara and Max.* Of course, in one sense, they *were* her life; nothing could erase them from her memory. *And Roger. Good old practical, always-there, unexciting Roger.* Try though she might, she couldn't picture him. All that she retrieved was some generic, middle-aged male face. *Ah, well…*It was just this murky mental fog. He'd be there when it finally lifted. That's the way the memory was, she thought: a simple matter of storage and retrieval. This alcohol or whatever had just messed up her computer, her memory retrieval mechanism. She found this perception—the fact that she could remember things about brain function, but couldn't compel her brain to *actually function*—extraordinarily ironic. Or was this just the manifestation of some subconscious process: had she repressed everything but work-related items? Well, what could she really recall about work? *A lot, actually.* Files, charts, forms. Countless sheets of film and printouts from the variety of scans. And, of course, the brain itself. Indeed, a remarkable organ—magnificent in design, proof enough in her mind of the existence of God. Synapses, axons, dendrites, myelin sheathing. Hundreds of millions of neurons. *Hundreds of millions!* The great brain in all it's wonder and complexity. Left brain, right brain. She saw that organ daily, in its perfection and in its damaged state. She'd seen the ravages of disease, the injury caused by blunt-force trauma and stroke, the little black dots representing transient ischemic attacks. And now this unintended intoxication was affecting her own brain's biochemistry. She tried to recall exactly what she had consumed, but nothing was registering. She repeated her name to herself, just to see if she could.

The van crested a small hill and then lurched to a stop. The driver switched off the ignition and climbed from the vehicle. JoEllen felt the passenger door swing open.

"Get out," the driver commanded.

She tried to lift her head but was unable. She felt the driver's arms wrap around her and pull her violently from her seat. Her feet touched the ground, but her legs collapsed under her. The air was hot and thick and sweet with the smell of pine sap.

"Walk, bitch."

The driver was supporting her, an arm under her limp right arm. JoEllen felt herself moving forward, one numb foot thrust in front of the other.

"What are we doing?" she rasped.

"I already told you what we're doing."

"Why're you doing this?"

"I told you. You're impure. You're like the others. You need to be purified."

She staggered forward, then fell face-first. She tasted pine straw in her numb mouth. Her stomach heaved and she spat up a mixture of chemicals and bile. Suddenly, even before she could spit the foul-tasting substance from her mouth, there was something around her neck—a belt or leather strap. With a powerful and violent motion, the driver dragged her forward. The loop tightened, cutting off her air.

"*The rat crept softly through the vegetation…*"

JoEllen tried to scream but was only able to make a low, moaning sound. She felt her body moving over the baked ground, scraping on rocks and exposed tree roots.

"*…dragging its slimy belly on the bank…*"

She felt herself being dragged down a slope. The loop relaxed momentarily as she rolled, affording her a precious gasp of air. She tried to scream, but all that came out was a strange, high-pitched squeal. She clawed desperately at the leather strap, but it tightened again. The ground was damp and cool, but she felt only the crushing pain in her neck.

"This is for your own good, JoEllen," the driver said. "Believe me. The world is impure and you, you JoEllen, have become extremely impure. All that is being done is in accordance with the book. Water purifies, indeed it does, my friend, but so does fire." The driver twisted the loop even tighter. "You are the third, JoEllen, and, thus, you will be purifed by fire."

She was on her knees now, sinking into the pliant earth at the water's edge. Her lungs and head felt like they were about to explode. Images flickered as dying neurons fired. Familiar faces flashed: her children again, her deceased parents, even Roger. And then she saw her friend, Carlyn. JoEllen remembered now that she was supposed to meet Carlyn. Her friend would be worried about her. And then she would eventually learn the cruel truth. It would be horrible for her, for everyone. She tried to say a prayer for them. She saw no point in praying for herself. She believed that she had been forgiven for her infidelity. And her brain, drugged and oxygen-starved as it was, could still recognize that there was no way she could possibly survive this ordeal.

The pain became unbearable, even through the sedative fog.

When unconsciousness came, her limp arms fell away from the leather loop and her body slumped forward.

Mickey and Leon Moran sat in the back of the unmarked Crown Victoria, patiently answering questions. Two investigators from the Lake County Sheriff's Office sat in the front, leaning back over the bench-style seat, their faces lit eerily by the dome light. The man behind the steering wheel had a wide, fleshy face and a gray moustache. He had previously identified himself as a sergeant. The other man had introduced himself only by his name, so the Morans assumed he wasn't anything important. The Crown Vic's engine was running, and the car's bright lights burned into the stark blackness where an ever-growing collection of officers and rescue personnel searched the area around the body of the woman. Mickey and Leon wondered why she was still there, lying on the ground like that. It seemed like they would have wrapped her up and taken her somewhere, if for no other reason than just respect.

They were brothers, Mickey and Leon, and co-owners of a transmission repair shop in Lake City. They sometimes shut the garage down early when business was slow and the weather was good. Mickey kept his boat, a faded blue twelve-footer outfitted with a Merc forty outboard and a full compliment of Fish Hawk instruments, in a custom-built bay at the rear of the garage. On a windless, partly cloudy, slow-business day like this one, they could be out of the shop and in the water in less than half an hour. Fishing was much more than a hobby to the two men. As Leon's wife, Trudy, put it, the brothers were "flat eat up with it."

On this particular day, Mickey and Leon were going after largemouth. They had begun the afternoon running crankbait deep, then had made a long, slow run along the bluffs just below the Talmadge highway. It hadn't been a bad day— Mickey had caught and released a twenty-five pound monster and Leon had hooked a pair of fifteen-pounders—but the two had decided to take a run at the laydown near the abandoned hotel before packing it in for the day. Fishing lay-downs—shallow water filled with fallen timber and other horizontal cover—was one of their specialties. Leon, in particular, had the touch and experience required to successfully navigate his line and bait through the timber without a snag. The men rarely left the hotel laydown without a big fish or two.

The brothers had lived their entire lives in Lake City, but neither man knew a lot about the old hotel. Leon could recall his father talking about how it had burned one night, many years ago. According to the standard account, a dozen guests had died in the fire. Mostly what Leon remembered was that the owner of the property had also died—mysteriously, according to legend—and then nobody would go onto the property to clear the ruins. The usual haunted house stories had circulated when he was in high school, but Leon had never believed them. To him, the decaying carcass of the old hotel was just a landmark—a navigation reference point when they were out in the middle of the lake.

"When did you first notice something unusual?" the investigator in the passenger seat asked. He had a long, narrow notebook balanced on the armrest.

"When we was reeling them in for the last time," Mickey replied. "Sounded like a child, choking or something. It was really weird. You hear all kinds of critters out there after dark, and you get to know all their sounds, even the strange ones. But this was different."

"Yeah," Leon agreed. "This sounded wild, but it sounded human, too."

"What did ya'll do?" said the man in the driver's seat.

"We didn't do nothin'," Mickey replied. "At least not at first."

"We kept listening for a minute or so," Leon said. "You know, to see if it would come again."

"Then there was this, like, chanting sound," Mickey said.

"Chanting sound?"

"Yeah, you know. Like this deep, growling voice saying these words over and over."

The man in the driver's seat asked, "Could you tell what he was saying?"

"No," Leon said. "It was just, like, strange words." He thought for a moment, then shrugged. "Hell, I don't know. Like one of them Indians doing some kind of tribal dance, or something."

"Native Americans," Mickey corrected.

Leon stared at his brother.

"What? We're part Native American our ownselves. Choctaw or Chickasaw. Or Cherokee. I get them confused. But 'Indians' ain't acceptable anymore. Unless you're from India."

The sergeant sighed audibly. "What did ya'll do then?"

Leon said, "I got the oar out and we kinda paddled to the tip of the point."

"Could you see anything?" The sergeant asked. He had clearly taken over the questioning at this pont.

Mickey said, "Nothin' more than it looked like something was on fire. Right there on the bank."

"What happened next?"

"Then I heard the engine crank up and seen the truck take off."

"It was a truck?"

"Yeah," Mickey said. "A truck. Or a van."

"I think it was a van," Leon offered. "All we could see really was the taillights. But, to me, it looked like the lights on an ol' Dodge van."

"Or a truck," Mickey said.

Leon shrugged. "Whatever."

"So it was a truck or a van?"

The brothers exchanged looks.

"Yeah, sure," Mickey said. "It wasn't a car, I know that much."

"But you think it was a Dodge?"

"Yeah," Mickey replied. "A Dodge or a GMC."

The two investigators exchanged glances. The non-sergeant cleared his throat.

"So what did ya'll do then?"

"Paddled up to the bank," Leon said. "It looked like the coast was clear, so we pulled the boat up at the landing down there and went over to see what was burning."

"That's when we seen it was a woman."

"We beat out the flames with a couple of towels we had in the boat," Leon said. He glanced at his brother, then his eyes fell to the floorboard. "It was pretty terrible."

"What happened next?"

"What happened next? Nothin' except we called ya'll on the cell phone."

"Like to *never* have got through," Mickey muttered.

"Did either of you ever get a look at the offender?"

"Nope. He was gone by the time we come around the point."

The investigators sat in a silence for a moment, then the man on the passenger's side flipped his notebook closed.

"I guess that's about it," he said. "Can we reach ya'll at these numbers?"

The brothers nodded.

"All right then, I reckon ya'll are free to go. Need a ride?"

"No, thanks," Leon answered softly. "We'll just take the boat back."

The two men climbed out of the patrol car and, with the car's headlights at their backs, shuffled toward their beached boat.

They paused when they got to the body, softly washed with the light from two sets of headlights, still sprawled where her killer had left her. The brothers stared at her now, for the first time really seeing her. She was dressed like a nurse, with white pants and shoes and a floral top. The knees of her pants were stained the color of the loamy lakeside soil. Her clothes were charred from her crotch up to her neck. Her eyes were open and her tongue protruded slightly from her lips.

"Ya'll probably need to just go on," a voice said. It was a Lake County crime scene investigator, there to photograph the body. "This ain't nothin' to be lookin' at, noway."

The two men carefully made their way along the bank. Leon paused when they reached their beached boat and glanced back at the menacing remains of the old hotel. A coyote began to howl. Leon began to shiver violently.

"What's wrong?" Mickey asked.

"Nothin'," Leon answered. He grabbed the boat's bow and began to push. "Let's just get the hell outa here."

Leon was still pretty sure he didn't believe in ghosts, but he was *damn* sure he would never be back to the hotel laydown again.

CHAPTER 9

▼

"Okay, hold it!" Avery May angled toward the rear of the O'Brien kitchen, camera held tightly to her face. "I want to capture this moment for posterity."

Con O'Brien, carrying his barbecue tools, froze at the door, a puzzled look on his face.

"You're capturing me with my spatula and burger fork for posterity."

The flash exploded in his eyes.

"What I'm capturing is you with that stupid apron on," Avery said. "So future generations can better understand our bizarre ways. Or, more accurately, they can attribute to the rest of us *your* bizarre ways. Now pout for me. Try to act sexy."

He glanced down at his stained "Kiss the Chef" cooking apron. "This is about as sexy as it's gonna get with me, Ave."

"That's what we all hear," Avery replied, not missing a beat. "Katie tells us you're all out of your little blue 'helper' pills."

The observers, family friends gathered at their home to honor Con on his fiftieth birthday, froze momentarily in a disintegrating semi-circle which now extended from the kitchen into the breakfast room. Most of the guests had known Con for a long time. Few had difficulty recalling occasions of lightning-stroke damage inflicted by the lethal combination of his agile wit, keen sense of irony, and legendary aversion to allowing his adversary the last, stinging word. A few were even able to remember a time when he and Avery had publicly exchanged brutal verbal shots. One such argument had all but ruined Con and Katie's rehearsal dinner. Faint connection to this history, even when consigned to the recycle bin of personal memory, momentarily paralyzed some of the guests. Eyes darted, fingers tightened around plastic drink cups as they evaluated that perilous interval between riposte and reaction. But when Con's face began to glow with appreciation—perhaps even *admiration*—the sound of laughter gradually began to spill out into the room.

In one sense, it shouldn't have been surprising that this would have been Con's reaction. As Katie put it, Conley Garrett O'Brien, version five-oh, was "a greatly evolved human being." At his half-century mark, there was little resemblance to the fiercely competitive young assistant district attorney who had once gleefully dubbed himself "Vlad the Inquisitor." The tightly wound firebrand who had earned a public reprimand from the state bar association and who had once spent three hours in a holding cell for contempt of court was gone forever.

There were many explanations for this new and improved Con. Like most mature adults, he had mellowed with age and experience. He had also absorbed many features of Katie's even temperament during their twelve years of marriage. And the birth of his only child nine years earlier had opened his eyes to new wonders and to a world not nearly as black-and-white as he had once imagined.

But, while all these things had exerted a substantial influence on him, two more recent events had absolutely hammered his personality into a completely new shape.

The first, the kidnapping of his wife and son and the attendant life-threatening ordeal, had made him cherish his family. Nobody could ever have doubted that he dearly loved Katie and Garrett. But, like many people with high-stress jobs and hectic schedules, he had found it all too easy to take his family for granted as frenetic days spun heedlessly into weeks, months, years. As with many tightly wound individuals, proximity made it all too easy to neglect or become annoyed with his loved ones. On a bad day, irritation spawned verbal birch-rods that lashed out angrily, then retracted just as quickly into limp fronds of regret. And then suddenly, in a single day, all of that changed. The brutal possibility that he might never see his wife and son alive again put a dramatic end to his domestic negligence.

The second event, his heart attack one year earlier, had made him cherish life and living. There was something about the life-altering lessons of a near-death experience—the pain and extreme urgency of the attack itself, waking up on life support in an intensive care unit—that simply couldn't be duplicated by any other social process or influence. Days that had once routinely begun with a mental inventory of obstacles to be crushed and opponents to be vanquished now commenced with quiet but fervent prayers of thanksgiving.

But while he may have, indeed, "greatly evolved," Con's core beliefs remained relatively unchanged. His experiences had refined, not re-created, him. A veteran prosecutor, he still viewed the world and the deeper motives of humankind with the jaundiced eye of the marginal misanthrope. In his opinion, there were precious few human endeavors that were immune to the powerfully negative influences of greed and pride. He was satisfied that many professional politicians were hubris-bloated ninnies who couldn't make an honest living in the private sector. He believed that professional sports had been ruined by the dominance of a few "megabuck" franchises. He was quite certain that a new and pervading stupidity was engulfing the world, as evidenced by the proliferation of certain voyeuristic "reality" television shows and so-called psychic phone services. And he claimed that appellate judges had amplified the Bill of Rights into a criminal-friendly engine of judicial oppression that James Madison wouldn't even recognize, much less ratify. The difference now with Con was that he finally understood that nothing could be gained—and much could be lost—by dwelling on things he couldn't change.

"I say—jolly good one, old girl," he said now, smiling and affecting his best British butler's accent. He set his barbecue tools on the kitchen counter. "Ah, yes. Very clever, indeed."

"Oh, I see. You're British now. Perhaps that will explain why you cooked all the burgers into hockey pucks."

Con just stared at Avery May, grinning and nodding. She was tall and slender, almost too thin, her hair currently a preternatural copper color and chopped off chin length. She was attired in characteristically offbeat casual wear: huge hoop earrings, an oversized Spongebob Squarepants tee-shirt, magenta capris and clogs. Wacky as she was, he really couldn't help but like her. Now, that was. When they first met, he was an archly conservative, beer-swilling, frat-boy graduate of Vanderbilt and the University of Alabama School of Law, she was a twenty-five-year-old bohemian of a decidedly liberal bent, with plenty of opinions and a penchant for sharing them. Con regarded Avery, Katie's longtime friend and former college roommate, as an obnoxious provocateur; Avery considered Con to be an arrogant bully. But both belligerents cared deeply about Katie Cowan, and this commonality of affection proved to be the great mediating influence. Then Garrett was kidnapped and things changed for all of them. Avery, who had been babysitting Garrett at the time of the abduction, fell into a deep depression prompted by intense feelings of guilt. Con, displaying compassion that most people never saw, befriended Avery May and single-handedly plucked her from depression's perilous grip. They had remained close ever since, although their nonstop verbal jousting made this difficult for others to see.

"Man," Avery complained, sagging noticeably, "you're absolutely no fun anymore."

"Not without my blue pills," Con said, glancing around. "Say, has anybody seen my beloved spousal unit?"

"I think she went to take a phone call," Betsy Malloy, the wife of one of Con's teaching associates, offered.

"When was that?"

"I don't know. About ten minutes ago."

Con sighed and pulled off the apron."Ah, hell. It's gotta be business." He walked around the granite counter and tested the empty cans gathered there until he found a half-filled can of diet ginger ale. He frowned and said, "I can't believe she's talking business at nine o'clock on a Friday night."

"How do you know it's a business call?" Avery May asked.

"Because the only other way she'd talk this long on the phone is if it was you on the other end." He poured the ginger ale into a plastic cup. He noticed a few blackened burgers left on a platter. He picked one up and let it drop with a disturbing thud. "Hockey, anyone?"

"I can go get her," Avery said.

"No, let her be. She's got a lot of heavy stuff on her at the moment. Let's just chill until she's through."

"Fine," Avery said. "Then let's all chill in the family room where we can begin our, ah, *tribute* to the birthday boy."

Almost all of the guests had already begun to migrate into the adjacent family room. It was, by far, Katie's favorite place in the twenty-year-old Victorian-style house. She had spent years decorating it, and, with its complex variety of styles and colors, it thoroughly represented Katie's personality. The guests had no problem finding places to sit. There was a traditional burgundy sauvage leather sofa along one wall, a billowing plaid fabric sofa packed with plump pillows along the opposite wall. Along the room's back wall, two comfortable chairs had been placed on either side of a brick fireplace. A mainspring-driven cuckoo clock from the Black Forest, a wedding gift from her parents, sat in the center of the mantel. A black mahogany Georgian-style stand holding a flowing fern occupied a corner near one of the chairs. A richly lacquered antique work stand had been positioned in the opposite corner. There was a sturdy oak coffee table crouching in front of the fabric sofa. A large and colorful Persian rug covered the polished hardwood floor in the center of the room.

Con stood in the doorway and sipped his drink while the guests seated themselves. Betsy and Roger Malloy sank into a large cushion on the fireplace end of the leather sofa. Mark and Clyda Ramsay, the O'Briens' next door neighbors on Kyle Ridge Road, took the corresponding positions on the fabric sofa. Chief Deputy D.A. Kevin Rose and his very pregnant wife squeezed in next to the Ramsays, while Berry Macklin sat in one of the chairs near the fireplace.

Avery May squeezed past Con holding several wrapped packages and a huge manila envelope. She set the gifts on the table and waved the envelope to get everyone's attention.

"All right," she said, "as this celebration's unofficial, ah, *ringmaster*, I'm faced with a difficult decision. It seems that my dear friend, Katie, has found something more interesting to do in the O'Brien's magnificent, some might even say extravagant, master suite."

"She's on the phone, Avery," Con said. "I thought everyone already understood that."

Ignoring him, Avery continued: "Being that, for all practical purposes, Katie's abandoned the celebration of a half century of her husband's life on earth, I'm making a unilateral decision to proceed with the entertainment part of the program in her absence. To be more specific, I'm prepared to share with you certain images intended to honor Con on this, the latest and most recent of his many, many birthdays."

Everyone laughed and Con bowed his head in quiet resignation.

"For starters," Avery declared, plucking a huge blown-up photograph from the envelope, "behold the essence of classical Greek manhood!"

She held up an image of Con at his pre-coronary weight, lying languidly on a vinyl-and-aluminum recliner sunk into a dazzling white beach. He was wearing woefully stressed swim trunks and had a faded Atlanta Braves cap pulled down low over his eyes. Ample thighs, spread wide apart on either side of the recliner, ballooned like plump sausages. In Con's right hand was a blue foam drink cozy from which protruded an open can of beer. Avery, enjoying the crowd's laughter, slowly walked the photo around the room.

"Another reason not to drink," she said, grinning broadly.

"Another reason not to take you to the beach with us," Con muttered.

"This next one happens to be one of my personal favorites," she said, producing another photo.

At that moment Katie, wearing a navy polo shirt and faded blue jeans, appeared in the doorway.

"Oh, hi, Katie," Avery said, feigning alarm, "I didn't want to start this without you, but Con just insisted—"

"I've got to go," Katie said. Her somber expression made it clear that her involvement in the birthday celebration had come to an end. "I need to run down to C.I.D. to meet with an investigator. I hate having to run out on ya'll. I know it's beyond rude for the hostess to ditch her own party." Her eyes jumped from Kevin Rose to Berry Macklin to her husband. "That was Bobby Franks. He thinks we might have a break in the Carry murders."

Con blinked. "So why does he need you?"

"He wants to lay the whole thing out before he arrests anyone. Plus, he wants to get a search warrant." She made a face. "Those homicide cops are great investigators, but they really suck at drafting search warrants."

Con said, "You're not going downtown by yourself. I'm going with you."

"No, Con. I don't want to ruin this. Why don't you just stay and enjoy the rest of the evening?"

"I'm going with you, and that's final." Then making a face at Avery, Con added, "Besides, it will keep me from having to take any more abuse from Cruella DeVil here."

"Sounds like you need me, too," Rose said. He cut his eyes at his wife and shrugged.

"What about me?" Macklin asked. "I mean, I'm only head of the violent-crime unit."

"Great," Katie said. "I'm sure Franks'll be glad to have every legal mind he can get." She paused, turning to the Ramsays and Malloys. "I apologize, ya'll. I really hate to break up the party. It's just—"

"Hey, you don't have to apologize," Betsy Malloy said. "This is something that's got to be done. Besides, if it'll help get this maniac off the street, we're one hundred per cent behind you."

Mark Ramsay added, "We probably need to be running anyway." He flashed a self-conscious grin. "First-time babysitter."

Avery May collapsed on the leather couch, the photograph curled in her lap.

"Fine," she said. "Ya'll just run out on me. Like I even care."

Everyone stood and began moving toward the doorway. Con patted Avery on the shoulder.

"Sorry, A-train," he said. "I was enjoying myself so much. I really hate to go off and leave you, but—"

"Leave me, my *ass*," Avery declared, suddenly popping to her feet. "I'm going with ya'll."

"I don't think so, Ave," Katie said.

Avery's face collapsed into a mask of dejection. "You never let me go anywhere good with you," she complained.

"It's law enforcement business," Katie said.

Avery glared at her.

"At a police station," Katie continued. "With case-sensitive information being discussed."

"It's my Spongebob shirt, isn't it?"

"No, Avery. With a case this important, you don't want to give a defense attorney anything extra to complain about to a jury."

"What about Con? He doesn't even work for the county anymore."

"He's got many years of experience. And he's an attorney in good standing—"

"He's a freaking *history professor*, for crying out loud!"

Katie sighed. "You can't go, Avery. It just wouldn't be right to show up with you. Besides, I need you here."

"For what?"

"Did you forget I've got a nine-year-old back in his room playing video games?"

Avery's defiant countenance faded quickly. She nodded solemnly, perhaps out of the sudden realization of some duty owed to her friend. It might even have been an expression of extreme gratitude to Katie for the reinvestment of trust.

"I guess I'd rather play video games, anyway," Avery said. She gave her friend a frail smile. "I'll make sure all the doors are locked."

She returned the photographs to the folder and, when the last person was gone, switched out the lights in the room.

There, the man thought.

In that house, having some kind of party, probably celebrating her many conquests. Fondly recalling sinners trampled beneath her feet. Anticipating glorious victories yet to be won. From his vehicle he had an excellent view of the house, the lights, the people milling about. Especially *her*.

He thought of her often, this woman. His personal inquisitor, the crusader who had once made it her sacred mission to bludgeon him into the penitentiary. He no longer had to imagine which room might be hers: he had caught a glimpse of her once through an upstairs window, just a glimpse, sitting at her dressing table, carefully brushing her hair. There in her safe house, on her crime-free little cul-de-sac overlooking the perfect world of which she imagined herself master.

An impressive house, he thought, huge and stately, with a wraparound porch and white picket fence. Floodlights burning away the hazy summer night. Hissing sprinkler heads popping up on cue, joining the buzzsaw chorus of the cicadas and crickets. Undoubtedly there would be a top-of-the-line security system armed and waiting. An abode truly worthy of the District Attorney of Bienville County. Doubtless she felt safe there, locked away from the wretched humanity she judged so ruthlessly. Ruthlessly and casually and with great finality.

But there was so much she didn't know. There was no way she could have known or understood him, for example. To her, he was just another common criminal, some variety of sick sexual predator. A "twisted user and abuser of people." She had used those exact words to the jury in her closing argument. And she had pointed at him and called him other names, dehumanizing him through the whole trial. He would not forget this condescending little flourish, part of the little influence game she had run on the jury. And, of course, she never really knew the so-called "victim," that emasculating little parasite. Katie had coached and packaged her and presented her as some traumatized paragon of virtue. She had been strategically placed in a chair behind counsel table, tissue in one hand, victim-service assistant attached firmly to the other. It had all been a charade, another carefully staged production in the finely choreographed theater of injustice. But did Katie O'Brien really understand what the truth was? She didn't, nor could she.

So why had she chosen to persecute him? For the benefit of society? For the so-called victim? No, it was for herself. Women like her were the real users, the worst victimizers in the world. Blinded by ambition, they used the crumpled bodies of unfortunates as their stair steps to the top. He'd seen this same vile process at work for years. He'd seen men who had been afflicted with this disease, but women were, as a class, much more adroit in the art of manipulation, much crueler in the execution of judgment. It began when they were girls, just discovering their claws and the raw power they had over men. Like all those girls from Carry. Cold-hearted little sexpots, completely spoiled by their tenth birthdays, arriving on campus with their trendy clothes and expensive foreign cars and their heads all full of themselves and Madison Avenue's bullshit. *Users, all of them.* Katie O'Brien wasn't any different. He could just see her as a teenager: homecoming queen, honor student, perhaps even a beauty pageant contestant, earnestly confessing her dream to one day serve the public. And it had all been made to happen for her. Because she was this willful, ambitious doctor's daughter with a pretty face, long legs, and a nice ass.

And then one day, surfeited with cases against addicts and simpletons, she turned her opportunistic gaze his way. Targeting him, picturing him—a person of substance and education—as the next rung on the ladder. In the end, it had all been a huge waste of time and ambition. All her work, her diligence, her steely-eyed self-righteousness had meant nothing. Because he had *not* been put away. To the contrary, he was right there where he had been—in the town she somehow perceived as hers, on that campus, and, at that moment, on her street. Thinking about her now, like he had thought about those self-involved Carry coeds.

He saw a light go out in the house, then another. The front porch light came on and a half-dozen guests were discharged into the darkness. He watched them outdistance the light and disperse—down the long driveway, past withering crepe myrtles and begonias, off into the suffocating, chirpy night. *Ah, the party's over.* What a shame to see the genteel revelry end at such an early hour.

And then there appeared the queen herself, standing regally in the electric corona, watching her loyal subjects disperse. For the time being, she still reigned over something.

Well, he thought, his damp hands twisting the steering wheel, her castle keep was beginning to crumble. People were talking, and the truth about her was beginning to circulate. The newspaper accounts pretty much told the story: the Killer was the master of this particular game, the D.A. and the police, mere hapless spectators. She was starting to realize that she couldn't just wave her little hand and make the ugliness disappear. This was much bigger than the little paint-by-numbers cases upon which she had built her career.

Of course, she had the power to put an end to it. All she had to do was seek him out, ask his forgiveness. She could use her power and discretion to actually perform a service for her terrified constituents. But she was far too arrogant to admit that she had a moral and intellectual superior. So she wouldn't do it. Not until it was too late.

Too late for all those women and others yet to come.

And, perhaps, even for Katie herself.

CHAPTER 10

▼

It was nearly ten when Katie's entourage arrived at the Metro Building, home of the Richfield Police investigative offices. Bobby Joe Franks met them at the front door. He wrestled briefly with the dead-bolt before realizing that the door wasn't locked. His visitors, meanwhile, waited patiently, smiling and swatting away the bugs swarming around the floodlights just above the door.

The seventy-five-year-old building, located at the eastern edge of the Richfield business district, had begun its life as a local retail outlet for a Birmingham dry goods company. Later it became the home for offices of various municipal department heads. A three-story brick building with arched windows on the top floors and a decorated entablature, it had once been considered a "building of interest" on the Richfield historical architectural tour. Now, more than a decade after C.I.D. had moved in, serious defects—inadequate heating, cooling, and ventilation, persistent roof leaks, and deadly radon gas wafting from the base-ment—were threatening to drive the investigators out.

"Glad ya'll could come," Franks said as he pushed open the heavy glass door. He was dressed in a threadbare oxford-cloth shirt and olive khaki slacks. A lit cig-arette dangled from his lips, the smoke curling up around his face. "I see ya'll brought a *veteran* prosecutor with you," he said, nodding in Con's direction.

"I'm just here to absorb radon," Con said. "I was told not to open my mouth."

"Except to the extent that it helps in the radon absorption process," said Kevin Rose.

Katie said, "The truth is, we let him come because it's his birthday. If we didn't bring him, he'd be at home, pouting."

"With Katie's crazy friend, Avery May," Berry Macklin added.

Franks began to herd the group across the lobby. To do this, they had to circle the only furniture in the room, a desk and a chair used in the daytime by the receptionist/operator, and weave their way through the stacks of bound documents littering the lobby.

Franks turned to Katie, the smoke making his left eye squint. "Avery May? That the ol' red-headed girl that nearly got arrested out at the Rollins farm last year?"

Katie sighed. "Yep. That would be Avery."

"What the hell's her deal, anyway?"

"God only knows. I think she was protesting the use of pesticides on that particular occasion. She means well. She's just—"

"A complete psycho," Rose said.

The group walked around a corner and into the south staircase. Two signs hung above the doorway. One said "No Smoking," and the other established a point beyond which unauthorized visitors were forbidden to pass. The group began tromping up to the second floor, the wooden stairs creaking under their feet.

"No smoking, eh?" Con asked.

"No unauthorized personnel, either," Franks replied, blowing a smoke ring in Con's direction.

The investigator pulled open the second-floor door and held it while the attorneys passed into the dimly lit hallway. The narrow passage had been created when contractors had, eleven years earlier, subdivided the open second floor into a fabricated warren of offices. The plasterboard walls, once painted bright white, were now scuffed and dingy yellow in color.

The group trudged past an open office door and glanced in. A woman wearing an orange sleeveless top was sitting in a chair positioned obliquely in front of an olive-drab metal desk. She had her head down and seemed to be weeping uncontrollably. A beefy man with a silver comb-over sat behind the desk, a ball-point pen poised above a yellow legal pad. An engraved name plate on the door read, "Det. Brant Woodley." The man shot Franks a look that said, "Thanks a lot, asshole."

"I wonder what her problem is," Kevin Rose said when they had moved a safe distance from the office door.

"I don't really know," Franks replied. "She showed up at the main station about an hour and a half ago, all hysterical. They sent her over here." He took the cigarette out of his mouth and flicked an ash into his left palm. "Lieutenant asked if I'd talk to her, but I had a report to do." He shrugged. "So Woodley got stuck with it."

Franks ushered the group into his office, or, more accurately, his demi-office—he shared an engineered work space with Rodney Massey, another Major Crimes investigator. His work "area" consisted of a desk, three side chairs, and a metal filing cabinet crammed into approximately one-hundred twenty square feet of green-and-white checkerboard floor space. A bulletin board hung on the six-foot-tall metal and plastic room divider. Colored push-tacks secured three FBI wanted flyers and a thick wad of subpoenas to the bulletin board. The surface of his desk was littered with stacks of files and loose papers. An open soft drink can sat on a monthly calendar-blotter with names and phone numbers scribbled in various colors of ball-point ink. A cow figurine, a black-and-white Holstein with a plastic toy police badge hung around its neck, stood on a stack of message notes just beyond the top margin of the blotter. Framed pictures of the investigator's three children were positioned at even intervals along the front edge of the desk.

Franks dropped his cigarette into the soft drink can and dropped wearily into his desk chair. Katie and her two deputies sat in the three side chairs. Con slumped against the filing cabinet.

"So what's going on?" Katie asked.

"Well, like I told you on the phone, I think we found Kerry Grinder down in Maynor County. In fact, I know it's her. They're waiting on some next of kin, whatever, to come in and identify the remains. But it's her."

"Her tattoo?"

"Yeah. On her left shoulder. An angel, and a pretty distinctive angel, at that. Voluptuous and scantily clad."

"An angel on her shoulder," Rose said. "Obviously not a guardian angel."

"Anyway," Franks continued, "the killer had done this same weird stuff to her. You know, the carving of a message in the skin, a calling card left in the mouth."

Kevin Rose's brow furrowed. "A calling card in her mouth?"

Franks grimaced. "Not an actual calling card, Kevin. An object. Something left to screw with us. You know, like the flower last time. In this case, a black plastic pawn from a cheap chess set."

"What's the cause of death gonna be?" Berry Macklin asked.

"They're not gonna post her until tomorrow, so nothing's official yet. She was all beaten up—bruises and cuts all over her face and head, big bruises on her legs, arms, and back, scrapes on her knees." He paused, picking up and examining a Polaroid photograph that had been sitting on his blotter. "But they're pretty sure the cause of death is gonna be strangulation. There's a fairly obvious ligature mark around her throat. Plus, the coroner down in Maynor County said the blood vessels in her eyes were damaged."

Katie asked, "What was the message?"

"'Let's play'" Franks snorted in disgust.

"'*Let's play*'?"

"Yeah. This is some twisted son-of-a-bitch's idea of a game."

"God, Bobby. This is getting a little too weird."

"Well, there's even more weirdness where that came from. First off, while I'm driving back, I get a call from the lieutenant saying they found another woman's body in Lake County. This killing just happened tonight. Two dudes bass fishing on the lake heard it going down. Again, it looks like she was strangled in just the same way—loop or ligature around the neck. Except this one had been set on fire."

"Set on fire?"

"Yeah. Sprayed down with lighter fluid or something and then set on fire. Our fishermen put the flames out."

"Did they get a look at the man?" Katie asked.

"Lieutenant said they never eyeballed the dude, but they saw a vehicle leaving. They think it's some kind of van or truck."

"Whew," Rose deadpanned. "Good thing there aren't many trucks or vans in Alabama."

"It's not much, smartass, but it's probably more than the killer wanted anyone to see."

Katie asked, "What's the story on the victim?"

"Don't know. She had no identification on her. She was definitely older than the other two women, probably mid-thirties." Franks took a pack of cigarettes out of his shirt pocket and began tapping one end with his right index finger. "I'm thinking she wasn't a student of any kind."

Rose asked, "Do you think this is gonna be the same dude?"

"Well, you got a female victim. And you got the same mechanism of death." He shrugged. "Nothin' else seems to fit the pattern."

"Maybe there's not really a 'pattern'," Katie offered. "Maybe this is just some opportunistic psychopath who's randomly attacking women wherever he's able."

"Or maybe it's completely unrelated," Con said. He paused, then added, "Or maybe it's a copycat."

Franks cringed and let the cigarette pack fall to the desk blotter. "Man, don't even *think* something that hideous," he said.

"I'm just saying—"

"You said there was more weirdness," Katie interrupted.

"Yeah, there is. When I got back here, there was a fax from the Birmingham lab waiting on me." He put on his reading glasses and scanned a document on his desk. "Miss Crawley's urine contained ethyl alcohol and several metabolites of...f-l-u-n-i-t-r-a-z—"

"Flunitrazepam," Katie interjected. "That's the generic chemical name for a popular sedative-hypnotic drug."

Franks peered at her from over the rims of the glasses. "Something like one of those 'date rape' drugs—what do they call them? Roofies?"

"Exactly. There's several of them out there, but this is one of the most popular. 'Roofies' and 'hyp' are just a couple of the street names."

"So how exactly does a person use them on someone else?"

"It's tragically easy," Katie replied. "It comes in pills that have no taste and dissolve easily in liquid. Plus, alcohol intensifies the sedative effect. You drop a couple in the victim's drink and, twenty minutes later, she's dizzy, nauseated, maybe on the brink of unconsciousness." She paused, reconsidering the circumstances of Anjanette Donna Crawley's murder. "It goes a long way toward explaining how these women are quietly disappearing."

Franks took his glasses off and chewed on an earpiece. "It would seem to suggest that the killer was someone close to the victim."

"Close enough to slip something into a drink."

"An ex-boyfriend, for example."

"I guess it's possible. What exactly are you thinking?"

Franks began playing with the cigarette pack again. "I'm thinking that someone dosed Crawley with this roofie drug, whatever. I'm thinking that whoever did that had to be around her, had to have access to what she was drinking. I'm thinking that whoever murdered Crawley also murdered Grinder." He paused, giving the pack a spin. "I'm thinking that Jamie Amerson is an evil little son-of-a-bitch who dated—and got dumped by—both these women. And he committed this crime because his ego was bruised and for no other reason." He leaned forward in his chair, his jaw set. "Mostly, what I'm thinking is that we need to get him off the street. Right now, tonight, before he can hurt anyone else."

Katie rubbed her chin. She hadn't had much time to think about Jamie Amerson since her conversation with Franks earlier in the day. But she'd conducted her own extensive psychological evaluation of him years earlier when she'd prosecuted him for the attempted parking lot abduction. From what she had been able to determine, Amerson was a classic "indulged psychopath," a narcissistic child of privilege whose superego pathology—his demonstrable lack of a conscience or concern for others—could have been the product of parental overvaluation or a valueless upbringing, or a combination of the two. His father, the owner of a heating and cooling monopoly in Bienville County, was a cigar-chomping blusterer who prided himself on his ability to manipulate powerful people in every milieu. His mother had died when he was a child; his stepmother was a society gadabout who was far more interested in her garden club and the Bienville Cotillion than her family. Jamie, who was significantly above-average in intelligence, had dropped out of Carry College after two years of uninspired academic performance. He had acquired a reputation as a "user"—of drugs and people—a self-indulgent and controlling Lothario who would not take kindly to being "dumped" by a woman.

But was he capable of these murders, these merciless acts of depravity? And the more immediate inquiry: Did sufficient legal cause exist to justify his arrest or the search of his house? Katie had grave doubts about that.

"Bobby, I'm not sure there's enough—"

"Enough *what*? Enough bodies? What do we tell the next victim's family—ah, sorry, Mister and Missus Jones, we were pretty sure that Jamie was the killer, but we hadn't collected quite enough little connecting bits of information—"

Katie tilted her head and frowned. "Come on, Bobby. Don't you start that mess with me, too. Please. I've already had to sit through an hour of Dean Wilker's indignant fuming today."

Franks eased back in his chair. "Oh, man. What a huge tool *that* guy is. He's been over here bitching to the chief, too." His eyes, still bloodshot and weary, met Katie's. "Chief's already been in the lieutenant's ear about this. And that ain't all. Did you happen to read the editorial in the paper today?"

Katie shook her head. "I haven't had time to read the clock today."

"They're all over us, Katie. The whole damn town's saying we're incompetent, we're just sitting on our hands, that kind of stuff. And they've started calling about the Lake County case." He took a deep breath and exhaled slowly. "I'm getting where I don't even want to leave my apartment anymore."

"Wilker mentioned us asking the feds for help."

Franks snorted. "The feds *are* helping us. We sent some of the evidence to the FBI lab for analysis. Beyond that, we don't need them. What the hell can they do to help make our case? Send some kind of profiler?" He lapsed into his oft-practiced "bureaucrat mode"—eyes wide and unblinking, words clunking out in a robotic monotone: "'Uh, your profile…is…thirty-five-year-old…white…male… loner…'"

"Yeah," Kevin Rose added, "just like the projected white male Beltway sniper."

Franks leaned forward again, his eyes now entreating the D.A.

"All we need is one little piece of physical evidence that'll link Amerson to the murders. One little thing. A wilted flower petal. A chess set with a missing pawn. A blister-pack of roofies. A drop of blood, a hair, a fiber. Anything. Help me put a search warrant together and I'll get that piece of evidence."

"All right, Bobby," Katie said. "Let's look at this totally objectively. Right now, this very minute, what do we have that directly or indirectly links Amerson to this crime?"

Franks rubbed his eyes and stared down at his blotter. When he began his response, his voice had a weary, almost defeated tone.

"He dated both victims," he said. "He was rejected by both victims. He's not unfamiliar with the world of illegal drugs." He paused a beat. "He's a freaking sociopath."

Katie gave him a sympathetic smile. "Bobby. Come on, now. We have to have probable cause to have a valid warrant. That means that you have enough information right now to believe that *probably* evidence of this crime will be found in his possession."

"I do have that—"

"What you have doesn't even add up to *possible* cause," Con interjected.

"Couldn't we at least put something together and run it by a judge?"

Katie frowned. "And then what? Suppose you search his house and vehicle and find something incriminating. We get to court and out it goes. Then what? You think we're getting tattooed by the media *now*? Just wait until everyone knows this is the guy, but we can't prosecute him because our key evidence has been thrown out."

"Because of a bad search warrant," Rose added.

Franks put his elbows on the desk and began rubbing his temples.

"All right. How much more do we need?"

Katie glanced at Rose and Macklin. Both of her deputies shrugged.

"I don't know, Bobby. Something more. Just something more than what we've got."

"I suppose asking Jamie to consent to a search is out of the question."

Katie frowned. "What do you think? A petulant shit like him who just spits at authority? His first move will be to call Daddy or his lawyer. And, of course, the answer will be, 'hey, screw you, go get a warrant.' And *then* what? Now he knows you're looking at him, he starts hiding stuff—"

"She's right," Rose said. "We're really gonna need the element of surprise with him. And everything's gonna have to be procedurally perfect."

Franks sighed and stared down at his folded hands.

"Well, then," he said, finally. Wearily. "I guess there's nothing more to talk about."

"We'll get him, B.J.," Kevin Rose said, as he and Berry Macklin got to their feet. "He'll mess up eventually and then we'll have his ass. It's just a matter of time."

Franks nodded solemnly. He stood with Katie and walked slowly to the door with the attorneys.

"I just hope he doesn't get someone else before then."

Katie nodded in grim agreement. "You and me both," she murmured.

Franks was smoking a cigarette and staring out his window when he became aware of Investigator Brant Woodley's huge frame filling his doorway.

"Hey, Bobby," Woodley said tentatively. "Can I interrupt for just a second?"

Franks sighed. "You're not interrupting. I'm just spinning my wheels here. What's up?"

"I thought you might want to talk to the lady in my office." When Bobby Franks gave him a puzzled look, Woodley added, "It may have something to do with your murder cases."

Franks bolted upright in his chair.

"Then hell yes I want to talk to her," he said.

Woodley called down the hallway for the woman. She appeared a moment later and the investigator steered her through the doorway. She was slightly built, with a great thatch of bottle-blonde hair, fried from too many perms. She had a pretty face, with a wide, expressive mouth, large blue eyes and a cleft chin. Dark mascara rivulets flowed down her cheeks from red-rimmed eyes. Her purse strap was twisted around her hands, each of which clutched a well-worn tissue. The investigator gave her a nudge and she sat in one of Franks's side chairs.

"Bobby Franks," Woodley said, "I'd like for you to meet Carlyn Bedsole."

Katie's bedside phone rang just after midnight, the shrill alarm sending an electric jolt through her. It hadn't awakened her—she'd been lying in her bed for nearly twenty minutes, assembling and then tearing apart the clues and bizarre circumstances in the kidnapping-murder cases—but the sound caused her heart to race, just the same. She answered it quickly before it could ring a second time.

"Katie, it's Franks," said the voice on the other end. "I'm sorry if I woke you."

"I wasn't sleeping," she said. "What's up?"

"You said we needed one more thing before we could get a search warrant for Jamie Amerson's house and vehicles?"

Katie sat up, adjusting her three pillows to support her. She glanced over at Con. He was sound asleep, his heavy, measured breathing evidence that the ringer hadn't disturbed him. She struggled to reassemble the details of their discussion a few hours earlier. All the conversations about the case were beginning to merge in her exhausted brain.

"I think what I said was we need something else. Whether one thing is enough, I guess, depends on what the thing is."

"All right, here's the thing. I just got through talking to a woman, a friend of the person who got set on fire down in Lake County."

"They've identified her already?"

"They were pretty sure two hours ago. I just got off the phone with the main case investigator down there and the woman's husband has just positively identified her."

"Okay, but it sounds like Lake County's gonna have jurisdiction on that case."

"On the actual murder, true. But we're pretty sure now that she got abducted from Richfield. Her car was found unlocked behind Breaux's. That's where my witness was gonna meet her. They were friends, just gonna have a drink and shoot the jive and socialize on a Friday afternoon."

Katie asked, "Who was this victim?"

"Nice lady, according to the witness. About thirty-five or so, worked as a technician for a radiologist, or something. Married with two kids."

"I still don't see how this—"

"She was screwing Jamie Amerson, Katie. This witness, Carlyn Bedsole, said the affair didn't last long, but this victim, JoEllen Russell, was the one who broke it off."

Katie sat in silence, trying her best to process this information.

"And," Franks added, "if that's not enough, guess whose place of business is just a block away?"

"Jamie Amerson?"

"That's a big ten-four, roger-dodger."

Katie rubbed her eyes with her right hand. She knew that by launching an official government action against the spoiled but well-connected Jamie Amerson, they'd be firing the first shot in a war that would be long and brutal and not quickly forgotten. Amerson's family had the wherewithal to fight the criminal charges by overwhelming the state with writs, petitions, and motions—counterattacks with civil lawsuits weren't even out of the question. And she also knew that Jamie's father had the ability to wreak havoc upon her political future. No, this promised to be an extraordinarily active and high-profile public battle. And, if they weren't able to find any additional evidence, a losing one, as well.

At the same time, if he *was* the kidnapper-murderer, then she and Franks had a sworn duty to take him down, to do whatever they could, legally and ethically, to protect the public. And the fact that the pursuit of justice would be unpleasant and possibly detrimental to her political future should have no bearing on her decisions in the case.

"Katie?"

"Yeah, Bobby. I'm here."

"What do we do?"

"Let's get the search warrants. If we're ever gonna find any physical evidence, now's the time. We'll need warrants for his house and personal vehicles. Does he own a van or truck?"

"No, none that are registered in his name. But his daddy's company has several vans and trucks and everybody knows that Jamie uses them from time to time."

"All right, then, we'll need another warrant for the company vehicles."

"You got it. Do you want to help put them together?"

"Go ahead and start getting the affidavits written. I'll look them over first thing in the morning."

"Ten-four. Anything else?"

She sighed. "Yeah. Hope to God we find something incriminating."

CHAPTER 11

▼

"May I help you?"

The receptionist at Amerson Heating and Cooling looked up from her morning paper and smiled at the two men standing at the chest-high counter. She was a plump middle-aged woman with her salt-and-pepper hair tied back into a tight bun. She evaluated the situation, her eyes jumping from Bobby Franks to Brant Woodley. Her smile began to disintegrate even before either investigator had uttered a word.

"We'd like to speak to Jamie Amerson," Franks growled.

She laid the paper on her desk and reached for her phone.

"Your name, please?"

Franks smiled politely. "I'm Bobby Franks. This here's Brant Woodley." He pulled his badge case from his windbreaker pocket. "We're investigators with Richfield Police Department."

She pursed her lips and pushed buttons on her phone console.

"Mister Amerson," she murmured into the receiver, "could you please step out here?" Her eyes locked in on Franks's. "I don't know. They're police officers of some kind." She hung up the phone and stared almost defiantly at the investigators. "Mister Amerson said he'd be right out."

Franks glanced out the glass window that ran along the side of the office. He could see that his two assist vehicles—an old black Plymouth and a black Crown Vic—were in position at the back of the property. Six officers, including two Special Response officers, and Craig Belew, a veteran RPD crime scene technician, awaited the signal to start searching the two vans and a truck parked at the back of the building. And he knew that two more units were "sitting on" Jamie

Amerson's house about two blocks away. The sight of the cars in position provoked a tingle of excitement, the gratifying adrenaline release that many police officers experienced as an important operation began to unfold.

"Is there something I can do for ya'll?"

Franks's attention was quickly redirected to the speaker, a large, middle-aged man with a cigar stub bobbing menacingly from the corner of his mouth. Franks had met him years before, at his first and last quarterback club meeting. He was quite confident that Wendell Amerson, who had spent most of that evening comfortably embedded in a circle of Richfield's more powerful and influential citizens, wouldn't remember him.

"Yes sir," Franks said. His eyes quickly shifted to the receptionist, then back to Wendell Amerson. "Maybe you'd prefer to step back into your shop for a—"

"This is my place of business," the man growled. "You got business with me, we can take care of it right here in my office."

Franks shrugged. "Actually, we'd like to talk to Jamie."

"Well, Jamie's not here. Does that conclude our business?"

Franks held the elder Amerson's defiant stare for a moment, then pulled the search warrants from his jacket pocket.

"Not exactly. I have warrants here authorizing us to search…"

"Search *what*?" Wendell Amerson bellowed. "Ya'll ain't searching a damn thing around here."

"…your trucks and vans. And I wouldn't make any bets on us not searching them."

Color rose from Amerson's neck into his face and scalp as defiance smoldered into rage.

"Get Rabon Creasey on the phone," he snapped at the receptionist. "I want him over here *now*."

A sudden flurry of activity at the back of the parking lot captured Franks's attention. He moved closer to the window and saw that the Special Response and uniform officers had broken into a run and had disappeared behind the company's sheet metal fabrication shop.

"Stay here with him," he said to his partner as he hurried out the front door.

"What the hell's going on?" demanded Wendell Amerson. He took one menacing step in Woodley's direction. Brant Woodley, a former college football lineman, was easily thirty pounds heavier than the powerfully built Amerson. He folded his arms across his massive chest and stood his ground. Wendell Amerson stopped in his tracks, balled up his fists, and scowled at the investigator.

"This is my place of business," Amerson fumed. "And that's my son."

"I thought he wasn't here."

"I'm going out there," Wendell Amerson snarled. He took another step toward the door and the investigator immediately blocked his path with a quick shuffle step to the left.

"You're not going out there," Woodley said. "Not until they get Jamie secured."

"Or what?"

"Or I'll arrest you."

"Arrest me? For *what?*" Amerson snarled.

"Interference with governmental operations. Hindering prosecution. Aiding and abetting." Woodely grinned and shrugged. "The list goes on and on."

Amerson sputtered something, then wheeled on his receptionist, who had hung up the phone and shrunk into a corner of the room.

"Where's Rabon Creasey?" he demanded

"He wasn't there. I got his machine."

"Try his lake house number," Amerson roared. "I want that son of a bitch *here.*"

"It's Saturday," Woodley said. "Rabon's had a tough week. Cut the man a little slack."

"I'm working. You're working. By God, for what I pay him, he can be working, too."

Woodley shrugged. "Whatever."

"Are you gonna tell me what this is all about?"

"Are you gonna lose some of the attitude?"

Amerson took a deep breath and unclenched his fists. He cast a sidelong glance out the window. His expression softened slightly and he nodded.

"We've got information about some criminal activity that may involve Jamie—"

Amerson's scowl returned. "*Criminal activity?* What kind of criminal activity?"

"I'm not at liberty to say."

"You mean ya'll come onto my business property, seize my son, hold me prisoner, and search my vehicles, and I can't know what the charge is?"

"You can see a copy of the warrant when Bobby gets done out there. Mister Creasey can get you a copy of the affidavit." Woodley stole a quick glance out the window, then met the owner's hard stare again. "That's all I can tell you right now. Except that neither you nor Jamie are under arrest right now."

"Then you can't make me stay here."

Woodley began to grin."Yeah, I can," he said.

"I got Mister Creasey," the receptionist said, her voice buoyant with triumph. "He's on his way and he'll be here in thirty minutes."

"Just tell me one thing," Wendell Amerson said. "This don't have nothing to do with them girls from the college, does it?" His tone, no longer confrontational, was almost fearfully expectant. "I know he went out with both of them."

The investigator did not reply, just stared down at the floor.

"That can't be right," Amerson protested. "Jamie's a good boy. He…wouldn't do nothin' to hurt—" His words, now confessing the helplessness of his situation, trailed off into a hoarse whisper.

"We're just investigating right now. That's all we're doing." Woodley cut another glance out the window. "If he ain't done nothin', then he ain't got nothin' to sweat. If anything, this'll clear him."

Wendell Amerson sagged, then collapsed into a chair next to the receptionist's desk.

"Get your damn hands off me!"

Jamie Amerson struggled to free himself from the grasp of the two young police officers who had pulled him from the fence behind the business. They had spotted him running from the fabrication shop and had caught up to him before he was able to clear the six-foot chain-link fence.

"Let him go," Bobby Franks said.

The officers, each of whom had a firm grasp on one of Amerson's arms, stared at the investigator.

"He's not under arrest," Franks said. "At least, not yet."

The two officers exchanged confused glances, then released Amerson. The suspect pulled violently away from them and, red-faced, began examining the damage to his clothing. His expensive polo shirt had been punctured by the barbs on top of the fence and his designer blue jeans had scuff marks on the knees.

Jamie Amerson was a handsome man, slightly over six feet tall and powerfully built like his father. He had curly blond hair and his dad's strong jaw and chin. He also had apparently inherited Wendell Amerson's conditional disrespect for agents of the government.

"You cops are in deep shit," he snarled. "Do you have any idea who you're fucking with?"

"Sure," Franks replied, calmly. "We deal with assholes all the time."

The uniform officers and crime scene tech burst into laughter.

"Ya'll are gonna think it's real funny when you get the shit sued out of you."

Franks shrugged. "Sue me and shit's all you're gonna get."

A new wave of laughter was drowned out by the rumble of a huge roll-back wrecker that was pulling into the lot.

"What's this?" Jamie demanded, gesturing at the wrecker.

"We're hauling ya'll's vans and truck to the city shed."

"For *what*?"

Franks waved one of the search warrants. "So we can process them, Jamie."

"This is bullshit! Ya'll barge onto my Dad's property—" He stood for a few seconds with his hands on his hips, too indignant to finish his thought. At last, he began marching toward the wrecker, now backing into position near the larger of the two vans. Franks quickly intercepted him, positioning himself between the suspect and the vehicle.

"What're you *doing*?" Amerson demanded.

"You need to come take a ride with me."

"I thought you said I wasn't under arrest."

"You're not. But we're gonna search your house next, and I'm giving you the chance to be there when we do."

The wrecker driver climbed from the cab and walked to the van, a red Dodge with the company logo, the words "Amerson Heating & Cooling" formed in a semi-circle above a cute ice-skating penguin, painted on both side panels. The back and driver's side doors were open, and the two crime scene technicians were inside, doing a preliminary inventory and search.

"Why're you searching my house?" Jamie asked. He suddenly didn't seem as confrontational. His hands, which only a few seconds earlier had been clenched into fists, were now thrust passively, almost protectively, into his jeans pockets. "I didn't do anything, man."

"Then why'd we have to drag you off the fence back there?"

"I don't know. I just didn't know what was going on. I guess I was kinda scared."

Franks snorted. "An Amerson who fears the police? Don't make me laugh. Meanwhile, let's take a ride over to your place."

"I'll have to get my keys, if you don't mind. They're back in the shop."

Franks turned in the direction of the fabrication shop. Two of Amerson's workers stood in the open doorway, watching the events unfold in the parking lot. Beyond the gawking men, the investigator was able to see piles of sheet metal from which flashing, ventilation pipe, and ductwork would be fashioned.

"All right," Franks said, gesturing toward the door, "let's go."

He actually *didn't* mind Amerson going back into his shop. Of course, he'd have to accompany him as a basic personal safety measure; even the restrictive search and seizure rules granted him this much authority. And, while he was in the shop, he'd be remiss if he didn't do a little looking around. Bottom line: he'd get a free look into a protected space for which he had no other legal authority to search. He didn't really think he'd find anything incriminating in the shop, but one never knew.

Amerson took a few steps toward the building, then suddenly turned back toward Bobby Franks.

"Listen, man," he said, his voice low, almost a whisper. "I need to tell you something."

"All right, Jamie. Tell me something."

Amerson jammed his hands deeper into his pockets and pawed at the boiling asphalt with the toe of a scuffed leather deck shoe. "If this is about…if you're looking for drugs, I can just get what you're looking for."

Franks stared at him. He knew that, at some point, he'd have to advise Jamie of his rights. But he was still just a suspect and was not actually in "custody," so a reading of the technical Miranda rights wasn't yet legally required. His instincts told him to give the young man some room to wander, just to see where he might go.

"What kind of drugs, Jamie?"

Amerson looked around him to see if anybody was within earshot. "Hell, I don't know. Just fun stuff. A little grass, a little coke. You know, party drugs,"

Franks's brow furrowed. "'*Party* drugs'?"

"Yeah, man. You know—nothing heavy, just a little mellowing-out shit." He gave the investigator an awkward smile. "Hey, you like to have a few beers to get mellow after work, don't you? This is basically the same deal."

"It's not the same deal, Jamie, because beer's not illegal."

"Yeah, right. I keep forgetting how fucking hypocritical our laws are."

"Whatever. It's still the law. What about pills?"

Jamie shifted uncomfortably. "Pills?"

"Yeah. You know, the little round and oblong things that come in pill bottles."

"I don't know. I guess there might be a few pills—."

"What kind of pills?"

Jamie shrugged. "Hell, I don't know. A lot of people have partied over there in the past few weeks. People bring stuff over and leave it. I can't keep track of it all."

"Any roofies?"

Jamie Amerson's face suddenly flooded with color. "Roofies? I don't know. Let me think." He swallowed hard and continued to paw at the pavement.

"We can make this easy, Jamie, or we can make it hard."

"All right. Yeah, I probably have a few. But not for what you're thinking about."

Franks adjusted his sunglasses and grinned.

"What's so funny?"

"Because you have no idea what I'm thinking about right now." He gestured toward the fabrication shop. "Now, why don't we just go and get them?"

Jamie Amerson lived in a turn-of-the-century craftsman bungalow located at the edge of the older and solidly middle-class Southpark neighborhood. The house, one-and-a-half stories with sharply angled gables and ornate braces, had belonged to his maternal grandmother and had been deeded to him two years earlier upon her death. A once meticulously kept yard had become a parched weed sampler; crape myrtles and unruly wisteria vines now nudged the rusting gutters. A towering magnolia tree, withering after two rainless weeks under a blazing sun, had begun shedding singed, waxy leaves all over the front yard.

Katie stood on the front porch with Rabon Creasey and watched the attorney as he studied the search warrant and supporting affidavit. Wendell Amerson had demanded that Creasey be present while the search was being conducted. Franks had agreed, but insisted that the attorney remain outside until the operation had been completed. So Creasey had sagged, warrant and affidavit in hand, against one of the porch half-columns, carefully positioning himself so that he could see his client through the front picture window.

He was dressed in tan shorts, a white golf shirt, canvas slip-on boating shoes. He had a slender white-gold wedding band on his left ring finger and a ten-dollar rubber running watch on his left wrist. A pair of sunglasses were hooked in the open collar of his shirt. He looked nothing like the domineering courthouse presence she had known for years.

But he had acted every inch the lawyer from the moment he had stepped from his Mercedes convertible, now parked in the street right behind Franks's car. He had sequestered his clients for a private conference; Katie assumed that he had instructed them not to make any statements or to consent to any searches or seizures. And he had demanded—and received—copies of legal documents authorizing the search. People didn't pay him fifty thousand dollars to make the job easier for the police.

When he finished reading the warrants, he sighed and looked wearily at Katie.

"Can you do one thing for me?" he said. "Can you just explain what's *really* going on here?"

"What do you mean?"

"Come on, Katie. This is a damn shakedown, and you know it." The attorney extended the warrant package in Katie's direction, barely grasping it between the thumb and index finger of his right hand, as though it were a piece of toxic waste. "There isn't reasonable suspicion to search this house, much less probable cause."

Katie made a face. "That's not true, Rabon. There're a bunch of things listed in the affidavit. They don't mean much by themselves, but added up, they're pretty significant. What do the courts call it—a 'layering effect'?"

Creasey flipped to the second page of Bobby Franks's supporting affidavit and began reading aloud. "'Affiant further avers that the said James Darren Amerson dated all three of the murdered women at some time during the past two years....'." He shook his head. "I don't care *what* you layer that with, it doesn't even remotely suggest that Jamie's house contains evidence of a crime."

Katie waved her hand. "Well, whatever. There's no point arguing about it now. A decision was made to get the warrants, the magistrate issued them, and now they're being executed. If there's a problem, I guess some court will tell us at some point down the line."

Creasey snorted derisively. "The problem is, they're not gonna find any evidence of a crime, because he didn't commit this crime. And the fact that Franks and his storm troopers barged in with an illegal warrant isn't going to help if— perhaps I should say *when*—Jamie or his Dad decide to sue."

"Gee, that's mighty generous of you, Rabon. I mean, giving us free legal advice, all on Wendell Amerson's dime."

At that moment, Franks called out from deep within the bungalow's interior.

"Katie!" he bellowed. "Get in here! There's something you need to see."

Katie and Creasey exchanged looks.

"I think I have a right to see this," Rabon said. He angled closer to the window and tried to see into the back rooms. "It *is* my client's house, after all."

"It's fine by me, but you heard Bobby. It's his scene, his prerogative." She shrugged and stepped past the burly patrol officer guarding the doorway.

"This isn't gonna help ya'll if there's a lawsuit," he called after her.

Katie stopped abruptly after entering the house. She found herself in the bungalow's living room, an area which clearly took up most of the front part of the dwelling. There were only three pieces of furniture in the room: a sofa, which ran along the wall facing her, an overstuffed chair, and a small coffee table. Three doorways provided access to other parts of the house. Katie could see several officers moving about in a room accessed by a door next to the sofa. The doorway on her immediate right led to a small kitchen. Another passage seemed to lead to the back of the house. Jamie and Wendell Amerson were sitting on the sofa. Jamie was slumped angrily, his arms folded across his chest; his father sat rigidly on the edge of a cushion, as though waiting for his opportunity to spring out at the first available government trespasser. Both men were staring at the district attorney with absolute hatred in their eyes. A young officer stationed between the sofa and the chair gazed vacantly out the window, oblivious to the threatening stares.

Franks appeared in the doorway of the room being searched.

"In here," he said.

Katie moved quickly toward the investigator, avoiding further eye contact with the two men. She entered the room and began to look around. A king-sized bed without a headboard took up most of the room's floor space. The four officers conducting the search were having difficulty moving about in the rest of the room. There was a dresser covered with message notes, envelopes, and other accumulated pocket cargo. All the drawers had been removed and were lined up on the bed. Katie's attention was quickly drawn to a large bookcase located in a corner of the room. There were well over a hundred books lining the five shelves, stacked on top of the bookcase, and crammed into available spaces above shelved volumes. Katie surveyed the titles and noted, with no small amount of surprise, that most of the books were novels, works of classical literature, and scholarly works dealing with literary and artistic subjects. She examined another pile of books on a bedside night stand. Her brow furrowed as she noted the odd mixture of titles: a recent best-selling novel, a copy of *Gray's Anatomy*, and, at the bottom of the stack, an annotated collection of T.S. Eliot's poems.

"Look at this," Franks said, lifting up several tee-shirts folded in a dresser drawer. Katie saw a carved wooden box which had already been opened. Inside the box there was a clear plastic sandwich bag filled with green vegetable material and another with white powder; a third bag held several blister-packs of white tablets. Next to the bags were two amber medicine bottles, each containing a variety of tablets, and a pack of rolling papers.

"Behold, the private stash," Katie said.

"In particular, behold *this*," Franks said. He reached into the box and pulled out the baggie with the blister-packs.

Katie leaned forward and squinted at the bag. "What's this?"

"Can you say, 'roofies'?" Franks said, grinning. "I thought you could."

"Whoa."

"And check this out." Franks set the bag back in the wooden box and opened a cardbox box sitting next the to the drawer on the bed. He pulled off the lid and displayed the contents to the district attorney.

"A chess set," Katie said.

"Not just a chess set. A cheap-ass set with plastic pieces, and a few pieces missing." The grin, again. "And guess what one of the pieces is."

Katie's jaw went slack. "Not the black pawn—"

"I think we have a winner!" Franks exclaimed. "And a loser, too."

Brant Woodley said, "That just might be Jamie's one-way ticket to ride ol' Sparky."

"My nieces and nephews play with the chess set, you idiots!" Jamie Amerson screamed from the living room.

Wendell Amerson suddenly appeared in the doorway.

"This is the most ridiculous thing I've ever heard of," he sputtered. "You're going through his personal stuff…this ain't got a damn thing to do with them girls goin' missing—"

Franks, still holding the chess box, scowled at the man. "Get your ass back on that sofa, Wendell, or I'm gonna put you in cuffs and leg irons. And tell your son to keep his mouth shut."

The uniform officer in the living room grasped Wendell Amerson by the arm and guided him back to the sofa.

"I'm gonna sue the hell out of all ya'll!" he hollered. "Every last damn one of you."

The cellular phone on Franks's belt emitted an obnoxious electronic snippet from the *1812 Overture*. The investigator frowned and answered it. He identified himself, then stood there for a long while, staring at his shoes and grunting in agreement.

Suddenly he turned toward Katie, his eyes wide with excitement.

"And ya'll did *what* now?" he said into the stub of a phone. His eyes danced from Katie to Brant Woodley. "Luminol? And what did you…" He paused again, plugging his free ear with a finger and cocking his head slightly to the right. After a few moments, his eyes found Katie's again. "You did? Damn, that's great! Ya'll got it goin' on, I'll tell you what. All right, that van's impounded." Another pause. "I don't give a shit if he's got Perry Mason for a lawyer. It's evidence in a murder and I want it impounded."

He hit a glowing button and returned the phone to his belt.

"That was Craig Belew," he said. He seemed scarcely able to contain his glee. "They did luminol tests on both vans and got positive reactions for blood in one of them. On some carpeting in the back, on the plastic dash, on the seat covers."

"Nothing off the doors or handles?"

Franks made a face at her. "You know better than that."

Katie pretended she was hitting herself on the forehead. She had momentarily forgotten that the luminol reagent reacted with the iron in hemoglobin, making an otherwise unapparent bloodstain glow under blue light. For that reason, it couldn't be used on metal surfaces. Now, what did this all mean? The big question would have to be: whose blood was it? The presence of blood in a place where it shouldn't be expected might be another small bit of information. But, by itself, it didn't prove a whole lot other than somebody's blood was present.

She asked, "Are we gonna be able to do DNA testing?"

Franks shook his head. "Doesn't sound like it. I mean, I'll check back with Belew, but it didn't sound like there was gonna be enough blood to extract DNA from the stain."

Katie nodded.

"Let's pop him," Franks said. "Right now. I'm mean, he's sitting in there, all smug and arrogant, with his big-shot mouthpiece out on the porch. Let's take him down right now."

"And charge him with what?"

"Well, Donna Crawley's murder, for one. I mean, we ought to be able to prove that one, at least, happened in Bienville County. And it'd be capital, so he won't be making bond. Then we could pop him for at least kidnapping on the others if the serology report shows they were drugged with the same stuff."

Katie stared at the floor and sighed.

"What's the matter, Katie? We got all this evidence." He gestured toward the items now being bagged by an evidence tech. "All these weird coincidences that he can't explain."

"I don't know," she said.

"The newspapers, the victims' families, and the college are out there cursing us, and Jamie's flipping us off."

"I understand that, Bobby. But do we really want to jump the gun on this thing?"

Franks's brow furrowed. "Do you really want to be sitting on your hands when another woman gets murdered?"

Blood rushed to Katie's face. That was really a cheap shot, something she would never have expected from Bobby Franks. At the same time, she understood that he was a warrior and that he would always try to fight his way out of a corner. And everybody in local law enforcement was beginning to feel a little cornered by the case.

"I need a few minutes," she said. "I can't think with all this static in the air."

She pushed her way out of the room and disappeared down the hallway.

She stood on the bungalow's back deck and stared out at Jamie Amerson's dying backyard. The things she saw there—a bench positioned under two tall oak trees, a birdbath, a sun-bleached plastic flying disc—were the kinds of things that could be found in many backyards. Nor had there been anything that unusual about the house's interior. She hadn't seen a single thing that might suggest a serial murderer lived there. Of course, she, of all people, knew that there was no universal personality template for serial murderers. And besides, while Jamie seemed to fit within the age, race, gender, and marital status demographics for these killers, he was anything but a loner. In any event, a case couldn't be based only on profiles, tendencies, or, for that matter, domestic accessories; there had to be evidence.

So what was the available evidence? It could certainly be argued that Jamie had a motive—a true violent psychopath wouldn't be able to handle the insult of repeated personal rejection. And the fact that he had the sedative drugs in his possession, access to a van, and the physical ability to drag an adult woman a significant distance clearly included him within the small subset of local men with the opportunity and means to have committed these crimes. And, of course, now there were two new items of interest: the blood traces in the van and the missing chess piece.

But did these discoveries clearly establish Jamie Amerson as the kidnapper-killer? Without some forensic linkage, no conclusions could be made about the presence of blood in the van except that blood was present in the van. And how many thousands of inexpensive cardboard-and-plastic chess sets had missing pieces?

Bobby Joe was absolutely right: there certainly were a lot of "weird coincidences" that Jamie probably couldn't—or, on the advice of counsel, *wouldn't*— explain. But, in his zeal, the investigator was forgetting that a defendant wasn't required to explain anything under the American system of justice. Once he was formally accused with these brutal crimes, it would become the prosecutor's responsibility to prove his guilt beyond a reasonable doubt. Could she do that with this particular string of circumstances? She knew that, under the law, circumstantial evidence could be enough to support a conviction if it was so strong that it excluded every other hypothesis except the guilt of the accused. Was this evidence that strong? She had to conclude that it wasn't. More importantly, there were still many things that had been uncovered in the investigation—the bizarre and seemingly ritualistic mutilations and other "clues" left at the crime scenes, for example—for which there was not even an indirect link to Jamie Amerson.

Katie watched a blue jay fly from one of the oaks to the edge of the birdbath. The bird seemed to consider the dry and pocked concrete basin, then flew noisily off in search of water. She wiped a bead of perspiration from her forehead and stared off into the haze that nearly obliterated Richfield's rolling hills. As much as she wanted to solve this case, as pathological and creepy as Jamie Amerson might be, it could well be a huge injustice to publicly accuse him of this crime.

She heard a sound behind her and turned to see Bobby Franks stepping onto the deck.

"We've just about got everything packaged up," he said.

Katie nodded.

"So, whadda we do?" Franks joined her at the rail, his boot heels thundering on the treated deck boards. "Lawyer Creasey is getting a little antsy."

Katie sighed. "I think we need to hold off, Bobby."

"For *what*?"

"I don't know," she said. "For something else. Something that ties it all together. Let's see if we can get the blood identified. See if he'll make a statement of some kind. See if the lab comes back with some kind of trace evidence or fiber match—"

Franks leaned wearily forward, resting his elbows on the railing. "We're not gonna get any blood identification back because we don't have enough blood," he growled. "Furthermore, he ain't gonna make any kind of statement, because his daddy's hired Creasey to tell him *not* to talk. I guess we could lie on our backs and wait for evidence to drop on us from the heavens. Short of that, I guess we'll just have to hope he doesn't kill anyone else."

Katie frowned at the investigator. "I really don't need your damn attitude, Bobby. Now, you do what you want, but my office isn't accepting this case without something more."

"All right, I'll hold off today. But I want you to meet with me and the chief on Monday—"

"I'm not going to be here on Monday, Bobby. My family and I are going to the beach for a few days."

Franks's jaw dropped. "The *beach*? We're all up in the middle of this shit and you're going to the damn...*beach*?"

"Yes, Bobby, I am. I didn't take a vacation all year, and I've just spent two weeks getting ready for trial and another week in court. And, if it's any of your business, I promised my son we'd go to the beach for a few days before he has to go back to school." She clambered down the deck steps and took a few defiant strides toward the back gate.

"Don't you care what the news reporters say?" Franks called after her. "Don't you care what everyone in town is saying?"

Katie stopped in her tracks and wheeled toward the investigator. "Hell, yes, I care what everyone says," she said, her voice quivering with anger. "But, unlike you, I'm not willing to do the wrong thing just to shut them up." She held his stare for a moment, then turned and disappeared behind a parched and ragged privet hedge.

CHAPTER 12

▼

Richfield Police Chief Brad Tarwater stood behind a mahogany laminate podium, watching with visible discomfort as the municipal courtroom slowly began to fill with reporters and other interested observers. Bobby Joe Franks stood just to the right of the chief, his arms folded, a scowl carved into his sharply angled face. Bienville County Sheriff Eddie Walton, making a rare appearance in his formal blue-and-gray uniform, was positioned on Tarwater's left. RPD public information officer John Earl Wiggins, looking, if it was at all possible, even more uncomfortable than his boss, stood stiffly at parade rest in the background. Wiggins had taken it upon himself to agree to the press conference after a television news reporter had accused the department of "keeping the citizens of Bienville County in the dark" about the Carry murders investigation. Chief Tarwater had fumed and sputtered when Wiggins informed him of the conference; in the end, he knew that he wouldn't be able to avoid the media forever—three women were dead, a killer was on the loose, and the anxiety level of campus and community had achieved critical mass. So he had summoned his veteran homicide investigator to give him a quick briefing on the case status and then ordered him to be present at the press conference. Tarwater told Franks that he was needed in case there were any "factual questions," but the investigator believed his primary purpose was to serve as the designated departmental lightning rod.

Franks surveyed the room, studying the various media representatives with a mixture of fascination and loathing. He had always been in awe of the media's raw power—the ability to almost instantly shape public opinion, particularly in areas where public access to specific information was quite limited. And it was this power—more accurately, what he perceived to be the arrogant wielding of that power—that was the source of his extreme distrust for anyone with a camera or a reporter's notebook. There are few negative beliefs more potent than those reinforced by bad personal experience, and, for Bobby Joe Franks, the media response to his beating of the Carry student had provided enough bad experience for a lifetime. He believed that the community's negative attitude toward him in the wake of that case's investigation was not based on the facts uncovered by departmental review boards and grand juries. To the contrary, he felt, public opinion had been shaped by critical editorials and interviews with indignant friends and family of the battered student. Moreover, in Franks's highly prejudiced opinion, the many accusatory editorials were simply the visceral reactions of cynical news veterans whose noses were perpetually wrinkled by the ever-anticipated odor of potential government malfeasance. He'd complain to whoever would listen that nobody had ever reported on his bruised testicles, the bite marks on his arm, or the spittle that dripped from his face. It was as though he was not even regarded as human, but some kind of robotic instrument of the evil government, incapable of being injured or feeling pain, impervious to every insult. In private, to his therapist and a few close friends, he had confided a loss of control and expressed regret over the injuries caused to the young man. Publicly, however, he still maintained that the force used was measured and appropriate, and he blamed the media for fomenting public ill will.

While he deemed all of the media coverage to have been unfair, he judged *The Richfield Ledger*'s reporting to have been unconscionably so. He could almost forgive the television stations for their coverage of the incident—the pieces all seemed to be formulaic and hastily cobbled montages of interview snippets and reporter observations, conveniently edited to fill the interstices between commercials and weather and sports reports. Furthermore, the stories, however they might have been judged in the court of media fairness, seemed to float harmlessly out into the ether as soon as the anchors took the newscasts to their commercial breaks.

The newspaper coverage, in his opinion, was another story. He knew that the *Ledger* reporters and editors also had deadlines and that news copy was, essentially, news copy. But, unlike stories on television news shows, the items appearing in the *Ledger*—especially the critical editorials and the stinging front-page, above-the-fold headlines—all seemed to Franks to reek of extreme premeditation and malice aforethought. Worse, unlike televised reports, the newspaper articles could be analyzed at the reader's leisure, even preserved for future reference; like other hazardous materials, they had, at least potentially, a half-life that could be measured in generations.

So it was not surprising that Bobby Franks was exceptionally edgy as he faced this assemblage of newspeople. The Carry College investigation had been the central focus of daily news reports for more than a month. A press conference, he feared, would give the local media an excuse to dispense with even the pretense of objectivity. Instead of asking educated questions that were sensitive to the dangers, the political considerations, and legal restrictions they faced, he imagined that the reporters would assume the roles of outraged citizens and college officials, and, fists pumping defiantly in the air, demand immediate answers. But what information was there to dispense? He'd spent nearly a hundred hours on the case and had only a raw theory and a few items of physical evidence—items already dismissed by the D.A. as insufficient proof of guilt—to show for his trouble. And he couldn't comment on the evidence, in any event—he wasn't about to tip his hand to the kidnapper, as deficient as his evidence might be. No, experience and intuition told him that this conference would not only not be helpful to the investigation, it was an open invitation to a public relations nightmare.

He scanned the room, evaluating the crowd. He recognized a number of faces, but very few belonged to sympathetic observers. There was a reserve deputy he knew from the FOP lodge. A female third-shift officer he had worked with on a couple of domestic assaults. And, in the front row, his old friend and ally, Lieutenant Gordy Childs. The sheriff's department had been conducting its own low-key investigation into Donna Crawley's murder, and Childs and his men had done much of the grueling post-crime-scene leg work: combing square miles of rugged terrain for trace evidence, walking door to door along Hazard Creek Road, questioning residents, hoping against all odds to discover the one shred of useful information that would break the case wide open. Childs had been in daily contact with his old partner, but, to date, the sheriff's investigation had made no case-breaking discoveries. Franks's eyes briefly met Childs's, and the lieutenant gave him a wink of encouragement.

Franks's attention was suddenly captured by a tall, attractive blonde working her way through the back of the courtroom. She was wearing a striped, sleeveless sweater top, navy pants, plain blue flats. A camera satchel swung from her left shoulder and she was clutching a tan canvas bag in front of her. His eyes were riveted upon her, sweeping over her strong and athletic body as she maneuvered through the crowd. He watched her closely as she paused and surveyed the room. She reacted, apparently spotting an empty chair in the front row next to Gordy Childs. As she began edging closer to the front of the courtroom, Franks suddenly recognized her. *Andy Renauld, from the Ledger.* He had first seen her at the Hazard Creek crime scene. She had somehow schmoozed her way past the deputies who had supposedly set up a security perimeter and was asking questions and taking photographs. Franks's eyes, admiring only moments before, narrowed quickly into angry slits. As good as she looked, with her golden hair, pretty, tanned face and great body, she was still, first and foremost, an agent of the enemy. Perhaps even *the* enemy. An inner voice sternly reminded him that she wasn't there to do him any favors. He turned away as she sank into the empty chair.

Tarwater leaned forward and tapped on the microphone clamped to the podium.

"I'm kind of on a tight schedule, folks," he said. His words and tone of voice confessed his impatience and frustration. "If ya'll could find a seat, I'd like to get this thing rollin'."

There was a ripple of laughter in the back of the room, the apparent response to a remark made by one of the reporters.

The chief's jaw tightened, but he didn't otherwise react to the laughter. He waited a full minute, giving the standing observers an opportunity to find seats, then began reading his brief prepared statement.

"The Richfield Police Department has been asked to respond to certain questions pertaining to the investigation into the kidnapping and apparent murder of Carry College student Anjanette Donna Crawley, and into the disappearance of student Kerry Jean Grider." He paused, never looking up from his notes. His blood-drained fingertips seemed welded to the sides of the slanted reading surface. "In response to these questions, I have this statement. First of all, this has been a joint investigation by the Richfield Police Department and the Bienville County Sheriff's Department. Both agencies have committed investigators to solving these crimes, and both agencies have made this joint investigation their top departmental priorities." He cast a quick glance in Sheriff Walton's direction; the sheriff, standing with his hands clasped in front of him, nodded in somber agreement. "Secondly, as the investigations have progressed, we have been able to uncover evidence and useful information which, we believe, will soon result in an arrest and a conviction."

"How soon?" a gruff voice from the middle of the room demanded.

Cameras and heads swivelled immediately in the direction of the voice. The speaker was quickly identified: a large man sitting in the middle of the fourth row. He was dressed in a red flannel shirt and had his arms crossed defiantly in front of a barrel chest. He had a wide face with ruddy cheeks and thick black eyebrows that seemed to be knitted into an unbroken emblem of disapproval.

"Sir," the chief continued, "I'm unable to give you—"

"Because I have a daughter, and she was supposed to start school at Carry College next week, and she's not gonna be there if this thing isn't fixed."

"Yes sir. I hear what your saying. What I'd like to use this time to say is that, with the new security measures in place and with beefed-up patrol in the Southpark neighborhood—"

"The last woman kidnapped wasn't even *in* the Southpark neighborhood," a man standing off to one side interrupted. "Isn't it true that her abandoned car was found downtown?"

"If you'd please allow me to finish," the chief said. His face was beginning to flush and his tone of voice had grown noticeably less warm. "We've increased patrols and taken other measures throughout the city, not just—"

"What other measures?" asked Dale Miller, a reporter for a local network affiliate. His photographer stood beside him, cementing the chief in his camera viewfinder.

The chief sighed. "I'm afraid I can't be more specific, Dale. If certain…measures are employed, then it would, ah, defeat their basic purpose to identify them publicly."

"So what are you talking about, then? Undercover officers? Roadblocks? Long-term surveillance?"

Bobby Franks groaned audibly. He wanted desperately to say what the chief couldn't: "*We don't want the killer to know what we're doing, you ignorant jay-bag!*" He glanced at Gordy Childs to note his reaction. The sheriff's supervisor was slowly shaking his head and glowering at the reporter.

Franks's glance shifted to Andy Renauld. In the brief moment before he jerked his eyes away, he was able to glimpse the barest hint of a smile and a slight, almost imperceptible, rolling of her eyes. As he turned back to Chief Tarwater, he felt the odd prickle of embarrassment. It usually took a lot more than a glance to fluster Bobby Joe Franks.

"As I was saying," the chief continued, "we feel like the streets of Richfield and Bienville County are safe. We're making progress in our investigation, and we don't anticipate any more, ah, crimes of this nature occurring."

"But then ya'll didn't anticipate any of the first three, either, did you?" Dale Miller said.

The room burst into laughter. Franks cut a glance at his boss. It was apparent that he was perilously close to his breaking point.

"If there are no more questions—"

"I have a question."

All eyes zeroed in on the speaker, a tall, gaunt woman with a chopped-off dome of silver hair that seemed to emphasize her severe facial features.

Franks groaned again. *Elena Daugherty.* The news director at WRTV, another local network affiliate. Franks knew her from many past encounters. She was a bright and well-educated news veteran with a seemingly innate distrust of government and a nose for controversy. She was a very qualified observer of such investigations because she knew a lot about law and police operations; Franks regarded her as potentially dangerous for the very same reason.

"Is it true that your department was prepared to make an arrest in this case, as recently as this past weekend?"

Chief Tarwater froze. If it was possible, his fingers gripped the podium even more tightly. His eyes rolled to his right.

"I'm gonna let my lead case investigator, Bobby Franks, handle that one," he said. His tone of voice and intense stare seemed to be commanding Franks to tread carefully on this potentially dangerous ground.

Franks grimaced as he shuffled toward the podium. He hated everything about this process, and knew that the chief was aware of his discomfort. Still, he couldn't fault the man for shifting the attention to him. If the chief of police couldn't trust his lead investigator to handle a few questions about his case, what confidence should the public have in the detective's basic investigative skills? Besides, Franks had always liked and respected Tarwater. The chief was a good man—a former Marine and Vietnam vet and Franks's onetime uniform division supervisor at RPD. More importantly, he had had the courage to bring Franks back into the department after the brutality accusation had chased him away. He'd decided long ago that he'd actually take a bullet for his chief. This meet-the-press drill was bad, but probably not as bad as getting shot.

He stood behind the podium and adjusted the gooseneck microphone.

"Miz Daugherty, it's true that we executed a search warrant this past weekend in connection with this investigation." Franks's deep voice thundered through the courtroom. "I don't think it's fair to say that we were close to making an arrest."

"Was that because no incriminating evidence was found in the search?"

Franks stared down at the chief's index card notes resting on the reading surface's paper stop. There was complete silence in the courtroom.

"Not necessarily," he said, at last. "Items of evidence were seized. Their exact value and significance to this investigation are still being, ah, evaluated."

"Would it be fair, then, to say that the focus of this investigation has narrowed to this individual?"

"I can't comment on that, ma'am."

Another reporter asked, "Well, you obviously have *something* on him, or else how could you have gotten a search warrant?"

Franks shrugged. "Draw your own conclusions."

"Who is this person?" another voice called out.

"No comment on that."

Andy Renauld suddenly raised her hand. Franks glanced at her and felt a strange discomfort. She looked so harmless just sitting there with her long legs crossed at the ankles and her reporter's notebook open on her lap. Maybe harmless wasn't exactly the right word. Non-lethal, perhaps that was more accurate. Like the attractive coed on the front row asking her professor whether there'd be any reading assignment over the homecoming weekend. And yet, the same could probably be said of all the reporters. They all looked like regular people, just standing out there. It would only be later, with the editing of tape and the hammering of keyboards, that their true diabolical nature would be revealed.

At last, he took a deep breath and pointed to her. "Miz Renauld?"

She lowered her hand and smiled at him. "Two questions, Investigator Franks," she said. "First, are you looking at just one suspect—that is to say, do you believe that the kidnappers and the murderers are one and the same person?"

Franks exhaled slowly and stared suspiciously at the woman. The question seemed harmless enough, but was he missing something? Or would it be the second question that provoked the response that would, eventually, be turned against him?

After a period of obvious deliberation, he said, "We believe that the individual or individuals responsible for the kidnappings and the murders are one and the same, yes, ma'am."

Seemingly satisfied with this response, Renauld said, "And secondly, do you feel like you're reasonably close to actually making an arrest?"

Again, Franks analyzed the question, turning it over in his mind until he was sure that there were no latent traps lurking there.

"I feel like—"

The father with the flannel shirt blurted out, "Why don't you call in somebody who knows what they're doing?"

Renauld, scowling, wheeled in her chair. "Why don't you let him answer the question? You're a rude and obnoxious person." Then, amid murmurs and laughter, she turned back to Bobby Franks. "I'm sorry. You were saying…"

Franks sneaked a look at Childs. The lieutenant was covering his face with his huge left hand.

"Yes," Franks said, finally. "Reasonably close."

"Thank you, Investigator," Andy Renauld said, flashing her brightest smile.

Chief Tarwater stepped back to the podium. "That's all we have today, ladies and gentlemen. As Bobby Franks indicated, we're close to making an arrest, and we certainly don't want to release any information that might jeopardize the investigation." He turned to Sheriff Walton. "Now if the sheriff has anything he wants to add—"

The sheriff held up both hands in front of him. "No, thanks. I'm leaving here in one piece, and that's more than I hoped for."

Most of the observers laughed. The media representatives, having accumulated quotes if not hard answers, stood and began moving toward the exits. Chief Tarwater, taking Bobby Franks by the elbow, steered him to a doorway behind the bench.

"I think that went pretty well," Franks said.

"'Reasonably close to an arrest'?"

Franks shrugged. "Fairly reasonably close."

"God, I hope so. They got that one on both audio and videotape. If we don't get this mother soon, we're gonna get *fried*."

Franks started to reply, but felt a tug on his sleeve. He turned and found himself looking into Andy Renauld's gorgeous eyes.

"Hi," she said. She turned to Chief Tarwater and extended her hand. "Hello, Chief. Andy Renauld. We've met before."

The chief shook her hand. "Yes, of course. Good to see you again."

"I just wanted to chat with Investigator Franks for a minute or so."

The chief nodded and stood there in the ensuing silence for a few moments, looking extremely uncomfortable. Finally he glanced at his watch and said, "Listen, you have your car. I'll just—" He gestured toward the door and began walking away.

Franks jammed his hands in his front pockets. "So. Andy Renauld from *The Ledger*."

She grinned. "So. Bobby Franks from the police department."

"What can I do for you?"

"I don't know. Go have a cup of coffee with me."

Franks stared at her.

"I'd like to talk with you," she said.

"I can't really add anything—"

She grasped his left hand and raised it slightly. "You're not married, or anything. Are you?"

Franks pulled his hand away. "No. No, I'm not married. Not anymore. It's just—"

"What, then? You think having coffee with a news reporter will somehow compromise your investigation?"

"No, that's not it." He traced a small circle with the scuffed toe of his boot on the polished tile floor. "What about you? Wouldn't this compromise *your* objectivity?"

She gave him a small smile. "I think it may already be compromised," she said.

Franks felt the blood rush to his face. "Give me a break," he said. "You work for the paper. They're never gonna cut me any slack."

"Come on, Investigator Franks. One cup of coffee. You name the place. That's all I'm asking."

"All right," he said, at last. He glanced around, as if he was looking for a secret emergency exit."You know where Prestwick's is at?"

Her brow furrowed. "The truck stop out on the Talmadge highway?"

He nodded.

"If you don't mind me asking—"

"I like their coffee."

She adjusted the bag hanging from her shoulder. "Okay," she said. "Meet you there in twenty minutes." She flashed a grin, turned, and marched toward the main door at the back of the courtroom.

Bobby Franks watched her go, wondering what the hell was going on.

Prestwick's Truk-N-Go was a plain cinderblock building just inside the southern arc of Richfield's municipal police jurisdiction. The business consisted of four gas pumps—two isolated pumps were exclusively for trucks and other commercial vehicles—a compact convenience-like store and a cook-to-order grill with a curved, six-stool counter and four red vinyl-upholstered booths. Bobby Franks had begun dropping in for the free coffee and pastries when he was a third-shift officer assigned to patrol duty on the south side of town. Because it was located in a remote and isolated area and open for business twenty-four hours a day, owner Johnny Mack Prestwick had long courted the patronage of area police officers. Prestwick, who also operated the all-night Waffle Barn in the Richfield business district, had a simple philosophy regarding survival in dangerous times: he believed that nothing discouraged criminals like the perpetual presence of cops and nothing encouraged the presence of cops like free food and beverages. After becoming police chief, Brad Tarwater had issued a departmental protocol forbidding officers to accept any free food, merchandise, or services. Franks and other investigators continued to patronize Prestwick's two establishments—as paying customers.

Andy Renauld had been waiting at the door when Franks arrived at 10:15. The grill was virtually deserted—the lunch crowd wouldn't begin to roll in for another forty-five minutes. When Franks and Andy Renauld seated themselves at a booth by the front window, they, a slow-moving waitress, and the short-order cook were the only people in the establishment.

The waitress shuffled over to the booth and offered a laminated menu to Renauld. She was wearing a white blouse with "Marguerite" embroidered over the pocket and a blue jean skirt. Her jet-black hair was pulled back into a ponytail.

Renauld considered the grease-stained menu and, smiling politely, refused. "Just coffee for me," she said.

Marguerite shrugged and turned to Franks.

"Same here," he said.

"I can get ya'll a grilled cheese," the waitress said.

Franks smiled. "No, thanks. Coffee and we'll be good." He sneaked a glance at his watch.

"Need to be somewhere?" Renauld asked.

"No, not really. I mean, I've got to get back on this case at some point." He gave her a weak smile. "I mean, you heard those folks at the press conference. We're obviously screwing around too much."

She waved her hand dismissively. "I wouldn't pay any attention to the Dale Millers and Elena Daughertys. They don't cover the cop beat day after day. If they did, they wouldn't ask such obtuse questions."

Franks folded a paper napkin into a neat triangle and didn't reply.

"You didn't have a lot to say at the press conference," Andy observed.

"Not a whole lot *to* say. Besides, reporters make me uncomfortable. No offense."

"None taken," she replied. "Although you don't know what uncomfortable is until you find yourself behind your gynecologist in the slow lane at the grocery store."

Franks's eyes flew open. "Whoa. I didn't see that coming."

She grinned. "What, that I mentioned my gynecologist?"

"No, the notion that gynecologists do the grocery shopping."

They both laughed, then Franks returned to his folding.

"So," Andy Renauld said.

"So."

"You're probably wondering why I wanted to meet with you."

The investigator laid the napkin flat and folded it again into a smaller triangle. "It occurred to me."

"Well, there're a couple of reasons. Three reasons, actually."

Franks glanced up at her briefly and continued folding the napkin.

Renauld took a deep breath and exhaled slowly. "Well, partly I wanted to let you know my…personal concerns."

Franks's brow wrinkled. "I'm sorry. 'Personal concerns'?"

Marguerite arrived with two steaming mugs of coffee and placed them in front of her customers.

"I know you don't take it black," the waitress said to Bobby Franks.

Franks nodded. The woman dumped a small mountain of sugar and non-dairy creamer packets in the center of the table.

Andy waited until she'd gone, then continued. "Before I get into my own personal matters, there's something I want to say. I don't want what the *Ledger* wrote about you eight years ago to be a problem between us."

Franks tore open three sugar packets and emptied them into his mug.

"I mean," Renauld continued, "I know what happened wasn't police brutality. I think that's pretty obvious. The grand jury, IA, and the Justice Department all cleared you." She blew on the surface of the coffee and took a sip. "I've pulled up the old articles and editorials and studied them. I really don't think you were treated fairly."

Franks emptied two creamer packets into his mug. He glanced at her briefly, then began to silently stir the coffee.

"I didn't have anything to do with the coverage. I was in high school in Birmingham when everything was written."

"I don't have a problem with you, personally," Franks said, at last.

"Good," she said, smiling at him. "Because I respect you and think you're very good at what you do."

His eyes rose to meet hers. He couldn't tell if they mirrored sincerity or camouflaged some sinister motive.

"Thanks," he said, at last. "I do the best I can."

She reached across the table and gave his hand a quick squeeze.

"So can we be friends?" she asked.

This sudden and unexpected overture made the investigator blush.

"I've never had any friends in the media before," he said.

"Well, you do now. Not just a friend—an admirer."

Temporarily rendered speechless, Franks began refolding the napkin.

"The next thing," Andy said, "is this—I have a very personal interest in this bastard getting locked up." She took a sip of coffee and carefully set the mug back on the table. "I live in Southpark, about a block from the campus. There hasn't been a night since this mess started that I haven't laid awake, listening to every creak, every dadgum car go by. I'm on the verge of buying a gun. It's ridiculous. A *gun*. My whole life, I swore I'd never own one. And now I feel like I might need one just to survive."

Franks nodded and stared down at the table.

"So I guess that's it," she said. "That's all I had to say." She smiled and pulled her purse onto her lap.

"So you're not gonna dog us out in the paper?"

She made a face. "Have I written anything unfair so far?"

Franks shrugged. "Hell if I know. I quit taking the *Ledger* years ago."

"Well, *I* won't do it. I understand ya'll's situation. I just wanted to let you know that I've got a personal stake in this matter. I may not be able to help you, but I won't do anything to hurt, either."

"That's good to know." Franks paused, his fingers tracing the outline of the cigarette pack in his shirt pocket. "If I tell you something, will you promise you won't write about it?"

She giggled. "You mean, can you speak 'off the record'?"

"Yeah, whatever the official term is."

"Yes. Of course."

Franks leaned forward, as if Marguerite might be able to overhear his comment from her post at the end of the counter.

"We're this damn close to arresting the son of a bitch, pardon my French." He indicated, his thumb and index finger spread about an inch apart.

"So, do ya'll know who it is?"

Franks snorted. "*I* do. Others aren't totally convinced yet."

She sighed. "Man, it would be a huge relief to me if you busted him," she said. "Have ya'll found any physical evidence?"

"Yeah. *Hell*, yeah. The D.A. thinks we need some more, so we're working on it."

She slung her purse strap over her shoulder. "Anything I can do to help?"

"Nah. Just write about it when we bust his ass."

"Deal." She got to her feet and stuck out her hand. Franks unwound his lanky frame, grimaced, and shook hands with her. "I'll spring for it," she said. "Company account."

The investigator shook his head. "Thanks, but no way. I'll wait on the ticket."

She thanked him and walked away. Franks drank her in, admiring her now fully and without reservation.

"Hey," he called after her as she was about to reach the door.

She turned to face him. Marguerite shuffled past her with the ticket in her hand.

"You said you had three things to tell me. I only remember two."

She flashed another smile, this one unabashedly flirtatious.

"I thought you'd be able to figure the last one out," she said.

She pulled open the door and headed out into the parking lot.

CHAPTER 13

▼

The menacing bank of clouds, darker than the twilight sky, seemed to simply appear over the Gulf of Mexico. It took only minutes for the boiling charcoal smear to reach the horizon, where angry spikes of electricity jabbed at the black water. The wind suddenly blew hard from the west, bending the sea oats and scrub vegetation on the white sand dune between the house and the shoreline. On the beach, seemingly oblivious to the increasing threat of the storm, two groups of crab hunters moved slowly along, their flashlight beams dancing across the wet sand.

Katie sat on the screened porch of the beach cottage and stared out into the night. The surf crashed and thundered in nonstop rolls. She slumped in her chair and stared straight ahead, seemingly hypnotized by the rhythmic rumble of the waves. But she was far from being anesthetized by the sounds—thoughts about the murder investigation swirled through her mind like the warm white froth teasing the feet of the crab hunters. As she had done nearly every waking moment for the past two days, she rearranged and reevaluated every relevant piece of information that had surfaced in the kidnapping-murder investigation. But it never quite added up. Even there, in that peaceful sanctuary more than a hundred miles from Bienville County, the specter of that frustrating case haunted her.

The cottage, a cozy two-room getaway, had been built by Katie's father, a successful Birmingham pediatrician, when Orange Beach was not yet a bustling resort community. Once isolated on a long strand of pristine beach, the cottage was now dwarfed by the high-rise condominium towers that had sprung up on either side. The unblemished strand Katie had explored during childhood summers was now, in the aftermath of hurricane fury and years of development, only a blurry memory. The parking lots of the motels and condos from Gulf Shores to Pensacola were now filled with cars with tags from every state east of the Mississippi, even from as far away as Ontario. The "Redneck Riviera," as the strip had once been known to area residents, had gone both commercial and universal.

The O'Briens had taken their annual vacation at the house on the Gulf almost every summer since they'd married. Katie's various professional responsibilities during the previous six months had made a structured "vacation," as such, a practical impossibility. And this particular escape—hard earned after the Hollins trial and the maelstrom of the current investigation—had been destined to be a "working vacation" for Katie: her laptop computer, cellular phones, pagers, and a cardboard case file caddy had been packed right along with luggage and groceries. Katie knew she'd never be able to truly relax until the maddening Carry cases had been both solved and resolved.

Even now, as nature staged its spectacular pyrotechnical display, her mind could see only the haunting images of the crime scenes, the bizarre flourishes and puzzling taunts, and, perhaps most of all, the unfinished portrait of a killer. Her mind seemed to recur, as it had done so often in the preceding days, to Jamie Amerson, the central player in the unfolding drama. No matter how she otherwise visualized him, she always first saw his eyes: dark, penetrating, and, well, *evil.* The one thing she knew for sure about these cases was that whoever had kidnapped and murdered these women had to be evil.

Evil. A subjective and elusive concept, to be sure. Katie had spent years debating both its philosophical significance and its place in the lexicon of the law. To some, evilness was merely an elusive abstraction—the fatal flaw of certain historical madmen or cartoon villains. To others, it was a common character failing found in everyone perceived as brash, cold, or uncaring. Katie understood that evil as a concept had long been consigned exclusively to the insular precincts of theology and ethics. Evil intentions and behavior, without more, weren't proscribed by any American statute. The psychiatric diagnostic manual, which had included in its menu of available afflictions "Overanxious Disorder" and "Stuttering," made no mention of an evil personality. And yet evil people caused most of the damage in the world. The Hitlers, the Eichmanns, the Stalins, the Ted Bundys and Gary Gilmores, the terrorists who unflinchingly murdered innocent people and, yes, the vicious predator who kidnapped and killed the Carry coeds, weren't legally insane. They were evil, pure and simple.

Was Jamie Amerson—his evil stare notwithstanding—truly evil? From her experience with him during his previous legal entanglement, she believed him to be the template of a psychopath—a totally self-centered individual who used others and who had little, if any, capacity for empathy or remorse. If this was the definition of "evil," then the label was certainly appropriately applied to Jamie. But was he capable of these terrible acts? This was the question that haunted Katie now. She had invaded his private living space and had seen no overt evidence suggesting that a violent sociopath resided there. What she had seen had surprised her—an unpretentious and relatively neat abode where the predominant personal effect seemed to be a collection of literary classics.

At the same time, she knew that a love of literature couldn't be the basis for any reliable psychological profile. There were probably tens of thousands of vicious and cruel people throughout history who, at one time or another, had a passion for the arts. And, of course, there were all the other curious discoveries that seemed to link Amerson to the kidnappings: the missing chess piece, the packets of drugs, the powerfully probative coincidence of his relationships with the victims. She shifted uncomfortably in her chair, as if this circumstantial dissonance caused her actual physical pain.

Sufficiently distanced from the crucible of the investigation, it was easy for her to torture herself over the correctness of her decision. *Had* there been enough evidence to justify his arrest? *Had* her objectivity been compromised by the fear of failure? Of professional reprisal? If he was the killer, had she jeopardized other women by opposing an arrest?

She angrily tried to jettison the lingering self-doubts. She'd made a judgment call and she'd stand by it. Hard decisions came with the territory. She'd known that when she accepted the district attorney appointment. Most of the cases brought to her office were straightforward and simple. Others featured briar patches and tar babies. This case clearly fit in the latter category.

She felt the sudden pressure of strong hands on her body. Con had slipped silently out of the cottage and was standing behind her, rubbing her shoulders.

"This is just great," he said. "We go three weeks without rain back home, come to the beach, and it's threatening to pour on us."

Katie smiled and grabbed his right hand. "It's sure acting like it wants to," she said. "Of course, this won't do our yard any good."

Con slid into an empty canvas-back chair next to his wife.

"You know," he said, "I've about decided to just write the ol' lawn off for this year. We've watered it every day and it still looks like fried rice."

She nodded and put her arm around her husband's shoulder. "My begonias, too. They look like poisoned dandelions."

After a few quiet moments, she asked, "What're Avery and Garrett doing?" Katie had wanted this to be a quiet family-only getaway, but Avery, who had become a more-or-less permanent fixture on their beach trips, convinced her that she desperately needed a vacation. Besides, Katie rationalized, Con didn't really mind her hanging around and Garrett considered her to be a second, much wackier, mom.

Con took a sip of beer from a can in an Atlanta Braves foam cozy. "Playing video games, I think. She's all bent out of shape because he keeps vaporizing her character."

"Silly girl. Doesn't she know Garrett's a video game Zen master?"

"Get serious. This is Avery May, the one true queen of denial."

Katie swivelled so that she could see back into the darkened cottage's den. Avery and Garrett were sitting on the floor in front of the couch, game controllers in hand, their blank faces lit by the shifting pattern on the television screen. In that light, Garrett's nine-year-old face—now absent the chubbiness of his pre-school days—still looked like that of a little boy. She found herself smiling as she watched his expressions cycle through intense concentration, anticipation, and, finally, complete joy.

In some ways, Garrett *was* still a little boy. At the age of nine, he was all too rapidly advancing toward adolescence, but she was still able to see vestiges of his childhood sweetness. When he slept, for example, he still had a handful of his favorite stuffed animals and cartoon characters arrayed around him in his bed. They vanished when friends came to spend the night, but, at least to that point, they had always returned. She knew, of course, that one day they'd disappear for good, just like all the things that had already been outgrown. The first to go were the cute toy train engines with their smiling faces and individual personalities. At about age four, they were supplanted by toy dinosaurs, which, in turn, had been replaced by model airplanes, monster figurines, and robot "transformers," in that order. Obsolescence condemned each class of toy to interment in a huge, plastic toy bin where they lay in preserved but ever-growing strata. The end result was a triumph of developmental geology: an almost perfect fossil record of the slow extinction of his childhood. She'd tried, on more than one occasion, to thin out the pile of plastic detritus, but found that each item represented a fond memory—of Garrett's innocence, of Con's loving indulgence, of their separate survival stories. So the bin remained full, an unsightly but reassuring reminder of the blessings that had been bestowed on her.

Even so, she remained painfully aware of the almost endless supply of threats and dangers lurking out in life's shadows. In addition to the everyday hazards she had faced as a child, life in post-postmodern America brought an array of terrifying new perils: drugs, gang violence, potentially fatal sexually transmitted and insect-borne diseases, an epidemic of crimes against children, and, in 9/11's chilling aftermath, the ever-present threat of global war and terrorism. And yet, she couldn't sequester Garrett in a protective bubble—somehow, life had to go on. Katie had finally decided that all she could do was love her son, educate and guide him, and watch over him from a respectful distance.

The rumble of the sliding rear door, barely audible over the crashing waves, pulled them back to the present. Katie turned her head and saw Avery and Garrett walking onto the porch.

"Okay, which one of you is the Ultimate Master of the Universe?" Katie asked. She put an arm around her son's waist and gave him a playful squeeze.

"I am, of course," Garrett replied. He gently pulled away from Katie and sank into the chair on the other side of his father.

"He's a stone-cold video game freak," Avery said, pulling another chair alongside Katie's. "It's like he's been playing *Alien Squadron* all his life."

Garrett, brow furrowed and lips compressed into a tight frown, shook his head. "I'm far from mastering the game. I've defeated the Level Five Vericon boss, but I can't figure out how to get past the Ion Shield Gate on Level Six."

Katie frowned. "Vericon boss?"

"Yes, ma'am. The evil, deformed pig monster boss of the level. He's almost impossible to defeat. I had to acquire the plasma net shield and fusion sword before I even had a chance." He regarded his mother with an earnestness she might expect from a job applicant.

"I'm sorry," Con said. "Did you say 'evil pig monster'?"

"Evil *deformed* pig monster. He's a mutant with two heads, one big and one little."

"All right," Con said unctuously, frowning at his wife. "Who's buying him these bizarre games with mutant creatures and themes of wanton destruction?"

"I believe that would be you," Katie replied, never letting her gaze stray from the crashing surf.

"Well, okay, then. As long as we were in agreement on the pluses and minuses of the game."

"*We* didn't agree to anything. *You* went to the electronics store with Garrett, supposedly looking for a portable CD player, and *you* came home with this game."

"Great," he said. "Just so long as we know how it happened." After a moment, he added, "I liked it better when *I* was a kid. We didn't have plasma shields and mutant, two-headed pig monsters. Our games had a certain elegant simplicity to them"

"Yeah," Avery said, "and it's a good thing too—sticking a proboscis on a plastic cootie probably pushed your intellect and stamina to the absolute breaking point."

Con flashed a phony smile at Avery May. "Garrett, could you please run back inside for a moment so Daddy can verbally abuse Aunt Avery?"

Garrett got to his feet and started back toward the door.

"I was just kidding," Con said.

"I know, duh," Garrett said. "But I have to beat Level Six."

"Level Six will have to wait until tomorrow," Katie said. "You need to read some while we're down here."

The boy leaned against the door and groaned.

"Come on," Katie said. "School starts back next week and you've completely abandoned your summer reading list. Your Hardy Boys books are on the dresser in your room."

Garrett sighed and disappeared into the house.

"So what're ya'll doing out here?" Avery asked. "Pondering the ol' metaphysical I-know-not-what?"

Con said, "Actually, I was just wondering if you wanted to go skinny dippin' with me later on."

Avery howled. "Right, Con. As if you would show up bare-assed in public. Besides, you've been here two days and you haven't come within fifty feet of the beach."

"I don't like the Gulf. It's like swimming in a bucket of warm goat piss. Besides, there's all that seaweed and shit. And all those wretched jellyfish." He shuddered and added, "A pack of those things got me in the crotch when I was eleven. I've never gotten over it."

Avery nodded. "Hmm. That would explain a great deal about your personality."

"All right," Con said, getting to his feet. "I'm going back inside where no one but Garrett can insult me." He took a long drink of beer and shuffled back into the house.

"I miss him already," Avery said.

Katie reached down and picked up a can of beer that was sitting on the porch. She took a sip and held the can in her lap. She and Avery sat for a long while in silence and watched the lightning show.

"What're you thinking about?" Avery asked, at last.

"Nothing. Everything." She took another sip of beer. "Sometimes I wonder if I have any business being D.A."

"Why would you say something like that?"

"I don't know. Sometimes I make a decision and it's like all the good ol' boys look at each other and groan. You know the look: *just another chick on a power trip, throwing her weight around.*" Katie flashed her friend a tight, ironic smile. "The bad part is, I'm starting to wonder if they might all be right."

"What're you talking about? I've never seen any man disrespect you."

"That's because you don't hang out at the country club. Or get over to the police station or to crime scenes."

"Only because you never let me go."

"The point, Avery, is that, after everything I've done, everything I've accomplished, I still feel like I'm a second-string D.A. You know: almost like the real one, but not really."

Avery pulled her legs up under her in the chair. "All right, girlfriend," she said. "Tell me what's going on here."

"Nothing really. We're at the suspect's house on Saturday executing a search warrant—"

Avery's overplucked eyebrows arched. "You execute search warrants now?"

"Not usually," Katie said, "but this was different. They—Bobby Franks, some of the other homicide investigators, and a few uniform cops—found some things they were looking for and wanted to take him down right then." She paused as the recurring cloud of self-doubt blotted out a few fugitive rays of self-assurance. "Franks didn't want to arrest without my approval."

Avery stared at Katie. "And you said ix-nay on the ust-bay."

"Basically."

"Don't you have to have, like, probable cause to search his house?"

"Yes."

"And all you need to arrest the dude is probable cause?"

Katie frowned. Everything Avery knew about criminal procedure had been gleaned from their job-related conversations over the years. Now she was attempting to assemble a full portrait from discrete splotches of color and detail wedges.

"Well, technically yes, but—"

"And on top of the probable cause you already had, ya'll found some incriminating things there at the house?"

Katie folded her arms and stared sullenly out at the beach. The lightning had stopped and the dark clouds seemed to be breaking apart. A solitary star twinkled in the clearing sky. New clusters of beachcombers sauntered by, light beams flashing.

"There were things that could *arguably* be called incriminating."

"Do you think he's the killer?"

Katie took a deep breath and exhaled slowly. "I don't know, Avery. A big part of me thinks he could be. I mean, I know the man. I've prosecuted him before. He's a psychopathic bag of crap."

Avery's brow furrowed. "All right, then. He's a psychopathic bag of crap. And there's evidence tying him to the crime." She shrugged. "What's the big problem?"

"I don't know. I've asked myself that question about ten times a day, ever since Saturday. And I get a different answer every time. Sure, we have probable cause to arrest him. But the case is weak. All circumstantial, and some of the circumstances are pretty questionable."

"You've tried weak circumstantial cases before."

Katie's eyes briefly met her friend's, then slowly fell away. So there you have it, she thought. Avery's implication was clearly the same as Bobby Franks's: *she was afraid to take this case on.* She'd convinced herself that holding off on an arrest until there was more evidence was the prudent course, the one that gave them the best shot at success at trial. And they would only have one shot. Moreover, analyzing the evidence objectively, it was obvious that a reasonable doubt about Jamie's guilt existed. Didn't the bar's ethical canons require her to "seek justice," not convictions? But what if Avery and Bobby Joe were right? Perhaps there really were unconscious motivations on her part—the fear of taking on the Amersons and an aversion to a high-profile pie in the face. If this is what her *friend* thought, what must everyone else be thinking?

Avery reached over and touched Katie's arm. "I'm sorry, Katie-bird," she said. "I didn't mean to upset you. I know this is probably stressful as hell—"

"Don't worry about it, Ave," Katie interrupted, patting her friend's hand reassuringly. "You know, even with Con and Kevin Rose to bounce things off, sometimes I feel like I'm all alone on an island somewhere. Sometimes it's good to hear somebody else's opinion." She broke into a grin. "A brutally honest, unedited, cruel-to-be-kind, gloves-off opinion."

"Oh, screw you," Avery replied. "You know, seriously, it wouldn't hurt to get some other opinions. Not just about general stuff, but specific things."

"Such as…"

"Such as these mysterious, so-called 'clues' that this scum-sucker left at the scene. You say ya'll are stumped by them. Then you say they're hush-hush super secrets that can be known only to three people with magic decoder rings. It seems to me, the more resources you harvest, the more ways you have to attack the problem. Sooner or later, somebody's gonna put it together."

Katie sighed. "Well, you're right about diversifying our resources. But, with investigations like this, you don't want to reveal to the public the things that only the cops and the killer know. You don't want some innocent schizophrenic coming in and confessing to something he didn't do. You don't want a clever killer making strategic decisions based on your game plan. And you sure as hell don't want some copycat out there." She paused, watching a group of crab hunters stroll past. "Besides, we have a bunch of cops, prosecutors, and forensic folks, even the FBI lab, looking at the evidence."

"Let me tell you a story," Avery said. "Long ago, in those halcyon, carefree days of youth, I had a bunch of dolls."

"Who didn't?"

"Did you have a freakin' James Bond doll?" Avery asked.

Katie laughed. "Well, no. You got me there."

"All right, then. Hush up your mouth and pay attention. Anyway, I'd make up these mysteries for him to solve. And James was too cool—Sean Connery in a white shirt and everything. So he'd investigate these mysteries, snoop around and all, then go hang with Q and Moneypenny—"

"You had Q and Moneypenny dolls, too?"

"Actually, Ken was Q and Midge was Moneypenney, but that's not the point. Sometimes they could help him out, sometimes not. So, do you know what he'd do when he got in a tight spot?"

"Not a clue."

"He'd climb in his borrowed pink convertible and go see all his buds back in Barbieville. You know: Barb herself, Skipper, Scooter, and everyone else. And they'd have sharing time. And you know what?"

"No," Katie said. She was laughing so hard she was almost in tears. "What?"

"Sometimes they'd know something James didn't and they'd end up solving the mystery."

"God, Ave. Your childhood was more desperate and lonely than I ever knew."

"Yeah, well. The point, dear friend, is that you can sometimes discover truths in unlikely places. Even if you're a big-shot super-sleuth."

Katie sighed and took another sip of beer. After a minute of silence, she said, "All right, I'm gonna tell you what was found at the scenes. It's not gonna do any good, but you'll just keep bugging me until I finally go crazy. But you have to promise me you'll never say a word to anyone. Not until after an arrest has been made."

"I promise, I promise," Avery said. "Now give it up."

Katie ran through a description of all the crime scenes, beginning with the Anjanette Donna Crawley case. She described the flower and the rocks and the chess piece and the mutilations. When she was finished, she took another sip of beer and rested her chin on her left hand.

Avery looked at her for a moment, then shrugged. "Is that all?" she asked.

"What do you mean?"

"I mean, where's the mysterious clues that ya'll can't figure out?"

"That's all of it, Avery. We don't know what those things mean."

Avery's brow furrowed. "It sounds pretty damn familiar. Like bizarre metaphors from some epic literary work we studied back in college."

Katie stared at her friend. Suddenly her eyes flew open.

"Wait a minute, Avery! You're right! All the references are from *The Waste Land*. You remember—the Eliot drought polemic." She held her face in her hands as she mentally connected all the dots. "It's like a T.S. Eliot primer gone insane. I mean, it's so obvious now it's—*stupid*."

"Well, pardon me."

"There's the deal about Belladonna, Lady of the Rocks. Don't you remember? And there was a Hyacinth Girl in that section, as well. And there's another section called 'A Game of Chess.' And then there's 'The Fire Sermon' section—that might explain setting the woman on fire." She shook her head in disbelief. "I can't believe it never occurred to me. It's all there."

Avery grinned. "See, I helped. I *told* you."

Katie's jaw suddenly dropped. "Oh my God, Ave. This man...the suspect, he had all these books on English lit. He even had a T.S. Eliot poetry collection right on his night stand!" She covered her mouth with her right hand. "It *was* him!"

"Can you tell me who it was now that I've solved the case for you?"

Katie stared, trance-like, out at the surf. "I can't. Not until he's arrested."

"Oh, well," Avery said. "I'll find out sooner or later." Then, grinning at her friend, she said, "I do find one thing mildly curious about all this."

"What's that?"

"That there'd be two *Waste Land* freaks in little ol' Richfield."

Katie gave her a puzzled look. "What do you mean?"

"Well, I went out with a guy a few months ago who was just eat up with T.S. Eliot. When he found out I'd been a lit major, that's all he wanted to talk about."

Katie stared at Avery. Her fingernails dug into the arms of the chair.

"What was his name?" she asked. She could feel her heart pounding.
"Jamie Amerson," Avery replied. "Why?"

CHAPTER 14

▼

Berry Macklin sat in the front passenger seat of Bobby Franks's Crown Victoria and stared at the investigator.

"Explain again to me exactly why ya'll needed me out here at one in the morning."

Franks tapped impatiently on the steering wheel with both index fingers. "You know good and well why, Berry. You're 'it,' at least for tonight."

"Why not get Kevin Rose's pimpled butt out here? And don't give me that, 'Because he's got a small kid and a pregnant wife and he went out on a crime scene call last night,' crap, either. Because I've heard all that—"

"It's because you're black, okay?" Franks pulled the brim of his ball cap down over his eyes and slumped down in the driver's seat. "That's why you're here and Kevin Rose, everyone's favorite honky prosecutor, is home in bed."

The head of the D.A.'s violent-crime unit glared at Franks for a moment, then broke into a grin. "Well, all right, then. Just so long as there's a reason."

The radio crackled and Franks leaned forward, totally focused on the dispatch. He and Berry had been parked at the end of Bienville Court, "sitting on" Jamie Amerson's house, for nearly two hours. Arrest warrants charging the man with capital murder, kidnapping, and three counts of possession of illegal drugs were tucked into the driver-side visor. Two patrol cars and an unmarked unit driven by Brant Woodley were cruising Richfield's south side, searching for any sign of Amerson or his late-model Ford Explorer. Franks decided that there wasn't anything about his man in the radio traffic and slumped back in the seat.

"I bet the chump ran," Macklin said. "I bet he got tipped off by someone and just booted it."

Franks frowned at the prosecutor. "He didn't get tipped off," he said. "You've been hangin' out with too many paranoid defense attorneys."

"It could happen. It's happened—"

There was another crackle and the investigator held up his hand to silence the prosecutor. Once again, Franks zeroed in on the radio. This time there was something for them. A vehicle matching the description of Amerson's SUV had been spotted heading east on Milton Boulevard, right toward them. The unit was closing, attempting to get a look at the tag. Less than a minute later, the officer called in the tag number and stated that the Explorer had turned south on Bienville Street. Franks bolted upright in his seat. There could be little doubt that this was Jamie Amerson and no doubt that he was headed right for them.

Headlights appeared in the distance. Franks turned the ignition key and the engine exploded to life.

"What's the deal?" Berry Macklin asked. His voice, normally deep and resonant, inched up slightly in pitch.

"The deal is that's our man."

"Great. We got our man. Do we have a plan?"

"There's a Tango unit right behind him," Franks replied. "Woodley's over on State Street, in case he tries to run through his backyard. We're gonna pin him in the driveway and, hopefully, extract him from the vehicle without incident."

Macklin stared at the investigator.

"Is there a problem?" Franks asked.

"No, I just—" The Deputy D.A. flashed a nervous grin. "In case there *is* incident, are we in any way…is there some kind of weapon—"

"There's a riot gun in the trunk." Franks's eyes remained glued to the approaching vehicle. "I'm sure it'll be fine, though. Remember, this is a dude who drugs his victims and chokes them when they're helpless." His right hand gripped the shift lever. "I really don't think he'll want to fight."

Macklin leaned over to check Franks for a weapon. "Do you even…you're not even wearing a gun."

"Nope," Franks replied, calmly. "It's in the glove compartment."

Macklin settled nervously back in his seat. "O-kay," he said quietly. He wanted to inquire further—why would an experienced investigator about to make a major felony arrest *not* have his weapon ready?—but decided to let it alone.

The Explorer neared Amerson's driveway and began to slow. Just as it was about to turn in, the vehicle came to a complete stop in the road. The headlights were trained directly on Franks's car. Macklin tried to slump down below the dashboard.

"Man, what's he doing?" he asked.

"I have no idea. He's probably trying to figure out who we are and what we're doing here." Franks could see another set of headlights appear further down Bienville. "That would be Mark Charles Mayweather and Eddie Davis in the Tango unit." He pulled his detachable blue light out from the center console and stuck it to the dash. "We've got the sumbitch boxed now," Franks said. He began singing, "Nowhere to run, ba-aby, no-where to hide—"

The Explorer suddenly lurched backward, then began racing in reverse the opposite direction on Bienville.

"What the—?" Franks jammed the Crown Victoria into "Drive" and the car began charging toward the fleeing SUV.

Macklin fastened his seatbelt and looked at the investigator with a concerned expression. "Um, this wouldn't be part of the plan, would it?" he asked.

"No, but the dumbass's got nowhere to go. He's about to get a surprise." He queued the radio microphone and alerted the patrol car. Officer Mayweather replied that he understood the situation.

Just then, the Explorer braked violently. With smoking tires, it veered off into the darkness between two houses.

"Son of a bitch!" Franks exclaimed. "I forgot there was an alley right there." He steered the Crown Vic into the narrow lane, completely dark except for one dim street light at the very end. His car fishtailed badly and he had to fight to regain control. Berry Macklin's fingers locked onto the molded grip above the passenger door.

"Sorry," Franks said. "I didn't get the deluxe pursuit suspension package on this piece of crap." He floored the accelerator and the car rumbled after the rapidly disappearing Explorer.

"You apparently also missed out on the deluxe 'attain the lawful speed limit package,' too," Macklin muttered.

"If he makes it to Feltner, we may have a problem," Franks said.

Feltner Avenue bypassed the business district and turned into a highway running west out of the city. Franks reached down and flicked two switches on a console control box. The blue light began flashing in his windshield and the startling yelp of the siren drowned out the chirping and whining of night insects.

"Well, this ain't gonna hurt the case any," Macklin said. "Trying to flee's not gonna make him look good at all."

"That's what I was thinking," Franks replied.

At that moment, the Explorer reached the end of the alley, which intersected at a right angle with Feltner. The vehicle veered north without slowing and immediately disappeared in a swirling cloud of dust.

"I think he lost it," Franks said, his voice taut with tension.

It was true. The first thing the two men saw when they reached Feltner was the Explorer lying on its left side in the median. A dense cloud of smoke rose from the crumpled hood of the vehicle, nearly obscuring a blinking amber traffic light fifty feet down the road.

Franks cursed softly and pulled up behind the disabled SUV. The marked patrol car roared up behind them. The flashing lights from both police units painted the area in a eerie blue glow. The investigator climbed from his car and began walking toward the vehicle. The two uniform officers, nine-millimeter pistols drawn and trained on the Explorer, followed, at least until they noticed that Franks was unarmed.

Jamie Amerson's head, bloodied from an apparent cut on his scalp, appeared suddenly in the open passenger window. Before Franks could react, he pulled himself out of the window and rolled over onto the pavement. Franks immediately straddled him, handcuffs in his left hand. He twisted the man's left arm into place and expertly popped the cuff over his wrist.

"See what you get for running, Jamie? Nothin' but a totaled ride."

"Leave me alone," Amerson rasped. The garbled words spilled out around his swollen and bloody lower lip. A powerful odor of alcohol made Franks wince.

"I have warrants for kidnapping, murder and two counts of illegal possession of controlled substances—"

"Stick 'em up your ass."

"You have a right to remain silent," Franks muttered, securing the other cuff to Amerson's right wrist. He took a deep breath, struggling to maintain his composure. "Anything you say can and will be used against you in a court of law."

"Go screw yourself. Why don't you use *that* against me in a court of law."

"I think I will," Franks snapped. He stood and tried to hoist the man from the ground. The two uniform officers stepped in to assist and quickly brought Amerson to his feet.

"If you decide you want a lawyer—"

"You damn straight I want a lawyer!" Amerson screamed. "I'm gonna get Rabon Creasey and sue the livin' hell out of every one of ya'll!"

Franks brushed off his hands and turned away from the man. To Officer Mayweather, he said, "Can ya'll transport his sorry ass?"

Mayweather nodded.

"Appreciate it. Take him to the hospital first. Richfield Center will do fine. I'll meet ya'll there in as soon as I get someone to work this mess." He opened his door and began to climb in his car.

"Why don't you beat me while I'm handcuffed?" Amerson snarled as the officers escorted him past Franks's car. "Isn't that your specialty—beating up helpless, innocent people?"

Franks froze, crouched with one leg already in the car. His jaw clenched and his eyes burned in anger at the prisoner.

"Let it go, B.J.," Berry Macklin said. "Don't let him mess up your case with all that smack talk."

Amerson let out a loud, demonic cackle.

Franks slid under the steering wheel, took a deep breath, and let it out slowly.

"You got him, Bobby," Macklin said. "That's all that counts. You did your job. Now we'll take it from here."

Franks nodded and slammed the door. When he went to turn the key in the ignition, he discovered that his hand was trembling.

CHAPTER 15

▼

Katie stood in the doorway of the Regent Cafe and strained to see over the wall of people crowded into the restaurant's narrow atrium. The Regent attracted lunch-hour patrons from virtually every social and vocational milieu. Farmers, businessmen, factory workers, laborers, and a representative sampling of Richfield professionals all ate there, and it wasn't unusual for local public officials, even members of Congress, to be found rubbing elbows with constituents. For that reason, nobody reacted to Katie's presence, even though she'd become an often-photographed and easily recognizable public figure.

Despite its popularity, Katie had never particularly cared for the Regent. In her opinion, the dining area was too noisy, the vegetables too overcooked, the entrees too unhealthy. On this day, however, she had been invited to lunch by Rabon Creasey, and when one lunched with the highly regarded defense attorney, one went to the Regent. Creasey, a long-time friend of the restaurant's owner and a devotee of the diner's exclusively country-style cuisine, was treated like royalty and could be found there almost every day at noon.

The hostess, a very tall woman with flaming red hair pulled into a tight ponytail, worked her way through the mass of waiting patrons and tugged on Katie's sleeve.

"Are you meeting Mister Creasey?" she asked.

Katie nodded.

The hostess grabbed her by the arm and pulled her through the bustling main dining area. Creasey was seated at his personal table in a secluded alcove at the back of the restaurant. The attorney stood as the two women approached. He and Katie shook hands and the district attorney slid into the chair that the hostess had pulled out for her.

"Thanks you so much for meeting me," Creasey said. "I know this is unusual, but then, why can't two old friends have lunch together every now and again?"

"Right," Katie said. "I suppose there's no reason why we can't."

Creasey grinned and dumped a packet of artificial sweetener into a red plastic tumbler filled with tea and ice. "I don't even think of us as adversaries, or even as lawyers," he said. "Just two folks who've known each other for a very long time."

Katie smiled and nodded. One couldn't help but like Rabon Creasey. That's part of what made him so successful in the courtroom. His countenance was paternal—the lines on his face and silver hair confessed his vast experience, his soft voice dispensed bite-sized chunks of wisdom lightly seasoned with "country horse sense," and his genial manner encouraged confidence that all his judgments flowed from a fundamental sense of honor and fair play. She knew that this presentation was, in some ways, genuine: as with her husband, time and illness had rounded once jagged edges.

At the same time, Katie knew that Rabon Creasey was also an extraordinarily willful individual. As is the case with most successful people, trial attorneys included, he had often overcome seemingly insurmountable hurdles by the sheer force of his immense will. He didn't always win the impossible cases—the Hollins trial was proof enough of that—but he had won enough of them to have established and marketed a myth of invincibility. His success certainly couldn't be attributed to erudition, for, although he liberally peppered his jury arguments with quotes from the great philosophers and writers, he had never pretended that scholarship contributed in any major way to his persuasiveness. Nor could his proficiency be credited to a great love for the written law—Creasey was rumored to have once said that any case that required a legal brief was one that should have been handled by a law student. He instinctively understood jury dynamics and whether a particular case required the quiet voice of reason or piercing invective. He envisioned himself a gladiator; the courtroom was his coliseum. His skill, his great and unique gift, was the ability to seduce jurors with shimmering possibilities. In his mind, objective truth was a pleasant but irrelevant destination. In the courtroom, the government had the burden of establishing guilt; he had the task of facilitating doubt.

But she also was aware that he hadn't always been regarded as a great master of trial advocacy. He'd come to Richfield in 1964 and set up a small general practice in a musty office building which, in earlier decades, had been used as a bonded cotton warehouse. After several years of struggling to make ends meet, he accepted a position with a small firm specializing in real estate, tax, and domestic relations work. He made a decent living doing occasional closings and representing aggrieved soon-to-be ex-spouses, but he was generally unfulfilled in that mission. In the probate record room or in a divorce hearing, he was just another legal technician with a briefcase and legal pad, one of dozens in the Bienville County bar. In the end, he couldn't have cared less about periodic alimony schedules, royalties, or non-commercial easements-in-gross. He wanted to be in the arena, the crucible of justice, working the jury like an evangelist.

Con had also told her about how a desperately longed-for opportunity had fallen into his lap in the fall of 1968. Glynnis Gruwell, a longtime member of the Richfield city Board of Education and wife of a Bienville National Bank vice-president, had been found dead—apparently from accidental carbon monoxide poisoning—in the garage of her fashionable Essex Street home. Her husband, Harrison Goodell Gruwell, told police that he had come home for lunch and found her unconscious on the floor of the garage. The engine of her Cadillac was running, according to Gruwell, and the enclosed garage was filled with exhaust fumes. He called an ambulance; efforts to resuscitate the woman failed.

Glynnis Gruwell was buried two days later in Richfield Gardens cemetery. There had been no investigation into the circumstances surrounding her death and no autopsy performed. The coroner had ruled her death "attended" and "unsuspicious" in nature. It had been, after all, a cold morning: Mrs. Gruwell had made a tragic mistake starting her car in the closed garage. A truly horrible accident, the coroner had reported, but nothing more.

The day after the funeral, friends of Mrs. Gruwell received an audience with Edwin Campbell, the longtime district attorney. The death, they reported, had been no accident: Glynnis Gruwell was a bright and knowledgeable woman who never would have left a car running in an enclosed space. Moreover, they said, Harrison Gruwell had, only weeks prior to her death, demanded a divorce from his wife; she flatly refused. The way things worked out, they claimed, Gruwell got exactly what he wanted without a protracted and messy divorce trial.

Campbell obtained a court order for the exhumation of Glynnis Gruwell's body, and an autopsy was performed. The forensic pathologist's report concluded that the manner of the woman's death was "homicide, based upon all related circumstances."

One month later, Harrison Gruwell was arrested after District Attorney Campbell had coaxed a first-degree murder indictment from the grand jury. Domestic relations lawyer Creasey resigned his position with his firm in order to represent Gruwell.

At trial, Creasey, quite simply, completely blind-sided the D.A. He had learned from his private investigator that Campbell intended to offer the highly incriminating testimony of a young female employee of Gruwell's bank. According to the investigator, the young lady intended to testify that Gruwell had asked her out for drinks and had even confided in her that "his miserable marriage" would "soon be over." Creasey had prepared an aggressive cross-examination of the woman, but was surprised when Campbell rested the state's case without having called her. Realizing that the prosecutor was opting to save her for "rebuttal"—an opportunity for the state to refute specific testimony given by the defense during its case—Creasey made a surprising strategic decision of his own: the defense would simply rest without offering any testimony. The murmuring of the trial spectators, packed into the small courtroom for the pedigreed bloodsport of a high-society murder case, confessed their confusion. But, across the courtroom from Rabon Creasey, District Attorney Campbell was stunned. No defense case meant that there was nothing to rebut; nothing to rebut meant no rebuttal witness. The jury would never hear the claims of his star witness—the one person who could have cemented the state's theory of Gruwell's motive. The banker was acquitted, and Creasey became the most talked-about lawyer in the county.

Now Katie recurred to the single truth that Rabon Creasy was, first and foremost, the highly paid legal representative of Jamie Amerson. She knew it'd be wise to heed Con's advice regarding the lawyer: enjoy his company, accord him the respect he'd earned, but never forget that he was, above all else, a warrior. His edges may have been rounded, but he was still very much in the Game and every inch a major player.

"So how's every little thing, Madam District Attorney?" Creasey asked now as he settled back into his chair and wrapped his hands around the plastic tumbler.

"Every little thing?" Katie laughed. "I guess you'd have to say it's business as usual. I run to put out one fire after another and usually succeed only in getting my hands badly burned."

"My friend, it seems we spend all too much time in this profession getting burned." Creasey gave her a fatherly smile and took a sip of tea. "The tragedy is, most of the time it isn't even necessary."

Katie nodded and returned his smile.

"So I take it, then, that you're keeping pretty busy at work."

"Are you kidding? I'm personally involved with three murder cases at the moment." She picked up a menu and quickly scanned the appended list of daily luncheon specials. She decided on the vegetable plate, folded the menu, and placed it back on the table. "And that's not even counting this mess with our friend Jamie Amerson."

"Ah, yes. Jamie Amerson. Funny you should mention him."

Katie's eyebrows arched. "Isn't that the main reason I'm here right now?"

"No, of course not. Look at me. How many opportunities does a beaten-up old man get to have lunch with a beautiful and intelligent young woman?" He took a sip of tea and studied the ice cubes swirling in the plastic tumbler. "On the other hand, we're both here, we're both reasonably well informed about the case. If the topic should come up, why not discuss it?" He flashed a sly grin.

"So let's discuss it," she said.

Creasey waved his hand. "Let's defer this unpleasant topic until the last possible moment. Right now let's just have lunch and chat."

"If it needs to be discussed, let's go ahead and do it."

He swirled the tea in his tumbler. "You know, it occurred to me that we really haven't tried that many cases against each other over the years."

"Two, in fact. You won the first one and, well, then there was the Hollins case."

Creasey laughed aloud. "Yikes. I'm still licking my wounds over that one. But that just goes to show you: it's all a matter of how good your facts are. If you have great facts and good police work, you'll beat me every time." He took another sip of tea.

"Yeah, and if I have marginal facts, I'll lose every time."

"Plus, it doesn't hurt to be hunting buddies with the judge," Creasey said, laughing again.

The waitress arrived, poured water into Katie's empty tumbler and took their orders.

"Anyway, Katie," he continued when the woman had gone, "I know Bobby Franks is a fine investigator. Good man, one of the very best. I've known him since he started policing way back when. I don't think he'd intentionally or maliciously try to misrepresent anything." He paused, took another sip of tea, then said, "However, in this case, I feel like he's made a huge and regrettable error. An understandable one, given the pressure that's being exerted on him, but an error, nonetheless."

Katie nodded but said nothing. Her worst fear as a prosecutor had always been the unwitting participation in the conviction of an innocent person. She knew that, in the vast majority of cases, the accused individual was guilty of *something*, if not the precise crime with which he or she had been charged. But she'd also seen occasions—*rare* occasions, to be sure—when totally innocent people had been sucked into the vortex of the system. And most of those cases involved scenarios wherein the defendant had been implicated solely by a single witness or where the evidence was mostly circumstantial. The case against Jamie Amerson was going to fit squarely into the latter category. Still, the individual bits of proof, when cemented together, created an easily recognizable mosaic of guilt.

"I wonder," Creasey continued, "whether you might consider recommending that a bond be set for Jamie."

Katie blinked. *So that's what this was all about.* She had hoped that, whatever it was, it would be something very minor, a matter of comfort or aesthetics. Like allowing him to have his favorite down comforter in his cell. That would have been an easy one to handle. *It's the sheriff's jail, Rabon—I'll be glad to put in a good word, but—*Or some basic technical or procedural issue. But asking her to agree to a bond? In a capital case? It was absolutely unthinkable. Nobody with a stake or interest in the case would agree to her making such a recommendation. This wasn't a minor drug possession charge or even a non-residential burglary. It wasn't even just a murder case. This case represented one in a series of atrocious killings. True, the evidence of guilt was not overwhelming. But there *was* evidence of his guilt. And Amerson's arrest had been like a sovereign remedy that had flushed the anxiety out of the community. Releasing him before his guilt had been adjudicated would be like injecting fear right back into Richfield's veins.

"Rabon, it's a capital case," she sputtered. "It just isn't—"

"I know it's an unusual request, but then, this is an unusual case. There isn't much evidence. You certainly have no admission of guilt—"

Katie frowned. She thought back on the statement they did receive from Amerson and Creasey—a neatly written and politely worded declaration of complete innocence. A stroke of genius: a testimonial surrogate, a device that could well permit Jamie to deny guilt without having to risk taking the witness stand. She understood that, technically, the statement should be inadmissible as hearsay. Still, most judges would probably allow the jury to consider it, especially in a case where death loomed as a potential punishment.

"Yeah," she said, "thanks to *you* we have no admission of guilt!"

Creasey sank slightly, a contrived look of hurt on his face. "Katie, I can't believe you'd say that. I can't believe you'd even *think* that. I mean, you were a defense attorney once. You know that you do what you have to do. Besides, he *is* innocent." He paused, gauging her reaction. "Did you actually expect him to admit guilt?"

"No," she said softly. "But I didn't expect a freaking self-serving press release, either."

The waitress arrived at that moment with two steaming plates. She set them in front of the lawyers, refilled the defense attorney's tea glass and placed the check on the table.

"Let's just enjoy lunch," Creasey said. "We'll talk about this later."

They ate their lunches, Katie picking unenthusiastically at her vegetables and Rabon devouring his chicken-fried steak and potatoes. Creasey made several attempts at non-business chit-chat; Katie responded politely, but seemed distant and troubled.

"You okay?" Creasey asked, at last.

"Yes. I'm fine—"

"I'm fine, *but*—" He waved his fork as a non-verbal prompt for her to finish her thought.

"It's nothing, Rabon. I understand what you're asking of me and why you're asking. It's just...I hate to think of the public reaction if Jamie Amerson got out of jail right now."

"When he's found 'not guilty,' will you still have the same aversion to his return to freedom?"

"No, of course not. If that were to be the result. But I'm not so sure—"

"It's a very weak case, Katie, and you know it." He sawed off a piece of steak and stabbed it with his fork. "You've even told people that he shouldn't be charged."

She felt blood rush to her face. Who would have told him something like that? Obviously someone close to her or the investigation. She knew who could be ruled out as suspects. It absolutely wouldn't have been Con or Avery; they'd die before betraying a confidence. And, although Creasey had many inside contacts at RPD, it wouldn't have been Bobby Franks, not ever. Her brow furrowed as she struggled to identify the source of this dated information. It could have been any other officer, anyone to whom Franks had complained. Or it could have come from someone in the Sheriff's Department. No matter, it was no longer true. Or at least not *completely* true...

"I may have had reservations in the early stages of the investigation," she said at last. "At that point, certain, ah, *things* hadn't yet been uncovered. But now I'm very confident that he's our guy. There's a great deal of evidence pointing straight at him."

Creasey lowered the skewered chunk of meat and made a face. "What evidence? A dried hyacinth? To the best of my knowledge, Jamie wouldn't know a hyacinth from a hula hoop."

"What about the plastic pawn they found—"

"First of all, *that* case isn't even in your jurisdiction. Secondly, you've got a completely different cause and manner of death—"

"Rabon," Katie interrupted, a look of amazement on her face, "you've got the exact same pattern of disfigurement. And you've got a kidnapping with the same sedative drug—"

"You're counting on the Rohypnol as persuasive proof of guilt? *I* wouldn't. Do you have any idea how much Rohypnol there is out there in circulation right now? Enough to sedate an entire army. And the college kids—female and male— are dosing themselves with drugs like that, just to get high. Who's to say these two girls weren't out partying with some folks from the college? They all take the drug to get high, then one psycho, maybe not even somebody with them, decides to take advantage of the disabled victim." He shrugged. "These scenarios are all possible, maybe even probable."

"What about the chess piece?"

"A pawn from a cheap chess set you can buy at any drug store? Give me a break. There're probably a hundred sets with missing pieces just like that in central Alabama alone. I probably have one at my house. Most of our jurors will probably have one at *their* houses."

"What about the fact that he dated all these women, and they all broke up with him? There's your proof of motive."

Creasey shook his head. "My investigator has interviewed dozens of friends and family members. They all say those relationships ended amicably. He was on speaking terms with both Donna Crawley and the other girl—"

"Kerry Grinder."

"Right." He took a bite of potato and chewed pensively. After he swallowed, he said, "It's not there, Katie. Some strange coincidences, perhaps, but that's about it."

"There's more, Rabon."

"There's no eyewitness, no DNA, no fingerprints, no confession. The kinds of things jurors like to have in a capital case."

"There're other things, too. Things of which you're probably not yet aware."

"You talking about that stupid poem, *The Waste Land*?" he snorted. "I hope *that's* not your ace-in-the-hole."

"The clues left at the crime scenes are all references from it. And I think it's clear he was obsessed by it—"

"He was no such thing. He was an English major, like thousands of other Carry graduates. He'd read it, even discussed it, but he was far from being obsessed by it."

Katie paused, wondering how much information to divulge at this stage of the proceedings. She knew that, this being a capital case, she'd eventually have to open her entire case file to him. Still, she didn't want to give up *everything* she had, at least not at that time.

"Rabon, he had the book, the T.S. Eliot collection with that poem in it," she said, at last. "It was right there in his bedroom bookcase. It was marked—"

The attorney again waved his fork. "That's easily explainable. A friend, acquaintance, whatever, had called him a few weeks ago and asked him a question about it." He laid the fork on the table and wiped his mouth with his cloth napkin. "It's highly relevant right now, you see, what with the drought conditions and all."

"What about him fleeing Bobby Franks? Flight can be used to show consciousness of guilt."

The lawyer took a sip of tea and smiled. "Sure, you can throw it out there, but we get a chance to explain."

"What's there to explain?"

"Simple. Jamie, of course, knew he was a suspect. I mean, after all, ya'll searched his house. And he's heard rumors that people—friends and family of the unfortunate victims—are out to get him. So he's coming home after meeting some friends for drinks, he sees a car with two men in it, he runs away." Creasey shrugged as if the merits of this defense were self-evident. "What juror wouldn't understand that?"

"Rabon, Bobby had his blues on him. His lights *and* the siren. How could he not know it was a cop car?"

"He didn't turn on his emergency equipment until they were well down that alley. As soon as Jamie noticed the lights, he tried to stop. That's when he lost control. I don't think what he did shows consciousness of anything but being chased by an unmarked car with two men it." Another shrug. "What would *you* have done?"

Katie frowned and poked a carrot with her fork. Of course, it didn't come as a surprise to her that he already knew so much about the state's case. Successful trial lawyers didn't sit back and wait for evidence to come to them. Nor was she shocked that he'd already fashioned explanations for every otherwise incriminating item of proof. This was another skill possessed by the best defense attorneys. But it bothered her that he was so supremely confident in the inadequacy of her evidence. Was she missing something? Had she become so numbed by outside influences—Franks's persistent handcuff rattling, Dean Wilker's implied threats, the political posturing of folks like Bru Nix—that she'd lost all her objectivity about the case's merit? This preview of the defense assault upon her evidence caused her to recur to her many early doubts about Amerson's guilt.

"I can't agree to the setting of a bond," she said, finally. "It's a capital case and we feel he's a threat to the community."

Creasey carefully folded the napkin and arranged it on the table next to his plate. "Very well," he said. He sighed audibly and gave a good-natured shrug of concession. "It doesn't hurt to ask." He paused, then added: "Of course, I'm going to have to file a writ. I think we're entitled to a hearing, given the nature and quality of the evidence."

Katie nodded. She understood that the courts would allow the defense to explore the strength of the prosecution's case at a bond hearing. She had hoped it wouldn't have become an issue, but she certainly understood why Rabon Creasey was going to do it. She would've done the same had she been in his shoes. She just hoped that the judge, whoever it might be, would see the same strengths in the case that she'd seen only a few days earlier.

"I understand and respect your position," she said.

"Sometimes the only place these things can be settled is in the courtroom." Creasey raised his tea glass in a salute to his adversary, then said, "At least let me buy your lunch."

"Thanks, Rabon, but I can't. You know: I have to avoid even the *appearance* of impropriety."

"But I invited you to lunch as my guest. You accepted. A contract was created."

"I'll tell you what," she said. "Let *me* buy *yours*."

Without hesitation, Creasey slid the check in front of Katie. "There's one thing I want engraved on my headstone," he said with a grin, "'Here lies Rabon Creasey, a man who never turned down a free lunch'."

"You'll get used to it," Joe Terry Hollins said to Jamie Amerson. Hollins lay on his side on his narrow bunk, one tattooed arm supporting his head. He turned slightly and nodded at the hollering inmates directly across the cellblock corridor. "Either that, or you'll go bat-shit crazy."

Amerson sat on the side of his bunk and stared at the floor, clearly ignoring his cellmate. He shifted his weight in an attempt to find a comfortable place to sit, something he had done with regularity since placing his flip-flop-covered feet on the painted concrete floor five hours earlier. He could feel the perforations on the metal bunk deck even through the three-inch mattress. Hollins's grating voice persisted, but Jamie was clearly lost in his own thoughts. The previous night—his first in the Bienville County Jail in some time—had been unpleasant, especially after the potent pain medication, administered at the emergency room, had worn off. He hadn't slept at all—the hideous antiseptic smell, the gray-green flourescent corridor lighting, the institutional clangor, and the ambient hostility of the place were far more powerful than either exhaustion or the gauzy warmth of the narcotic drug.

While Hollins had slumbered, Amerson had taken a silent inventory of his cell. Things had changed since he had last been a guest in the "Bienville Hilton." And for the better, in his estimation. The walls, once peeling institutional gray, had been painted a glossy beige. The ceramic toilet and sink—insipid and open invitations to inmate abuse and sabotage, in his opinion—had been replaced with a consolidated stainless-steel unit that seemed indestructible. And there was a stainless writing desk, another new feature, bolted to one wall and a metal stool secured to the floor in front of it.

But he also knew that some things—some damn *important* things—would be very much the same as they had been. His daddy, who knew the current sheriff from the Quarterback and Lion's clubs, had always been able to see to it that nobody bothered him in the jail. Indeed, Jamie was aware that he was safely segregated from the general population. Not that he needed protection. He shot a quick glance at the faces leering at him through the bars across the corridor. *Punks.* There wasn't one of them he couldn't kill with his bare hands in a fair fight. His years of prep wrestling and jujitsu study had made him a formidable opponent in any fight. Still, it was nice to know that Daddy was looking out for him. During the night, one of the old guards, a veteran third-shift detention officer named Glidewell, had stopped by to see if he needed anything.

"Thanks," Jamie had said, "but what I need you can't get for me."

Indeed, he felt far more threatened by the justice system's functionaries than he did the other inmates. This Katie O'Brien—he had to remind himself that she was no longer Katie Cowan, the obnoxious assistant D.A. from his past—had been after him for years. The same was true with the case investigator, Bobby Franks. Obviously, putting him in the electric chair had become some kind of joint crusade for them. Never mind that these so-called victims were all users who had gotten what was coming to them. But this wasn't about them anymore. Maybe it had never been about them. This case was really about power, political pressure, and a couple of megalomaniacs out for personal revenge. And, even though Rabon Creasey had convinced him that the state would never be able to prove its murder cases, Jamie worried that the felony drug charges could pose a problem.

Well, he had decided, Daddy and Rabon Creasey would just have to make that problem go away. He couldn't pull any state time—a prison sentence was simply out of the question.

"So what was it like?" Joe Terry Hollins's irritating voice pulled Jamie back to the stark reality of the cell.

Amerson's eyes rose and locked on the speaker. Hollins was still propped up on an elbow. He flashed an awkward grin.

"How was *what?*"

"Chokin' out them ol' girls."

Amerson laughed derisively.

"What? What's the matter?"

"I don't know what you're talking about."

"I want to hear about the deed, man. Seriously, I enjoy hearin' details. Did they beg for their lives? Did you hit some of that before you—"

"Go fuck yourself, you ignorant clown."

Hollins frowned and held Amerson's hard stare for a moment. Then the lop-sided grin slowly returned. "Oh, I get it," he drawled. "You think I'm just playin' you. You know, workin' you, then turnin' State." He cackled. "Well, that's all wrong, inmate. Think about it. First of all, what would be the point? I mean, I've already been convicted. I've already been sentenced. It's already a done deal. I'm doing all day, and there's nothin' can be done about it."

"You're doing *what?*"

"All day. You know: Life without." Hollins pulled himself up and swung his feet over the side of the bunk. "In other words, nobody got nothin' to offer me now. And that's the other thing. Do you really think I'd help out Katie O'Brien for free?" He snorted. "I wouldn't piss on her if she was on fire."

Amerson's brow knitted. "Don't you have some kind of motion for new trial pending?"

"Why would you say somethin' like that?"

"Why else would your ugly ass still be here in the county lockup? The way the sheriff bitches about lack of cell space, seems like he'da shipped you south by now if he could have."

"I might have something left in circuit court," Hollins said. "Technical shit."

"All right, then, Mister Technical Shit. Please understand why I don't have anything to say about my case." Amerson cocked his head and smiled. "Besides, I really don't think my lawyer would appreciate it."

The grin again. "Me and you have the same damn lawyer."

Jamie laughed derisively. "Not really. You got the less-productive, court-appointed Rabon Creasey. I, on the other hand, am getting the deluxe, paid-for version."

The crooked grin slowly became a tight and angry gash cut into a week's worth of beard stubble. "You got a mighty smart mouth for such a pretty boy," the convict snapped.

"Really? Well, you're unbelievably stupid for such an ugly piece of crap."

Hollins jumped to his feet, his hands clenched into tight fists.

The prisoners across the hall began hollering for Hollins to take care of the new inmate.

"Stick the pretty boy!" one of them yelled.

"Slide him some steel," another cried.

Amerson, unperturbed by the taunts, got slowly to his feet. He stood face to face with his cellmate.

"You need to learn some respect, boy," Hollins hissed.

Jamie laughed. "From *you*? From someone whose most manly act is murdering a ninety-year-old woman?"

Hollins gave out a growl and struck out at Amerson. A massive right fist traced a long overhead arc in the direction of his cellmate's head.

Amerson reacted with lightning speed, dropping his center of gravity and shooting his shoulders at his attacker's midsection. He had practiced this takedown so many times in training exercises that he was able to execute it almost effortlessly. His head drove hard into the side of Hollins's right hip as his hands grasped the backs of his attacker's legs. With one powerful lifting step, he took the man quickly and violently to the hard concrete floor. Hollins twisted slightly as he was falling and thereby managed to keep his head from absorbing the full force of the impact. But he was clearly stunned by the force of his fall, and Jamie Amerson had little trouble maneuvering himself into position to apply a rear choke hold. Hollins struggled briefly, but clearly was not going to be able to break the hold.

The hostile prompts of the other prisoners quickly turned to murmurs of surprise. They watched in disbelief as the "pretty boy" held Hollins's life in the crook of his right arm.

"Now you can tell *me* how it feels," Jamie whispered into the fallen man's ear. "Wasn't that what you were curious about?"

Hollins clawed desperately at the arm, but Amerson pulled the choke even tighter. The convict's face began to redden and swell.

"Let him go," one of the other prisoners now complained. "You're gonna kill him."

The palms of Hollins's hands were now on the floor in a display of complete submission. Strange noises squeaked out of his compressed throat. Clearly he was begging for his life.

"You are the hollow man," Amerson whispered, taking liberties with one of his favorite T.S. Eliot poems. "Your dried little voice is quiet and meaningless."

"Five-oh!" hollered a prisoner from across the corridor. The standard inmate code for an approaching guard.

Amerson released his hold on Hollins. The convict tumbled to the floor and began gasping for air.

Two corrections officers appeared at the cell door. One was Deputy Glidewell, the other a slender man named Miller. Glidewell was clutching a baton; Miller had a cannister of pepper spray in his right hand.

"What's going on?" Glidewell demanded.

"Nothing," Amerson said as he got to his feet. "My friend here was just helping me look for a contact lens."

The guards opened the door and entered the cell. They examined Hollins briefly, then assisted the wheezing man to his feet.

"We better get him to the nurse," Miller said. He grasped Hollins by the elbow and led him from the cell.

Glidewell turned to Jamie Amerson. "You better be careful, hoss," he muttered in a low voice. "We're tryin' to watch your back, but shit like this ain't gonna help your case."

"He jumped me, man. What was I supposed to do?"

"I don't know. Just try to lay low." Glidewell pulled the door behind him and trudged back down the corridor. The soles of his shiny boots squeaked on the polished tile.

Amerson walked to the cell door and grasped the bars. "This is how Joe Terry ends," he bellowed after the departing prisoner. "Not with a bang, but a damn whimper." He shot a reproachful glare at the prisoners across the way and snarled, "It's T.S. Eliot, you ignorant buttwands! He was a poet!" Then he turned and lay down on his bunk.

He closed his eyes and relived the thrill of the moment. Of humiliating someone like Joe Terry Hollins right in front of all his friends. Of holding a person's life in the crook of his arm. The sense of power was overwhelming.

He grinned and rolled over on his side. Within a few minutes he was asleep.

CHAPTER 16

▼

Katie sat at a small table in the corner of the courthouse coffee shop and swished a tea bag back and forth in a polystyrene cup half-filled with tepid water. She stole occasional glances at her watch and at the rather odd and strangely familiar man who seemed to be staring at her from his position at a table in the far corner of the room.

She had made this rare appearance at the coffee shop at Avery's request. Her friend was in the neighborhood to do a photo shoot at a nearby architect's office. But Avery, as usual, was running late and, with the bold surveillance of this stranger and the press of her professional obligations—a hearing on Jamie Amerson's habeas corpus petition was less than two hours away—Katie was beginning to regret the decision.

This latest configuration of the shop had evolved from a rather unimpressive operation—three tables, one self-serve coffee pot, and a limited selection of time-expired wrapped pastries in the courthouse's early days—into a bustling nerve center of the downtown business, political, and legal world. The driving force and principal beneficiary of the shop's expansion was an Indo-American gentleman, a Mr. K.V. Patel, who, along with his brothers and cousins, already operated convenience stores, restaurants, and a movie theater in Richfield. With the expert legal assistance of the Nixes, father and son, he was able to negotiate the murky waters of county politics to secure the exclusive license for the courthouse concession operation. Patel and his team also managed to get the designated floor space for the shop increased by some four hundred square feet, allowing the addition of a refrigerated drink box, an ice-cream freezer, a microwave oven, an expanded service counter complete with a dozen towering product

racks, and three new tables. Almost overnight, the shop went from being an austere courthouse employee break room to an indispensable pit stop for jurors, witnesses, lawyers, and ordinary citizens called to pay taxes, renew licenses and tags,
or handle real estate or probate matters. And, as is the case with many designated
gathering spots in public buildings, it also became a magnet for what Con had
once insensitively labeled "the odd squad"—representatives of the lunatic fringe,
homeless men and women, and the growing ranks of wandering schizophrenics.
Although she felt compassion for many of these people, Katie, mildly introverted
by temperament, shuddered at the prospect of being buttonholed every time she
entered the shop. In fact, the likelihood of a sudden encounter with an aggrieved
eccentric bothered her far more than the pricey snack food, bitter coffee, and
periodically crushing crowds.

     But this is where Avery wished to meet, so Katie had wedged herself against
the wall and slowly shrank in her chair, trying her best to become invisible. The
tactic had apparently failed. She had been noticed, and by someone who was
doing his level best to substantiate her aversion to the coffee shop. Of course, she
didn't know the man and therefore couldn't objectively quantify his strangeness,
but his appearance and demeanor strongly suggested that he understood and
enjoyed flaunting his outrageous nonconformity. The most apparent external
indicator of this engineered contrariety was the oversized heavy wool beret that
seemed to have consumed the top of his head. The beret was, in and of itself, a
stylistic anomaly in a place like Richfield, where the most frequently observed
headwear was the baseball-style cap. Beyond that, it was nearly ninety-six degrees
outside—hardly wool hat weather. And the beret was just, literally, the crowning
point of his weirdness exhibition; almost everything else about him seemed
equally peculiar. He wore glasses with heavy black frames and dark lenses tinted
almost eggplant purple. The glasses prevented her from seeing his eyes and therefore confirming that she was the precise object of his attention; she felt his penetrating stare, nonetheless. A shaggy gray beard climbed up his face almost to his
cheekbones and seemed to bush out in every direction from there. His mouth,
largely concealed by the beard, appeared only as a small gash twisted into a
tell-tale smirk of superiority. An oversized ribbed turtleneck sweater hung down
well past his waist and curled up under the beard. A number of medallions, pen-
dants, and amulet-like objects hung from a leather cord that had been tied
around his neck. He wore dirty and threadbare bell-bottom jeans, an obvious
relic from more or less the midpoint of the previous century, and a pair of cheap
running shoes tied with salvaged sections of dirty, broken laces. She collected this
identifying information in a number of discreet glances, each expertly executed as

critical minutes in a series of sweeping visual arcs. While she was unable to identify the man, there was something vaguely—eerily—familiar about him. She stared down at her cup and scrolled through her mental database. Faces, names, and contexts spun like images on a slot machine; nothing registered with her. Putting names with faces had become a frustrating task for her. She dealt with so many people—witnesses, attorneys, victims and their families and friends, potential jurors by the hundreds and sitting jurors by the dozens, concerned citizens, community leaders—that it had become impossible to remember everyone. Of course, many of these people approached her as if they'd been best friends for years. But this man, this brooding, rudely gawking individual, was hardly behaving like a long-lost friend. To the contrary, his conduct was more consistent with that of another class of individual she often encountered: the criminal defendant. It was this particular awareness that gave her an ever-increasing reason for concern.

A colorful whirlwind slicing through the crowd suddenly caught her eye. *Avery May.* Katie's friend was wearing a sleeveless saffron top, navy capris and sandals. A huge satchel purse and a camera bag swung from her torso like loose saddlebags. A delicate bead of perspiration ran down the side of her ruddy face.

"I'm sorry," Avery said, gasping for air. "The architect dude was, like, twenty minutes late, and then he started giving me the tour of all the historic district buildings they were renovating and—" She sank into the chair at one end of the table, effectively blocking Katie's view of the bearded man. She took a deep breath, seeming to melt as she exhaled.

"It's okay," Katie said. "Except for the fact that this guy's been staring at me for the last fifteen minutes." She took a sip of tea and jerked her eyes slightly in her observer's direction. "Don't make a big deal or spin around to stare at him," she added, as Avery began to look over her shoulder. "I think, to quote my terminally sensitive husband, 'he ain't quite right in the head'."

"Well, I don't care," Avery said. "I mean, he's staring at *you.*"

"I know, I know. I just don't want to get anything started with him. He looks like the abnormal psychology poster child."

"Fine," Avery said. "I'll just move over there where I can see."

She grabbed her bags and moved to the opposite side of the small table. The man was reading—more accurately, he was pretending to be reading—a newspaper that he held open in front of him like an observation blind. He tipped the paper fractionally and seemed to be gazing at her over the top of the pages. Avery stared right back at him.

"I'll show you what crazy is, you lice-ridden freak. You don't know what kind of a day I've had so far. I'm bleeding like a stuck pig, I've been up to my ass in silverfish—"

"The thing is," Katie said, deliberately interrupting her friend, "I think I know him from somewhere. I just can't remember where."

"I think he might have been one of the Fabulous, Furry Freak Brothers. Elwood, or something. Remember? From the ol' head shop comics back at school?"

Katie frowned. "That was *your* deal, Ave. Back at school, I was the one soberly studying while you were out raising hell, don't you remember?"

"Oh, yeah. How could I have forgotten that I roomed with the person voted Most Likely to Become the First Queen of America? And what did it get you? A good job and good money. Maybe a little prestige. Okay, power and respect, too. But so what? Now you're one of those boring parents who have to truthfully admit to their child they never did drugs in college."

"I did a drug, once."

"Oh, yeah, I remember. It was, like, half a caffeine pill the night before an exam. I think you started hallucinating or something and I had to talk you down."

"You're so full of it. And, by the way, I think Elwood was one of the Blues Brothers."

"What-*ever*," Avery said, rolling her eyes and feigning a look of extreme disinterest. "Speaking of drugs, I'm gonna go get some in a cup." She jumped to her feet and headed over to the coffee warmer, which was on a counter next to the bearded man. She plucked a white cup from a stack next to the coffee pot and glared at him. He seemed to hold her stare briefly, then everything but the floppy beret sank beneath the paper's security barrier. Avery filled her cup with coffee and flashed a grin at her friend.

"Target acquired and neutralized," she declared triumphantly when she got back to the table.

Katie was about to respond when she noticed Andy Renauld enter the coffee shop. The reporter glanced quickly around the room and, when she spotted Katie, waved and headed straight for the D.A.'s table.

"What a surprise!" Andy exclaimed. "I don't think I've ever seen you down here before. You slumming with the common herd?"

"Just making an appearance. I usually just choke down the office coffee."

"Have ya'll got room for me?"

"Sure," Katie said. "But I have to be going in a few minutes." She grimaced. "Gotta meet Bobby Franks and some family members. Get everyone up to speed on the big hearing."

"Which would be why I'm here," Andy said. "My editor's only given me five things to cover this afternoon." Like Avery, she had a huge satchel and a camera bag. She dumped them in an empty chair and headed to the counter to get a soft drink.

"Who is *that*?" Avery mouthed.

"I'm sorry. I thought ya'll already knew each other. It's Andy Renauld with the paper."

Avery nodded even as she studied her. "She's pretty," she said, at last.

Katie agreed. She watched her standing at the counter, talking to Mister Patel. The diminutive shop manager was barely visible, his dark eyes and shiny bald pate framed between a tower of chips and a case of slanted plastic racks filled with cracker "sandwiches" in a variety of geometric shapes. He scooped ice into a cup for Andy and then money, the drink, and rapid-fire pleasantries were exchanged.

Andy walked back to the table, stopping to avoid a collision with two men carrying cups of coffee to a table in the rear of the room. She muttered something, then slid into the chair facing Katie.

The district attorney introduced Andy to her friend and the two women exchanged greetings.

"I think I've seen you around," Andy said. She bit the end off a straw wrapper and expertly extracted the straw with her teeth. "You must work downtown somewhere."

"I wish. Our office is out on Feltner, in the old mill area." She made a face. "I think it's zoned 'Struggling Ventures That Don't Mind Violent Crime Only'."

Katie said, "Avery's the photo editor for *Bienville Life and Leisure*."

"Cool," Andy said, taking a sip of diet cola through her straw.

"Actually," Avery replied, "I'm really a bunch of stuff. I'm the photo editor and also, at least for the time being, the only staff photographer." She grinned. "I'm also the assistant copywriter, the restroom attendant and after-hours security person."

"Tell me about it. I'm doubling up as downtown reporter and photographer, at least until we hire a new person. I've got the courthouse, city hall, crime, housing authority—anything going on down here. All that and I get to shoot my own pictures, too."

"You're here for the Jamie Amerson hearing?"

"Oh, yeah. I wouldn't miss this for the world." Her eyes narrowed and her nostrils flared. "Not for the world."

Avery shot her friend a furrowed-brow, "what-the-hell's-going-on" look. It was an expression Katie had seen a thousand times over the years.

And why shouldn't her friend be puzzled? Ever since the beach trip, Avery had seen herself as a survivor—perhaps even as the sole survivor—of Jamie Amerson's murderous campaign of personal retribution. She understood both his motive and the pattern of his attacks: It was obvious that he was killing off the women who'd rejected him. And, being one of the members of that unfortunate class, she was now on the presumptively very short list of potential future victims. She certainly had her reasons for wanting to see Amerson locked away forever. Her question had to be: Why would Andy Renauld feel such hostility toward him?

"I don't ever want him to get out," Andy continued. "*Ever.*"

"Andy lives in the Southpark area," Katie said to Avery, locking into her friend's radar. "That's where two of the victims were from. She can finally sleep again and she'd like to keep it that way." She fixed a narrow-eyed stare at her friend. The message was clear: "Andy's covering this case for the paper—let's not share too much personal information just yet."

Avery sipped her coffee and quietly nodded.

At that moment, the bearded stranger got to his feet, unfolding to a height of well over six feet. He tucked the newspaper under his left arm and began shuffling toward the door. For the first time Katie noticed his hands: huge and hairy with blue, poorly defined letters tattooed across the knuckles. These markings, probable jailhouse tattoos, certainly helped explain his apparent hostility toward her; they did nothing, however, to help identify him. He lumbered past them on his way out the door, his eyes fixed on Katie.

"Getting warmer," he mumbled. "Warmer, warmer." Then he cackled and disappeared.

"Okay," Andy said, as she watched him sidle toward the public elevators. "That was a little weird."

"He sat over there and stared at me the whole time I've been here," Katie said.

"I've seen him around," Andy said. "I think he works somewhere over near my house. I've seen him driving a beat up old van."

"He actually is employed somewhere?"

"Well. Sort of like a part-time junk man, or something." Andy shrugged. "I mean, it's not like he's the CEO of Southern Power, or anything."

"What did he mean, 'warmer, warmer'?" Avery asked.

Andy shrugged. "Maybe we were just getting our own customized weather report. Or maybe he's just crazy."

"He looks sort of familiar to me, too," Katie offered. "I'm wondering if I prosecuted him. Not recently—back when I first went to work up there." She stared fiercely at her coffee cup, as if trying to dislodge a case name or history by the sheer force of will. Finally she shook her head and glanced at her watch. "I don't have time to worry about it now. I've got a hearing to go to." She took one last drink of coffee and got to her feet.

"Me, too," Andy said. She stood and grabbed her bags off the chair. "I don't want to miss anything."

"Are you gonna come upstairs and take a look at Jamie?" Katie asked Avery. "You need to go grab a seat if you are because it's probably gonna be a packed house."

Avery slowly pushed up from her chair. "No. I'm not interested in becoming a drowning victim." When Katie and Andy looked at her with puzzled expressions, she added, "That's the next section in the poem. *Death by Water.* I looked it up." She shook her head. "If he gets out, I guess I'm next on the list. I'd kind of like for him just to forget I ever existed."

Andy fixed Avery May with a perplexed look. "Why would you be next on the list?"

Katie, knowing well her friend's tendency to state exactly what was on her mind, quickly intervened. She handed Avery her bags, gave her a hug, and pushed her out the coffee shop door before she could make her expectedly revealing reply.

When Avery had disappeared into the courthouse atrium, Andy asked, "What did she mean, 'it's the next section in the poem'? *What* poem?"

"Oh, who knows? I think she was just goofing on us. She does that sometimes."

Andy brushed her hair away from her face and shrugged. "Oh, well. Guess she got me."

The two women walked a short distance into the atrium together. Katie suddenly stopped as she prepared to head toward the stairwell.

"Gotta stop off at the clerk's office," she said. "I guess I'll see you upstairs."

Andy nodded and began to walk away.

Katie was puzzled by the woman's troubled expression and sudden change in demeanor. Andy had seemed so vibrant when she arrived at their table. What had suddenly changed her attitude? She decided that it had been Avery's comment about being the next target in the killer's catalog. It unquestionably had provoked a harsh recurrence to a fact that Andy surely had been repressing: this was a deadly and very real game being played by a cunning psychopath. One that, quite obviously, had to be removed from the streets of Richfield.

Katie said, "Don't worry, Andy. You're gonna be fine."

The reporter forced a smile and nodded, then turned toward the elevators.

"All rise again, please."

Clayton Cauthen, bailiff for Circuit Judge Robert Stiles, stood on the elevated pedestal of the bench and watched as the principals and spectators in the packed circuit courtroom got to their feet. Almost simultaneously, the judge, black robes flowing as he quickly covered the ground between his chamber door and his high-back chair, ordered everyone to be seated. The result was a courtroom full of observers comically frozen for a moment in an awkward squatting posture. The murmuring spectators looked around the courtroom with puzzled expressions, finally settling back into their molded plastic chairs a few seconds after the judge was seated.

Katie watched Judge Stiles carefully, attempting to read his facial expressions and body language. Stiles had heard testimony from Bobby Franks and two women offered by the defense, received a half-dozen documentary exhibits, and heard arguments from both sides. Rabon Creasey, as expected, hadn't put on any evidence that might reveal his ultimate defense strategy. He offered the testimony of the women primarily to establish that Jamie was a longtime resident of Richfield, that he had strong ties to the community, and that he was no threat to run, despite Franks's testimony that he had already fled the police not once, but twice. But Katie was not unaware of the additional purpose of this testimony, namely, the subtle psychological impact of well-educated, intelligent women who demonstrated absolutely no fear of this alleged accused predator.

The legal issues weren't particularly complex. The thrust of Amerson's petition was that the state's case was totally circumstantial and so weak that the refusal to set bail amounted to a deprivation of liberty without due process of law. The state countered that bail was seldom permitted in capital cases, and that the continuing or serial nature of the underlying crimes made it imperative that bail be denied in this case. The law gave the court the discretion to set bond in capital cases when the available evidence was less than compelling. Despite the uncomplicated nature of the proceedings, Katie had expected the judge to take the matter "under advisement" and issue a ruling at some later time.

But Stiles informed the crowded courtroom that he would decide the case that day, and, after taking a brief recess to consult with his law clerk, was back on the bench and ready to announce his ruling.

Katie had no idea what might be coming. She'd done her best to prepare the relatives and friends for the unpredictable roller-coaster ride that lay ahead of them. The criminal justice system, she explained, was not designed to achieve true justice or to placate victims and their families. To the contrary, the system, or at least the system's most recent incarnation, seemed to have two primary objectives: to move cases as swiftly as possible and with the smallest chance that an innocent person—or a person whose rights had been violated—might be convicted. Insofar as the habeas corpus hearing went, she told them that Stiles wasn't "likely" to set bond, but she had also cautioned them that anything was possible. Now, as she watched the judge slumped in his chair, vigorously massaging his temples with blood-drained fingertips, she had an uneasy intuition that the news wasn't going to be good.

"Before I announce my decision in this matter," Judge Stiles declared, "I want to caution the parties and observers to refrain from any public displays or outbursts. I know this matter involves a great deal of emotion on both sides." He paused, his wide face flushed, his fingers still working the sides of his head. "This is a court of law and I must make my decision based on the law and not on emotion."

Franks leaned toward Katie. "What the hell does *that* mean?" he whispered.

"I don't know, Bobby. But I don't like the sound of it." Her eyes darted about the opposite side of the courtroom, coming to rest on the defendant, who sat smugly next to Rabon Creasey at the defense table, and, sprawled behind them with arms crossed and a defiant scowl on his face, Wendell Amerson.

The first words of Stiles's ruling hit Katie like a body shot from a professional prizefighter. As the order's details spilled out, the stunned D.A. was only able to absorb critical bits and fragments of judgment: "…the evidence…enough to justify an arrest…not of such quality or quantity…warrant holding Mister Amerson without bond…not a threat to absent himself…therefore…two-hundred fifty thousand dollars…"

Katie turned to the large group taking up the whole left side of the courtroom. These were the mothers, fathers, sisters, brothers, cousins, friends, and neighbors of the murdered women. She saw shock, confusion, and anger on their faces. She knew she'd have to meet with them and try to explain the ruling, but what was she going to say? She'd been through this dance of defeat with victims so many times during her career that she could almost write the debriefing script. The first question they'd ask would be whether Amerson could make a quarter-million bond. Her answer would have to be yes, and, if she chose to be bluntly honest with them, she'd have to add that he was probably already on the street. Then they'd ask if they had any way to appeal the judge's ruling. Her answer again would be yes, but that it would be an exercise in futility—in such matters, the judge had been vested with great discretion. Beyond that, she'd have to be careful how she chose her words because there was no way she could completely rule out Amerson's innocence in her own mind. At the same time, she also knew that the ruling would send an immediate and potent shock wave through the community. These good people, of course, had been standing at ground zero, but there'd be many others impacted: the students, teachers, and administrators of Carry College, concerned citizens of Richfield, and, of course, Avery May and Andy Renauld. In the end, she'd simply have to assure them that this was merely the first round; the fight would definitely continue.

She turned to look over at the defense table. Wendell Amerson was clapping Rabon Creasey on the back, and the attorney was shaking his client's hand. But Jamie Amerson was glaring directly at Katie. She stared angrily back at him. He held her glare, then, after several seconds, puckered his lips and blew a kiss in her direction.

Blood rushing to her head, Katie turned toward Bobby Franks, but before she could speak, she was startled by a sudden disturbance in the back of the courtroom. She looked up to see the man from the coffee shop standing near one of the rear doors, waving his hands and calling out to her.

"Not even warm, Katie O'Brien," he called out. He laughed again, that harsh and grating cackle, then disappeared out the door.

"Please find out who that is," Katie said, touching Franks's arm.

The investigator darted for the door, but, by the time he reached the hallway, the man had disappeared.

Katie stirred restlessly in her bed, turning from her left side to her right and back, finally settling on her back, her collection of "helper" pillows bunched around her in the bed. Convinced that sleep was nowhere near, she clasped her hands behind her head and stared at the dark shadow that was her ceiling fan. She had tried to clear the Amerson case from her mind, but it refused to go away. *There were so many questions.* Despite the ever-expanding inventory of circumstantial evidence, she was still not convinced beyond a reasonable doubt that Amerson was the murderer. It wasn't hard to see how Rabon Creasey's argument that no single piece of evidence, taken by itself, pointed unerringly to his client's guilt had swayed Judge Stiles; it certainly provoked an uneasy distrust of the state's evidence in her own mind.

Still, if Amerson *wasn't* guilty, the knot of implication had been tied from an amazing, perhaps incredible, string of coincidences. Either that, or he was being set up. Carefully, methodically. But by whom? Bobby Franks? That notion was almost laughable. The man was not without fault—his temper had occasionally gotten him into trouble and had a tendency to compromise his objectivity. But he was a dedicated investigator and, given time for reflection, generally was able to collect his thoughts and make the right decision. More importantly, he was an absolute straight shooter: "getting it right" was a higher priority than getting a collar. No, there was no way Franks would ever knowingly participate in a frame-up. What about peripheral police players, such as Brant Woodley? Highly unlikely. Like Franks, Woodley was a "by-the-book" kind of cop. Besides, he would have had little opportunity and absolutely no motive to do such a thing. It was equally difficult to imagine that Amerson might have had an enemy resourceful, dedicated, and pathological enough to have engineered such an elaborate plot. No, a set-up didn't seem to be a plausible explanation for all the available proof.

Still...

"Hey," Con whispered.

Katie rolled her head toward her husband. He had propped himself up on an elbow and his face was faintly illuminated by the light from the digital clock on the table next to his wife.

"Hey," she said. "What're you doing awake?"

"I'm mentally calculating the gravitational pull on each of Jupiter's moons. You?"

Katie laughed. "Yeah. Me, too." She turned away from him and draped an arm across her forehead. "Actually, right now it'd be kind of nice to do that for a living. Calculating gravitational pull and escape velocities, all that stuff. Or teaching, or treating illnesses, or finding a cure for disease. Actually *helping* people. Some noble profession in a perfectly ignoble time. Instead of just bashing my head against a brick wall."

"What're you talking about? You *are* doing something noble. You help people all the time."

"No, Con, I don't. I *can't*. The system won't let us help anyone. Name one person I've helped in this Amerson mess."

"Sometimes it just takes time before people realize that they've been helped. Right now everyone's just caught up in the raw emotions of it all."

"I don't know. I've worried about this every day for weeks, and what does anybody have to show for it? The killer's out there, right now, maybe plotting his next murder, everyone's terrified, the Carry administration's freaking out, the victim's families are disgusted, and Bobby Franks—" She paused, remembering his face as he left her office that afternoon. "Bobby Franks is *so* pissed off."

Con reached out and began to massage her neck and shoulders with his left hand. "Come on, Katie. This was one minor setback. *One.* Not even a setback, really—you'd be tickled with a quarter-million bond in just about any other case."

She didn't reply immediately. Instead, she buried her face in the crook of her right arm while the many troubling issues in the case continued to swirl through her thoughts.

"Katie?"

"It's not just that the judge set a bond," she said. "Although it guarantees that the killer is out there somewhere tonight." She turned back toward Con. "But what if Jamie *didn't* do it? What if all these circumstances are just part of a gigantic, ridiculous string of coincidences? Not only would we have damaged him in this community, we've spent virtually all our energy making a case on him. There are no other suspects."

Con withdrew his massaging hand and sighed.

"What?" Katie asked. "What is it?"

"That's just the way it is sometimes in this business, girlfriend. You know that. Some days you eat the bear, some days the bear eats you. You can't always know everything beyond all doubt. You can't always emerge the unscathed, triumphant gladiator. Like you said, the system ain't designed for that. You just have to take the hand you're dealt, then play it intelligently and with integrity."

Katie didn't reply immediately. She knew that Con believed what he was saying, and that this code had always been his professional guiding light. But she also knew that there was a great deal of truth in this belief. Nobody who anguished over every unsettling case development could last for long in that business. Prosecutors had to be ethical and fair, but they didn't always have to know that they were one hundred percent right. Indeed, there were certain cases—one-witness identification cases came immediately to mind—where the prosecutor might *never* know if the accused was guilty.

But now there was something else, something bizarre and unforeseen and certainly beyond the creeping doubts generated by the circumstantial proof. She couldn't get the man in the coffee shop out of her mind. His cryptic comments and his rough, almost feral, image had lingered in her thoughts ever since she'd left the courtroom. Who was he? Why had he been present at the hearing? What, if anything, did his bizarre comments mean? Was he trying to tell her something about the case? About Jamie Amerson in particular? Or was he just another mentally ill courthouse denizen wandering through a typically ragged day without his medication? She desperately wanted to mention the event to Con, but she didn't want him to think the job had finally gotten to her. She loved him and respected his judgment, but, at some point—and she decided that she'd arrived at that very point—she was going to have to cinch it up and act like the D.A.

She rolled toward him and laid her right hand gently on the side of his face.

"You're right," she said. "There's no point worrying about it. I'll just deal with it as it comes. Thanks for listening."

"That's my girl." He leaned forward, kissed her, and sank back into his pillow.

Katie lay awake long after his heavy and measured breathing let her know that he was asleep.

He sat in the darkness in his idling van and watched her house as he'd done on a dozen previous occasions. The last light had gone out more than an hour earlier and now the hulking mass of the house seemed to have receded into shadow, with only the cream-colored trim clearly visible in the dim glow of a distant streetlight.

He wondered how Judge Stiles's ruling had impacted her. Had she lashed out at her subordinates, actively plotted her next move, or just quietly seethed? Whatever her reaction, she wouldn't know how it felt to be the prisoner—the pathetic sub-human in the ugly orange jumpsuit sitting at the defense table. She couldn't even comprehend how it might feel to be thrown in a cage, to have one's identity stripped away, to be herded about like some kind of dumb animal. She probably viewed this as a bad day, but to her, a bad day was having her imperious will defeated.

But it would get worse for her, much worse. It was obvious now that this thing would devour her before all was said and done.

For one thing, she wasn't bright enough to figure this one out. She performed quite satisfactorily when she had ten eyewitnesses, a confession, fingerprints, and a DNA matchup. But who wouldn't? Any ten-year-old of reasonable intelligence could have won a case like that. This time she had only bits and pieces, discrete items intentionally left for her dim-witted investigator and which might or might not be imbued with meaning. Using jigsaw chunks from three separate puzzles, she was trying to fashion a single, coherent picture. True, she—or someone—had figured out the arcane *Waste Land* references, but she didn't, and *wouldn't*, get the big picture. And still she postured for the cameras, playing D.A., putting on a dog-and-pony show for the equally clueless members of the community. Even as the judge was rejecting her pathetic argument, she was setting her jaw for her audience to behold.

But did she really believe in her case? Not that he could tell. She had no confidence in her evidence, in the appropriateness of the charge; perhaps she even doubted her ability. She was imperious, true, but imperiousness was not the same as confidence. He could see this doubt in her eyes from across the courtroom. She was struggling, and she knew it. And she also knew that her struggle was going to end badly for her.

He, of course, could solve her problem. He, alone, had the power to do that. And he'd do it, too, because now he almost felt sorry for her. *Almost.* All she had to do was apologize. Admit that her persecution of him was fraudulent from the inception. And she also had to ask for his help. If she did these things, it would all end. And it'd be so simple.

He slipped the van into gear and began rolling slowly up the street. As he passed her house, he began laughing.

He knew that she'd never call him, that she'd never apologize, and she'd never admit she was wrong. *Hubris.* Insipid, excessive pride. That's what it would come down to. It would be her fatal flaw, just like all those fallen heroes in Greek tragedy. It would take her down and all the others, too. "I know I'm right," that's what she probably was telling herself just then. She probably said it to herself in the mirror in the morning and repeated it a hundred times to help her fall asleep.

Maybe her husband could have that inscribed on her headstone.

CHAPTER 17

▼

Bobby Franks stared down through his reading glasses at the newspaper folded in his lap. He held a ball-point pen in his right hand; his thumb nervously worked the point retractor button as he sat deep in thought. The surface of the small table next to his chair was cluttered with objects: a heavy glass ashtray packed beyond capacity with ash and cigarette debris, a beer can, a pack of cigarettes, a plastic butane lighter and a half-eaten Swiss steak microwave dinner were balanced on a stack of folded newspapers and unopened envelopes. Cigarette smoke spiraled into heavy air through the light from a brass floor lamp. A bookcase, television stand, and sofa had been wedged into a corner of the room. The bookcase was completely full; even the spaces between the tops of the book covers and the shelves had been filled with slim, sideways-lying volumes and notebooks in a variety of sizes. A professional wrestling match raged almost unnoticed on the twelve-inch screen of his television set. Occasionally the pen dipped toward the crossword puzzle, hovering tentatively an inch or so above the paper. Less often, in intermittent bursts of inspiration, the point struck out at the empty squares, filling them with scarcely recognizable blue-ink characters. With each conquered set of spaces, the investigator reached for his cigarette and, tipping the growing ash into the ashtray, allowed himself to savor a small measure of satisfaction.

Franks had lived in this small apartment, alone, since his divorce. He had discovered that life was easier, if not more enjoyable, now that he had been relieved of the responsibility of a marriage. He had been in love with his wife, Nancy Jean—indeed, he maintained that he still loved her—but found himself unable to leave his work-related issues at his home's threshold. His ever-increasing sense of persecution had combined with mounting debt and workaday vocational frustrations to produce a fatal synergy of domestic stressors. After Nancy Jean moved out, he engaged in a frenzied campaign of self-improvement. He enrolled at the local community college, taking courses in criminal justice and computer sciences. He even submitted to multiple therapy sessions with a psychologist—potent evidence, given his persistent doubts about that profession, of his determination to save his marriage. In the end, his valiant struggle against his personal demons wasn't enough. Nancy Jean filed for divorce after a six-month separation and remarried less than three months after the decree became final. With his marriage over and his children off at school or married, Franks found it pointless to remain in his farm house in the country. He sold the house, paid off his bills, and moved into the small apartment in town. He dated occasionally; in each case, he found the flow of love and tenderness occluded by danger, stress, frustration. He thus came, at the age of forty-six, to a life consisting of his frustrating work, fitful sleep, and, in whatever time remained, reading, television, or his puzzles.

There was a knock at the door. Franks's brow furrowed as he glanced at his watch. He created a space for the newspaper on the table and rocked out of the chair, wincing as his chronically injured back straightened. He moved slowly across the room and peered through the door peephole. He was stunned to see Andy Renauld standing in the breezeway, her hands thrust into the back pockets of her tight black jeans. He ran his fingers through his hair, cracked open the door, and mumbled an awkward greeting.

"I really hate just showing up like this," she said. "I just needed to see somebody. Well, not just somebody—*you*." She paused, evaluating. "If this is a bad time—"

Franks leaned against the half-open door, the pen still in his hand. "No," he said. "I was just trying to catch up on my crossword puzzles." He opened the door and motioned for her to enter. "I got a little behind with all the craziness going on."

Andy stepped into his apartment and flashed an awkward smile. She was wearing a pink top that did not quite conceal her trim midriff. She glanced around the room and nodded.

"Yeah. This is sort of what I expected."

"I apologize for the way it looks. I haven't been here but a few hours every day." He snatched up the plastic microwave dinner tray and the stack of folded papers and began walking toward the adjacent kitchenette. "Have a seat."

Andy sank into the end cushion of the sofa.

"Can I get you a beer or anything?" Franks called out from the other room.

"Yeah, sure. Whatever you got. Something cold."

"It's gonna have to be a beer," he replied. "I'm fresh out of everything else."

"That's fine. I think I feel more like a brew now, anyway."

He shuffled back into the room with two long-necked, amber bottles. The cigarette was gone. He handed her one of the beers and eased himself back into his chair.

"So," he drawled, "I guess the obvious question would be, why is it me that you need to see at nine forty-seven at night?"

"Why is that the obvious question?"

"I don't know. Usually, the only folks hunting me down at this hour are my sergeant or lieutenant." He took a deep drink of beer and grinned. "Also, the word 'need' has officially never been uttered by a beautiful woman in this apartment."

"I'm scared, Bobby," she said. "Pardon me for cutting to the chase, but that's it. He's out there tonight, and I'm scared to death."

Franks nodded and tapped the beer bottle with his index finger.

"How the hell could he make bail so fast? I mean, a damn quarter of a million dollars!"

Franks shrugged. "It's easy. The man at the AA-Acme Bonding is a friend of his dad's. And he's crazy as a run-over dog, on top of that. He'd sign a bond for anyone. He probably let Daddy sign a note for ten-percent of the quarter mill, and bam—just like that, your murderer is back on the street. What he doesn't know is that, if Jamie runs—and he's already tried to run twice—I think Judge Stiles will probably stick it to ol' AA-Acme for the whole quarter million."

"I don't know what to do," she said. "I'm terrified all the time. I hear a sound in the middle of the night and I can't get back to sleep." She took a sip from her bottle and paused a moment, reflecting. "I've almost considered looking for a job with another paper. One on the other side of the continent."

Franks changed positions in the chair, wincing as pain shot through his lower back.

"I don't think you need to worry, Andy. For one thing, Jamie knows now that the whole county's watching his every move. And Rabon knows that, too. I wouldn't be surprised if he stays hunkered down in his little cottage until the trial starts. Secondly, he's had personal relationships with these other women. It's not like he's just crashing into houses like some kind of barbarian and running off with screaming women slung over his shoulder. He somehow seduces them into having a drink with him, then he drugs 'em. I'm still not sure exactly how he pulls that off. Maybe he finds them out walking and talks 'em into gettin' in his van." He stared with a wrinkled brow at the wrestlers on the television screen.

"That just occurred to me. That might explain why nobody put these two together." He shrugged and took another slug from the bottle. "Either way, you don't figure to be a target."

She nodded and stared down at the beer bottle. After a long silence, she said, "What you're saying probably holds true for most of the other women in Richfield. But my situation is a little different." She sighed wearily and began peeling the label off the bottle's neck. Her eyes finally rose and locked onto his. "I've never told anyone this before," she said, her voice low and filled with mortification, "but I slept with Jamie."

The investigator stared, slack-jawed. "You've got to be kidding."

She shook her head. Franks thought he saw a tear running down her cheek.

"I'm sorry, Andy," he said. "I didn't mean...that was rude of me. I was just very surprised—"

"I know, I know." She swiped at her cheek with the back of her right hand. "Looking back on it now, it all seems so stupid. But back then—" She paused, eyes glazed, fingernails picking at the bottle label. "I don't know. I mean, I was single, he was single. I met him at a party and he asked me out. He seemed pretty intelligent and was *very* nice looking. We went out to the movies, out to eat. You know, the usual boring Richfield date stuff." She took a deep breath and exhaled slowly. "I ended up sleeping with him a few times. Nothing seemed that abnormal. Except that he was a totally self-involved jackass." She laughed ironically. "I, of course, thought I could change him."

"So how long did this...*relationship* last?"

"A month, maybe two. Then I saw him out one night with another woman and I realized he was worthless. I went over to his house the next day, got my things, and that was that. About a week later he started leaving messages on my machine. He was all, 'I'm sorry, I screwed up, give me another chance,' at first. When I didn't call him back, the messages became more frequent. Also, more disturbing and hateful. In the end, he actually threatened me."

"Threatened you? In what way?"

"Just, 'come back or there's no telling what I might do.' Different things like that."

"Do you have any of these threats recorded?"

"No, I erased them all. I guess I wanted to believe he was only running his mouth, that he was really harmless. If I'd only have known—"

"When was all this going on?"

"In the late spring, early summer. About a month before he started his killing spree."

Franks finished off his beer and tried to let this information sink in. It certainly filled in some blanks in the state's case against Jamie Amerson. It also gave him a new and different evaluation of the possible risk to Andy. But it also raised a number of disturbing questions.

"I know what you're thinking," she said, at last.

"What am I thinking?"

"You're wondering why I didn't come forward with this information. And how I can still cover the case."

"I think that would be pretty accurate."

She sighed. "Hell, Bobby, I didn't know *what* to do. I mean, I'm stuck covering the case—I didn't ask for it, it got assigned to me—and, all of the sudden, ya'll had Jamie in custody. Suddenly everything made sense. But then I realized that, if I came forward, I might be called as a witness, and so—" She carefully placed the bottle on a pile of newspapers on the coffee table. "I haven't told anyone about this. I have my reasons. I think it would be the end of me down at the paper." Her eyes, large and gorgeous, blinked back tears. "For a lot of different reasons."

Franks rubbed the salt-and-pepper stubble on his chin. His eyes, locked on hers for a long while, slowly drifted to other areas of her body.

"I reckon I understand," he said, finally.

"More to the point, I think you understand now why I'm afraid to stay at home. Not only am I probably on his 'hit' list, he probably hates me more than ever for all the stories I've written about the case." A sharp, bitter laugh. "I never really expected him to get out."

"Yeah. Me, neither."

Her eyes drifted casually toward the bookcase. She leaned in that direction, squinted, and plucked one of three framed photographs off the top. It depicted Bobby dressed in a ball cap, flannel shirt and blue jeans, standing between a cow and a calf.

"Who's the cowboy?" she asked.

Franks laughed. "Uh, that would be me."

"You raised cattle?"

"Affirmative. Once, long ago. Sometime in a prior life."

She put a hand over her mouth. "I can't believe it! Here I am, a committed vegetarian, and there you are—"

"A barbaric animal killer?"

Her face reddened. "Well, no. I mean, I wasn't gonna be so harsh about it."

"Well, I haven't been a cattleman for years. In the end, it got the best of me. My marriage, my finances, my health. And, like I said, me."

She stared down at the picture. "Who're your friends in the picture?"

"It's kind of a long story."

"I'm not in a hurry."

Franks again ran his fingers through his hair. "Well, the little guy's name was Chip." He laughed. "Short for cow chip. Kind of a private joke. Anyway, the cow's name was Beulah—"

Her brow wrinkled. "You named all your cows?"

"Oh, no. Just three or four, the special ones."

"Chip and Beulah were special?"

"Yeah, they were. We had taken Beulah's calf away. Sent him off to a feed lot as soon as he was weaned. Beulah just wandered around for a few days, looking for her calf. She finally went up to the barn and just stayed there by herself. Wouldn't have anything to do with the rest of the herd. We couldn't get her to eat or anything. Finally I put Chip, this orphaned calf, up there with her. We'd been bottle-feeding Chip for a few days, and he was kind of pitiful, too. I didn't know what would happen, but I thought I'd give it a shot. It took a couple of days, but she finally let him nurse. Next thing you know, it's just like they were natural mother and calf." He folded his hands in his lap. "That picture was taken when Chip was about seven months."

"That's a sweet story," she said. "Please don't tell me they ended up in someone's taco."

"No, no way. I kept them, at least as long as I had my farm. Beulah went back to the herd, and Chip, well. Chip was still hanging around, even if a couple of his essentials weren't, if you know what I mean."

She nodded, then said, "Answer a question for me."

"It ain't gonna be in the newspaper, is it?"

She laughed. "No, this is just for my own…understanding."

He shrugged. "Okay. Shoot."

"Can you still eat beef after that?"

He stared at her for a moment. "Of course, I can. Why wouldn't I?"

"Because you've been able to see the love a mother cow has for her baby, and for another baby. It's like humans. The decent ones, anyway. You can't eat animals who feel that way."

He made a face. "They don't feel that way, or any way, for that matter. They have brains about the size of tennis balls. And it *ain't* love. It's instinct, pure and simple."

She sighed and placed the picture back on the bookcase. "It's obvious I'm not gonna convert you." Then she flashed a grin at him. "Not today, anyway."

"Nope. I'm a hardcore carnivore. Probably always will be."

They sat in silence for a few moments. Finally, Andy sighed wearily and got to her feet.

"I guess I'll head back," she said. "I'll just have to protect myself the best I can." She walked to the door and pulled it open.

"Hold on a second," Franks said. He got up and went into the back of the apartment. A few minutes later, he emerged with a pistol in his hand. "Have you ever handled an automatic before?"

She shook her head. "I've never handled any kind of gun before."

"It's really easy," he said. "You just insert the magazine, pull back the slide to put a round in the chamber, aim, and shoot."

Eyes open wide, she took the weapon from him. "This is yours?" she asked.

"Yeah," he replied. "One of them. I have about ten pistols. This one is not what you'd call top-of-the line. But it'll blow a hole in Jamie Amerson."

"Is it loaded now?"

"Got a full magazine. All you have to do is pull back the slide, jack one in the chamber. Then hold the weapon with both hands, aim and squeeze the trigger."

She held it in her right hand, testing its weight. She grinned at the investigator.

"Thanks, Bobby," she said, at last.

"You just gotta promise me two things. First, go down to the Sheriff's Department and get yourself a permit. I'll call Gordy Childs and grease the skids for you."

She nodded.

"Next, I want you to agree to meet me within the next week for shooting lessons." He grinned. "And, after that, maybe for dinner and a few drinks."

"You got it," she said. "Just call."

She gave him a hug, kissed him on his right cheek, and walked out into the stifling night.

CHAPTER 18

▼

"I think that went pretty well," Kevin Rose said. His voice, an engineered mono-tone, floated from the back seat of Katie's Jeep. The remark broke the silence that had enveloped the prosecutors since their meeting in the Bidewell women's dor-mitory's conference room had concluded four minutes earlier.

Katie shot a quick and annoyed rear-view-mirror glance at her chief deputy. He was reclining languidly in the back seat, staring out the side window. As it happened, there was nothing to see out that window but the dorm's ornamental shrubbery—squat juniper, prickly-leafed holly, and cadaverous, fried azalea bushes—which confirmed to her that he had lapsed into his distant, ironic mode.

"Are you trying to be funny?" she asked. She returned her attention to her immediate task—maneuvering the vehicle through the dorm-lot maze created by illegally parked student cars.

"Hmm. Interesting question. Funny? I think not. I think it's fair to say that I was trying to be *something*. Maybe it was pungently satirical. Perhaps it was face-tious. Although I find that it takes the fun out of either satire or facetiousness when you have to explain—"

"Maybe you were just being an insensitive jay-bag," Berry Macklin offered from the front passenger seat.

Katie sighed and merged into the active late afternoon traffic on Park Drive. Two things were clear: The meeting *had* gone very poorly, and Kevin Rose had urgently warned her of this possibility in advance. The idea of the meeting had begun as a sensible concept on a very small scale: a face-to-face between Katie and her top lawyers and the roommates and close friends of Kerry Grinder and Donna Crawley, the last people besides the killer to have seen the women alive.

Although each of the coeds had previously been interviewed by Bobby Franks or Brant Woodley, it remained possible that some obscure but critical piece of information had been overlooked. An offhanded comment, an interrupted confidential report, a brief sighting—anything that might directly and dramatically link Jamie Amerson with his victims. For the sake of the case, for the victim's families, for her own peace of mind. And what better dynamic for dislodging an overlooked tidbit than collective sharing in some neutral and non-threatening environment?

But it hadn't taken long for the simple information-sharing session envisioned by Katie to degenerate into a quasi-public gripefest. When family, neighbors, college officials, and other "concerned citizens," enraged by the adverse bond ruling and determined to be included in the information loop, learned of the meeting, they insisted on attending. Thus, Katie and her contingent arrived at the dorm to find, in addition to the coeds, a small community of people, including Dean Sherman Wilker, attorney Bru Nix, and several frustrated relatives of the murdered women. Kevin Rose had immediately cautioned that this infusion of belligerents would impede the free flow of information and advised his boss to postpone the planned session. But Katie had already been accused of incompetence and stonewalling; she didn't want to do anything that might further alienate these theoretical allies. Besides, the meeting was taking place on the Carry campus, so she'd be hard put to exclude Wilker or Bru Nix, the school's counsel. So they had proceeded as originally planned, with Katie positioned at the head of the huge conference table, and the Carry women arrayed in a semicircle between her and her glowering critics.

It had been a disaster from the onset. Ima Grinder Lee, who had initiated her public campaign of outrage before her sister's body had ever been discovered, set the general tone when she suggested that a special prosecutor should be retained by the victim's families in order "to put them on an equal legal footing with the defendant." Before Katie could respond, Dean Wilker had added, unctuously and with large eyeballs rolling, "perhaps we should give Madam District Attorney another opportunity to justify the taxpayer's investment."

Things had gone downhill from there. The coeds, clearly confused and intimidated by the hostile preemptive strikes directed at the D.A., had very little to add to their previous statements to police. Marcia Rainey, Kerry Grinder's sometime roommate, rocked in her chair and sucked on bunched-up ends of her hair as she mumbled a few nearly unintelligible remarks. Yes, she said, Jamie and Kerry had "dated." The relationship had lasted "about three, four, maybe six weeks." When asked about the specifics of the relationship, she had shrugged and stated that

Kerry had "dumped" Jamie "because he was wanting her to do a threesome" with "some dude he hung with," and that this suggestion had "totally made her want to break up with him." She concluded by saying that she hadn't seen Kerry for several days before her disappearance, and had no idea who she might have been with. Ronda Mattice, one of Donna Crawley's friends, offered that Donna "seemed to be on decent terms" with Jamie, and that she "never really talked a lot" about their breakup. Despite Katie's diligent follow-up questioning, no additional information had been volunteered. The students soon retreated completely into an arms-folded, foot-wagging silence. In fact, no one in the room spoke again until a middle-aged woman suggested that Katie "had no business being D.A., much less the prosecutor in this important case." That sentiment was echoed by others in the room. At last, Bru Nix—a most unlikely ally, to be sure—rose, and in Katie's defense, suggested that it was a difficult case and that the D.A. should be given time to "get it put together." After this flirtation with fairness was greeted with furrowed brows and low grumbling, Katie thanked everyone and abruptly announced that the meeting was concluded.

"Screw all those assholes, anyway," Berry Macklin said now, as the Jeep rolled down Park, along the edge of the Southpark neighborhood. "I mean, we get paid to use our professional judgment and discretion to handle criminal cases. We don't have to jump just because a bunch of snoots got their trunks all in a wad."

Katie didn't reply as she brought the vehicle to a stop at a traffic light at Park and State. She leaned over the steering wheel and stared sullenly out into the intersection. The afternoon sun torched the abandoned sidewalks. Convection waves shimmered from the steaming asphalt.

"You okay?" Macklin asked.

Before she could reply, a battered van, its red paint faded from wear and the sun, rumbled through the intersection, heading west on State. The outrageous scene that followed unfolded so quickly that it took her a full fifteen seconds to respond. The driver, clearly the bearded man from the courthouse coffee shop, leaned out the open window and, mouthing some apparently angry words, jabbed his middle finger insolently in Katie's direction. When the full import of this act finally registered on her, Katie turned to Berry Macklin, her jaw slack with disbelief.

"Did you see what he did, Berry?"

Macklin nodded. "The ol' half-a-peace sign. Who the hell *was* that?"

The car behind the Jeep honked angrily. The light had turned green. Katie stomped the accelerator and wheeled quickly west on State. The engine roared and the tires squealed as the vehicle began making up ground on the speeding van.

"It's the fool who yelled out in the courtroom the other day."

Kevin Rose said, "I guess the next question would be, what are we doing chasing him?"

"I'd like to know who he is, Kevin."

Berry Macklin braced himself against the dashboard. "I cannot believe this. Momma talked me into going to law school so I could have a respectable job, and I'm in my second high-speed chase in two weeks. I should've been a funeral director, like my uncle. Then everybody treats you with respect, and they all get their butts out of the way when you're on the road."

Katie maneuvered in and out of the thick flow of traffic, but she wasn't able to gain on the speeding van. When the light at the next intersection turned red, Katie slowed her vehicle and abandoned the pursuit. She could see the van steer sharply to the right and disappear behind a row of businesses two blocks down the road.

"Don't tell me you're giving up," Kevin Rose moaned from the back seat. "I was just starting to get into it."

"It's not worth endangering some innocent motorist," Katie muttered. "Besides, Andy Renauld told me he works around here somewhere. I'll find out who he is."

Macklin struck a prayerful pose, his eyes cast heavenward. "Thank you, Jesus."

Katie turned the Jeep back toward the courthouse.

"Don't you at least want to cruise the mean streets to see if we can find the van?" Rose asked.

"No. I'm dropping ya'll off at the courthouse, then I'm taking it home. I think I've struck out as many times today as I care to."

"All right," Con snarled at Garrett. "Try it again, only this time, make it for real."

Katie was curled up with a *Southern Living* magazine on the leather couch while her husband and son grappled and practiced self-defense techniques in the open area between the family room and the extended kitchen. She flipped through the pages of the magazine, mechanically, her mind clearly elsewhere.

"Watch this, Mom," Garrett called out. "I'm gonna give Dad the head-butt."

Katie looked up with an annoyed expression. "What on earth are you teaching that child, Con?"

"It's part of his self-defense training. We've already covered eye-gouging and jewel-smashing." When his wife only scowled at him, Con added, "He's old enough to know some of these techniques."

"*Head-butting*, for crying out loud?"

"Hey, a boy needs to know certain things. Someone bigger, stronger tries to hurt him, it's the perfect defensive move."

"Watch, Mom," Garrett said. He pushed close to his father's chest, flexed his knees and sprang upward, his forehead targeting the center of his pretend "attacker's" face. Con pulled his head back at the last second, avoiding serious injury.

"You're a dead-beef goner, sucker," Garrett crowed. He followed up his attack with a flurry of pretend punches to his dad's unprotected midsection.

Katie shot a fierce look at her husband, then frowned at Garrett. "Have you finished your homework yet?"

Garrett turned to his father, a worried look on his face. "Dad said I could finish it after—"

Katie glanced at the mantle clock. "It's almost eight. You need to finish your homework and take your bath. Now get going. Your daddy and I have something to discuss."

"Aw, Mom. Dad and I—"

"Garrett! Don't argue about this. I'm not in the mood."

The boy shuffled off, muttering to himself. Con sighed and collapsed against the door frame.

"I made him promise me he wouldn't ever use it unless he was really in trouble—"

"He's not even ten years old," Katie protested. "You know how those kids are. My God, that could kill someone!"

"If he'd known that technique when those bastards kidnapped him—"

Katie's jaw went slack. "Are you insane? When he was four years old? When a bunch of fully grown professional killers grabbed him?"

Con shrugged. "Well, if it ever happens again, he'll be ready."

Katie threw the magazine on the coffee table. "My head's killing me. I'm gonna take some aspirin and get ready for bed." She picked up a glass of water from the table and pushed past her husband.

Con followed her to the staircase. Katie marched up the steps and Con stayed just behind her.

"Okay, what's the matter?" he asked when they reached the bedroom.

"I don't think it's very smart teaching a nine-year-old how to inflict serious physical injury on another child."

"He has to learn sometime. It's a brutal world out there. Besides, he's gonna be ten next month."

Katie walked into the vanity area of their master suite and got a bottle from the medicine cabinet. "Maybe the world's brutal because all the fathers are teaching their sons how to be brutal."

"Oh, c'mon. All dads have to teach their sons about fighting at some point. My dad taught me, his dad taught him. All dads since Piltdown Man. It's a testosterone-drenched rite of passage. Besides, do you really think his friends don't discuss all this stuff? He's the one that first brought up the topic of head-butts. I was just showing him the proper—"

Katie popped two tablets into her mouth and chased them with a gulp of water from the glass. "I don't want to discuss it, Conley. I think it's wrong, and that's all I have to say." She tried to push past Con again; this time he grabbed her and wrapped his arms around her waist.

"Okay, girlfriend. What's really the matter?"

"Nothing." She pushed against his chest, broke free, and sat on the edge of their bed. "I just don't want my son going around school head-butting everyone."

"Uh-uh. There's something else. You called me Conley. You never do that unless you're super-pissed or super-depressed."

Katie sighed and rubbed her face with her hands. "It's everything," she said. After holding her head in her hands for a minute, she looked up at him with weary eyes. "How could you ever have let me become D.A.?"

He sat next to her on the bed. "You said it was something you wanted to do."

"Well, I must have been delusional at the time." A tear rolled down her cheek and she brushed it angrily away with the back of her left hand. Con plucked a tissue from a box at the end of her dressing table and handed it to her. "It's just been awful the last few weeks."

"Wanna tell me about it?"

She took a deep breath and dabbed at her eyes. After a moment, she began describing the disquieting moments of her very recent past, beginning with the details of the disastrous meeting at the college. She finally got around to the bearded man—his obnoxious staring, his comments, and the van stunt from earlier that day.

"You have any idea who it might be?"

"He looks so familiar, but I can't place him."

"Did you get his tag number?"

She shook her head. "He didn't have one. At least, not one that I could see."

"Does Franks know about this?"

She shook her head again. "I just came straight home. I…I didn't really know who to tell." She paused. "Or whether I should say anything at all—"

He made a face. "My God, Katie! Why *wouldn't* you say something about that? I mean, in one sense, he's been stalking you. At a minimum, it's harassment."

"Because you wouldn't have worried about it if it'd happened to you."

He stared at her for a moment. "I'm not so sure that's true," he said, finally. "But even if it is, that's me, not you—"

"See…that's what I'm talking about. I'm the district attorney, Con. I'm not supposed to get all freaked by stuff like that. It's not supposed to make any difference that I'm a woman." She paused, twisting the tissue. "All I need is everyone saying, 'The new chick D.A. not only can't get a murderer off the streets, she's scared of her own shadow'."

"Katie—"

She got to her feet and walked over to her dressing table. She threw the tissue into the wicker waste paper basket tucked away in the table's kneehole.

"It's true, Con. You know it, and I know it. It shouldn't matter that I'm a woman D.A., but it *does* matter. To some people, anyway. To the mac-daddies at the country club, to the Nixes and the good ol' boy network, to the big dogs over at the college. And that's fine. I never imagined that everyone would like or support me. I just never dreamed I'd be the town laughingstock." Her eyes met his. "If I unravel, I want it to be private. I don't want to be some quivering spectacle on the six o'clock news."

Con stood behind her and began to massage her shoulders. "You're being too hard on yourself, baby. All anyone can reasonably expect is for you to be diligent and fair. And you've been both of those things. And more. Sure, this stuff is kind of sticky right now. But it'll work itself out. It always does. A year from now, Amerson will be convicted and nobody'll remember any of these details." He kissed her lightly on her head. "You wait and see."

She turned to face him and wrapped her arms around his neck. She knew that he was partly right—she had been an effective trial lawyer and a decent office administrator. But there was much more to being a good D.A. than those two tasks. She knew she also had to be a leader—strong, independent, and unafraid. She had played the role, but she was really weak and indecisive. It had taken the Amerson controversy to draw out her weaknesses, but now playtime was officially over. Now everyone could see the empress was naked.

"It's not that simple, Con," she muttered, finally.

"What do you mean?"

"I don't even know how to tell you." A long pause. "I'm not sure Amerson did it."

He pushed back slightly from her. "I don't understand—"

"I can't explain it, Con. Call it intuition—"

"No," he said. "Let's don't call it that. Not intuition. Intuition won't play in Richfield. That's the one thing that *will* get you voted out of office."

"I don't know what else to call it. I've just had this feeling, this gnawing but persistent feeling, ever since the day we executed that search warrant. It's like there isn't one single cinching piece of evidence. There just *isn't*. There're all these other things. Little things, all neat, all perfectly arranged. Maybe a little too perfectly arranged. Do you know what I mean?"

"Not exactly. It sounds like Rabon Creasey's gotten inside your head."

"No," she replied defiantly, "nobody's gotten inside my head. It's just experience and common sense. Yes, and intuition, too."

"Well, what are you saying, then? That Amerson's being framed?"

"I don't know, Con. I really don't. I'm starting to wonder if I even know what I'm talking about anymore."

Con squeezed her tighter. "Come on, girlfriend. Shake it off. You'll get past this. You're just dealing with a bunch of unhappy and anxious people. They think they're being helpful, but they're not." He kissed her again. "Every prosecutor doubts himself or herself from time to time."

She held onto him tightly, rocking gently in his strong arms.

"Did you ever doubt yourself when you were a prosecutor?" she asked.

"Me? No. Never did. I guess I should have said, *almost* every prosecutor—"

She playfully bumped his chin with her head. "How'd you like one of your head-butts, butthead?"

He grinned. "If you're gonna do it, do it correctly," he said. "Flex your knees, then, using your forehead—pow! Right in the old nose."

"That sounds painful."

"Oh, it's painful, all right."

She bent her knees and was about to explode upward when she froze in place.

"What is it?" he asked.

"Shhh. Listen."

There was a low rumble in the street outside the house. It sounded like an old truck slowly cruising Kyle Ridge Road. She stepped to the window and pulled the curtains apart. She could see a dark-colored van with its lights turned off slowly negotiate the turn in the circle at the end of the street. As it passed under a dim streetlight—the only operating lamp on that end of the street—she could tell that it was faded red in color. She could also see damage to the left front fender. The vehicle came to a stop when it was facing the side of their house.

She shut the curtains and turned to her husband. Her heart began to pound. "Con—It's him! It's the van! The man with the beard—he knows where I live!"

Con switched off the overhead light and moved to the window. He opened the curtains and peered into the darkness.

He stared for a minute, then muttered to himself. He walked briskly to the closet and reached under a pile of sweaters stacked on the top shelf. After feeling about for a few seconds, he retrieved a chrome-plated pistol. He carried the gun to his dresser, opened the top drawer, and began searching under socks and folded underwear for the weapon's magazine.

"What do you think you're doing?" Katie asked.

"I'm gonna go block off the street with my car. Please call RPD and get a unit headed up here." He continued to search for the loaded magazine he'd hidden months earlier.

"It's not in there," Katie said. "Garrett wouldn't have any problem getting into that drawer. I put it up in my closet. But it doesn't matter. You're not gonna go out there and start shooting up this van."

Con frowned at her, then laid the pistol on top of the dresser. "I wasn't planning on 'shooting up' the van. It was just for protection. You know, just in case." He slipped into a pair of deck shoes and began clambering down the stairs. "But I'll be fine. If he pulls a gun on me, I'll ward off the bullets with my secret plasma force field."

"Don't you think you should just let the police handle it?"

"I don't want him to get away," he replied. "I want to know who this bastard is."

"Be careful, Con," she called out to him as she dialed the number of police dispatch. "If he tries to go, let him. We'll find out who he is eventually."

Garrett stuck his head out of his door. "I wanna go with Dad."

"You're not going anywhere," Katie said sternly. "Go back and finish your homework."

Garrett scowled and closed his door.

Katie cradled the phone in the crook of her neck. Suddenly learning the man's identity didn't seem so immediately vital. She knew that Franks would be able to track him down—Richfield wasn't that big a town.

Right now, more than anything, she just wanted Con to be safe.

Con jammed his Ford Taurus into reverse and screeched out of the garage. He backed out a little too forcefully, however, and struck Garrett's basketball goal. The metal pole swayed precariously but didn't fall. Without turning on his lights, Con slipped the car into "drive" and floored the accelerator. Again, he was unable to control the vehicle and it crashed into a thick privet hedge that lined the driveway. As he was attempting to back out of the hedge, he saw the van fly by on the street.

He sped down the long driveway and fishtailed into the street, but he soon realized that it'd be futile to pursue the van. Kyle Ridge was a curvy and narrow road and the van had too much of a head start. Too many things could happen during a high-speed chase on a dangerous road, and almost all of them were bad.

He pulled back into the driveway, cursed aloud and pounded the steering wheel with his fist.

CHAPTER 19

―――――――――――― ▼ ――――――――――――

Franks took a drag on his cigarette and leaned over the steering wheel of his Crown Victoria. He gave a quick glance down a deserted alley, blew a smoke ring out his window, then angrily punched his accelerator. The vehicle lurched and then, gathering speed, rumbled toward the College Street intersection. Franks braked at the corner, tossing quick glances up and down the street. He checked his watch and muttered to himself. Damn waste of time, he thought—committing police assets and time to a search for something that was probably nothing. And it had all been Katie O'Brien's doing. After an agitated early-morning plea to the chief of police, a BOLO—a dispatch advising officer's to "be on the lookout"—had been issued for an old red van and its bearded driver. Precisely which crimes the man was supposed to have committed remained a huge mystery to the investigator. The "suspect"—or someone else in a red van—had parked near Katie's house. Not a crime, to the best of his knowledge. This person had also stared at her in the courthouse coffee shop. *Stared at her*. That one almost made Franks laugh. If he was given a dollar for every time some crackhead or gang-banger had tried to stare him down, he'd never have to work again. But Katie, who usually dealt with the unsavory element from across a well-guarded courtroom or with an armed D.A. investigator by her side, found this rudeness unacceptably threatening. Unlike the average citizen, she happened to have the political stroke to set this low-scale dragnet into action. As a result, he'd spent the best part of his morning cruising the alleys and back streets of the Richfield business district looking for a beaten-up van or a man with a shaggy beard. Instead of working on the open investigation files stacked in an ever-growing pile on the corner of his desk.

As much as he liked and respected Katie, it was becoming increasingly obvious to him that the Amerson case had already gotten the best of her. And this development wasn't really all that surprising. She'd been tortured by doubts about the case since her first involvement. She'd questioned the quantity and quality of evidence he'd gathered, only reluctantly approved the search and arrest warrants, and now was emitting paranoid blather about being stalked by a savage bearded man in a red van. Whether she realized it or not, she'd already inflicted serious damage on the state's case by creating a new "alternative" suspect. And, despite the chief's philosophical dismissal of Katie's report as "just something to rule out," Franks knew that this complaint and investigation would come back to bite them. It wouldn't matter now if the mystery man had absolutely nothing to do with the murders—the simple fact that *he'd been targeted* as a possible suspect would be seized upon by the defense. Rabon Creasey seldom overlooked such investigative distractions; once he identified a weakness, he exploited it. Reasonable doubt was all he needed to win, and an investigation that veered wildly off course almost always reeked of doubt, reasonable or not, to Bienville County jurors.

Franks turned onto College Avenue and cruised slowly east until he reached the Carry campus. He pulled into a parking place directly in front of James Hall, the administration building, took a drag off the cigarette, and let his eyes drift over the row of buildings that symmetrically framed the campus's arched and wisteria-draped entrance. The college had buildings of almost every architectural style, but these elegant Greek Revival buildings—the president's home, the administration building, two sorority houses—and meticulously landscaped grounds created an impressive and distinctively southern image for the world outside the campus.

Which was, Franks understood well, very much *his* world. He had lived in Richfield ever since his discharge from the service twenty years earlier. He had often walked or driven down this block and envied the students, books tucked under their arms, languidly shuffling under magnolias and towering moss-swaddled oaks, seemingly immune to the trouble that seemed to be contained north of College Street. He often wondered what it might have been like to have been installed as a teenager in such an idyllic sanctuary, to have been granted a reprieve from the harsh sentence life had arbitrarily imposed on him. But the campus had remained a foreign land—distant, forbidding, unattainable. For a few years following the birth of his children, he occasionally allowed himself to indulge in the dream that they'd one day stroll in his stead on that sacrosanct expanse of ivory and green.

But his tenure as a uniform policeman had compelled him to observe the campus with a less idealistic eye. He had stood on the steps of the stately buildings and seen that the pediments and friezes were cracked and peeling. He'd arrested drunk and boisterous students and had been caught in the crossfire between his sworn duty and the politics of privilege. And, of course, there'd been that one exceptionally unfortunate episode—the brutality charge that, although unwarranted in his own mind, had forever changed his career, his life.

Now, all these years later, Franks looked out on the campus and saw nothing more than desiccated greenery and underappreciated space. And, of course, fear. Frazzled from the unresolved menace and baked by drought and relentless heat, Carry College looked more like a desert wasteland than a bustling and verdant campus.

He pulled back onto College and continued to roll slowly east. A few prematurely brown leaves scuttled and tumbled across the road in front of his car. He turned south onto Park, cruised the edge of the campus, then turned east again onto Poplar. Andy Renauld lived on Poplar, two blocks down on the right. He thought he'd swing by there and check on the house as long as he was in the area. It was the least he could do, under the circumstances.

Andy. He'd been with her the previous afternoon, having sneaked off during his "lunch break" to meet her for a shooting lesson. But they had never gotten around to guns and ammo. They hadn't even made it past the living room. They had made love where they had tumbled—on the living room rug. Now, as he approached her house, the thrilling details of that encounter filled his veins like a powerful drug: Andy naked except for her open cotton blouse, his hands, exploring her firm body, the taste of her as his tongue explored her smooth skin. She made love like he imagined she did everything in her life: mounted on top, passionately, in control. Afterward, as she lay against his body, her heart beating wildly against his chest, he realized that he was hooked. As unlikely as their relationship had once seemed, it now felt absolutely right. Her power over him was simply overwhelming.

But this episode had also convinced him of her odd vulnerability. He recalled now that, as they lay in lovemaking's narcotic afterglow, she seemed strangely tense. When a wind gust caused the bare tip of a tree branch to peck on a window pane, she reacted visibly.

"What's wrong?" he had asked.

She had pushed up on her left arm and stared wide-eyed at the window. At last she had replied, "Every time I hear a sound, I just know Jamie's about to break in." When she had identified the source of the pecking sound, she settled back into Franks's arms. "I know it's stupid," she murmured. "As long as he's out there, I just can't help feeling afraid."

"It's not stupid," he had replied. He gently kissed her cheek. "But he's not gonna come to your house. Like I told you, that's not his...M.O." After a moment, he started laughing.

"What's so dadgum funny?" she had asked.

"I don't know. A couple of things."

"For example..."

"Well, I don't think I've ever actually said 'M.O.' before." He had laughed again. "Also, Jamie's especially not gonna come here when *I'm* here."

She had smiled and melted into him. They lay there, in silence and each other's arms, for a long while. Outside, the sky darkened and the wind grew stronger.

Franks suddenly began to sing: "*You and me and rain on the roof...*" He blushed now as he recalled this uncharacteristic rhapsodic interlude, the old Lovin' Spoonful tune done great harm by his raspy, off-key rendering. "Are we actually gonna get some rain?"

"Probably not," she had replied. "I'm convinced it's never gonna rain again."

Thunder swelled and rolled, then receded into the distance.

"Not gonna rain, huh?" he had asked.

"Nothing but fake thunder, dry and sterile."

He made a face at her. "*Dry and sterile?* Where the hell did *that* come from?"

She shrugged. "Can't say. Somebody said it once. Thought it sounded cool."

He noticed a photograph in a frame on top of a speaker cabinet. It depicted a man standing in the doorway of a small log cabin in the middle of the woods. He appeared to be in his twenties, medium height and build, dark hair. Franks propped himself on an elbow and studied the photo more closely. In the upper-left corner, there was a blur of red and white in a gap in the oak and pine trees. Nothing in the photo looked familiar.

"It's my brother," Andy said, anticipating Franks's question. "Half-brother, actually. He's at his hunting cabin on the mountain."

"What mountain?"

"How should I know? I'm not sure it even has a name. It's out that way." She pointed toward the back of her house. Before the inevitable flurry of follow-up questions began, she added, "He's in the service, stationed in Germany. Haven't seen him in a while. I go up there occasionally, mostly when I need to be alone."

"Is it in Bienville County?"

"I think so. I'm not sure." She glanced at her watch and, with a panicked expression, bolted upright. "Oh, man! I've got an interview in ten minutes!"

And, just like that, the moment's magic had expired. They had dressed hurriedly and in silence, and with a perfunctory parting kiss, returned to their professional responsibilities.

Her house was in the middle of the long second block of Poplar Street in the leafy Southpark section of Richfield. The neighborhood had come into being just after the arrival of the twentieth century and many of these houses had been built in that century's first decades. Most of the homes on Poplar were cottages or colonial, prairie, or California-style bungalows, medium-sized, mostly one-story dwellings with posted porches and sloping gables. Andy had a California bungalow, a compact house with a broad gable positioned symmetrically above a weathered stone porch. Directly across Poplar Street from her driveway, a short cul-de-sac provided driveway access for the two houses on either side.

Franks slowed his car and studied Avery's house as he passed. He noticed that a few shingles were missing from the roof and that the trim was in need of paint. And the yard was in terrible shape—hedges and bushes were ragged and the grass appeared to be dying of thirst. He made a note to himself to check back with her about helping with yard work.

He was so preoccupied with the house and yard that he almost missed the vehicle parked at the end of the cul-de-sac.

In fact, only his many years of police training and experience allowed him to piece together the discrete units of sensation—fragments of color, shape and size—accessed through his peripheral vision as he passed the stretch of road. These snippets of information fused instantly into a perception of something threatening, out of place. He slammed on his brakes and threw the car into reverse.

And there it was: a GMC van, faded red in color, left front fender crumpled and rusted. The vehicle was parked at the end of the street near a concrete drainage ditch, a man-made boundary separating the Poplar Street houses from the park. Franks could see a man behind the steering wheel. He could tell only that he seemed fairly large and had a graying beard.

The investigator called in a backup unit and swung his car into the cul-de-sac. He positioned the Crown Vic sideways, essentially blocking the van in. He knew enough about search and seizure law to realize that this act probably amounted to a de facto arrest of the man, but he couldn't worry about procedural details at that particular moment. There was a BOLO for the man; more importantly, he was obviously watching Andy's house.

A sickening wave of anxiety washed over him. Could it be that Katie was right, that this individual might actually be involved with the kidnappings? It really couldn't be possible—the evidence against Amerson was simply overwhelming. Katie had argued that this evidence might be nothing more than a string of coincidences, but what bizarre coincidence could explain the strange man's surveillance of Andy's house? Franks angrily shook off these annoying conflicting thoughts. There'd be plenty of time later to search for the truth, to make all the pieces fit. Right now his mission was to secure this stranger, identify him, and seize any case-significant evidence.

The man suddenly jumped from the van and began running toward the park. Franks opened his door and ordered him to stop, but his command voice only prompted the stranger to run faster. The investigator quickly collected his Beretta, his handcuffs and a canister of O/C spray, and began to give chase. He grimaced as each booted footfall caused crippling explosions of lower-back pain. Franks soon realized that he really didn't have much of a chance in this foot pursuit—the object of the chase was exceptionally agile for a large, middle-age person. Still, Franks was able to keep the man in his sight, at least until he veered into a thickly wooded area at the northwest edge of the park. Franks continued the chase until his back and scarred lungs finally gave out. Then he sagged against a tree and cursed the fact that he had neglected to grab his hand-held radio. He breathlessly issued another order for the man to stop, but knew the stranger couldn't even hear him.

Rubbing his aching lower back, he began trudging back toward the cul-de-sac. He figured the patrol officers would have a decent shot at rounding up the suspect. After all, if the man was even half as winded as *he* was, he wouldn't get very far.

Besides, he'd had left behind a critical piece of evidence—the suspect van.

And Bobby Franks knew that, even though he was no longer worth a damn in a foot pursuit, he could still search an impounded van with the best of them.

CHAPTER 20

▼

Katie and Kevin Rose followed Bobby Franks down the narrow hallway that led to his office. Franks had met them at the entrance to the stairway on the first floor. He had nodded to the two prosecutors as they crossed the vestibule, but he seemed sullen and preoccupied. Katie had worried that the doubts she'd expressed about Amerson's guilt might have strained her working relationship with Franks. His uncharacteristically flat affect did nothing but confirm her suspicion.

Franks had left a message a half hour earlier that he had "the bearded man" in custody at the investigative division office. The man had been apprehended by two uniform officers after a woman discovered him crouching behind a shrub in her backyard. Now the man was being guarded in the interview room just down the hall from Franks's office.

"All right," Bobby Franks said, "here's what we know about our friend in there." He reclined in the chair behind his desk and played with the cow figurine. "For starters, he basically refused to talk to me, so this isn't gonna be easy. He said *maybe* he'd talk to Charlotte, whoever the hell that is. I think the bastard's just crazy. His name appears to be J.P. Marat. We got that from a handful of receipts we found in his van. He apparently makes his living selling scrap metal— aluminum, copper, whatever—to a couple of salvage businesses around the county. He had pieces of flashing, chunks of copper tubing, old faucets, all that kind of stuff in the van."

Kevin Rose asked, "Have you talked to any of these salvage dealers?"

"Just one, so far. Tommy Rowell from Bienville Salvage down in Talmadge. He said they have no personnel records on him because they pay him on a contract basis. He also said that this dude just showed up about six weeks ago with three bags of aluminum cans. He said they bought them, and he keeps coming back with more stuff. I think that's probably gonna be true for all the folks he's dealt with."

"Any idea where he might live?"

Franks grinned. "In my opinion, he's been mostly living out of his vehicle. We found boxes of crackers, empty sardine and tuna cans, stuff like that. Also, there was a ratty-ass sleeping bag. Looked like he'd found it in a garbage can. Rowell told us he sometimes stays at the rescue mission."

"What else did you find?" Katie asked.

Franks rocked back in his chair and threw his boots up on the desk. They landed with a disturbing thud. "Crap, mostly. We found a leather strap, looks like it might be a guitar strap, or something." He shrugged, as if to say that he'd already dismissed this article as being utterly without significance. "I got it bagged up, ready to go to forensics. I think I, myself, can rule it out as the murder instrument. I mean, it's pretty wide and the strangulation marks were all narrow, maybe an inch, tops. Otherwise, we're still processing the van—prints, trace evidence, the works. I looked it over pretty good and didn't see anything obvious. No clothing, hair, visible blood stains. Crime scene did Luminol sprays on the dash and doors and seats. Most of the interior is bare metal, so we're not gonna get anything there." Franks shrugged again. "As you know, Luminol don't work on metal." He paused, rotating the cow between his index fingers and thumbs, his brow furrowing as he mentally inventoried the evidence. At last, he added, "That's all I can think of right now."

Katie leaned forward, resting her elbows on the edge of the investigator's desk. "Did you run the vehicle?"

"Of course we did. Although we're still trying to figure out what we've got. It's registered to a woman in Tuscaloosa—" He leaned forward to check out a scrap of envelope sitting on his desk blotter. "—name of Alice Butler. I got a friend with the P.D. there checking her out."

"J.P. Marat, eh?"

"Right. J.P. M-a-r-a-t. That's the name on the invoices. I can't really say if that's really his name."

"Well, I can," Katie replied, "and it's not." This blunt declaration, issued in a flat voice, leaden with the weight of great certainty, landed like the thud of Franks's boots.

The investigator shot a quick look at Kevin Rose, then locked eyes with the district attorney.

"What makes you so sure?"

"For one thing," she said, "it's an obvious pseudonym. Jean-Paul Marat was a Nineteenth-century French political extremist. He was, if I recall my history, a leader of the Jacobins, a radical political group at the beginning of the revolution."

Franks cut another quick glance at Rose, then smiled patronizingly at Katie. "Do you really think some whacked-out junk dealer living out of his van would know about leaders of the French revolution?"

Katie returned his smile. "This one would. His real name is John Paul Fourier. He'd have reason to know all about Marat because he was once a rather distinguished professor in Carry's history department. The French Revolution and the Age of Napoleon were two of his specialty courses. At least they were until he broke into the apartment of one of his students and tried to rape her." She paused, making sure that this fact's raw significance wasn't lost on the investigator. "I was his prosecutor," she continued. "This was back when I was only two, three years out of law school. I was just doing property cases then. The file came to me as a routine burglary third. After Con realized that there was an attempted rape involved, he asked me if I felt comfortable keeping it." She shrugged. "As it happened, I did."

Franks didn't reply, but his expression confessed equal parts surprise and interest.

"He was tried and convicted," Katie continued. "Judge Caldwell sentenced him to twenty years. The last I heard of him, he was denied parole. We objected, but I think a handful of prison disciplinaries was what kept him in. I suppose he could be out by now."

"Wouldn't the parole board have let you know before they turned him loose?"

"Not if he EOS'd." Katie understood that the Alabama parole board often released prisoners who had reached their technical "end-of-sentence" without notifying victims or prosecutors.

"I'm sure they'll run his prints through the computer," Franks said. "So we'll know for sure—"

"I already know for sure, Bobby. That's him."

Franks shrugged. "All right. So it's this For-yay dude. That doesn't mean he did these murders."

"No, not by itself. But he's got a van and he's got a violent criminal history. He'd certainly have at least a passing familiarity with *The Waste Land*." She held his skeptical stare. "And he's one each disturbed dude. Even you have to admit that."

"He has no motive, Katie. We can prove all the above plus motive on Jamie Amerson."

Katie sighed. "What are you holding him on?"

"I guess that's where ya'll come in." He nodded in Kevin Rose's direction. "There's no way of knowing if any of the junk in his van had been stolen. And I don't know what the story on the van is. We didn't get a hit on it." He eyes searched the ceiling. "I don't suppose staring at people or their houses is a crime."

"Not to my knowledge."

"You can't think of anything?"

Katie shook her head.

He tossed the cow figurine onto his desk. "Well then, I guess we gotta cut him loose."

"We can't Bobby. At least not until we get the forensics back."

Franks let his boots drop to the floor and ran his fingers through his hair. "Well, all right, then. We'll just let him sit in jail. And when we get sued—"

"What do *you* think?" Katie demanded. "Why does this all have to be on me?"

"You're the one that called the chief with your trunks all in a wad—"

"And you're the one who caught him watching your girlfriend's house."

Blood rushed to the investigator's face. He crossed his arms defiantly and stared at the doodling on his desk blotter.

As if immediately regretting her remark, Katie quickly added, "I don't know *what* to think anymore, Bobby. I know you've worked your ass off on the case. I know there's a bunch of evidence pointing right at Jamie Amerson. But now we've got this other asshole to consider." She paused, choosing her words carefully. "I wish he'd never come along to complicate things, believe me. But he did, Bobby. He came to Richfield, he's got a history of predatory behavior, he's been seen acting suspiciously. We're just gonna have to deal with it. If we call him a suspect, Rabon Creasey will cram it down our throats. If we just disregard him, he'll make *that* an issue."

"So…"

"So I want to talk with him," Katie said.

Franks shook his head. "You'll be the only one talkin'. He said he'd only speak to *Charlotte*, remember?"

Katie's eyes bore into Franks's. "I think it may be me," she said. "I might be Charlotte."

Franks's brow knitted. "I don't understand—"

"He's pretending to be Jean-Paul Marat. That's the little game he's running. Marat was killed by a woman named Charlotte, a member of a rival political group."

Franks still look puzzled.

"Perhaps he thinks of me as his symbolic murderer. Because I helped put him prison." She paused. "Or maybe he *is* just crazy."

Franks got to his feet. "All right, Katie. Or Charlotte. Whoever you are. I'm ready anytime you are."

"You're not going in there. It's just gonna be me and him."

Franks blinked. "All by yourself?"

"I'm a big girl, Bobby. Despite what you might think."

"Well, I'm gonna be watching through the mirror. I'm at least gonna do that."

She shrugged and turned to leave the office. "Suit yourself," she said.

The interview room at CID had been constructed substantially to law enforcement standards. There were only four pieces of furniture in the room—a small desk, a chair for the subject being interviewed, and two chairs for interviewers. The office was arranged so that the interviewer would be positioned between the suspect and the door. This arrangement reduced the likelihood of escape, and also helped foster the symbolic notion that full disclosure might be the suspect's only way out. A small, hand-held micro-cassette recorder and two microphones sat on the table. A two-way mirror had been installed in a hole in the wall behind the suspect's chair. Investigators sitting in the adjoining office could observe the interview and operate the audio and video recording equipment.

Katie entered the room and asked the uniform officer, an apple-cheeked, second-shift rookie, to wait in the hall. He gave her a strange look and seemed frozen in his chair; when Franks appeared and motioned for him, he slowly got up and headed for the door. He lingered in the doorway.

Fourier was slumped forward in his chair, his arms crossed defiantly and his elbows propped on the table. He was wearing the same turtleneck sweater and bellbottom jeans that he'd worn in the coffee shop. The beret was gone, as were the pendant and amulets. The jeans were badly torn at the knee. Katie thought she saw crusted and dried blood on the margins of the tear. One of the earpieces was broken off the dark glasses; they sat in two pieces on the table's dull surface. His lower lip was fat and purple. In his phone message, Franks had mentioned that the arresting officers had had to fight him. Without the beret, she could see that his hairline had receded and that the remaining hair had turned almost white. She had little difficulty recognizing him now as a greatly aged version of the man she had prosecuted a decade earlier.

"Ma'am," the officer said, "if you need me for any reason—"

"I'll be fine," Katie said. She gently pushed him away and shut the door. She had only managed two steps toward one of the empty chairs when Fourier spoke.

"*Je ne voudrais pas parler avec vous,*" he snarled. "*T'est pas Charlotte.*"

Katie kept her eyes on him as she pulled out the chair and sat down. She had not expected to hear him speaking French, although it was certainly no surprise to hear the words roll off his tongue so effortlessly. Seeing him, unkempt, dirty, and ragged, it was easy to forget that he had written his doctoral thesis on some arcane aspect of the French Revolution. She also recalled now that he had been born and raised in Louisiana's Cajun country and had learned English as a second language. In fact, he was using the Cajun idiom at that very moment. Katie had studied "classical French," but knew enough of each variation to figure out what he meant.

She folded her arms and inclined her body toward him, replicating his body language. "I know I'm not Charlotte," she said. "You know perfectly well who I am."

He shrugged, as if utterly indifferent to her or her presence.

"Why were you parked near my house the other night?"

"Aren't you supposed to advise me of my rights before you question me?" He paused a moment, then sneered at her. "Or doesn't it matter, since all my other rights have already been violated?" With a knuckle on the back of his right hand, he gently massaged his swollen lip.

"Franks already read you your rights, asshole." She leaned back in the chair. "And I think you understand them quite well, in any event. My question was, why were you parked on my street the other night?"

He snorted defiantly. "For the record, I don't know what you're talking about. But I am somewhat startled to learn that you own the street." He broke into a slow grin. Katie could see that his teeth were badly discolored.

"What do you want?" she asked.

He snorted again. "Screw you. If you're so smart, go figure out what I want."

She glared at him, then angrily pushed back the chair and got to her feet.

"I don't have time for this," she said. She began walking toward the door, then turned and added, "Bobby Franks told me this'd be a waste of time."

"Franks is King of the Dicks and you're Queen of the Cunts." He began cackling, a rasping, unhealthy sound that soon degenerated into a consumptive cough.

She tapped on the door and turned back to Fourier. He was still coughing violently, his eyes bulging and red.

"*Elle avez trés peur, cela appellez Donna.*" The words were punctuated by agonized coughs.

The uniform officer opened the door, but Katie gestured for him to remain where he was. She was focusing now on the man's last utterance. *She was afraid, this woman named Donna.*

"Was it Donna Crawley?" she asked.

No reply.

"Where did you see her, Doctor Fourier?"

"I saw everything," he said. "Everything. I saw her face, I heard her voice. But I have nothing else to tell you. Not until I get what I want."

Katie turned again and walked into the hallway. Franks met her just outside the door.

"Did you hear that?" she fumed.

"I did better than hear it. Got it on tape. Sounds like a load of shit to me."

"I want him locked up," she said. Her eyes burned with indignation.

"Katie—"

"I'm serious, Bobby. Let him cool his heels for a day or so, then let's see if he's willing to talk."

"He doesn't know nothin'. He's just jerkin' you around."

"We'll see."

"What would we even charge him with?"

"Let's start with felony Hindering Prosecution. You oughta be able to get the magistrate to go ten thousand on his bond. No way he'll make that."

Franks sighed and stared at the floor. "You have any idea what this is gonna do to the Amerson case?"

"I'll worry about that when it goes to trial." She set her jaw. "*If* it goes to trial."

She began walking toward the staircase. Kevin Rose, who had been with Franks in the observation room, silently fell into step with her.

CHAPTER 21

▼

Andy Renauld slumped in her chair, two open reporter's notebooks in her lap. She cursed at her computer screen and slapped the side of the monitor with an open left hand. Yellow sticky-notes flew across her tiny cubicle.

Ed McKee, the city editor, appeared at the cubicle's opening.

"Everything okay?" he asked.

"Hell no, Ed. Everything's *not* okay. I'm trying to finish this stupid story on the power outages and the damn power blinks. I lost everything I put in."

McKee struggled to suppress a smile. He was a slightly built man in his early fifties. He wore a wrinkled shirt with a skewed tie hanging from the open, buttoned-down collar. His hands were thrust into the front pockets of loose-fitting khaki trousers. What little hair remained on top of his head had turned gray. He wore wire-rimmed glasses and had a perpetual look of concern on his face. Any expression remotely approaching a smile was so alien to his face's harsh terrain that it was almost impossible to conceal.

"It's not funny, Ed," Andy snapped. Her cheeks burned crimson. "I've been working all day trying to finish this story—it took the guy from the power company four hours to return my call—I got another story to file before I go home—" She turned away, her voice quivering at the edge of rage. "And now I gotta start all over again."

"I know it's not funny," McKee said. "But you have to admit it's ironic—a power outage interrupts your story on the inconvenience of power outages."

Andy shook her head and flipped the pages in one of the notebooks. "I guess I'm just not a big fan of irony right at the moment, Ed."

McKee rocked back and forth in his crepe-soled suede shoes. After an appropriate interval of apparent reflection, he asked, "Can you spare a few minutes to talk?"

Andy glanced at her watch. "I guess so. A few minutes." She shot an irritated look at her computer monitor. "Because the ancient equipment in this dump won't autosave for me, I'll be working all night." She tossed the notebooks onto her desk and swivelled her chair to face him.

"Let's go to Jim's office," McKee said. Jim Donnelly was the *Ledger*'s managing editor. He had gone home at six o'clock and his roomy office overlooking the maze of cubicles in the newsroom was vacant.

Andy sighed and followed the shuffling editor past two other cubicles and into the office. Phillip Henry, the business reporter, stuck his head up over the top of the partition and pretended to shudder with fear. Andy shot him a fierce look. McKee opened the office door and gestured for his writer to sit on the floral print love seat against one wall. She sagged instead into Jim Donnelly's high-back leather chair.

"I've always wondered how it would feel to sit in this chair," she said.

McKee eased into one of the two chairs facing the editor's desk. "Well? How does it feel?"

"Good. It feels good. The feel of power and control, for a change." She swivelled back and forth a few times then crossed her legs and smiled at McKee. "So what's up, Ed?"

The city editor, plainly not at ease, brushed his lint-less trousers and focused on the framed photograph of Jim Donnelly's wife and two children. McKee had worked his way up through the ranks at the *Ledger*, starting out as an overworked beat reporter, covering education and various county and municipal boards, authorities, and commissions. He had earned a reputation as competent—though not necessarily tenacious—and fair, and was generally well respected by the individuals he regularly interviewed. But he had never savored confrontation; he especially disliked having to reprimand or critique the reporters he supervised. He always thought that he'd enjoy being an editor if all he had to do was assign stories and edit copy. Instead, he found himself spending most of his time wearing other official hats: guidance counselor, psychologist, and, as now, clucking inquisitor.

"I need to talk to you about a possible problem that's been brought to my attention."

"A problem?"

He shifted in his chair. "Well, to be fair, I'm not sure it's actually a problem. A potential problem is more accurate." He carefully smoothed the trouser crease, finally letting his eyes rise to briefly meet Andy's. After a few seconds, he adjusted his glasses and his gaze drifted upward, as though he was searching the ceiling tile for inspiration. As his thoughts apparently organized, he continued with his remarks, although the color in his cheeks confessed his obvious discomfort. "I've been told that you've recently established some kind of...*relationship* with the principal investigator in the Amerson cases."

Her eyes narrowed. "Where did you hear that?"

"It doesn't matter, Andy. The only question—"

"Perhaps it doesn't matter to *you*, Ed. But me, I'm very interested in knowing who feels obligated to report the details of my personal life—actual or imagined—to my supervisors."

McKee took a deep breath and exhaled slowly. "I'm not at liberty to divulge the source of the information. The thing is—"

"How can this possibly be the business of anybody at the *Ledger*?"

"Because, Andy, if it's true, if you *are* currently seeing Bobby Franks, you have a major conflict covering the progress of the case." He paused, his fingertips beating a furious cadence on the edge of the desk. "And that's where it becomes very much our business."

She stared at the papers on Jim Donnelly's desk and didn't reply.

"So is it true?"

"I've seen him socially, if that's what you're asking. I fail to see how that's a conflict. My stories have been impartial and unbiased."

McKee shrugged. "Well, Donnelly disagrees. About the conflict and about the unbiased reporting." He paused and swallowed hard. "And, for the record, so do I."

She snorted in derision. "Have ya'll just been sitting around discussing my personal life? Isn't there anything more significant to talk about around here?" When McKee didn't answer, she said, "It would really be nice if ya'll could take a few minutes to discuss the real issues at the paper. Like, whether or not I'm ever gonna get a photographer, or when you're gonna hire a new staff writer, or when we're gonna get a dental plan. Or you could talk about getting us a decent computer system, or just getting the fucking newsroom back up to room temperature."

The color in McKee's face spread to his whole face; even his ears were crimson.

"So, what are you saying then?" she asked him. "Are you telling me I have to quit seeing Bobby Franks?"

"No. Of course not. We would never even suggest such a thing. Like you said, who you socialize with is pretty much your personal business."

"Well, then *what*?"

Another deep breath, another heavy sigh. "Andy, we're...we're gonna have to get someone else to cover the Amerson case."

She rolled her eyes and crossed her arms. "Great. That's just great. The only interesting thing I've got to write about, and ya'll take it away." She stared at him for a minute, then said, "All right. Fine. Give it to someone else. I'll just cover birthday parties, booger-eating festivals and pool closings for the rest of my career."

"I'm sorry, Andy. It's just—"

"It's fine, Ed. Don't worry about it." She ran her fingers through her hair, then got to her feet. "Now if you'll excuse me, I've got a story to write all over again."

She marched angrily past him, leaving him welded to the chair, muttering to himself.

Andy left the office at a few minutes after nine. The power outage story had been filed and was ready for Ed McKee's review. As far as she was concerned, the other story, involving a complaint by the city sanitation workers, could wait until whenever. She was tired, angry, and disgusted.

The stifling air hit her like a wall. She'd been freezing in her cubicle since early afternoon—an air-conditioning register directly over her head discharged frigid air on the side of her face—and the sudden change in temperature and humidity value was an absolute shock to her body. She stood on the concrete loading pier and tried to remember where she'd parked her car.

Phillip Henry came out onto the pier and lit a cigarette.

"Getting the ol' one-on-one with McKee, eh?" He took a deep drag off his cigarette. "Been there, at least a dozen times. I wouldn't worry about it, if I were you."

"I'm not worrying about it," she replied.

"I mean, I don't know what it was about or anything—"

"That's right, Phillip. You don't." She walked down the steps and into the parking lot.

"Be careful about locking horns with Donnelly, though," he hollered after her. "Ed's a pussycat, but Donnelly'll mess you up."

She turned the building's corner without replying. She had never really cared for Phillip Henry. She regarded him as a geek who had nothing else to do but work and nowhere else to go but his miserable cubicle. He had asked her out once; she had flatly rejected this proposal. She imagined him as he must have been in his high school days—his face ravaged by acne, immersed in geeky role-playing medieval dungeon games with his geeky friends.

She took a deep breath, desperately trying to find oxygen in the blast-furnace air. Her head and neck hurt from working at the keyboard for nine hours. She knew she had to get away from the *Ledger* building—for her own good, and for the good of everyone around her. It'd been a long day, one of those days when nothing went right. Mercifully, it was almost over.

She spotted her car, a 1989 Toyota, parked at the end of the row farthest from the building. Almost every other car was gone; the remaining two vehicles belonged to guys from the back shop.

She was suddenly aware of the low rumble of an engine behind her. She kept walking and didn't look around. The rumble grew closer and headlights blazed across the parking lot. She turned to see why the vehicle was following her to the end of the lot. She could tell that it was large, probably a van. She assumed that it was probably one of the night-shift back-shop guys. Whoever it is, she thought, I wish he'd quit following me.

The van pulled alongside her. She got her keys out of her purse and fingered the pepper-spray cylinder that dangled from the chain. She picked up her pace. *Fifteen more feet.*

"Hey, there, beautiful."

A familiar voice, nasal and irritating and slurred. She glanced at the van. The first thing she saw was the Amerson Heating and Cooling penguin logo. Then she saw Jamie Amerson. The passenger window was rolled down. He grinned and lifted a beer can to his lips.

"Go away, you bastard! I mean it! I swear I'll holler for help."

He rolled along with her, the fat tires breaking apart loose pieces of gravel.

"Hey, c'mon. Don't be like that," he said. "I just want to talk. You know, have a cold one and talk." He laughed. "Just like the good ol' days."

"Leave me alone!" she snapped. "I'm not kidding, Jamie." She stood at her car door and fumbled with the keys. *Where was the damn door key?*

He rolled to a stop alongside her car. "You know you're supposed to have your key out and ready before you get to your car. It's common parking lot safety." He cackled and took another swig of beer.

The keys dropped onto the asphalt.

"You want me to help you?"he asked.

"I want you to go away. I'm about to call the cops!"

Another cackle. "Your boyfriend? Or should I say, your *old-man* friend?"

She retrieved the keys and, with shaking hands, tried another one.

"You know, I've been reading the stories you've been writing about me." He hiccuped. "Not very nice, Andy. Not very nice at all."

"Leave me alone, asshole!" Andy snapped. She slipped a key into the lock and the tumblers turned. She quickly jumped into the driver's seat and locked the door. She grabbed her cell phone from her purse and began hammering numbers.

The van began to roll away. Slowly, almost defiantly, at first, then gradually picking up speed.

Soon it disappeared around the corner of the building.

"Thank you for agreeing to see me at this ungodly hour," Dr. Britton McHugh said. He settled into one of the side chairs in Katie's office. "After the Hollins case, I'm surprised you'd agree to see me at all."

The defense's psychiatric expert in the Joe Terry Hollins case was dressed in a blue cotton shirt and lightweight tan suit pants. His jacket was folded in his lap under a green file folder. His silk tie had been loosened at his open collar. There were dark circles under both eyes.

McHugh had called Katie that afternoon from his car phone, requesting a meeting with her later that night. He told her that he would be in Richfield for the remainder of the day, meeting with a group at the rescue mission and several prisoners in the county jail. He had not disclosed the subject of the meeting, only that it was urgent. Katie had agreed to see him at eight o'clock, but it had been closer to nine when her investigator, Robert Miller, had escorted McHugh into her courthouse office. Katie had waited at her office window, watching the breathtaking sunset yield to the gauzy night. But her mind had not been on the magenta sunset or the passing time. Instead, it had been spinning with thoughts, all of them related to the troubling murder investigation. She thought about the fact that Rabon Creasey already knew about John Paul Fourier and that he was a "person of interest" in the kidnapping/murders. She wondered what Fourier actually knew, whether he had any direct involvement with the kidnappings, and, if not, whether he would ever agree to help the state. And she desperately prayed that the case could be finally resolved before there were any other victims.

"How may I help you?" Katie asked now, as she inclined herself physically in the psychologist's direction. She sat in the chair next to him with her legs crossed at the ankles, trying her best to look at ease.

"I was actually hopeful that I could help *you*," he said. Then he grinned and added, "Believe it or not."

Katie returned his smile, but her expression still reflected her confusion.

"Before I actually get to the precise reason for this visit," he continued, "please indulge me as I attempt to settle one matter." He paused, his elbows resting on the chair arms, his steepled fingers tapping each other. "For starters, I want you to know that I'm really not some unprincipled whore, as our previous and only encounter might've led you to believe."

Katie's face turned crimson. "No, I never said...I don't...believe that. I never—"

"Please. I don't want to make this awkward for you. That's not why I'm here. We were only doing our jobs, you and I. Only you were doing yours much better than I."

"I'm sorry if I was too harsh," she said. "I didn't mean—"

McHugh held up his right hand to stop her. "Please, Missus O'Brien. You were entirely within your rights to vigorously challenge my testimony." His eyes suddenly seemed out of focus, trained on some archived ideal in a distant dimension. "I believe that my profession does a lot of good for a lot of people."

Katie nodded in agreement.

"On the other hand, as you're well aware, it's not a precision science. It never was, it probably never will be. The people who were the driving forces behind the diagnostic manuals, Spitzer and Frances, have called that instrument 'empirical,' but it's scientific only in the broadest possible sense of that word. I'm sure you know that it's based on consensus and observation and clinical data, but—" His eyes rose to meet Katie's. "—it's nothing like the scientific method that calculated gravitational pull and helped put men in space."

"Or determines which gun a projectile came from, for that matter."

He gave a shrug of concession. "Still, we're able to help some folks. We help people who're depressed, who can't sleep, who have learning disabilities—" He paused after reading agreement in Katie's face. "You understand what I'm saying."

"I do, indeed."

"The problem comes when we cross the street and take the witness stand on behalf of some accused criminal. Then we're out of our element, like neurosurgeons treating reflux."

Katie smiled appreciatively.

"Our classification system doesn't connect well with most issues that arise in the legal process. And the manual admits this, right there in the precautions.

Even those of us who're certified forensic examiners learn how to cope with the differences, but we never master them." He paused, collecting his thoughts. "That's what happened to me with Mister Hollins. Rabon Creasey came to me, gave me a laundry list of symptoms, asked me to make a diagnosis. I interviewed Hollins, observed many of these signs and symptoms—" He shook his head slowly. "At that point, it's very hard to get a read on what's real and what's programmed into the subject's head." He shifted in his chair, as if the memory of the case caused him actual physical discomfort. After a moment's somber reflection, he met Katie's sympathetic gaze and seemed to rise above the unpleasant memory. "So, anyway. That's that. You were well-prepared and very knowledgeable and you handed me my head." The grin again. "And now, here we are."

"Right. Here we are."

"So, without taking any more of your valuable time, let me get to the reason I'm here." He opened the worn folder. "I do volunteer work with several shelters and rescue missions, here and in Birmingham. While I was seeing some clients in Birmingham the other day, I met with a woman I'll call Ava. She had some very interesting things to say. She said she'd met a man at the mission who'd called himself J.P. Marat. She said she'd seen on television that he was being held in Richfield in connection with the Carry murder cases. I'm not betraying a confidence when I tell you this because she asked me to follow up on it. Supposedly this Marat man told Ava that he thinks he saw one of the kidnapped women in a van. He was in an alley near the campus, collecting junk out of a dumpster, at the time. And maybe he saw the kidnapper, as well. All that is unclear to me."

Katie bolted upright in her chair. "He told me that he saw the first victim, the one named Donna." Her nostrils flared. "The son of a bitch also said that he wouldn't tell me any more until I 'gave him what he wanted'."

"That's another thing Ava said. She said he'd talk to you if you'd just apologize to him."

Katie's face collapsed into a mask of disbelief. "*Apologize to him?*"

"He apparently feels he was treated unfairly—"

"That's ridiculous! He broke into a student's apartment, woke her from a dead sleep, and pinned her down in her bed. He only put her into therapy for the next two years. I think he was treated pretty darned leniently, all things considered."

"His story apparently is he had no intention of raping her. He just wanted to 'teach her a lesson,' because, as he told Ava, 'she was a bitch on wheels'."

"Well, what if she was? He had no right to terrorize her. He broke the law, got caught, got an appropriate punishment. He's getting no apology from me."

McHugh smiled. "Fair enough. And that brings me to the next thing. It's my opinion, again subject to the limitations we both know exist, that he did not commit the murders."

"Based on what?"

"For starters, I believe Ava. I've worked with her for years and she's always been truthful to a fault."

"Did he tell her anything else about the kidnapping?"

"I got the impression that he did. She didn't, however, share this information with me."

"He could've just been shining her on about the whole thing."

"He could have been, but I don't think he was." His eyes bore into Katie's. "At Ava's request, I went and had a little visit with him this afternoon."

"How did you even know who to ask for?"

"I knew his name was John Paul. And, of course, there was his unusual appearance—"

Katie nodded. She was beginning to feel some of the tension leave her neck.

"I talked to him for more than an hour. That's part of the reason I was late tonight. It took a while to build rapport, but he finally warmed up to me. I was able to eventually learn a lot about him—what he wants and needs, how he interacts with others. And I asked him about the kidnapping victim. He told me essentially the same thing he'd told Ava. And he also told me that he thought he could identify the van." His eyes bore into hers. "But he said he'd only tell you, and then only if you apologized."

Katie stared back at the psychologist. "And you believe he's being truthful with you?"

"Absolutely. And, furthermore, I don't think he's capable of committing these crimes. He's a psychopath, but he's a social psychopath. He has grandiose thoughts, he's self-important, very glib, and, in some ways, quite superficial—"

"And he's manipulative."

"Yes, manipulative, too. Just about every category in Hare's Psychopathy Checklist. He's clearly enjoying the fact that he has something you want, and the sense that this gives him the upper hand—"

Katie snorted. "The *upper hand*? He's in jail, for crying out loud!"

McHugh shrugged. "Jail's nothing to him. Remember, he's used to living under overpasses and in the back of his nasty van. In jail, he's got a bed, a toilet, three hot meals a day. No, he clearly believes he's gotten the best of you on this deal. He's got something you want, whereas you can't take anything from him."

"So why shouldn't he be regarded as dangerous?"

"He's not a Malevolent psychopath. Are you familiar with Millon and Davis's essay on psychopathic subtypes?"

Katie turned to her bookcase and pulled out a blue, hardback copy of *Psychopathy: Antisocial, Criminal, and Violent Behavior,* edited by Theodore Millon, Roger Davis and others. She showed McHugh that the chapter he had referred to was marked by half an index card.

The psychologist laughed. "No wonder I never stood a chance."

"So you're saying he's a psychopath, just not a violent one?"

"Exactly. I think he fits most closely into the 'Covetous' subtype. He's resentful of what he perceives as being ignored, not getting his due. He thinks he should have been made a department head, and, yes, that his young, attractive female students should have paid him more attention. And he sees his hurtful behavior as completely justified because of those perceived slights. At the same time, he clearly lacks physically violent intentions. His smug sense of entitlement caused him to break in the young woman's house, and also to torment you with his demands. It also keeps him from understanding how he has, in fact, hurt others. But he never intended to physically harm his burglary victim. And I honestly believe that he would never hurt you or these women who were murdered."

Katie stared down at a thin spot in her carpet. McHugh's assessment of John Paul Fourier seemed to be fully supported by much of the literature in the field. And he was absolutely right about who had leverage on whom. Fourier was, indeed, offering the one commodity she absolutely coveted—the single piece of evidence that could solve the mystery of the case. If it pointed clearly to Jamie Amerson, it could be the key that locked him away forever. And if it could do that, it'd bring her the first peace of mind she'd had in weeks. But should she pay the price that was being asked? And was this commodity genuine? Or was it just a twisted manipulation, another instrument of revenge generated by and justified within his disturbed mind?

She asked, "Do you know enough about the case to have a killer profile in mind?"

"I know the basic facts. I also know that a Mister Amerson, a onetime Carry student, has been accused and Rabon Creasey's representing him. As far as a profile goes, I'm sure that it's going to be another psychopath, to be sure, but someone in the Malevolent subtype. Cold-blooded, ruthless, vindictive. Fully capable of violent behavior, all of it self-justified. It's not your typical serial killer. Count on that. I've pored over case studies on dozens of serial killers and this is unlike all of them. It's certainly not random, not opportunistic. The victims seem to be clustered, somehow connected. In my opinion, there was a common motivation involved. Some kind of sick and twisted motivation."

"Would being rejected by these women give this person such a motivation?"

"It's certainly possible. It wouldn't be a notion a healthy mind would entertain. But a malevolent psychopath? I don't see why not."

"What about all the *Waste Land* references?"

McHugh rubbed his chin. "I've been very interested by that, but I don't really know enough about the poem to intelligently comment."

"Well, it was written during a major drought, for one thing."

The psychologist's eyebrows arched. "There's one kind of obvious connection."

"Beyond that," Katie said, "I'm really pretty stumped. Each killing has been coded to one section of the poem. So far, three killings, three sections."

"How many sections to the poem?"

"Five."

He made a face. "That's not good."

"I agree. Especially because I know two more women who fit into the target category." She paused a second, then added, "One happens to be my good friend."

"What's the poem's central theme?"

"Who knows?" Katie said. "As I recall, it's about emptiness. It's sort of the anti-*Canturbury Tales*. I read once that Eliot claimed it was nothing more than his personal bitchings about things in general."

McHugh sighed. "I'm afraid I can't help you with that part of it."

"All right," Katie said, after a long period of quiet reflection. "I've got to see if Franks has any heartburn with Fourier's plan. I'm assuming he won't, since he didn't want him locked up to start with. Of course, things like this are always potential trouble. Whatever he says will have to be disclosed to the defense. If it turns out to be pure bullshit, we're screwed. Then we'll have a circumstantial case on Amerson, a wrongly arrested suspect, and a wild goose chase, to boot." She groaned and rubbed her temples.

"And if it turns out to be something meaningful…"

"Then it'll probably help us turn the corner on this thing."

"You said yourself that there're two more sections to the poem, and two more potential victims out there."

She nodded. "You're right. I don't see that I have any choice. If Bobby doesn't care, I'll do it—I'll issue him his stupid apology. What the hell. It's not like it's gonna undo his conviction, or anything. And if it gets a killer off the streets, it'll be worth it."

"He did have one additional, ah, demand."

Katie sagged visibly. "I hate to even ask."

"He said he wanted to be released from jail before you talk. He told me it was demeaning for him to have to carry on a 'substantive conversation' in 'the presumptively oppressive context of incarceration'." McHugh shrugged. "His words."

"What's to prevent him from running after we release him?"

"Well, for starters, you have his van impounded and he has no money. He wouldn't get too far. Secondly, I think he really wants to hear you say the words. I think that's his main motivation for existing these days."

Katie tossed the demand around in her mind. At last, she said, "If Franks doesn't care and if forensics doesn't turn up anything in his van, he's got a deal."

Dr. McHugh got to his feet and stuck out his hand. "Katie, it's been a pleasure. I'll let Mister Fourier know, first thing in the morning. He said he would want to go to the Feltner rescue mission when he got out. You and Franks can take it from there." He handed her his business card. "Please call if I can be of any help."

Katie firmly shook his hand and thanked him for his information. Then, as McHugh was about to join investigator Robert Miller at the office door, Katie said, "May I ask you one more question, Doctor?"

He turned to face her. "Of course."

"What if Fourier identifies the killer and it turns out to be Jamie Amerson?"

He shrugged. "What if it does?"

"Isn't that gonna be awkward for you, knowing that Rabon Creasey represents him?"

McHugh looked puzzled. "Awkward? Absolutely not. Why should it be awkward?"

"I don't know," Katie replied. "I guess because of your past...association. I mean, in the Hollins case, and all. I just thought you might feel like you owed him—"

"I was asked to put my professional integrity on the line for an ungrateful murderer. I did what was asked of me, and, as a result, you made an issue of that integrity. I feel like I let my colleagues in the profession down." He slung his suit jacket over his shoulder. "No," he said, finally, "at this point, truth is the only thing I owe anything to." He gave her a quick smile, then patted Miller on the arm and disappeared down the main office hallway.

"I'm sorry," Avery May said to Bobby Franks. "I'm usually not easily freaked about stuff like this, but that asshole scared the hell out of me."

Avery sat across the desk from Bobby Franks, who was leaning over his desk blotter, busily making notes on a legal pad. He glanced at his watch and noted that it was nearly nine-twenty. He had been on his way out to meet Brant Woodley at the Truk-N-Go for supper when he had literally run into Avery on the sidewalk. He almost hadn't recognized her—she was wearing glasses with thick, black frames, purple capri pants, unlaced combat boots; her terror-frozen, unmade face was framed in a nest of untamed, preternaturally red-orange hair. She had pushed her way into the safety of the building's lobby, then breathlessly informed Franks that Jamie Amerson had threatened her in the parking lot of her apartment complex. Franks had ushered her into his office and now was alternating between listening intently (with crumpled facial features that made him appear to be in great pain) to Avery's fractured and emotional narrative and reducing the relevant information to writing.

According to Avery, she'd been en route to a nearby convenience store when a red van belonging to Amerson's Heating and Cooling had blocked the complex's only exit. She indicated that she wasn't particularly alarmed by this, since Amerson's often did work on the apartments' air-conditioning system. But then she had seen Jamie, leering at her from the driver's window. She said that he appeared to be drunk—he seemed barely able to hold his eyes open—and he ordered her to get in the van with him. She told Franks that she had rolled up her window and made an attempt to back away, but he turned the van and began driving directly at her. At one point, she said, he held up a belt formed into a noose shape and waved it at her through the windshield. He finally drove away when another vehicle from the next building began approaching. She had tried to call Katie twice from her cell phone, but had gotten no answer.

And now that her statement was complete, Franks remained slouched over his desk, wondering what to do about it.

Avery noticed his worried expression and apologized again for interrupting his plans.

Franks waved his hand dismissively. "Hey, I'm a cop and I'm on duty," he said. "Besides, I think this'll help convince the judge to put the fool back in jail."

The phone rang. Franks answered it, spoke for a moment, then cradled the receiver between his left shoulder and ear as he furiously jotted more information on his pad. After a few minutes, he looked up at Avery and mouthed, "It's Katie." He listened with increasing interest while Katie related the substance of her con-

versation with Doctor McHugh. He told her that he agreed wholeheartedly with
the arrangements she'd made and looked forward to hearing what Fourier had to
say. He then told the D.A. that Avery was there, and summarized her frightening
experience. Katie asked to speak to her friend, and Franks handed the phone
across the desk.

While Avery and Katie were talking, Franks heard his partially opened office
door creak. He looked up to see Andy Renauld. Her expression of relief turned
quickly to shock as she noticed Avery curled up in the side chair.

Franks jumped to his feet. "Andy! What—"

"Oh, I'm…sorry," she stammered. Her now frozen facial features were washed
in crimson. "I'm interrupting—"

"No," he protested. "Avery and I were just talking about the case. She's talking—" He gestured toward Avery May. "That's Katie on the phone.
They're…also discussing the case." He felt as flustered now by Andy's quite obvious discomfort as by the situation's inherent awkwardness.

"I'll just get back with you later," Andy said. She waved to Avery and left the
office.

Franks followed her out the door and down the hallway. He called after her
and she stopped just short of the interview room and turned back toward him.
Her eyes were red and a tear was rolling down her right cheek.

"What's the matter?" he asked.

She wiped the tear away and shook her head. "I mean, Jamie Amerson has
just, basically, threatened me. I came up here because your line was busy and I
didn't know what else to do." She fought to keep the tears from flowing. "Then I
find Avery all curled up—"

"Tell me exactly what Jamie did. What, when, and where."

"It doesn't matter," she said. "I'll just go someplace he'll never find me."

He took her by the left arm. "It matters a lot, Andy. This is the thing that's
gonna get him put back––"

She pulled angrily away from him. "Can you explain to me what…she's doing
all cozied up with you in your office at nine-thirty at night?"

He put his hands on his hips and frowned. "All right, first of all, we were not
'cozied up,' whatever. Secondly, she's here for the exact same reason you're here.
Amerson was also threatening *her* tonight."

She brushed the hair away from her face. "I don't understand. Why would
Jamie be after *her*?"

Franks took her by the elbow and steered her into Brant Woodley's office. He
shut the door behind them and said, "Avery had an affair with Amerson. It didn't

last long, but it happened." He watched Andy's facial expression cycle through shock, hurt, anger. "If my theory of the case is even halfway on track, she'd be exactly the kind of victim Jamie'd stalk."

Andy stared down at the floor and muttered something else to herself.

"So that's why she's here," Franks said. "The important thing is you're okay, and we've finally got Jamie Amerson by the short ones."

"Right," Andy said. She seemed subdued, now, almost pacified. "That's the important thing."

"The best part is, Katie just called and she's got someone who possibly witnessed one of the abductions. We're gonna talk to him tomorrow."

She blinked. "A witness? I thought there weren't any."

"So did I. But then this strange man shows up—a big, hairy junk collector—and he apparently saw something."

Andy's eyes widened. "The dude with a beard in the courthouse coffee shop," she murmured.

"Exactly! Katie told me she saw him there. And he was also at—"

"—the bond hearing. I know, I saw him making a scene in the courtroom."

"That should drive the last nail into Amerson's coffin," he said, grinning. He reached out and pulled her close. She resisted briefly, then wrapped her arms around him.

"What a relief," she said. "You're sure this man can identify Amerson as the kidnapper?"

"Well, he won't actually talk to us yet. He said he'd tell Katie what he knows, but first she has to apologize to him."

"*Apologize* to him? For what?"

Franks snorted. "For putting him in prison. That's what our justice system has come to. Anyway, Katie's gonna arrange for him to be released at nine in the morning. He's gonna be taken to the rescue mission out on Feltner, then she's gonna meet him there at one P.M." He pulled back and looked at her. "What did you mean you'd 'go somewhere he could never find you'?"

She didn't answer immediately. Her eyes briefly met, then darted away from the investigator.

"*What?* You can trust me."

"My hideaway," she said finally.

"You mean that ol' cabin from the photo? Your brother's place?"

She nodded. "Jamie doesn't have a clue it even exists. And he'd never find it even if he did."

"Well, I don't think you'll have to hide out," Franks said. "We're *gonna* get him."

She laid her head on his shoulder. "I'm so tired of being frightened," she whispered.

"It's all gonna be over with tomorrow," he said, gently kissing her. "You've got to believe me."

"I believe you, Bobby,' she said. She closed her eyes and melted into him.

CHAPTER 22

▼

Katie had begun to think that the twenty-eighth day of August was going to be the best day she'd had in a long time.

At nine o'clock, she learned that Judge Robert Stiles had overruled Rabon Creasey's motion for a new trial in the Hollins case. At nine-fifteen, Judge Stiles agreed to release John Paul Fourier on his own recognizance; twenty minutes later, he issued a bench warrant for the re-arrest of Jamie Amerson on a probable violation of his bond release conditions. These rulings, although welcomed by Katie, had been more or less expected.

The ten o'clock visit from Bru Nix, on the other hand, had not.

The attorney had shown up just as the sheriff's department was verifying that Fourier had been delivered to the community shelter. Nix had arrived alone and without an appointment, all smiles and apologies and firm handshakes, exuding genteel southern charm like a sorghum fountain. He had been to a nine o'clock motion docket, he had explained, and wanted to stop by since he "didn't get by the courthouse all that much anymore." Katie had seated him in one of her leather side chairs and collected loose files while Laurie Ross fetched coffee from the scorched pot in the office kitchenette. Then they had sat next to one another and chatted while the haze-filtered sunlight painted her office walls a warm, autumnal shade. Katie noted that Bru, wearing a white oxford cloth shirt, a silk club tie, navy braces, a lightweight pincord suit and gleaming brogans, seemed, as always, impervious to heat and professional stress. Katie had sipped her coffee and contributed to the cordial conversation, as she waited for the badinage to turn suddenly to accusation.

But, once again, Bru Nix distanced himself from his perceived role as critic-in-chief of her administration. He told Katie that he respected her for the job she was doing, fully supported her, even offered the services of his law firm to assist her office in her preparation of the murder case. Katie had sputtered awkward thanks for the unexpected compliment and extravagant generosity, even as she evaluated the attorney's sincerity. Nix, anticipating Katie's suspicions, quickly explained that he had, "perhaps, been somewhat unfairly critical" of her in the execution of her professional duties. But, he continued, after observing her deal with "the frankly maddening turns of the coed murder cases," he had changed his mind about her. When Katie mentioned rumors of his political ambitions, Nix laughed and replied that "they couldn't pay him enough money to put up with that kind of mess."

Thus assured that they were allies in the troubling cases, Katie updated the attorney on the status of the investigation, providing detailed information, right down to her afternoon meeting with John Paul Fourier. Nix thanked her for the information, assured her that he would "handle" Dean Wilker at the college, and was on his way.

Katie was one hour into a case review with Berry Macklin and Kevin Rose when the perfect day began unraveling.

The first dose of bad news came at noon courtesy of a Bobby Franks's phone call. The tone of his greeting immediately informed Katie that something was very wrong.

"You're not gonna believe this," he continued. "For-yay's dead."

Katie held the receiver and stared in disbelief at Kevin Rose. "What do you mean?"

"He's been shot. Point-blank range. He was at the mission and, according to a witness, another guy—he was described as about six feet tall, medium build, wearing tan coveralls, sunglasses and a baseball cap—called him around to the back of the building. The witness heard a shot, and they found For-yay lying on the ground. One shot, right in the chest. He was dead by the time the EMTs got there." There was a long pause. Katie could tell Franks was sucking on a cigarette. "The guy in the coveralls just disappeared."

"I'm stunned," Katie said. She slumped over her desk and ran her hand through her hair. She fought through the fog of shock, attempted to isolate and evaluate information that might explain why this had happened.

Her first coherent thought on the subject was a most troubling one.

"I told Bru Nix about him being there," she said. These words, imbued with the portent of some unforeseen conspiracy, emerged as a hesitant murmur. Her hand covered her face as if to symbolically seal the source of the perceived betrayal.

There was no reply.

"The person, his killer, must've known he was gonna be there," she offered, as if Franks required additional information in order to comprehend her initial declaration. "Someone who knew what was gonna happen must've told him. I told Nix, just two hours ago, that Fourier had been taken there."

"Why would you've done that?" Franks asked.

"I don't know. He came here this morning. He offered us the help of his law firm. We…I thought we were on the same side."

"I think there's more than two sides to this mess, Katie."

She didn't answer.

"It doesn't really matter, though," he said, at last. "I don't think he's gonna be your leak."

"What do you mean?"

"The sheriff's department knew everything. The guys in the jail all knew we were talking with Four-yay. They knew what he was in for, what we we're talking to him about. They knew we got him released on his own recognizance. They transported him to the damn shelter, for crying out loud." There was a pause, as if Franks was drafting the indictment of betrayal even as his thoughts were unfolding. "Think about it, Katie—Amerson's daddy and the sheriff are tight. Same with the chief. Tighter than a buncha thieves, all of 'em. And you saw how those deputies were joking around with Jamie when he was in court." He snorted and cursed as this possibility seemed to gel into a probability. "One phone call is all it would've taken."

"So what're we gonna do now?"

"Hell, I don't know. I've gotta find Amerson, for one thing. He might've just stepped over the edge. After last night, he figures, what the hell—at the very least, he's going right back into the jail." After he covered the mouthpiece and spoke to someone else, he suddenly announced that he had to go. "There're some folks here at the shelter I still gotta talk to."

The line went dead. Katie hung up the phone and held her head in her hands.

Franks pulled his car into Andy Renauld's driveway and frowned. He hadn't heard from her since they spoke at his office the previous night. Nobody in the *Ledger* newsroom had seen her. Her editor, a man named McKee, said that she just hadn't shown up that day. When Franks had asked if that was unusual, McKee had laughed and said, "unusual for the past year, but usual for the last few days." Franks had mulled that one over as he had steered his car south on Park and east onto Poplar. As he neared Andy's house, he had tried calling her for the third time; each time her machine had answered. Now that he was there, he could see that her car was parked in its usual place.

Something definitely wasn't right.

He slipped his vehicle into park and redialed her number. Again he was greeted by her recorded message. He called out her name this time and waited for her to pick up. When the recording cycle ended and an irritating tone sounded, he pressed the disconnect button.

He got out of the car and gave the property a walk-around. Her Toyota was locked, as were both house doors. He peered into two of the rear windows, but wasn't able to see anything unusual. He could actually see into Andy's bedroom; the bed was made and nothing looked out of place. He stepped off the deck and surveyed the parched backyard. The sun had plenty of heat in it, even with the thick layer of haze. He stood on the grass, sparse and the color of straw, and scratched his head. Cicadas screamed from the trees at the back of the lot. Sweat ran down his forehead into his eyes.

He walked back to the front of the house and climbed back into his car. He sat behind the wheel for a good minute, struggling to find an explanation for Andy's bizarre and sudden absence. She seemed to have just disappeared. *Just like Amerson's three victims.*

He didn't want to believe that this could have been her fate. Andy was smart, physically fit, very capable of defending herself. And she had his gun.

But tormenting questions continued to boil in his mind. What if Amerson had somehow managed to lure her into a situation where he could drug or other-wise incapacitate her? What if she was, at that precise moment, bound at the wrists and ankles, just like the others? Neither the gun nor all the savvy in the world could help her then. She'd be completely at his mercy. And he'd already made it abundantly clear that there was no mercy in him.

He knew he had to find her.

He started the car and backed out of the driveway. He began driving, not yet sure where he should go.

CHAPTER 23

▼

Katie tried in vain to focus her attention on the young couple and the attorney sitting on the other side of her desk. They had made the appointment weeks earlier, back when the abduction murders were just a troublesome collection of loosely related circumstances. Now, as they earnestly pitched their case—they were accusing a local general building contractor of cheating them out of thousands of dollars—Katie's mind was fully occupied with thoughts of a killer who remained on the streets. Even worse, Katie had learned only minutes before the couple arrived that neither Andy nor Avery could be located and that a presumably fugitive Jamie Amerson had disappeared from sight.

Katie had considered postponing the meeting; a delay would've been both justified and understood, given the dire circumstances. The postponement certainly wouldn't have been because of her lack of interest in consumer fraud. Indeed, as the former head of the property-crimes unit, she knew well how such crimes could cripple its victims, both emotionally and economically. In the end, it was this awareness that prompted her to proceed with the conference, as scheduled. Now her challenge was to redirect her focus to the complainant's words, their charts and graphs and accordion files brimming with documents, and the blueprints now spread across her increasingly cluttered desk.

Her phone rang, just as the couple's attorney began referring to a financial flow chart he had created with the help of some presentation software. He had placed a laminated blow-up of the chart on Katie's sofa and was standing in front of it, poking the critical numbers with a telescoping metal pointer. Katie gave the phone an annoyed glance; she'd asked Laurie Ross to hold her calls until the meeting had concluded.

"Excuse me," Katie said, as the ringing persisted. "I'm afraid I need to see who this is."

The attorney sighed and returned to his chair.

Katie answered the phone and swivelled obliquely away from her visitors. As she had suspected, the call was from Bobby Franks. He told her that he still was unable to find the two women, nor was there any sign of Jamie Amerson.

"I'm worried, Katie," he said. "He threatened both of them last night."

Katie bolted upright. "What do you mean? He threatened Andy, too? What…*happened?*"

"Yeah, and that's what bothers me," Franks muttered. "I should've just picked Amerson up last night. I guess I never thought he'd do something crazy with the heat on him. But now it looks kinda obvious. He got word about For-yay, took him out, then went after the girls. I guess he figured, what the hell, he might as well go out and complete his demented little murder project."

"Avery never said anything to me about being threatened," Katie protested. The observation seemed to be, at least in large part, an effort to convince herself that her friend couldn't possibly have been targeted by the killer. "I can't imagine her not calling—"

"She said she tried to call you two or three times. She said she couldn't get you."

Katie realized that she had been in her office during that critical time, meeting with Dr. McHugh and reviewing the Amerson file. A chill swept through her. It suddenly seemed not only possible, but probable, that Amerson had killed McHugh, then grabbed Avery and Andy.

"What…are you gonna do?" she asked the investigator.

"I'm gonna keep looking," he said. "I don't know what else to do right now." He paused, then said, "I'm wondering if Andy might have gone off to her brother's cabin."

"She has a brother?"

"A half-brother, actually. She told me he was off on active duty somewhere. He has a log hunting cabin up in the hills. She told me she goes there sometimes when she needs to escape."

"But you said her car was still in her driveway."

"Yeah, I know. I've got another theory now. What if Avery came by in her car, picked Andy up, and they went up to the cabin *together?* You know, to hide out, whatever, until Amerson was down again. I mean, they left my office last night acting pretty chummy."

"You really think it's possible?" she asked.

"Hell, I don't know. Let's just say I want to believe it is. At this point, I'm kind of running out of other possibilities."

Katie asked him to keep her posted and hung up. She turned back to the visitors who had been silently staring at her.

"I apologize for that," she said. "It's...about some missing people."

They continued to stare.

"It could have something to do with the Carry murders," she added.

The couple nodded. "I guess that takes precedence," the man muttered.

Katie took a deep breath. "Would it be possible if I let my investigator and property crime lawyers continue this conversation? I really need to follow up on some things."

The couple looked at the lawyer. He sighed again and began collecting his exhibits.

"As long as they'll listen," he said.

She called Robert Miller and asked him to meet the complainants in her waiting room. She gave her visitors her assurance that she would follow up on the meeting. Seemingly satisfied with this pledge, they took turns shaking her hand, then walked out with the investigator.

As soon as they'd gone, Katie pulled Dr. Britton McHugh's business card out of her purse and quickly dialed the number. When his receptionist answered, Katie explained who she was and that her call was an emergency. The woman connected Katie with the psychologist.

"I need your help," she said, when he picked up the phone. "You said to call if I—"

"Absolutely, Katie. Whatever I can do."

"Do you think Fourier provided this 'Ava' woman with more details about the kidnapping than she shared with you?"

There was a long pause while McHugh apparently evaluated the ethical implications of his answer. At last, he said: "I'm not sure, although that would be my distinct impression. It seemed like she was giving me the *Reader's Digest* version."

"Do you know how to get in touch with her?"

"I believe so. She does cleaning for a woman in Hoover. I think I have the number here. What—"

"Fourier's dead," Katie said. "Someone shot him right after he got to the rescue mission." In the intervening silence, it occurred to her that this unemotional rendering of this fact must have seemed particularly cold to Dr. McHugh. In all truthfulness, she had little regard for the man she had prosecuted—an individual she clearly regarded as a self-centered user of other people—other than his potential value as a source of information. Even in his offer to help with the murder probe, however, he had demonstrated his manipulative and controlling nature.

The silence lingered. "That's terrible," McHugh eventually said.

"Yes," Katie said, struggling to imagine that Fourier must have had some decency in him. "I feel at least partly responsible."

"As do I."

"I'd like to meet with Ava," she said.

"When?"

"This afternoon. As soon as possible."

"I'll see what I can do. This will have to be her decision, of course."

"Of course. But please tell her that there could be other lives on the line."

"I'll do what I can," he said. "Give me about ten minutes."

Katie thanked him, hung up the phone and sank back into her chair.

Franks steered his car onto the two-lane rural road leading up the side of Fraley Mountain. This "mountain," like the others in the isolated cluster of slopes, rises, and hillocks that anticipated the flattening of Alabama into plateau and coastal plain, was scarcely nine-hundred feet above sea level. But the settlers of Bienville, Maynor, and Lake counties, who honored their kin by naming their unspectacular bodies of water and relief elevations after them, apparently found the "mountain" appellation significantly more majestic than "hill."

Franks followed Martin's Gap, a narrow and gently sloping two-lane road that curved up the hill's side. After the first sweeping turn, he found himself in a strange, densely wooded world, where the residences, mostly simple structures with rusted tin roofs and cedar siding, had no trouble hiding beneath the sylvan canopy. He noted that the color of the trees was clearly more autumnal than vernal—the browns, oranges, and yellows of fall seemed far more prevalent than the deep green of the forest in mid-June. Franks leaned over the steering wheel as he drove, his head swivelling constantly from right to left and back. He had no real idea what he might find at the top of the mountain. The area was well outside Richfield police jurisdiction; as a result, he rarely had the occasion to travel there. He only knew that he had to find Andy's log cabin.

He glanced at his watch and grimaced. It was almost three in the afternoon. He knew he was running out of time. He queued the radio microphone and called Brant Woodley. After a few seconds, the investigator's voice crackled back over the speaker. He reported that he was "sitting on" Amerson Heating and Cooling. All he knew, he said, was that one of their vans was missing and that nobody had heard from Jamie since the previous afternoon.

"Is the chief aware of the situation?" Franks asked.

"Ten-four. He'd like you to check in with him if you find anything. What's your twenty?"

Franks made a face and tapped the mike against his forehead. He didn't want to let Woodley—or anyone else monitoring this traffic, for that matter—know that he was following a hunch outside Richfield's jurisdiction.

"I'm on Bradley, near the college," he said, at last. "Then I'm heading out toward the mall, just to see if anybody's seen anything."

"Ten-four," Woodley said.

Franks tossed the microphone onto the bench front seat and ran his fingers through his hair. Up ahead, tucked away into the vegetation in yet another curve, a building came into view. It was a square cinder-block structure with a flat roof. A rusted metal sign identified the place as "Ed's Country Grocery." Franks steered into the gravel parking lot and pulled alongside the only other vehicle, an old Ford pickup. He got out of the Crown Vic, grimacing as he stretched his screaming back. He lurched toward the front door, where an "Open" sign hung at an angle just at waist level. A tarnished cowbell, clumsily rigged to the door, jangled as he stepped into the store.

There was a long counter directly in front of him. Two men with baseball caps sat in chairs behind the counter. One was dressed in a white undershirt and bib overalls. The other was almost obscured by a huge glass jar filled with pickled eggs. An oscillating fan on the floor turned toward the men, sweeping an anticipated wave of cooler air their way.

"Afternoon," Franks said to the men, nodding to them one at a time.

They nodded back, almost in unison.

"Hot enough for ya'?" asked the man in the overalls.

"Yessir," the investigator said. "Hotter 'n a three-balled tomcat."

"What can we git for ya'?" the man in the overalls asked.

Franks pulled his badge case out if his pants pocket and flashed the gold shield at the men. "I'm Bobby Franks, an investigator with Richfield P.D."

"Name's Ed Cowley," replied the man in overalls. "This here's my cousin, Revis."

Revis nodded.

"I was wondering if ya'll might know if there were any log cabins up there on the ridge." "If there's one up there, I don't know nothin' about it," Ed Cowley declared.

"Me, neither," said Revis.

"Any idea where I might find one out this way?"

The two men exchanged glances.

"Why you lookin' for a log cabin?" Ed asked, his eyes narrowing suspiciously.

"I'm trying to find some folks. I don't know where they live, just that it's in a log cabin out this way."

"They in some kind of trouble?" Revis asked.

"No. I mean, I just need to talk to them, that's all."

Ed swatted at some kind of flying insect. "Can't help you," he said. "They ain't but three houses up on that ridge, and none of them's made of logs."

Franks bought a cold drink and a pack of cigarettes, thanked the men and left the store. He cranked up his car and headed back down the hill. He paused at the highway, looked north and south, trying to decide where to go next. He thought back to the photograph, struggled to remember the details. Anything that might help him locate the cabin. Lot of trees—absolutely no help there. And judging by the amount of sky showing in the photo's background, it was more than likely situated on the top of a hill. He drained the soft drink from the bottle as he searched his memory for any other salient information.

And then he remembered the blur, the slightly out-of-focus streak of copper and silver visible among the trees in the left corner of the picture. What the hell was it? It almost looked like a low-flying UFO, caught by pure accident on film.

Suddenly it hit him: it had to be the microwave relay tower on top of Skelton Mountain, several miles to the north. So far as he knew, it was the only one in that area of the county.

He pointed the Crown Victoria north and stuck the accelerator to the floor-board.

CHAPTER 24

▼

Katie met Dr. McHugh and the woman he had referred to as "Ava" at a waffle restaurant in Bessemer, a city in Jefferson County, just southwest of Birmingham. When Katie arrived, just after two-fifty, Ava and the psychologist were already waiting at a table by the window. McHugh introduced Ava by her pseudonym, but the woman promptly offered her true identity.

"My name's Jane Corbett," she declared, standing and pumping Katie's hand. "I didn't want the doctor to call my real name, but he told me I could trust you."

Katie glanced at McHugh, then flashed the woman a sincere smile.

"I've already broken the news about Mister Fourier," McHugh said. He reached across the table and patted Jane's arm as she sank into the cushioned vinyl seat.

Katie slid onto the bench next to McHugh and across the table from Jane. She studied the woman, evaluating her. She had wispy, shoulder-length blonde hair. Her face was slightly weathered and generally unremarkable; the only striking features were her wide, coal-black eyes. She wore a blue tee-shirt, cut-off sweat pants, striped athletic socks and cheap sneakers. Katie judged her to be in her late thirties or early forties. She watched her expression when the topic of John Paul Fourier's fate came up. The D.A. observed only that her eyes blinked and that she seemed to let out a tiny, almost unnoticeable, sigh. Katie guessed, correctly, that she was a woman well practiced in the art of absorbing pain.

"Doctor said you was in a hurry," Jane said. Her hands, clasped on the table, flexed and squeezed rhythmically. "If you want to ask me whatever it is—"

"Did he explain the problem to you?" Katie asked.

She nodded. "He said whoever it was that done this to J.P. might be fixin' to hurt someone else."

"Two people, I'm afraid."

Jane shrugged. "I don't know for positive that I can help you, but I'll do what I can."

"I guess I need to know exactly what J.P. told you about the kidnapping."

The hands quit flexing for a moment as the woman seemed to lose herself in the theater of memory, then began again. "He said he was going through a dumpster in an alley next to some kind of club or bar, whatever. He did that sometimes, you know, just lookin' for stuff. Anyway, he was right there, across the street from that college. He said the two of 'em, the one in coveralls and cap and the girl, cut through that alley, and walked right past where he was at."

"Could he see the people?"

"Well, he said it was night and the lighting wasn't no count in that alley, so he couldn't see all that great. But he was pretty sure it was that girl, the one they showed the pictures of. Pretty girl, kind of long, blonde hair."

"Donna Crawley?"

"Yeah, I'm pretty sure that's the one. The other one—I reckon it was a man, based on what he saw—he couldn't see that well, on account of the lighting, plus the dude had that ball cap pulled down low. Anyway, J.P. said the girl was *messed up*, if you understand what I'm saying. He said she couldn't hardly walk. The guy was having to hold her up, almost carrying her. The girl got sick right there, near the dumpster. J.P. said she nearly puked right on him."

"Did J.P. see where they went?"

"Yeah, he was kind of curious, so he followed them out of the alley. There was a van sitting there—he said he was pretty sure it was an older model Ford Econo-line—and he said the guy shoved her into the passenger seat. Then he climbed in and they took off. J.P.'s van was parked right near there, so he climbs in his and starts a-followin' them." She noticed Katie's strange look, so she added, "Hey, I don't have no idea why. J.P.'s just that way. You know, all curious and every-thing."

Katie cleared her throat and nodded slowly.

"Anyways, he kind of lays back so the man don't know he's being followed, then he follows them until they head off up into the hills."

"Did he mention any particular streets or roads?"

Her head dropped and her eyes narrowed as she searched her memory. Finally she said, "He might have, but I really don't know nothin' about Richfield—" Her mouth twisted into a perplexed frown.

"That's okay," Katie said. "I just thought—"

"Wait—I do remember something. He said he followed them out of town until they headed off up this hill, then he turned around in the parking lot of this lumber yard."

Katie blinked. "A lumber yard?"

"Yeah. I can't remember if he called the name of the place, but he said there was, like, a statue of a giant lumberjack—"

"Bunyan's!" Katie interjected. "They have a big Paul Bunyan next to the building. They must've headed up Skelton Gap Road."

The woman shrugged. "I suppose that coulda been it."

Katie shot a glance at her watch. *Three-ten.* "Listen," she said, reaching across the table and grasping Jane's right hand, "I have to run. I've gotta call the investigator and pass this along. And I also need to get back to Richfield to help find these people." She squeezed the woman's hand and gazed earnestly into her eyes. "I want you to know that I appreciate you helping us out this way. You didn't have to do it, but you did. And it may be the thing that helps get this guy off the streets."

She shrugged. "I just don't want nobody else to get hurt."

Katie got to her feet. Britton McHugh and Jane Corbett rose with her.

"Thanks so much again," she said to the psychologist.

"Like I said, I'm just happy to be able to help."

"I'll be in touch," Katie said. "I promise."

She waved to them and ran to her Jeep.

Franks's car rolled to a stop near the end of Skelton Mountain Road. He was able to glimpse the top of the microwave relay tower in the distance—two drum-like objects hung from the side of a four-legged, orange-and-white structure—but he hadn't seen anything that looked like the cabin from Andy's photo. Then he saw what looked like a logging trail: twin tracks worn into the gray loam, veering off the road into the woods. When he was unable to locate any other familiar landmarks, he steered the car onto the trail.

He followed the tracks as they curved through the trees. At times, the trail was so narrow that limbs scraped his windshield as he squeezed between trees.

And then, quite suddenly, he caught a glimpse of the cabin. It was almost perfectly camouflaged in the distance by the mottled rust-color smear of the parched woods. As his Ford jostled closer, he was able to observe that another structure, tall and wide enough to be a small barn, stood just past the cabin. The hood of Avery's Chevy Lumina was visible beyond the larger building's far side. When he turned off the main logging road, he was able to see that a gate, secured with a chain and lock, blocked the trail. The investigator pulled up to the gate and breathed a heavy sigh of relief. His theory had obviously been correct—Avery had picked up Andy at her house and they'd driven up to this sanctuary together. It was clear to him now that they were safe and all his worry had been for nothing. He only wished they would have taken a minute or two to let somebody know where they were. His hand briefly gripped the radio mike on his seat before he decided against reporting his discovery. He didn't want to admit that he'd kept his partner and three uniformed officers searching all day for no real reason. He decided he'd just make sure they were all right, then head on back to town.

He got out of the car and stretched. He grimaced as the leather handcuff case rode up his back and pressed into the tender lumbar region. He gingerly worked his way around the gate and began walking toward the cabin.

He was halfway there when he saw Andy.

She came running from the cabin door, something streaming from her left wrist. Franks stopped and waved to her. She didn't stop running until she reached him. She grabbed the investigator and held him tightly while she struggled to catch her breath. Franks could feel her heart racing as she crushed against him.

"Glad to see ya', too," he said, as he wrapped his arms around her. "Although it would have been nice if you coulda—"

"He's...got...Avery!" she gasped. She pushed away from him, her eyes filled with terror. She had a crust of blood in her left nostril and noticeable swelling of her right cheekbone.

He froze, confusion apparent on his face. "I don't...*who's* got Avery?"

"Jamie! He was waiting for us." She bent over, her hands on her knees.

For the first time Franks identified the thing that had been flying from her left arm as duct tape. He took the end of the tape in his hand and examined it. "Did he—"

"I got away," Andy said. "He beat me with his fists and was trying to tie me up, but I got away. But he's still got Avery and—" She covered her face with her hands. "You've got to get him before he hurts her."

Franks reached back and felt his waistband. His cuffs were still there but he'd left his Beretta in the car.

"I forgot my gun," he said, turning back toward the Crown Victoria. He felt his mouth go dry as he anticipated the fight to come. Anyone as bold as Jamie had been was not about to quietly surrender.

"I've got the gun you gave me," Andy said. "It's in my purse in Avery's trunk."

"Is her car unlocked?"

Andy nodded.

"Which way did they go?"

She pointed in the direction of the large outbuilding. "There's a cave partway down the backside of the hill," she said. "I bet that's where he's taken her."

"All right. I'm gonna get the gun and go down after her. I want you to get in my car and lock the doors. There's a radio mike in the seat. Do you know how to queue the mike, with the little button?"

Andy nodded.

"Okay, listen, Andy. I want you to call until you get the dispatcher, anybody. Tell them where you are and what's going down. Can you do that?"

She shivered and nodded again.

"If you see him, I want you to sit on that damn horn, do you hear me?"

"Yes."

"And if I haven't gotten there first, my gun's in a holster under the passenger seat. It's just like the one I gave you. Rack the slide back and it's good to go." He took her by both shoulders. "If you have to, blow his damn head off."

She told him that she thought she could do it, if she had no other choice.

He kissed her on the forehead and gave her a gentle shove in the direction of his car. He watched her take several steps up the dusty trail, then he began running for the white Chevrolet.

Avery May's eyes opened halfway, but nothing came into focus. The blur of shadow and shape she apprehended represented nothing to her—the gauzy continuation of her troubled sleep. She lay on her side on the building's dirt floor for a long time, staring in a vacuous and non-comprehending way at the dimly lit wooden slats in the wall of the ersatz garage. Her hands and feet were bound, but she had no particular awareness of her body position or condition. She was numb, paralyzed for all practical purposes, and locked into a dreamy insensibility from which she had no particular urge to escape. When she was finally able to focus on particular objects, visual images were formed and assigned meaning without any conscious process. A knot on a cedar board became, along with its concentric rings, one of her photographs—a black-and-white portrait of an elderly woman. Scattered beams of rich afternoon light in which motes spun and swirled became ethereal javelins. These objects had no particular meaning to her, no perceived purpose. They were just there, like she was. They were all merely random items suspended in a diaphanous and self-sustaining matrix.

She became vaguely aware of voices, distant and unintelligible. These, too, were without meaning to her. Like the persistent drone of insects and the crunching of boots on dried twigs, sounds alien and yet familiar, nothing more than an element of her ambient dreamscape. A horsefly buzzed around her face landed on her cheek. She moved her head slightly and the fly departed. Either way, the event was of no real consequence to her.

A fragment of a thought briefly occurred to her. A horrifying notion, or one that certainly might have horrified had it impacted her in any meaningful way. It was, like most fleeting thoughts, a synthesis of conscious and unconscious processes, the transient firing of critical neurons. For just a second or two, she was able to glimpse her recent past, her present, and her immediate future. She assessed her current predicament, recalled the circumstances of her incapacitation, identified her probable fate. This troubling thought made the briefest appearance in the spotlight of her consciousness, then was blotted out by the dense narcotic fog.

When the thought had gone, there was nothing left but the shadowy, meaningless matrix.

She closed her eyes and fell back into the comfort of her drugged sleep.

Franks stood at the side of the Chevy, listening for any sound that might indicate the whereabouts of Avery and her abductor. After a full minute, he quietly opened the driver's door and pulled the trunk release. He noticed that there was a woman's handbag on the front seat; he could only assume it belonged to Avery May. He walked to the back of the car and lifted the trunk lid. He saw bound stacks of flyers, a bag of charcoal briquets, a sleeping bag, and a variety of loose garments, shoes, and personal items. He wasn't, however, able to find a woman's handbag. He lifted several items, shuffled others, then straightened up and scratched his head. He was quite sure that Andy had said that the gun was in her bag in the trunk.

He suddenly felt a presence behind him.

Before he could turn, he felt something hard pressed against his lower back. He turned his head, his eyes now filled with confused alarm.

"You pathetic moron." A gravelly voice, low and menacing.

Franks raised his hands, more a gesture of confusion than fear or surrender.

There was a rumble of thunder in the distance. Clouds darkened and lowered and the wind bent the pines and oaks.

"What do you want?" Bobby Franks mumbled. His mouth was suddenly completely dry, his tongue swollen.

"Nothing," the voice growled. "Except for you to be dead."

Franks stood there helplessly, his hands half-raised, his eyes unfocused and searching. His mind raced, scrolling quickly through the very short menu of survival options. He suddenly wheeled, his right hand grabbing the weapon's slide. For a fraction of a second, for as long as it took for the powder in the chambered cartridge to be ignited by the primer, his eyes met those of the killer. When the barrel exploded from within his grip and the bullet pierced his side, he staggered backward. His right hand fell away from the weapon and groped wildly for the trunk lid, or anything else that might keep him from falling.

He landed in a half-sitting position on the car's rear bumper. He stared down in dumb amazement at the hole in his shirt, the nucleus of a rapidly creeping crimson cell.

"It's all your fault, you stupid prick," the killer snarled. "You should've just left everything alone."

The investigator looked up with glazed and unfocused eyes at the blurry figure. He tried to speak, but it was difficult enough for him to breathe.

"No," he finally whispered, before pitching forward to the rock-hard earth.

CHAPTER 25

▼

Katie pulled her Jeep into the Bunyan's Lumber parking lot and, under the giant statue of the lumberjack, frantically hammered on her cell phone number pad. She'd been trying without success to reach Avery and Bobby Franks ever since leaving Bessemer twenty minutes earlier. Her anxiety level climbed with each passing minute. A large part of that apprehension derived, of course, from the fact that one of her closest friends was missing. Avery's frequent unplanned absences had never been a source of great alarm for Katie—although her friend was a free spirit and an eccentric idealist, she was also remarkably streetwise. She'd lived for years in Atlanta, Los Angeles, and New Orleans; more importantly, she seemed to have an uncanny knack for avoiding trouble. Under the current perilous circumstances, however, Katie found her unexplained disappearance more than a little disturbing. A strong inner voice instructed her that something was, indeed, very wrong.

Of course, she hoped her intuition would prove to be mistaken. She hoped Franks had been correct and that Andy and Avery were together somewhere, their security assured by a synergy that Amerson would be both unwilling and unable to penetrate.

But where were they? And where was Franks? The maddening uncertainty of the situation was beginning to get to her. As always, the less hard information she possessed, the more dependent on intuition she became.

At that moment, the inner voice was ordering her to get help.

She stared down at the phone, its eerily glowing message window beckoning her to enter a number. It was hard to know who to call—she hardly knew what specific assistance she required. She was, after all, essentially flying blind; she didn't know if she was en route to a reunion, a rescue, or nothing at all. The one thing she *did* know was that she had only the most general idea about where to look. She scanned the names and numbers scribbled in her pocket phone directory, finally settling on Brant Woodley's entry. She remembered that he was a hunter; perhaps his outdoor experience might've made him familiar with the area's rugged terrain. Besides, she thought, he just might've made contact with Bobby Franks.

She heard five rings before Woodley answered. The investigator told her that he hadn't been able to reach Franks, but that he had Jamie Amerson in custody. He reported that he had caught him a half hour earlier, as he tried to sneak his van back onto the Amerson Heating and Cooling lot. And, although the van was still being processed by crime scene investigators, there didn't appear to be any trace of either Avery May or Andy Renauld.

"Did he tell you anything?"

"Nothing more than he wanted to talk to his lawyer." He paused. "Where you at?"

"I'm out here in the south county, in the Bunyan's parking lot."

No reply.

"I'm looking for Andy's cabin, but I don't have a clue where to begin."

"You think them girls might be holed up there?"

"That's what I'm hoping."

"Well, I'm afraid I can't help you with directions. There's so many sneaky little nooks and crannies up there—"

Katie's disappointed silence echoed on the line.

"If I was you, I'd call the county. They got people that actually patrol up there."

Katie thanked Woodley and pushed the "end call" button. She knew the investigator was right: rural Bienville County, even the remote coves and rugged aeries, was the sheriff's everyday workplace. But who in the SO to call? She ran a quick mental inventory of department employees and finally decided on Lieutenant Gordy Childs. Not only was he a friend of Franks, he knew Bienville County like his own neighborhood.

She dialed in the investigative division number, put her vehicle into gear, and began rolling up Skelton Gap Road. The division secretary answered and promptly transferred the call to Childs, who was about to leave his office for the day. The lieutenant told her that there were, indeed, a few log cabins atop Skelton Mountain, but he couldn't give her specific directions. She thanked him, ended the call, and continued to negotiate Skelton Gap's climbing curves. The road ended soon after leveling off at the top of the hill. Katie paused at what appeared to be an entrance to an unpaved logging road, then carefully guided the Jeep's front tires into the deep ruts.

The road twisted through the woods; where it ran along the ridge, there were occasional glimpses of the Cold River valley and the heat-seared ridges beyond. As she neared the top of the hill, however, the oak and hickory trees seemed to swallow the narrow trail. She leaned forward, staring intently through the foliage and hanging branches for some sign of human activity. Or, more apropos to the killer, inhuman activity.

Suddenly, through the imperfect filter of dying leaves, she caught a glimpse of something utterly alien to that bosky habitat—an object that was squat, metallic, midnight black. *Franks's unmarked unit.* Filled now with a sense of hopeful expectation, she steered around the last dense clump of trees. The entire scene now unfolded before her: Beyond Franks's car was a log cabin with the barn-like building a short distance away. The front end of Avery's Chevy was visible in the clearing behind the larger structure.

She gave an excited yell and turned onto another path that appeared to lead to the cabin. As amazed as she was that she'd been able to track her friends and associates to this remote location, she was even more relieved that everything appeared to be under control. After all, Bobby Franks was there and, perhaps even more importantly, there was no sign of Jamie Amerson's van. She almost couldn't wait to tell Avery the story of her wild mountain search, then mercilessly scold her for her heedless behavior.

Katie pulled as close to the gate as she could, lowered her window, then switched off her engine. She sat perfectly still and listened—for her friends's voices, for any sound at all. The silence of the woods, absolute and overwhelming, turned her feelings of relief to a pervading and leaden sense of dread. With all the noise her car had made, crunching and snapping dried twigs and branches, the three of them should have easily been made aware of her arrival. There should have been three people out to meet her.

Something had to be wrong.

Katie gave her watch a quick glance. It was nearly four-thirty. Once again, she needed to call someone for advice. She briefly entertained the notion of calling Gordy Childs again, then abandoned it just as quickly—he would have left the office by then and she didn't have his mobile number. Still, she knew that something had to be done. Her friends could be up there, imperiled—or worse. There wasn't time to go for help: it was a five-minute trip back to the highway, and even then, there was no guarantee that she'd find anyone to assist her. She suddenly cursed her aversion to guns, wished she'd taken Con and Franks's advice and carried one in her car. After her terrifying experience with the equipment thieves years earlier, she'd assumed that she'd never again be placed in the position of needing one.

Katie realized now that she had two choices: she could drive away or investigate. She wasn't about to abandon these people. Not there, not under those circumstances.

Grabbing her phone, she climbed from the Jeep. She quietly closed the door and began to make her way along the worn path to the cabin. She walked cautiously, hopeful that a friendly face would emerge from the cabin or the woods. The possibility of this deliverance diminished with each solemn footfall, however. She sensed that it was much more likely that she was marching squarely into the teeth of danger.

But who, exactly, was the villain? Despite her persistent questions about his involvement with the killings, she had more or less assumed that Jamie Amerson was the person responsible for the most recent attacks. After all, he was, by her own diagnosis, a psychopath. But, as Dr. McHugh had pointed out, there was a small constellation of psychopathic subtypes, some of which were inclined to violence and others whose psychopathy manifested itself in other socially hurtful ways. Jamie was clearly a self-involved user who was incapable of feeling remorse or empathy. She remained unconvinced, however, that he was capable of the atrocities involved in this investigation.

If not Jamie Amerson, then who? As McHugh had noted, the crimes were probably not random; rather, they'd been executed by someone with a specific motive. Certainly, when it came to motive, the fact of Amerson's involvement with the victims was powerfully persuasive. But could a view of these very facts from a fresh angle yield a different result? Who else might have been motivated to victimize this particular class of people? Someone jealous of Amerson or otherwise determined to set him up, just for two. These troublesome possibilities had flitted through her mind on a number of occasions, but she'd always dismissed them as being almost outlandish stretches of prosecutorial imagination. Besides, Jamie didn't really seem to have any real enemies, his "user" personality, notwithstanding.

She froze as another, even more disturbing, possibility occurred to her. What if he did, in fact, have an "enemy" who was neither a jealous nor angry male, but a member of the group he was supposedly victimizing? Someone who'd "dumped" Amerson, but who was also pathologically jealous of the other women he'd dated.

A survivor, obviously.

Which left, to the best of her knowledge, only Avery May and Andy Renauld.

Katie could automatically rule out Avery. She'd known her for more than twenty years. Avery was, by nature, an idealist, someone who yearned for peace and harmony and who found violence, conflict, even competition, harmful to the human spirit. True, she had her moments of unbridled goofiness and had never had a problem publicly venting her frustrations. But *kill* another person? Not just one person, but *four*? It wasn't just unlikely, it was absolutely ludicrous.

Which left Andy.

It just *couldn't* have been her, she told herself. Although she didn't know the reporter nearly as well as she knew Avery May, she'd been around her enough to hold in her high esteem, professionally and personally. She reminded Katie a lot of herself at that age: decent and hardworking, with normal goals, aspirations, and, yes, fears. She reflected back on their various conversations on the phone, in her office, in the courthouse snack bar—

A disturbing thought now shot through her mind.

What had J. P. Fourier meant when he muttered "warmer, warmer" in the snack bar that day? At the time, she'd dismissed the remark as the incoherent prattle of a schizophrenic. But she knew now that Fourier wasn't delusional. She also knew that he'd gotten a look—possibly a very good look—at the killer. Was he trying to tell her that this murderer was nearby? If so, he could well have been referring to Andy.

What about Andy's intense interest in the case? Was it truly actuated by fear? Or was it just her way of keeping a finger on the pulse of the investigation?

And who had murdered Fourier? Someone who knew he'd be at the rescue mission.

Andy knew he'd be there because she had told her.

She shuddered now as the terrible possibility began looking more like a probability.

With trembling fingers, Katie re-dialed Brant Woodley's number.

"You've got to let Amerson go," Katie half-whispered into the phone when the investigator answered.

"Say again?"

"I don't think he did it, Brant."

"What in the world are you—"

The line suddenly went silent. Katie stared at the display screen and saw that the light was out. She cursed and set the phone at the base of a nearby tree. She'd intended to charge the battery the previous evening but had forgotten about it.

And, of course, she didn't have her adapter cord with her. Screw it, she thought. *I'm halfway to the cabin, there's no going back now.*

A knot tightened in her stomach when she stepped onto the cabin's small porch. She moved tentatively to the front door, took a deep breath, knocked twice. She listened intently for any sound; there was none. Grasping and slowly turning the doorknob, she gave the heavy, windowless door a slight push. To her surprise, it creaked open. Katie paused, not sure what to expect. She could see the back of the room, where an old wood-burning stove sat, functionally useless, its primary ventilation pipe severed. She called Andy's name, then Avery's. *Nothing.* Her voice echoed through an empty and wooden chamber.

She pushed the door all the way open and stepped cautiously into the cabin. There appeared to be only two rooms in the structure: this barren front area, and a smaller cell accessed by a doorway on the left side of the main room. There was only one window—actually just a square hole covered by semi-translucent vinyl sheeting. The meager light made available by this inconsiderable opening barely illuminated the front room; the interior of the back room hid mostly in deep shadow. She was unable to locate any electric switches, fixtures, or outlets. There was only one piece of furniture in the room, a crude, handmade table constructed of two-by-fours and a sheet of particleboard. She angled toward the back room, the dusty, uneven floorboards creaking beneath her feet. She stopped just short of the doorway and called Andy's name again. When there was no response, she took a step into the room. Her right foot touched something; she gasped and jumped to the side. The dim light fell on an object that Katie identified as a canvas tote bag. She grabbed it by a strap and pulled it toward the doorway. Papers, notebooks, and several black-and-white photographic proof sheets protruded from the bag's opening.

She stood in the doorway with her back to the dark room and peered down at one of the shiny sheets. She squinted at the shadowy images, her eyes struggling to adjust to the dim lighting. When she was finally able to identify the scenes depicted, her jaw dropped.

There were multiple shots of the three kidnapping-murder victims at their crime scenes. All three, even the women found in other counties. Her eyes revisited the photos again. The first major shock that hit Katie occurred with the realization that the bodies of Kerry Grinder and JoEllen Russell would have been removed from the crime scenes *long before Andy could have arrived to cover the stories.* But there was more. The body of Donna Crawley was photographed nude on the ground, before the object had been placed in her mouth and before the words had been carved in her chest. The same was true of Kerry Grinder's picture. And the photograph of JoEllen Russell had been taken with a belt around her neck, before she'd been set on fire...

The glossy sheet fell to the floor as a chill swept through Katie. Even though there were strong circumstances pointing toward Andy as the killer, she had desperately wanted to discover that it wasn't true. The proof sheet, however, removed all doubt.

Katie's head was suddenly snapped back by a hand clasped over her mouth. At the same time, she felt a sharp pain as a hypodermic needle was jammed into the back of her upper arm. She flailed, throwing elbows and kicking at her unseen attacker, but she was quickly overtaken by the more powerful assailant. She crashed to the floor and felt herself being pinned from above. She tried to twist away, but she was trapped.

As a strange numbness began spreading through her body, she heard the voice of her attacker.

It was a voice she recognized, although artificially deeper now, and raspier.

It was the voice of Andy Renauld.

"You're next," she said. "You didn't have to be, but you are now."

Katie tried to reply but found she was unable to speak.

CHAPTER 26

▼

Con O'Brien stretched out his legs on the floor in his son's bedroom. He had a video game controller in his hands, and his back was supported by the lower unit of a bunk bed combination set. Garrett, also gripping a game controller, sat cross-legged near the bed's footboard. Their eyes were glued to the screen of a small television set elevated two feet above the floor on an inverted plastic storage box. Thumbs and index fingers hammered at a dozen buttons on the controllers. The only sounds in the room were the strange electronic tones emitted through the television speakers and the occasional grunt of disgust. Finally, after a prolonged stretch of manic button-pushing, Con tossed his controller onto the floor and collapsed in near-exhaustion against the bed. A replay feature, which displayed the loser's inglorious unhinging from a completely new angle, flashed obnoxiously on the screen.

"Good game, Dad," Garrett said. He flashed a tiny, engineered smile that said, "Not bad for a completely outclassed middle-aged man with limited game-playing skills."

Con shrugged. "These new games and systems are ridiculous," he sniffed. "Back in the day, when games were simple and controllers only had one button, I was the man." He gave the M-shaped controller a symbolic nudge with his shoeless foot. "You almost have to have a doctorate in button management to play these days."

Garrett grinned and nodded. "I wouldn't worry about it," he said. "You play very well for an older man."

Con frowned at the boy, then glanced at his watch. It was after five and he still hadn't heard from his wife. He knew that her trip to Bessemer would take a few hours, but he had expected her at least back in her office by four-thirty. He pulled himself to his feet and padded out of his son's room.

"You giving up?" Garrett asked.

"I gotta call your mom."

"Ask her if we can have pizza for dinner."

Con walked into the family's walnut-paneled study and picked up the cordless receiver from a phone base sitting on the surface of his desk. He tried Katie's cell phone number but only got an out-of-service message. He stood for a moment with the phone earpiece resting against his chin, then quickly pecked out Laurie Ross's number. He knew that she worked late from time to time, a vestigial ethic from her days as Katie's assistant in a busy civil firm. He was about to give up on the call when Laurie's stressed-out voice came on the line.

"Laurie, it's Con."

"Have you heard from her?" Laurie quickly asked.

Con stared at the floral pattern in the Persian carpet under his feet. "No, Laurie. Not since she was leaving for Bessemer."

"Me, either. I'm getting worried, Con."

He took off his glasses and pinched the bridge of his nose with his right index finger and thumb. "All right, let's just think this through. What time was her meeting in Bessemer?"

"Don't know exactly. She never told me. Probably about three."

Con stared at his watch. "Okay. So Bessemer's what, about thirty, forty minutes from here?"

"I guess."

"And her meeting lasts, let's say about an hour. Give or take. That puts her leaving at around four. Forty minutes back, add ten minutes for school buses, lumber trucks, afternoon rush, whatever—that puts her due back just about, well, *now*."

"She hasn't called, Con. I haven't heard a word. She *always* checks in—"

"Maybe she's just been too busy. Maybe she forgot her cell phone. Who knows?"

"So you're not worried?"

Con stepped to the nearest window and pulled back the curtain. There was no sign of her Jeep on the street or in the driveway.

"No," he said. "I'm not worried."

A pause. "Really?"

"Really. I'm really not worried. I'm concerned. There's a difference."

"What if you haven't heard from her by six o'clock?"

Con shifted his weight from one foot to the other. "Then," he said, "I'll be worried."

Katie realized that she was free.

She had managed to escape whatever remote peril had threatened her, and she was free.

More remarkably, she had somehow been transported to a place she remembered well, a park she knew in her adolescence. A safe place, a sanctuary she used to wander with her father. It was a late afternoon in spring and minutes after a shower had passed overhead. The towering trees, all of them fifty to sixty feet tall, surrounded her, their limbs hanging perfectly still in the windless dusk. Leaves, coated with moisture, dotted her with cool rainwater as she wandered a familiar trail. The sun, a huge orange ball, hung in the gossamer screen that seemed to hang just above the horizon.

She was alone as she strolled, but she felt completely safe there. Nothing bad had ever happened in that park, as least as far as she knew.

But it was somehow different this time. This time, she felt vaguely threatened by some powerful and occult force, some evil lurking beyond the glistening oaks and dripping wisteria. The sun suddenly disappeared and menacing darkness rapidly enveloped her. She felt a knot tighten in her abdomen.

She became aware of two tiny blurs of fitfully glowing light.

She struggled toward them, not knowing what fate awaited her.

"Here she comes. Wake up, sleeping beauty."

Katie blinked, trying to make the blurry objects come into focus. Within a few seconds, she realized that her vision wasn't the only thing that was fuzzy. She was having tremendous difficulty remembering how she had come to be there, wherever that might be. She could see a face weirdly painted by the glow from two candles. There was enough flickering light to reveal that this was a woman's face, but not enough to permit identification of the person. Suddenly, almost inexplicably, she was reminded of a minor point of interest from her college art history classes—Toulouse-Lautrec's teenaged self-portrait, the pensive face alternately concealed by shadow and revealed by the crescent of illuminated flesh. Except this light danced and shifted and never twice shone on the same face.

"Good," the woman said. "You're awake." She got to her feet and laughed. "I wanted to see your expression when you died."

With chilling abruptness, Katie recalled her perilous situation. She was on her right side on the floor, her shoulder, arm, and hand completely numb. She tried to move, quickly realizing that her hands were bound. She felt the heavy metallic pinch that indicated that her hands were cuffed, not tied. She knew from the space between her wrists that these weren't the new "hinged" handcuffs, but the old-style, linked type.

"They're Bobby Franks's," Andy Renauld said. "I figured he wouldn't be needing them anymore." She took a few steps toward Katie.

Katie twisted her neck to look up at her captor. She recognized her and a shiver ran down her spine. She could see that Andy was holding a roll of duct tape in her hands.

"What did you do to Bobby?"

"He had an accident, poor bastard. Shot with his own gun. It was just terrible."

Katie recoiled, the shock of this news causing a wave of nausea to sweep through her. "Why are you doing this?" she asked, at last.

"Why am I doing this?" Andy took a long, pensive breath. "Hell, I guess I really don't know. That psychiatrist—what's his name, McHenry?—could probably come up with something interesting. Hmmm. My dog bit me when I was a child, my father was a drunk who molested me. There're a couple of reasons for you. Then, too, there's the seemingly endless line of narcissistic men and avaricious women I've had to deal with all my life. I could go on and on. I'm truly a sick person. My God, Katie, *you* couldn't even convince a jury of my guilt!" Another snarling laugh. "Which, it turns out, is a moot point, since you're not gonna be around."

Katie moved her legs and realized that her ankles weren't bound. She cut her eyes left and right, making a quick assessment of her environment. The room wasn't large, maybe twenty-by-twenty. There was an object, some kind of wooden crate, turned on one end not far from her feet. One of the candles sat atop this makeshift table. There was a sleeping bag or blanket roll on the floor. Another candle, short and squat, burned on some type of metal can lid on the floor. And there was a small fabric chair positioned against the wall next to the overturned crate. She considered what it would take for her to get her to her feet. Obviously, with her hands bound behind her, it wouldn't be easy. But the crate, possibly the chair, could prove useful for that purpose. As long as her legs were free, she felt she had a chance to escape.

"Where's Avery?" she asked.

"She's in the van, all ready to go."

Katie stared at her. "What van?"

"Oh, the mystery killer's van, of course. I have it parked in my little detached 'garage,' where it's been for the last month. Just for your information, since you tortured so over this, it's a Ford Econoline, mid-eighties model. It belongs to my brother."

"What do you mean she's 'all ready to go'?"

Andy twirled the roll of tape around her index finger. "Well, as your buddy, Avery, the skanky hootchie-mama, accurately predicted, she's due to drown. That's the next section in the stupid poem. *Death by Drowning.*" She gave a drawn-out, sarcastic sigh. "Although, perhaps I'll arrange something else for her. I'm really tired of having to play out the T.S. Eliot thing. I never cared for him, not in the least. He was just some self-indulgent asshole deeply in love with his own ridiculous words. *Goonight, goonight, weilala, lala...*all that bullshit." She paused, the tape still twirling. "But I really had to act out the *Waste Land* jive. It was the thing that really tied Jamie to the murders." She cackled. "The one thing that wasn't right, of course, was the whole April thing. It turns out that *August* is the cruelest month, wouldn't you agree? It's just that...well, I actually couldn't wait for April." Another laugh, this one a sharp, staccato burst. "None of this really matters now, though, does it?"

"You killed these poor girls just to get even with Jamie?"

"Gracious no, girlfriend. That'd be shallow, vindictive, and just plain small-minded. No, this actually gave me the opportunity to pay my respects to all these whore boyfriend-fuckers *and* to deal with Jamie." Katie could see her grin, unmistakably evil even in the flickering light. "Kind of a variation on the old two birds with one stone deal." She knelt at Katie's side. "You, on the other hand, are an unfortunate casualty of war." She set the tape on the floor, undid her narrow leather belt, and pulled it free from the loops on her jeans.

Katie snorted. "*War?*"

"Yeah. My personal war on the vermin of Bienville County. I actually kind of liked you. But you couldn't leave shit alone. You couldn't just let Amerson go to trial. I mean, it was the perfect case—"

"You stole the pawn from him?"

"Yeah. And I picked the hyacinth from his little garden out back. Hyacinths, actually. I have more. I got them back in April. That took some planning, don't you think? And I got the drugs there, too. I got a month's supply of hyp from him." She formed the belt into a loop. "You know he tried to use that shit on me once? Put two pills in my drink. Unbelievable. I mean, it's not like we weren't having sex anyway. He just liked his women unconscious. Well, it didn't work on me. I saw him do it and threw the drink in his face." There was a long pause. "And this is the dude you were trying so hard to protect."

"I wasn't trying to 'protect' him, Andy. I just couldn't bring a man to trial for murder when I didn't believe he was guilty." She grimaced as she shifted to get her weight off her right shoulder. "And, as it turned out, he wasn't."

"Yeah, oh, well. None of that matters now. It doesn't make any difference." She gave the belt loop a sharp, threatening snap. "You appreciate irony? Bobby Franks undid this very belt. Unhooked it with his trembling, gnarled, old fingers. Held the murder weapon in his very hands. Never had a clue." She slowly shook her head. "He *was* pretty clueless, you have to admit."

"They'll know it was you, Andy."

She shrugged. "Maybe they will and maybe not. It occurred to me while you were sleeping that Bobby Franks might be just as likely a suspect as me."

Katie's brow furrowed. "How do you figure?"

"Well, he's got a history, if you know what I mean. A hothead, violent type. The media won't be kind to his memory. He hardly tried to make amends with anyone. And who was the person doing his level best to build the fraudulent case against poor ol' innocent Jamie? Why, Bobby Franks, of course. Then, of course, it was his gun that killed our bearded friend, Professor Bigmouth." She paused, stretching the belt loop wide. "But wait, it gets even worse. I think the other cops will find some interesting things in his car when they finally get here. Some roofies, your wedding band, some of Avery's jewelry. More withered hyacinths and plastic pawns." Another pause, this one more ominous than the last. "Some of my jewelry. And of course, they'll also find my torn and bloody clothes. They'll find everything but me. Then they'll find him, dead, gun in hand, shot at close range by his own weapon." Another sigh. "Poor bastard. The heavy toll of conscience—"

Katie suddenly spun on her right hip and lurched forward into a sitting position. She quickly crossed her legs and started to stand. Reacting just as quickly, Andy threw the looped belt over her head and pulled the strap tight. Katie ducked, tucking her chin against her neck. With her left hand, Andy punched the district attorney as hard as she could in the face. Katie hollered out and jerked her head back. Then, using both hands, Andy Renauld jerked the loop tight around Katie's neck.

Katie fought the urge to shut her eyes, but felt a crushing force to her windpipe. She sagged slightly, and the loop tightened even more.

She now was unable to get any air at all. Her head felt like it was about to explode; the pain became unbearable. She tried to kick out at her attacker but only managed to graze the outside of Andy's leg. Enraged, Andy twisted the loop and yanked Katie close to her.

Katie thought about Garrett and Con, the two loves of her life. She tried to hold them in her mind as long as possible, even as consciousness began slipping away.

CHAPTER 27

▼

Lieutenant Gordy Childs stood at a window in the squad room of the sheriff's patrol division headquarters and stared at the threatening skies to the southwest. It was growing ominously dark even though there was still more than an hour before official sunset. The air was heavy with moisture but very still; the menacing storm clouds seemed to have simply materialized out of the harmless afternoon haze.

Childs was supposed to have gotten off work at four, but the possibility of severe weather had extended his shift. Now he was trying to coordinate the placement of deputies in strategic locations around the county. The sheriff and emergency services director both liked to have their personnel already in place when dangerous storms lashed the vulnerable countryside.

"Call for you, Lieutenant," one of the deputies hollered from his office across the room. Childs was barely able to hear him over the amplified crackle of traffic on the radio, the loud voices of deputies gathered around a long conference table, and the manic juddering of the suddenly useful television meteorologist. "It's Brant Woodley, with the city."

Childs shuffled across the room, past the conference table where four uniformed deputies sat with their eyes fixed on the televison set. He paused to check out the radar picture, noting that the meteorologist was projecting that a long line of very heavy storms would move in a northeasterly direction, right through the southern part of the county. He ducked into his glass-enclosed office and took the phone from the deputy.

"Have you seen or talked to Franks today?" Woodley asked.

"No, not today. Had supper with him yesterday." Childs stuck a finger into his right ear to block some of the noise from the squad room. "Why? What's going on?"

"Hell, you tell me. I talked to him earlier today, but he went ten-seven at some point this afternoon. Nobody's heard from him since then. We were all out, driving around, looking for this van that may or may not exist. Then I went and sat on Amerson Heating and Cooling for a while. And guess what?"

"What?"

"Jamie Amerson come driving up in his ol' work van. Been off somewhere on a bender, I reckon. Smelt like a damn brewery. Anyway, there's this outstanding bench warrant, so I went ahead and popped him."

"You put him back in jail?"

"Yep."

Childs snorted. "I bet Wendell wasn't too tickled about that."

"I didn't hang around to see, but I imagine he was pretty chapped." He paused a beat. "Anyway, I've been trying to let B.J. know, but I can't raise him. Tried his pager, the radio, his cell phone. Nothing. It's like he just vanished."

"That sure don't sound right. If Bobby Joe's out and about, he's usually all up in somebody's ear about the first thing or another."

"It gets stranger, Gordy. Katie O'Brien called me from her car and said she was looking for her friends down around Skelton Mountain—"

"I talked to her, too, maybe an hour and a half, two hours ago. She was asking me about log cabins up there."

"Then she calls back and tells me to cut Jamie Amerson loose. Her phone give out before we finished talking."

Childs rubbed his chin and stared at a map of the county on the office wall. "It all smells funny to me. I mean, not that she'd want Jamie cut loose—she's never really been comfortable with ya'll's case on him. But why the hell would she be interested in *anything* on Skelton Mountain? There ain't nothing up there but the Dacys and Harkinses and Filyaws. Them and that ol' microwave relay station."

"Beats the hell out of me. Maybe she's lookin' to buy one of them refrigerators off Royal Filyaw's porch." He chuckled at his little joke. "Anyway, I'm sure she's okay."

"Yeah," Childs replied. "You're probably right." With his right index finger, he traced the twisting line on the map that represented Skelton Gap Road.

"Well, guess I'm gonna run. Ya'll be careful out there."

"Same to ya'," Childs replied.

He hung up the phone and continued to stare at the map. *Skelton Mountain?* What was it that she was after up there? The few clans who made it their home didn't much care for outsiders. It wasn't the kind of place Katie needed to be. Not alone and with the sun setting. Especially not with a bad storm tracking the mountain, dead on.

He grabbed his rain slicker, his keys, and two deputies from the conference table and headed for the door.

"What are you thinking right now?" Andy growled. Using both hands, she'd managed to pull Katie up to her knees. Now her intended victim's face, contorted with agony and purple with pooled blood, was at her belt level. "I bet you don't think you're so damn important now, do you?"

Katie could hear Andy's voice, but couldn't make out the words because of the roar in her ears. It didn't matter what she was saying, anyway. Her intent—to kill her, as she had done with the others—was now manifest. And, through the randomly firing neural sequences of a brain about to die, Katie knew that her end was not far away. Her windpipe was close to being crushed and her head was about to explode. Her visual field had been reduced to a series of dots; her assailant's face was nothing more than a shape-shifting smear of light.

Memories of her life began racing as her unconscious mind emptied itself, perhaps for one final time, into the constricted vessel of her consciousness. Familiar faces appeared to her, a silent montage of patrons, angels, and loved ones. There was, of course, her father, the kindly pediatrician with his strong hands, gentle spirit, and wise words of advice. And then her mother appeared, not frail and pallid as in her febrile last days, but strong and vibrant, as she had been when Katie was a child. Then, of course, her friend and confidante, Avery May, her nonconformity and gay insouciance simply a camouflage jacket for her wounded and conflicted inner child. And there were others as well: cherished college professors, mavens, professional role models.

Most importantly, though, there were her boys. They alone seemed multi-dimensional and real, more than just elements of her personal history, actually part of her. She saw them from every angle: in rapturous joy and unspeakable sadness, buoyant with confidence and withered with fear. She saw them now in serious moments and cutting up with one another. Both of them, teaching and learning. And she saw them at play—maneuvering video game characters, practicing ball, or just crashing into each other, roughhousing like boys will. Falling headlong into furniture and appliances. Grappling, throwing, punching, kicking, and head-butting.

And head-butting.

Katie suddenly scrambled to get her feet under her. Gathering her remaining strength, she shot upward, aiming her forehead at the center of Andy's face, the classic head-butting technique just as Con had described. She felt the impact and, under the circumstances, the strangely satisfying crunch of cartilage, followed immediately by Andy's release of the belt. Katie found herself able to breathe again. She slumped over, greedily sucking air into her lungs. When she finally looked up, she saw Andy Renauld standing six feet away, blood pouring out of each nostril.

"You *bitch!*" Andy screamed. She swiped at her nose and watering eyes with the back of her left hand. "How dare you!" She grabbed an object from the chair and angrily kicked the box. It crashed on its side sending the burning candle tumbling across the plywood flooring. Then, quickly circling the gasping prosecutor, she took up a position in the doorway, blocking the only way out of the room.

Katie shook her head to further loosen the loop. She stared in horror at the flame spreading quickly across the bare floor. She made a decision to just rush her assailant, using her feet and head if necessary to bash her way out of the cabin. She knew that Andy had to be at least partially disabled from the blow to her nose. That might not put them on equal footing, but it was the best situation she could hope for. Katie took a step toward the doorway, then suddenly froze.

Andy had an object in her hand. As the spreading fire began to light the room, Katie was able to recognize it as an automatic-loading pistol.

"I'm tired of screwing with you," Andy growled. Blood continued to run in twin streams down her chin. She raised the gun and pointed it at Katie's head.

The D.A. flinched, then noticed something unusual about the pistol. A shell casing appeared to be protruding sideways from the ejection port on the weapon's side. Katie immediately recognized this as a "stovepipe jam," a malfunction that would render it incapable of firing. Franks had taught her that this type jam often occurred when the weapon was held too loosely or when the slide was not allowed to move normally. She couldn't know that Franks had caused the jam when he'd grabbed the slide as Andy was shooting him. But it didn't really matter to Katie how the jam had occurred. The important thing was, *the gun wouldn't fire until the jam had been cleared.* Franks had taught her how to do this; she just hoped he hadn't taught Andy.

She made the decision to try to smash her way out of the cabin.

As Katie charged at her, Andy pulled the trigger. Before Andy could react to the gun not firing, Katie kicked her in the left knee, then jammed her shoulder into her midsection. Andy sagged for a moment, but recovered quickly and smashed Katie above the left brow with the butt of the gun. The D.A. doubled over in pain, but, realizing that this might be her only chance to escape, crashed full into her assailant once again. Andy wrapped her arms around the lawyer and the two women fell to the floor. Katie heard the dull thud of the weapon as it struck the floor.

Katie struggled the best she could, using her knees and feet to strike out at her captor. But, with superior strength and two good arms, Andy was rather easily able to get control of her. Avoiding her earlier tactical mistake, Andy maneuvered behind her and began to re-tighten the loop. Katie lowered her chin and, for a few seconds, was able to keep the belt from closing on her windpipe. But Andy gave the strap another twist and soon Katie was choking again.

"Go ahead and fight," Andy hissed. She wrapped the belt around her clenched fist and pulled her victim backward. "It's just gonna make it that much better for me."

Once again, Katie felt herself begin to lose consciousness. She groped madly for the gun with her cuffed hands. It was her chance, she thought. *Her absolute last chance.*

And then she felt the smooth, wooden grip plates of the pistol. Andy yanked her to the right, and Katie was able to close her restricted right hand around the grip. With her head feeling like it was about to explode, she tried to remember what Franks had told her about clearing a stovepipe jam. She rotated the gun to its right so that the ejection port and casing were facing the floor. Then, with her left hand, she pulled back on the slide.

She thought she heard the sound of the expended shell hitting the floor.

"What the hell..." Andy muttered. She momentarily stopped twisting the belt.

Once more, Katie told herself, as she teetered on the brink of unconsciousness. Now that the jam had been cleared, she needed to strip a round from the magazine and jack it into the chamber. She tried to pull the slide all the way back, but the device, anchored by a powerful spring, slipped from her fingers. *Pull it back or die!* As the belt again tightened, she tugged on the slide with every remaining ounce of strength. The slide finally yielded, snapping all the way to the rear of the weapon. She knew a live round was in the chamber. But there was still more that had to be done. With her right thumb, she pushed the magazine release mechanism. The clip fell loose, about one-half inch from the bottom of the grip. That task accomplished, and with no way of aiming the pistol, she did the only thing left for her.

She squeezed the trigger.

A deafening explosion shattered the eerie silence. A few seconds later, Andy Renauld began screaming in agony. The bullet had passed through her leg, just below the knee.

Suddenly the loop was loose again and Katie filled her lungs with air. She slumped forward, her head striking the floor. She sucked in air, inhaling dust and dirt from the floor. Her sweat and blood from the wound above her left eye ran down the side of her face, into her eye, and pooled under her cheek. She glanced back and saw that Andy was in a sitting position, her legs splayed in front of her. The fire was beginning to run up the wall a few feet behind her. Katie tried to get to her feet, but didn't have the strength or balance to accomplish that task. She began to slither toward the door on her belly, the gun still clutched behind her in her right hand.

Andy suddenly lurched forward, landing just behind Katie. Her labored breathing consisted of a series of tiny, squeaking gasps. She leaned forward, grabbed the gun's slide, and yanked the weapon out of Katie's hand.

"You...miserable...bitch!" she gasped. She raised the pistol with a shaking hand. "The only thing they'll find of you—"

She pulled the trigger and, once again, the only sound was the sterile metallic snap of the hammer. She pulled the trigger again and again with the same result. Sensing that this was her last and best opportunity to escape, Katie rolled onto her left hip and, with every ounce of strength she had, kicked her right leg back in her attacker's direction. Her shoeless foot caught the woman squarely on the jaw. Andy's eyes rolled back in their sockets. She crumpled without a sound, falling backward into a circle of rising flames.

Katie began crawling—out the door and through the front room. When she reached the cabin door, she sagged to the floor. She had nothing left, not one ounce of energy remaining to struggle with the heavy door.

Behind her, black smoke and angry tongues of flame jabbed out of the darkness. Katie could feel the heat searing her cheek.

She closed her eyes and began to pray.

Gordy Childs raced his Chevy Impala up the side of Skelton Mountain, his concern growing with each passing minute. He and his deputies had paused at the end of Skelton Gap Road to look around, still unsure what they might be looking for. Childs was about to drive away when one of the deputies spotted flames in the distance. He crashed the Ford through the brush and the men rushed to the burning cabin.

Childs pulled open the front door and recoiled from the blast of heat and smoke. One of the deputies standing behind him raked the floor with the powerful beam from his halogen-bulbed flashlight. Thunder from rainless clouds exploded in the air above the men.

"It's Missus O'Brien!" the deputy suddenly hollered. The light beam had been able to penetrate the smoke shroud well enough to illuminate the facial features of the woman lying, unconscious, a few feet from the door.

Childs and the two deputies quickly pulled Katie out the door. As they lifted her, the magazine from Franks's gun, still loaded with five live rounds, fell from her limp left hand.

CHAPTER 28

▼

"The doctor wasn't kidding," Berry Macklin said, as he stared down at Bobby Franks in his hospital bed. "You *do* look like the wrath of God."

Franks turned his head slightly so that he was looking directly at the district attorney and her deputies. It was standing-room only in his small room—Katie, Kevin Rose and Macklin were lined up on the right side of the bed, while RPD information officer Pam Green and Gordy Childs flanked him on the left. Avery May slouched against an air-conditioning register adorned with a floral arrangement at either end.

"Give me a cigarette, Berry, and I'll forget you said that," he rasped, in a voice even more hoarse than his usual chainsaw drawl.

"Yeah, right," Katie said. "You're getting oxygen piped into your nose and we're gonna give you a cigarette." She laughed. "I guess you'll just have to always remember what Berry said."

"Besides," Kevin Rose added, "truth is an absolute defense. I was talking with God earlier today and He certified that you looked *exactly* like the wrath of Him."

Franks did, in fact, appear to be in very bad shape. A nasogastric tube running out of a nostril was taped to the tip of his nose and pinned to the front of his hospital gown. Two clear plastic chest tubes, each partially filled with vile-looking fluid, protruded from gashes in his left side and anchored him to a large drain box sitting on the floor between Pam Green and Gordy Childs. A Medusa-like sprouting of intravenous lines connected his left arm to two poles heavily laden with drip bags and bottles. A feeding line had been established in the subclavian vein just below his neck. His lifeless and support hose-clad legs protruded from the blanket that he had bunched up around his chest. Wires connecting him to the unit's monitoring console and the oxygen line and cannula further tethered him to the room. He had dark circles under his eyes and a heavy growth of beard. The NG tube made it difficult for him to raise his head or turn more than a few inches to the left or right, but he insisted on trying anyway.

Despite these inconveniences, Franks now had every reason to acknowledge his exceptional good fortune. The bullet had narrowly missed his spine, liver, heart, and major blood vessels. It had, however, splintered a rib, nicked his spleen and stomach and perforated a lung; as a result, he'd lost a large amount of blood. His surgeon had told him that, had he arrived at the hospital ten minutes later, he probably wouldn't have survived. As it turned out, an ambulance had reached the top of Skelton Mountain only minutes after Gordy Childs's frantic call for help, and the subsequent surgery to repair the damage had been an unqualified success. His condition had been upgraded to "Fair," and his doctors were hopeful that he might be discharged within a week.

Physically, at least, he was on the road to recovery.

"So how're *you* doing?" Franks asked Katie.

The D.A. shrugged. Her lower lip was swollen and purple. The blow with the pistol butt had resulted in a gash over her left eye that required twenty tiny stitches to close. And the belt had left a horrifying purple bruise around her neck.

"I don't think I'll qualify for the Missus Alabama pageant, or anything," she replied, "but I guess I really can't complain."

"She pulls these stunts just so she can get the pain dope," Avery offered casually.

"Thanks a bunch, Ave," Katie said, glaring back in mock anger. She turned to Pam Green and Gordy Childs. "Avery, here, is one of my best friends. Can you imagine what kind of stuff my enemies say about me?"

Franks rasped, "Speaking as someone with a morphine button at his disposal, I can assure you all this suffering ain't worth it."

"All I know is, a couple of ya'll'd be residing on the other side of the ground right now if it hadn't been for her," Gordy Childs said, nodding in Katie's direction.

"Believe me, that occurs to me about fifty times a day," Avery said.

"I didn't do anything ya'll wouldn't have done," Katie protested. "Besides, Gordy and his men actually got us all out of there."

"But we all might've been goners if you hadn't popped that magazine out of the gun," Childs protested. He paused for a moment as one of Franks's IV regulators began emitting an annoying beeping alarm. "That was some pretty quick thinking, especially under the circumstances."

Katie's face began to turn red. "I wouldn't have known anything about pistols if Bobby hadn't taught me—"

"Enough, already!" Kevin Rose cried out, clamping his hands over his ears. "It's like I accidently walked into the Kissymouth Club's Smooch-Off award banquet, or something."

"My boss is a stone-cold sharpshooter," Berry Macklin interjected. "Trick-shootin' like Annie Oakley. Poppin' a cap on that girl, blind, her hands tied up. Maybe you could join a Wild West—"

Everyone, Macklin included, could see Bobby Franks's face suddenly collapse. He cleared his throat and made a feeble attempt at a smile. But his eyes began to mist over and dart uncomfortably, as though he was desperately attempting to stanch the flow of complex and unresolvable feelings.

Katie knew then that he had loved her. She could only imagine what he must have felt at the instant the near-fatal shot had been fired. Had he been consumed by fear, or had that emotion been a mere ripple, quickly obliterated by the simultaneous jolts of rejection and betrayal? However his heart may have then charted that moment, here, with unfilled hours and the crushing weight of recent memories, the pain of loss must have been unbearable.

A nurse, dressed in a floral print top and white pants, breezed into the room, parted the standing gallery, and shut off the alarm. Avery and Kevin Rose applauded this act.

"If a gunshot doesn't get you, the irritating beeping will," Avery observed.

"Ya'll probably need to give him a break," the nurse said to everyone and nobody in particular. She slid a blood pressure cuff around Franks's arm. "He didn't get a whole lot of sleep last night."

Franks snorted. "It'd help if ya'll wouldn't wake me up every ten minutes to take my freaking blood pressure and prick my finger. Or make me suck on a plastic tube filled with cold smoke." He cut his eyes in Katie's direction. "Although I suppose cold smoke is better than *no* smoke."

The nurse put her hands on her hips. "Let's go, folks," she said. "I'm serious. Everyone but immediate family needs to clear on out. Ya'll can come back after six tonight."

The attorneys and police visitors gave the fallen investigator a few parting words of encouragement, then began shuffling toward the door. Katie stopped in the doorway and glanced back at Franks. She knew that he'd had no recent contact with his children and his ex-wife was living in New Mexico, and that he had no other family in the area. If it hadn't been for his friends—mostly cops and prosecutors—he'd be going through this difficult recovery with nobody at his bedside.

Suddenly Avery curled up in the chair next to Franks's bed. The nurse stared at her with a puzzled expression on her face.

"Immediate family," Avery declared. When the woman's eyes narrowed, she added, "We's common-law now, but we's gonna get hitched up, all proper-like, soon as ya'll spring him outa here." She squeezed an object into Franks's left hand. "Ain't that right, Bobby Joe?"

The nurse shifted her now baleful glare to the investigator.

Franks stared for a moment at the tiny cow figurine in his hand, then smiled weakly. "I reckon so, Miz Elly May."

When Katie saw the nurse roll her eyes and shake her head, she waved goodbye and disappeared down the dimly lit hallway.

Katie let her two assistants off at the courthouse door, then pulled away in her Jeep. She drove east on State, then turned south on Park, moving almost randomly at right angles away from the courthouse, her office, and the dozens of message slips waiting on the corner of Laurie Ross's desk. She had no particular destination in mind. She just needed some time away from the press of humanity, the persistent questions, the steady accretion of human conflict. Her harrowing experience on Skelton Mountain had given her much to think about. She had used her newly installed transceiver-based car phone to call Con and let him know that she'd be picking up Garrett from school. And, until the final bell rang, she would drive and think, hoping to make some sense out of her insensible recent history.

She couldn't stop thinking about Andy Renauid, the woman she had once regarded as an industrious and well-meaning professional. *The woman she had once regarded as a friend.* Her inner-psychologist wondered what processes had brought Andy to that monstrous final form. Had she been abused as a child? Had the humanity been hammered out of her later in life? She was familiar with most of the historical formulations of psychopathy, from the early theories of Koch and Kraepelin to the those of Birnbaum, Kerberg, and Millon. She knew all about limbic-cortex disconnections and other psycho-biological explanations for impulsivity. But what theory could adequately explain Andy's single-minded vindictiveness, her savage cruelty, her utter lack of humanity? Katie was sure of only one thing—whatever diagnoses might be made after her psychological post-mortem, Andy Renauld hadn't been legally insane. She'd been able to appreciate the nature, quality and wrongfulness of her actions. She understood the difference between right and wrong and deliberately—one might even say *single-mindedly*—chose wrong. Common sense instructed Katie to disregard all the theories, formulations, and mutable Diagnostic and Statistical Manual categories. In the end, Andy Renauld was, quite simply, evil.

Andy's half-brother, George, had been able to provide a few answers. Andy had told Franks that he was on active military duty overseas but, in truth, he'd been working on an oil rig just offshore of his native Louisiana. He had departed for Richfield immediately upon receiving news of his sister's death. He arrived as her only surviving family member and, although Andy had not designated him as her fiduciary, he undertook the grim task of burying his half-sister's fire-ravaged remains and settling her estate. When he spoke with Katie and her staff, he had worn the same stunned expression as those who had known and worked with Andy. He said that they had grown up in rather austere conditions in a two-room house in Marksville, Louisiana. Andy's natural mother had died when she was a toddler; her father and George's mother married a few years later, then disappeared, never to be heard from again. He said that they'd been raised by an alcoholic and rather neglectful father. After Andy accused him of sexually abusing her, the two children were taken from him and eventually installed in the home of an indifferent aunt in Birmingham. From there, George and Andy completed high school and went their separate ways—Andy to college on an athletic scholarship, George to work. They'd kept in touch over the years and, when George collected a substantial sum in settlement of a worker's compensation claim, Andy persuaded him to invest in the Skelton Mountain real estate. She had convinced him that the mountain would eventually be developed and the property would become "worth a small fortune." In the meantime, he granted Andy unrestricted use of the cabin and the old red van stored in the barn-like outbuilding.

He never imagined that the property or his sister would become what they did.

Clearly George had become another of Andy's victims. Katie recalled his face, sequencing through a range of emotions, as he was asked to identify the items collected by crime scene investigators from the back of his impounded van. There were the harmless personal effects that reminded him of Andy's ordinary humanity—clothing, a sleeping bag, the contents of her purse, including her reporter's notebook, packets of cheese crackers, tampons and migraine medication. There were the other possessions—her stereo and CD collection, a cosmetics bag, garbage sacks filled with her shoes, clothing, and jewelry, and a box of books (including a well-marked copy of *The Waste Land*)—which strongly suggested a plan to leave Skelton Mountain that night, never to return to Bienville County. And there were also lengths of rope, duct tape, Amerson Heating and Cooling coveralls, and other evidence of her destructive enterprise. After official property release forms for Andy's personal effects and the van had been handed to him by Gordy Childs, George had wandered through the CID parking lot, stunned by grief and confusion, tears welling in his eyes.

But George Renauld, of course, was only the last of the casualties of Andy's deranged campaign of personal retribution. The faces of the others scrolled through her mind as she steered without conscious thought through the deserted Southpark streets. There were, of course, the murdered women, Donna Crawley, Kerry Grinder, JoEllen Russell. There were the faces of their friends and family members as Katie had last seen them, their blank stares and rigid features suggesting only that the grisly resolution of the case had done little to assist the healing process. And there was the Rasputin-like J.P. Fourier, neither true hero, nor true villain; murdered by Andy so that her dark secret might survive a few hours longer.

And, oddly enough, she also thought of Jamie Amerson. Social psychopath that he might have been, he too had been victimized by Andy. He hadn't been physically injured and he hadn't lost a loved one, and he certainly hadn't been subjected to any public process with which he didn't already have more than a passing familiarity. But he had, nevertheless, been falsely accused of terrible crimes and subjected to public humiliation, and, whatever else he might have been and done, he'd been deeply wronged. Would he file a lawsuit against the police department and Bienville County, as he, his father, and Rabon Creasey had threatened on more than one occasion? She had no way of knowing for sure. She couldn't imagine Creasey encouraging that course of action: the government had certainly not "rushed to judgment" and there had been probable cause to believe he was the offender, if not enough proof to get a conviction. It seemed highly unlikely that a Bienville County jury would hold the government liable, given the circumstances. Moreover, his bizarre and characteristically impulsive actions on the last days before the confrontation on Skelton Mountain—getting drunk, harassing Andy and Avery, then disappearing in his father's van—did nothing to help his case. And, of course, he still had certain felony drug charges lurking in the system. In the end, Katie knew that the only thing she could do was issue a formal and public apology to Jamie on behalf of local law enforcement. If that wasn't good enough for him, he'd just have to take his best shot.

She thought she might be able to do more to help the murder victims' families. She planned to set up scholarships in the names of Donna Crawley and

Kerry Grinder at Carry College. And, perhaps with Roger Russell's assent, she could help Carlyn Bedsole implement her plan to do things with the Russell children. She knew she couldn't do anything to erase the hurt Andy had caused; maybe, however, she could do something to help the survivors move forward with what they had left.

Katie shifted in her seat as the pain from her bruised legs and lower back began to return. She glanced at her watch and saw that it was almost three o'clock. She worked her way back to Feltner and headed in the direction of Garrett's school. She'd have plenty of time to think once she fell into the line of pick-up vehicles.

Her car phone rang. She glanced at the caller window and saw that it was Laurie's number. She started to reach for the receiver, then pulled her hand away. No, she thought—not this afternoon. On this day, she'd be there for her son, and she'd hug him and take him for a milkshake or a smoothie and, if he wanted, she'd get on the floor of his room and let him cream her at *Alien Squadron*. One thing she knew to be true was that there wasn't any office crisis that couldn't be solved without her. She'd been one stovepiped nine-millimeter round away from never returning to her office, period. And, of course, from ever again sharing an afternoon like this with Garrett.

She turned a corner and a saw the line of cars already well formed along School Street. She joined the queue and began waiting, her Jeep end-to-end with a hundred other cars, vans, and SUVs, a hundred other moms and dads and grandparents. Her radio blasting, dark glasses on, slunk down low so that someone would have to look hard to see her battered face. She was just happy to be there, happy to be anywhere. And when she saw Garrett's face, flushed with surprise and joy, there was nowhere else she would have wanted to be.

As she drove away, the sun disappeared behind a bank of threatening clouds—gunmetal gray and distended with hoarded moisture. Within a few minutes, fat raindrops pelted her windshield. Katie looked over at Garrett and the boy grinned at her. Everything was good, she thought, even the rain. *Especially the rain.*

Soon the water came down in diagonal sheets, filling the gutters, breaking the city's summer-long fever.

The End

0-595-31908-4